THE CHANGING OF THE GUARD

The Changing of the Guard

A NOVEL

JOHN EHLE

RANDOM HOUSE NEW YORK

Copyright © 1974 by John Ehle

All rights reserved under International and Pan-American Copyright Conventions. Published in the United States by Random House, Inc., New York, and simultaneously in Canada by Random House of Canada Limited, Toronto.

Library of Congress Cataloging in Publication Data

Ehle, John, 1925–
    The changing of the guard.

    I. Title.
PZ4.E33Ch   [PS3555.H5]   813'.54'   74–9083
ISBN   0–394–49499–7

Manufactured in the United States of America
9 8 7 6 5 4 3 2
First Edition

to Bella Spewack,
who makes almost all things possible

THE CHANGING OF THE GUARD

One

A T H E A T H R O W he and Kate had been seated last, had been given the two front seats. There was no first-class section, but British Airways, to help them maintain their privacy, had been thoughtful enough to close off the two seats across the aisle and the two directly behind them. Also the airline had supplied an extra stewardess, apparently solely to wait on them, a star-struck, somewhat eager, rather pretty young blonde. She brought them cocktails and a tray of cheeses and crackers, then stood beside his seat, obsequiously alert for any further need.

He waved his hand, merely to shoo her away; realizing he had hurt her feelings, he smiled at her, his famous, friendly smile, murmured a polite apology, and turned toward his wife. "They won't leave us alone, will they?" he said quietly.

"She has now," Kate said.

He leaned his head against the back of the seat, closed his eyes, sighing gratefully. "They worry you to death," he said. "But what if suddenly they didn't, Kate?"

Fondly she watched him as he rested, watched his chest rise and fall with each breath. He was in his fifties, but there were no wrinkles in his face or on his hands, no signs of age or even inherent weariness. He was still compellingly handsome, as handsome as ever, with Northern European features, a clean-shaven, long rather than round face, a high forehead, bright, intelligent gray eyes, thick brown brows, thick brown hair with gray highlights, a rough stubble in one or two spots under his chin where he had been unusually careless that morning. He had a long, elegant English frame. He was superior, he possessed an aura of superiority, which fit him as neatly and tightly as his tailored suit, while she, though pretty enough, was not striking; she was much younger, had more energy, more vigor, perhaps.

He sighed again, contentedly. "At least I'll be working again. The long vacation is over."

The loudspeaker: "We have just passed over the town of *Lou Uf*." With that information, a lady back in the plane a ways, a gray-haired matron, promptly rose from her seat and took her coat off the rack; then, taking a lingering look at Richie, one filled with romantic kindness—it was as if he were a bit of nostalgia come to life—she plopped back down. She had seen him, she had seen him close up, in real life, she had almost touched him and later would claim she had.

"No houses yet," Kate said. "Not that I can make out."

"You always get to sit by the window, don't you, Kate?" he said.

"I can see six towns just now."

"All the way from Los Angeles you've had the window. Do you arrange this beforehand on the phone, or am I simply outmaneuvered in each aisle?"

"Larger towns now," Kate said, her nose pressed against the glass.

He took her hand, rubbed it, warmed it with his fingers.

"Now a dark patch, like a lake," she said.

"Farmlands, most likely." He was becoming rather excited actually, arriving once more in Paris. He had never lost his sense of excitement, his capacity for excitement—thank God for that. Arriving in Paris had always been pure pleasure, no matter how tedious the trip.

The plane slowed, circled. The wing uncurtained Paris below. "Ahhh," he said, pleased. She was not brightly, gaudily lighted; rather sedately she lay there, the dear creature, each light discreet, tamed in color and intensity, nothing with the sheen and boastfulness of Los Angeles, for instance.

The plane was still circling.

He could see cars on the highway now.

The English pilot said, "Ladies and gentlemen, from the right side of the aeroplane you will see Orly Airport, with Paris beyond."

The far-flung city, the lady of the world.

His special hostess, English accent, breathless: ". . . get wraps—this is your coat, sir. A car will be waiting for you at the plane, so you deplane first. And your wife, of course. Money will be exchanged for you by the manager, if you wish; the banks are closed. Straighten seats now, that's nice. Fasten safety belts."

Still circling.

"You have any French money, Richie?" Kate asked him.

"Oh, yes."

"Going to give me my fifty francs for the week?"

He smiled. "Wouldn't buy your lunch, dear. Or pay the bartender. See here, now, Kate, let's have less drinking, you hear? No excuse, now that you have work to do."

She turned abruptly to look out the window. "Oh, hush."

"I mean it, Kate," he said. "Drinking *can* get the upper hand, you know."

Paris was spread out before them, mile after mile of the fabled city, sedate, decorous, nothing dazzling, all tastefully done, the French way.

"Make a wish," Kate said.

"I wish for an earthshaking film, this time round," he said. "My Lord, Kate, I'm taking a chance on this one."

She closed her eyes tightly, feverishly, held her crossed fingers against her face.

"What are you wishing for?" he said.

She held her trance a moment longer, then relaxed, leaned her head back against the seat.

"What you wish for, Kate?"

"It's a secret. It's my secret," she said.

"Have anything to do with me, Kate? Does it?"

Touchdown: gentle, smooth, the heavy plane rolling with a sense of true trajectory. Terminal building off to the left. Soft music on the loudspeaker. Lights along the runway red, yellow, white, blue. Why, he wondered, did he bother to notice such details? "My mind is one detail after another," he said to Kate. The plane was still rolling swiftly; the runway seemed to be more bumpy. He could distinguish individuals now, walking about, one man running. They swept past a Lufthansa plane. The airport did seem to be one of magnificent distances. "Poplar trees all in a row," he said softly.

"It's none of your concern, really."

He looked at her. "No?"

"One should keep a secret," she said, "not blurt it out like you do."

"Maybe in Scotland, but in America we blurt out our secrets. Always have."

"You're English."

"Yes, but I've lived in America for decades, seems like."

"I wished that our marriage would stay happy," she said.

He considered that, nodded. He took her hand and kissed it. "That's a better wish than mine. I do so want your wish to come true, Kate. I do, indeed. If only we both can continue to be happy. That's the main thing."

The plane had landed at 10:00. A bus waited to take the other passengers to the terminal building, but a long, black Citroën limousine waited for him and Kate. As they were leaving, the special stewardess asked Richie to autograph an airline napkin; stepping out of the plane, he noticed that she put a lipstick imprint on it.

A uniformed French attendant came forward, eager to welcome them and to shake Richie's hand. He said something in French about how honored France was.

Hal Vorono, Richie's male secretary, moved them swiftly through a special customs office, them and their luggage, then led them down a back stairway to their own car. Richie remembered the chauffeur from somewhere, some previous assignment, perhaps. "Good to see you again," he said, ducking past him and into the Rolls sedan, the first one in. Kate climbed in behind him. The chauffeur shut the door, waited outside to keep away the curious while the luggage was loaded in a waiting taxi. Vorono swung into the seat beside the driver. An airport official and the customs official both came forward to wave at Richie through the closed window. He opened the window, shook hands with them, murmuring in English his thanks for the privileges extended him at Orly.

The car moved forward, gently edged into the lane of traffic. "Let's see, driver, was it New York?" Richie said. "Where did I know you?"

"I drove you on the Riviera, sir," the driver said. "It wasn't New York."

"Which time? How long ago?" Richie said.

"Nine and one-half years ago, almost to the day, sir. Mr. Douglas Fairbanks was with you."

"Right. Perfect. I recall," Richie said, satisfied.

There was almost no traffic on the highway, Kate noticed. "Is the house secluded?" Kate asked. "I do hope so."

"The French always know how to be secluded," Vorono said.

"Where's Richie's dog?" Kate said. "Is he in Paris yet?"

"Yes," Vorono said.

"Then we're all here," Richie said.

"Go through Paris on the way to the house," Kate said.

"Through Paris?" Vorono said, surprised. "Do you really want to?" When neither she nor Richie replied, he shrugged and turned to watch the road.

"Don't teach your grandmother how to suck eggs," Richie said suddenly to her. "Doesn't help my image, does it?" He waited tensely for her reply.

"I never know what to tell reporters," she admitted defensively.

"Vorono, she told the *World-Telegram* reporter she was coaching me on my lines, the ones for this French film, trying to *improve* my interpretation, and that I had said to her, 'Don't teach your grandmother how to suck eggs.' "

"Doesn't help your image," Vorono said dutifully.

"Headline: Grandma Richie returns to films. Marvelous, darling, helpful."

Kate shook her head fretfully. "You did say those very words to me."

He pressed her hand. "My dear, it doesn't matter."

"How big is the house, Vorono?" she asked, leaning forward, toward him.

"Two or three bedrooms, big sit-down dining room,

two-story living room, library, servants' rooms," Vorono said.

"You say Kolisch is in town?" Richie said.

"Probably," Vorono said.

"Well, surely the producer is here by now."

"The director's been shooting in Spain," Vorono said. "Maybe Kolisch is there, too."

"Yes, yes, we'll have a lot of shaky, hand-hold footage to get rid of, I suspect," Richie said. "Why does Spanish footage have to tremble?"

"I told the Spanish servants you'd want a Reuben sandwich tonight," Vorono said.

"Every night. See here, why are we moving about the Arc de Triomphe? Are we going to the house or *not?*"

"Turn right into Avenue Foch," Vorono told the driver.

"A Reuben and a bottle of Dom Pérignon," Richie said, "every night of my life, from here out. I've earned the right to have what I want, haven't I, Vorono? *Whatever* I want. Haven't I, Kate?"

She said, "Isn't it wonderful to be here, Richie, in the city of romance, the Virgin City . . ."

"*Virgin* city. Darling, you're in Paris."

They drove past the fashionable apartment buildings and into the Bois de Boulogne, which was, of course, black as pitch. He still held her hand. She put both of hers around his, marveling at the sense of contentment she felt. They had spent the past five or six years in Beverly Hills, sitting by the pool and talking with other celebrities about past laurels. They would spend each day the same way, would sit by the pool and let the morning creep by till lunchtime, then a cocktail and a poached bass; maybe a guest would be present—Danny Kaye or Loretta Young or Myrna Loy . . . Then the afternoon: a drive, a swim, a nap. The cocktail hour began at half past six. Dinner was at eight, there at the

house or at a friend's house—but no parties; Richie had
developed an aversion to the tumbling about of numer-
ous personalities in a room, the chitchat about who was
going to do what property as actor, actress, director, producer. He was retired. He had announced six years ago
that he was through with films. The rough-and-tumble
battling with directors and producers, the study and op-
tioning of properties, the courting of the public, was
over.

Silence as they crossed a bridge.

"Like a Matisse," Richie said. "I wonder if Matisse
learned his technique by studying reflections in the
Seine. We're riding like a ghost through the night. We
are all ghosts, aren't we, happy, prosperous ghosts, all
shadows of the Master who made us, willed us, and is
himself less interesting, I suspect, more predictable. Or
did we grow from seeds, darling? Some novelist once
told me that in his writing he peeled a character like an
onion and never found a core there. Who was that?"

"James Jones," Kate said simply. She knew all his
stories, even all his whims by now.

" 'What did you want to find?' I asked him. And he
grew still and silent. He only found pretensions, he said,
and he hated pretensions. But see here, the pretensions
are part of a man, I told him, often the best part, and are
signs of good instincts within; I have always admired the
pretensions of the better Englishmen, for instance."

They rode in silence considering that. "He probably
thought you were *bats*, Richie," Kate said.

Richie. She called him that, as did everybody who
knew him well, a nickname he had acquired when as an
impoverished actor he had spent his first four pay checks
on a party for the cast. She rarely called him dear or
darling. She had no special name for him, but was still
foolishly in love with him and admitted it. Most everybody liked him—he was often witty and had world-wide

fame—but she loved him. She alone loved him. She had not loved the Beverly Hills life, not really, and she had helped Edward Kolisch persuade him to do one more film. And she had persuaded them both to let her play a supporting role in it. She had been an actress—not terribly successful or well-known—before marrying him. Professional name: Kate Holland.

"Is Annie Logan here in Paris yet, Vorono?" Richie asked.

They were passing by lines of darkened shops, each one with its glass and brick personality, yes, and its awning, its broad hat, as Kate saw them.

"She should have come with us," he said.

"She—probably wants her independence," Kate said.

"Beautiful film test. Seeing her swimming in our pool last summer, I never knew she could act at all."

"Nor needed to," Kate said dryly.

"Of course, you never really expect seriousness of the Irish, anyway."

"You were so kind to let her have the part, Richie."

"Why, she was marvelous. She's to be Marie Antoinette, Vorono."

"A friend of mine from Liverpool Rep days," Kate said.

"Been at Universal for years, lost in the maze," Richie said. "Nice bosom, I must say."

Vorono said, "Expect that of Marie Antoinette."

"It's the bloody director that worries me," Richie said.

"Oh, let him have his chance, Richie," Kate said. "Won't you?"

"He did a Florida swamp film, Vorono, about a lad who kills his parents in order to remain in that—uh—isolated world, and of course he can't."

"Beautiful nature scenes," Kate said.

"But Lord, the violent scenes are—beyond acceptability. What he will want to do with the French Revolution—"

"Only one way to cut your head off, Richie," Kate said.

"Yes," he said. "Always have arranged to avoid that in previous films."

"And you've avoided acting with any of your wives, too."

He patted her knee. "Just do as I tell you, darling," he said.

Richie had rewritten the script, had taken out most all the deaths. He had clothed the beautiful, naked duchesses being dragged through Paris streets. "They were clothed in history, actually," he had told Kolisch. He put them in carts, also, and deleted the more explicit shots at the guillotine. He had reversed the order of his and Annie Logan's death so he could go last; later he deleted her death entirely. "By giving an unknown a chance, I don't mean for her to steal my film from me, you know," he had told Kolisch. He was a dear man, Kolisch, now in his sixties, very cooperative after forty years of film-making. He had insisted only on this certain young director, a man named Sigler, and he flew to Spain to start him on filming crowd scenes and fill-in shots. Sigler was doing *Desire Under the Elms* there, and hoped to do a film on the I.R.A. next. He read the proffered script and threw it out his hotel window. Even so, the studio's publicity department began issuing news releases about the new dynamic team, meaning Richie, a romantic artist of world standing, and the naturalistic, tough Doug Sigler: "The best of the world's screen actors and the best of the new young directors." Sigler had even been flown to New York to be interviewed on the *Today* show. A hulking, splenetic creature of about thirty, handsome of face, black-haired, sweaty, a Southerner who seemed to spill over his belt and threaten the seams of his clothes, he mumbled his answers and looked askance at Miss Walters and the camera. When asked what the idea of the film was, he said, "I sense films."

"What does that mean?" she asked.

He scratched his chest through his sports shirt and sniffed uncomfortably. "I d-d-d-don't *think* films," he said.

Miss Walters asked him if he and Richie were in agreement on the nature of the film.

"What nature?" he said.

Miss Walters reflected on that. "He is notoriously difficult to work with; such famous stars *are* difficult to work with."

Sigler shrugged. "I'll m-m-make something out of it."

The studio had been embarrassed, had apologized to Richie, had canceled Sigler's scheduled appearance on a nighttime talk show. They flew him back to Spain, where he arrived in Madrid drunk and went through customs with a bottle of whiskey in one hand and a shopping bag, his only luggage, in the other. Kolisch later told Richie by telephone that Sigler's bag contained a change of underwear, two pairs of socks, two sweat shirts, a pair of Levis, a pair of loafers, three Hershey almond bars, a copy of Thomas Wolfe's *You Can't Go Home Again* with passages underlined in red and green, a copy of Dylan Thomas' poems, everything beer- and whiskey-soaked, dog-eared and dirty, and a copy of Thomas Carlyle's book on the French Revolution.

"I phoned several film people to ask what to do with this director, Vorono," Richie said. "I asked what his reputation is, but he has none."

They were in a residential section now, driving past the gates and walls of the Paris houses of the wealthy.

"Also, I was nervous, wanted assurance. Hell, I *am*

nervous. It's been a long time for me."

"Oh please, Richie. You and the Burtons and Olivier—"

"Why must I always be compared with the Burtons, who are two people?"

"And they're divorced, anyway," Vorono said.

"I phoned Rex Harrison. The whole bloody thing has changed, and Rex has kept up with it. He never did like Hollywood. He kept flinging himself into projects elsewhere, everywhere. Olivier never would go the Hollywood route, either."

"Which you did," Kate said gently.

"He got offered character parts for years, too, until this duel thing—"

"*Sleuth,*" she said.

"Yes, that's it. He and Rex and the others have remained English, and I miss being English, Kate. If it hadn't been for the income taxes, I just might have done work in England."

"Well, you did. I saw you when I was a little girl, playing on Shaftesbury Avenue."

"Oh well, well yes, before I succumbed and was typed as a—a bloody gentleman."

She was fond of telling others that he would sometimes stand for half an hour in front of a full-length mirror grimacing, smiling, reciting lines from plays he had done in his youth, remembering parts from thirty years ago: Sylvius in *As You Like It*, Fluellen in *Henry V,* Dogberry in *Much Ado About Nothing*, Puck in *Midsummer Night's Dream*, Launcelot Gobbo in *Merchant of Venice*, Friar Laurence in *Romeo and Juliet*, Polonius in *Hamlet.*

"My son, Vorono, is he by any chance in France?" Richie asked suddenly.

"No, sir. He's in Greece."

"You send him his check each month?"

"Yes, sir. I've increased it to eight hundred dollars, inflation and all."

Kate said, "Invite him to Paris, Richie." The son was in his early twenties, was from Richie's second marriage.

"No, no, dearest," he said. "I have enough to be concerned about."

They arrived at the house. The car stopped before a closed green garden door. Kate was out of the car at once, was banging on the door.

"The Scots tend to be overly demonstrative," Richie told the driver, rather proudly, too, and fondly. He stood waiting for her to work out the arrangements—just as she had done with this new film, even to getting her closest friend a part in it. Well, she needed Annie Logan with her, to give her support and confidence, and make her control the gin. He was pleased to think he was helping the two of them, two younger, less experienced people who trusted him to make no serious errors in this risky venture. As Rex had told him, or maybe it was Monty, every film while in production is a new assault on everything at all reasonable.

The Spanish butler opened the gate and Kate rushed inside the garden. Richie followed along, smiling at the notion of her vigor, her enthusiasm.

He noticed that the entrance hallway had a beautiful eighteenth-century portrait of a royal figure, maybe a king. The French had always been infatuated with royalty. He gave Vorono his hat, stood there gazing at the portrait, wondering what characterization he should give Louis XVI. "Vorono, a bourbon on the rocks might relax me," he said.

"Yes, sir."

"Suppose they wouldn't have Jack Daniel's over here. Or I'll take Glenlivet Scotch," he said.

"Yes, sir."

On the hallway table he happened to see a handwritten note.

Dear Sir:
　　Here is a new script for the film. Hope you approve.
　　　　　　　　　　　　　　　　　　　Sigler

Later, Kate, laughing at the predicament of having for servants a Spanish couple who spoke no English, found him standing in that entrance hallway, stationed under the chandelier, typescript open in his hands, a baffled frown on his face.

"It simply won't do, Kate," he said, looking at her. "This young director has done his own version of my film."

Two

THE STUDIO DE BOULOGNE, the preeminent film studio of France, is situated east of the Bois de Boulogne, not far from the house Kate and Richie had rented the year before in 1972. Much of it had been torn down to make way for apartment buildings, but three studios remained. Kolisch had put a commissary dining room in the smallest of them, and the large ones, A and B, were filled with the needed sets.

The cobblestoned courtyard was only large enough for seven or eight cars, and it would become the daytime home of Richie's Rolls sedan or his Rolls convertible—both had been brought to Paris—as well as of the studio sedan assigned to Kate, the one assigned to Miss Annie Logan, the one Kolisch had assigned to himself, and the one assigned to Publicity. A group of French chauffeurs would be conferring here each morning, standing in the summer sun, snickering and chuckling and looking mildly bored. Also, perhaps, there would be a chauffeured sedan for Sigler, though none had as yet been requested by him, or assigned to him. The private cars of the crew and the lesser cast members, the noblemen and revolutionary leaders of the drama about to unfold, were to be parked outside the gate.

The first car to arrive on this particular Friday morning was the black, sleek French Citroën sedan assigned to Miss Annie Logan, a strikingly feminine-looking, pretty woman in her early thirties. Her lips were full and pouting, particularly the lower one; her eyes sky-blue, her hair black and worn in a bun, unadorned. She never wore jewelry, rarely wore make-up, except when make-up was needed for a character in a film, which had not occurred recently. She was, to be honest, simply not in demand in Hollywood. She had had a brief, modest career, playing perfectly ordinary parts in ordinary police films and detective stories. Then one day she realized no producer had phoned her for a year. She began to face the fact that she had been at sixteen a brilliantly promising actress at the Abbey Theatre in Dublin, as Sean O'Casey had noticed, and at twenty-three a promising actress at the Liverpool Repertory Company, but now at thirty-three she was stuck in the cultural backwater of Hollywood, where even her agent acknowledged no hope remained.

Then Kate had managed to launch her on this new, high road, which had stunned her agent and estranged husband.

Her driver parked near a paneled door, then came scurrying around to help her out. "Dressing rooms upstairs," he said, pointing toward the door.

The hallway had two or three tiny, bare offices to the right. The cleaning lady stopped her lazy sweeping and led her up a narrow stairway—no wide stairway to the stars, this, Annie thought—to a blank, plain hallway along which were four closed doors, each one numbered.

Annie wouldn't take the first dressing room, certainly, she decided. As for the second, well, no doubt Kate would want to be next to her husband. So she paused outside the third door, tried to imagine what her French dressing room would be like. She pushed it open ever so slowly; she meant to pass considerately into this new world of Marie Antoinette.

Before her was a room about fourteen by fourteen feet, larger than any dressing room she had ever had before. Two windows looked out over the courtyard. An ornate French dressing table was set against the right wall, placed so that the windows' light would fall on the subject's face. On the floor was a dark blue rug. Against the left wall was a blue couch, and flanking it were two upholstered French chairs. The paintings above the sofa were not contemporary, she was pleased to see; they were of a garden and a child. On the right wall near the door were mirrors, a bank of mirrors, and beside them were photographs of three actors she recognized, but could not just now identify, who must have used this room. One signed his picture: "To Cher Ami, Studio de Boulogne, Charmed."

She opened a door. A large bathroom with pink fixtures, even a pink tub, even a pink bidet. She opened the only other door. A closet, large enough to hold a family's clothing, just now housing her wardrobe. She took out a billowing lace and satin costume and stood before the mirrors, holding the magnificent dress in front of her.

"Marie Antoinette, I believe," a man's voice said.

She swung about and saw in the doorway the smiling, dignified King of France. "My husband, the King," she said and curtsied.

He offered his hand. "Sorry not to be in costume. Not even a sword."

He had an extraordinary smile, always extraordinary

charm, Annie thought. "Are we—are we to rehearse—anything today?" she asked.

"Costumes. We try on the costumes, I believe," he said.

"These?" she said, indicating her closet.

"Not for me, thank you. I have my own things."

She tilted her head questioningly. "I wish you luck, sir."

"Ah?" He smiled warmly. "My, you are pretty. This is going to be a pleasure for me; Kate told me I would be amazed at how well you would play Marie Antoinette, and when I saw you in the screen test . . ."

A magic in him as always, in his expression, his expressiveness: At last I have found you, he seemed to say, the promise he had for every woman, all women, world-wide.

He took two of the dressing rooms, selecting the one at the front for his visitors and interviewers and office matters, the second for changing; therefore, her dressing room actually did adjoin his. She could hear his laughter now and again, as well as the fretful, high-pitched noise of his comments as he talked to his dresser.

Her own dresser spoke no English at all. She was French, a professional who knew about court costumes and motion-picture wigs, but was not graceful or beautiful, and since grace and beauty were in everything else, Annie resented her at once. Oh, go on home, she thought. But the lady was as obedient as a big sheepdog, and probably needed the work, and her sad eyes seemed to mirror much deep suffering, so Annie let her be.

About 9:30 Kate arrived, began calling, yelling gleefully from the courtyard. Annie got a window raised, and they shouted happily at each other, each gasping with pleasure at this fairyland world, all the drivers smiling, laughing. "You look the same in Paris . . ." "You're not a day older . . ." "Isn't this a happy place?" "Isn't it like play-acting as children?" "Did you see Richie?" "It's a fairyland, fairyland, fairyland . . ."

"Richie," Kate shouted imperiously from below. "Which window are you? Show yourself at once."

Richie's head appeared.

"Oh, you two are together already, are you?" Kate said.

The three of them gathered in Kate's dressing room, the corner room. She hugged and kissed Annie, and fixed Bloody Marys for everybody. Yes, Doug Sigler *was* in Paris, *was* even at the studio, her driver had told her. Sigler had arrived in a Volkswagen which he parked on the sidewalk. He had a Spaniard with him, a young man who spoke no French, and the back seat was full of camera gear and wine. Sigler, because he was so unkempt, had been refused admittance for over an hour. He had gone through Studios A and B criticizing the sets.

Of the three of them, Richie was the only one displeased with the costumes. He and his trusted Portuguese dresser soon decided that Sigler must have had a voice in their commissioning. First of all, there was far too much padding, and secondly, the costumes were scruffy. "See this," he said to Kate and the dresser. He stood before his dressing room mirrors, the padding strapped to his belly, clothed in a baggy court costume which looked as if the King had lived in it for days. "There even appear to be splotches of ketchup on it," he said. "Do the French even use ketchup?"

"It's the new realism," the dresser said distastefully.

"Your stomach's off-center, Richie," Kate said.

He tugged haplessly at the padding. "Can you imagine my appearing before eighty million fans in this comic opera suit?" He pulled the padding out from under his belt and tossed it aside.

At once the Portuguese fell to work with pins, taking tucks at the back of the costume. "They take the romance out of everything."

"It is *all* going to have to be redone *completely*," Richie said.

At 2:00 Kolisch's secretary, an elderly, companionable woman named Marge, came upstairs to escort "our stars" to the commissary. She was neatly, conservatively dressed in a tweed suit, was sad of face and manner, as was her wont, but when Richie asked about Kolisch's health she suddenly became kindly. "Now, he is sick," she said, "but is as active as ever, and, as you know, he doesn't complain."

RICHIE had never even seen a photograph of Douglas Sigler, but the man standing alone at the commissary bar, dressed in a baggy, dark suit, no tie, scowling, drinking a beer, had to be he. If he recognized Richie, he gave no notice of it, though Richie stood only five feet from his elbow and coughed twice. Kolisch came forward, greeting Richie, and this happy, noisy ceremony also took place near Sigler, but the young genius managed to ignore it too.

The man was intolerably rude, as Richie saw it; so often these young people were, even while claiming to be of the common sort, out of the earth and all that. A pity. His own son . . .

Kolisch got Richie, Kate and Annie seated at his table and ordered drinks all around. "How was your flight, Richie?" he began. "No trouble, surely."

Richie was still staring at Sigler, considering the arrogance of the man.

"He's eating prawns with his fingers," Annie whispered to Kate.

"He's a bear," Kate said. "Most directors are horses, but this one's a bear."

"Did he like the studio sets?" Kate asked Kolisch.

"No," Kolisch said unhappily. "But maybe we can fix them. 'This is not a musical,' he keeps telling me, and I know he's right."

Marge said, "He's a man of few words." She turned to Richie. "Did you see his new script?"

"One more film," Kolisch said, interrupting—he didn't mean to broach that subject here. "I've made forty-five. Is that right, Marge? No two ever seem to me to be alike."

"Forty-four," Marge said.

"Forty-four, is it? Each one is a foreign country with its own population." He chewed on a sliver of pâté while he waited for his cocktail. "When do you want to start the shooting, Richie?" he said.

"The costumes don't fit, Kolly," Richie said, as if mentioning the most casual consideration.

"Oh, not that too," Kolisch said. "Poor man. I'm sorry, Richie."

"The wigs are mangy. Does your studio think Louis had lice?"

"We'll have to redo them, Richie."

"As for the effort to rewrite the script," he said to Marge, "it has become incredibly brutal."

"Yes, he's working at a—an approach—" Kolisch began, "an interesting, contemporary—"

"We'll use draft four," Richie said bluntly.

There was a long pause as his measured words sank in. A nervous burp escaped from Kolisch. He took a vial from his coat pocket and selected a pill. "Anybody else want one? They're chewable."

"Can you come to lunch Sunday?" Richie said. "I'll show you the costumes."

"Ulcers," Kolisch said. "Yes, Marge and I would love to come."

"It just won't do," Richie said to him. "I do mean to make King Louis a distinct character. I'm not going to play him as a stock figure, but if he's unlikable, unattractive, what's the audience paying for?"

UPSTAIRS Kate kept glancing out the dressing room window at Sigler, who was in the courtyard below, tossing a football back and forth with a Spaniard. He was intriguing to her, animalistic and sexy. She moved to Annie Logan's dressing room, next to Richie's, and watched from Annie's window. "He's an animal, a crude animal," she said. "Richie will dislike him for that too."

Annie, in euphoria, ecstatic over her first fairyland day as a film star, was not even remotely aware of Kate's worry.

"It's another world, the film world today, and the animals understand it," Kate said. "Don't they?"

"I rather enjoy film-making," Annie said happily.

Kate moodily considered that. She shrugged finally. "Don't tell Richie," she said.

"What?"

"That I'm going to invite Sigler to lunch Sunday."

NOBODY knew how the schedule of shooting would go, or even if Sigler would show up. It was known that he had entered passionate appeals to Kolisch about his script; they had been overheard. Not generally known was that Kolisch had replied, had asked for patience and compliance, at least for now. Kolisch was, certainly, an experienced diplomat, and he respected Richie's power.

Sigler did post the Friday schedule, calling for Kate and Annie only; the scene he called was in draft number four. He scheduled Richie for Monday, and those scenes were also from the approved draft four.

Kate at once suffered a terrible siege of stage fright. When she first saw the call on the board, a chill went through her. My Lord, what had she got herself into? She marveled at Annie Logan's calm. All day Annie was in a lovely, complacent mood, seemed to have no concern about anything, really. Of course, Annie was one of those pretty women who didn't need to feel deeply or intensely. Kate felt intensely about everything.

Richie was no comfort, either. Friday morning as he lay in bed, propped up on both his and her pillows, he was speculating pleasurably, philosophically, about having won the battle of the scripts. She fumbled nervously with her clothes—she simply must hurry, wanted to arrive early at the studio—while he urged her to be calm and detached, as he was.

Trembling in every muscle, she was at the studio by 8:00. At 9:00 Alexandre himself came to dress her wigs. "They say Sigler rehearses each scene all the way through, then shoots it all in a run-through," she told Alexandre, who hadn't the faintest idea what she was talking about, nor did he in the slightest care.

By 10:00 she and Annie were dressed in their "court" costumes and waiting in Studio A on as perfect a reproduction of an eighteenth-century Versailles room as money and talent could arrange. They were giggling and snickering, flicking open their ornate fans and oohing and aahing about their necklaces and rings, marveling at each other's coiffures.

Kolisch came out of his niche of an office and waddled onto the set. "I'm startled to be so pleased," he admitted.

The camera crew came in from the commissary. Steve Houston from Hollywood was the cinematographer, a veteran of scores of films, winner of two Academy Award nominations, friend of Richie's—or at least an acquaintance from previous films. The big dolly was rolled in place, bright lights were flicked on.

"Kill those hot lights," Houston ordered in English. A dozen crewmen translated his command into French, and a moment later the lights were out.

Two young actresses, both French, hired to play ladies-in-waiting, entered from the maze of cables and daintily stepped onto the set.

"Sinful how pretty they are," Kolisch said to Houston.

"Sinful how old I am," Houston said. "I'm too old for any erections except on cranes, Mr. Kolisch. I've even got so I enjoy my own privacy, you know. The most overrated thing in the world is sex, and the most underrated is good cinematography."

Kolisch, laughing contentedly, moved around the big dolly to the chair marked PRODUCER, then moved past it to Annie Logan's. "You're beautiful, Marie Antoinette," he said.

"*Merci,*" she said, smiling up at him.

Sigler's big hulk came through the far door of the studio, and at once all conversations came to a stop. It was as if a gloppy syrup had threatened to engulf them all. The grips held their places, still and quiet. Sigler studied the set from a distance, then moved toward it. "Jesus," he said. "A birthday cake."

Kolisch belched. "You know Houston?" he asked Sigler. "He's the world's best cinematographer."

Sigler said nothing to either of them. He picked up a copy of the mimeographed script, flipped it open. "What's the number we're set up for?"

"Shot number ninety," Houston said.

Sigler located the shot and read the description, one eye closed, one hand massaging the side of his head. He was a passionate creature, a sweaty Thomas Wolfe even when riffling pages.

The script girl, a frail, pretty brunette in her teens, came alongside and knelt on a pillow. "What we do, monsieur?"

"Break the ice," he said. "Get over the fright."

She looked at him, nonplused.

"My script has shot ninety as a bakery's tail, a bread-line," Sigler said to Houston.

"Try one ninety," Houston said, apologetically.

Sigler sought it out, his big hands mauling the pages of the script. "One ninety. Well, that'll do. Where's Antoinette?"

"Miss Logan," an assistant, a young Frenchman, called.

Annie came forward. After a while a yawning Sigler turned to look at her. What he saw was a quite pretty, even royal Marie Antoinette, her hair swept upward, powdery white, a single strand of large pearls interwoven into it, crowning it finally. Around her bare neck was a broad blue ribbon tied in front in a bow, much like a man's bow tie. Her dress was cut low, so that the full contours of her breasts were seen; yellow and white lace overlapped, covering the otherwise bare breasts. A floral wealth of color and ruffles billowed out at the waist to stop just above the blue and yellow dancing slippers. The pretty face was puckish, playful, alive with interest and curiosity, the face of a woman who would like to be amused and would wink delightedly at most anything.

"I don't know," Sigler murmured. "This isn't a musical."

Annie sank into a chair, stunned by disappointment.

Kate moved on set, nervousness radiating from her; she was dressed as the Princess de Lamballe, mistress of the Queen's household. Her hat was a swirl of green lace and ribbons, her pink dress was bordered with tan velvet, the pink yielding to tan near the slippers. The crewmen gaped, made whispered and not-so-whispered comments in French about both women.

"All right. Where you lighting Antoinette, Houston?" Sigler asked, ignoring Kate.

"The script says she's sitting on that stone bench," Houston said.

"We'll work close," he said. "Anything to avoid showing all this color."

Houston turned to him, surprised. "You mean the room?"

"Go sit down, Antoinette," Sigler said.

Annie managed to sit down as directed, but her skirt flounced up. Her French dresser hurried forward and smoothed it down appropriately.

Sigler had his hands poked deep down in his pants pockets, his head lowered, as if preparing to ram somebody. "You're angry, upset with this P-P-Princess Lamballe," he told Annie Logan. "You're testy. She's your closest friend, but you're sending her on a journey to Austria to see your mother. So you're testy."

"With her or with my mother?" Annie said.

"You're sending the P-P-Princess to your mother, who is critical of the flighty way you act as queen. Here you, Princess, come past those cables. Somebody help her. Where you going to stop, Princess?"

"She's to be at the window," Houston said.

Sigler looked through the viewfinder. "We're not close enough to Antoinette."

"If we're close to the Queen, the Princess is out of focus," Houston said. He turned wearily to Sigler. "You want both of them or one of them?"

"Both," Sigler grumbled.

"In focus or out of focus?" Houston said.

Sigler, annoyed, turned away from him. "Work it out." He approached the Queen, walking in the manner of a man who has in the past been even heavier than now. He bent over her. "You ready to go through it?"

"I've never—" She stopped. "Yes," she said. "I guess so."

He nodded, then moved to his chair and sat down with a sigh. "All right, go ahead, Queen."

The Queen sat stiffly on the stone bench. "I know

it's silly, but I've forgot my line," she said.

" 'When you see my mother' is the line," Sigler told her.

"Yes," Annie said, but still hesitated.

"All right, Queen," Sigler said. "Can't you talk? 'When you see my mother' is the line."

"When you see my mother, will you give her my respect," Antoinette said.

"Only your respect?" the Princess replied, her voice trembling.

"What's more appropriate than respect for an empress?" Antoinette said. "Would I send an empress love, endearments?"

"She is your mother."

"Tell her I do not intend to be bored with my own court, as she is with hers."

"Yes, Antoinette," the Princess said.

"I will continue to speak my mind about ladies and gentlemen of this court who are uncharming. If a man can't dance gracefully, if a woman has a penchant for violets—"

"She only counsels you from her own experience as a queen to make friends."

"Friends? They would all kill me if they could."

After a pause: "Indeed, Your Highness, that is what your mother knows."

That was the scene. The two actresses waited in place.

"Well, maybe," Sigler said. "Now, let me ask you, Antoinette, to use half volume and go slower. Princess, speak less formally and use half volume. Let's try it that way. It's not a stage play. All right, 'When you see my mother . . .' "

"When you see my mother, will you give her my respect?"

Sigler interrupted. "Pause before 'respect.' That is,

start to say 'love,' hesitate, then say 'respect.' "

"When you see my mother, will you give her my . . . respect?"

"Not a good line," Sigler said. "She would be more imperious. Cut the 'will you.' "

"When you see my *mother*—"

" '*My* mother,' try that, with the emphasis on the 'my,' " Sigler said.

"When you see *my* mother, give her my—"

"Not so heavy. And look up slowly as if rising to a decision, then coldly . . ."

". . . respect."

"Your *respect?*" the Princess asked, surprised, her voice still trembling.

"What is more appropriate for an empress—"

"Not so loud," Sigler said. "She's more . . . personal. Don't project your voice, Queen. You are only talking to *that woman there,* and you are Antoinette, so powerful that even a whisper can put a person in a tremble. Now what are you two ladies-in-waiting going to do?"

"They were to pass in the background," Houston said, "but if we have only a close-up of the Queen, they can go home."

"You two walk through in the background," Sigler said. "That is—Antoinette, you start your first line and stop before the end because you realize these two attendants are passing. You hear me, Antoinette?"

"Before I finish?" Antoinette said.

"Yes. Now try it."

"When you see my mother, give her my—"

"Now walk on through, ladies," Sigler said. "Damn it, don't you speak English?"

"No, monsieur."

"Tell them, somebody. No, not everybody. One person tell them."

"Tell them what?" the script girl said.

" 'When you see my mother . . .' " Sigler said. "Talk to one another. You walk, but stop as you come near the Queen. Let's see fear in your manner, in your faces. Tell them, somebody. And curtsy, even though she doesn't even glance at you, be abashed to be near the Queen."

They pass on through, confused.

"Give her my . . . respect," Marie Antoinette said.

"Yes, of course," Sigler murmured.

"Your respect?" the Princess said.

"You're too damn loud," Sigler said. "Why the hell are you projecting? She's only right there."

Kate sank down on the floor of the set, her legs trembling so much she could not stand.

"Just do it like I tell you." They rehearsed it over and over, Sigler hammering away unrelentingly, unfeelingly. Everyone was surprised to hear him after about two hours say, "We won't shoot it till last thing today. Put it down for four o'clock."

Houston turned on him, stunned. "Why, for God's sake? We're all set up now. I can set the lighting in fifteen—"

"Shoot it at four," Sigler said.

"But we'll need to dress and make up again," Kate said.

"Keep the outfit on, the wigs, all of it," Sigler said.

"Keep it *on?*" Kate said.

"*She* did," Sigler said, "that princess of yours, she wore it all day, didn't she? Eat your lunch in your costumes. Keep the corsets on. Keep the tight little slippers on."

"It's too bloody hot, Sigler," Kate said defiantly.

"It's no hotter here than at Versailles," he said. "How far is Versailles—ten miles from here? Lie down and take a nap, but keep the dress, the wig, the jewelry on."

"It'll wrinkle the costume," Annie said.

"Antoinette wouldn't have cared, would she?" He turned to the two ladies-in-waiting. "Stay in costume and make-up and be back at four."

The French costume designer was distraught. The French hairdresser, an assistant to Alexandre, put in a formal complaint to a lighting technician—of all authorities. Sigler himself ignored everybody around him, even Kolisch. A burly, fat giant, he beat off all objections. Use script number four, he would, at least temporarily, but he would not do a pretty film.

BY late afternoon all four of the actresses had got food on their costumes, had smudged their make-up, were perspiring profusely, were exasperated with their corsets, but they dutifully, sullenly appeared.

Sigler had them take their places. The lighting was arranged. He had the scene slated. "Now, roll it, Houston," he said.

"I don't have my dress straight," Antoinette said from the bench.

"You don't mean," Houston said irritably to Sigler, "to shoot it right now, do you?"

"Roll it," Sigler said angrily. "Do your best, Houston, to turn the damn thing on."

Houston turned the camera on with a defiant slap of his hand.

The Queen was still getting her clothes in order. She was obviously hot, bothered by the heat. Drops of perspiration stood on her royal, pouting face. Without emphasis she said, "When you see my mother, give her my . . ." She waited for the two maids to pass by, two tired young ladies just now.

The Princess de Lamballe was preoccupied, engrossed in her own wilting concerns, pampering her hair into place.

"My respect."

The scene was natural, unemphatic, conversational, rather stray and wan. Houston was not even bothering to look through the viewfinder. Everything was being done sloppily, Sigler's way, nobody else knowing just what Sigler was after.

"Yes," Sigler said once the scene was done. He frowned at Annie, then at Kate. "It'll do," he said grudgingly.

"I thought it was a run-through," Kate said.

"No, no. That was it."

No compliments from the lord, no smile, no encouragement, no second take, and no consideration of anybody's complaints or pleas. The women, both of them furious and close to tears, stormed out of the studio.

"Astonishing," Kolisch said to Sigler. "You work for disintegration, seems to me."

"Brilliant," Houston said sarcastically. When Sigler ignored him, he moved on off in the direction of the commissary bar, cursing softly.

Kolisch said, "Antoinette really bit the nail in two on the last line: 'They would all kill me,' she said. She meant it."

"She scratched her neck, too," Sigler said. "The guillotine."

"I didn't notice. You want a print of this by when?" Kolisch said.

"Next Tuesday," Sigler said, "with the Spanish footage."

"And what about Monday, about Richie?"

"What about Monday?" Sigler said.

"You can't direct him the same way, you know that."

"What other way is there?" Sigler said.

*   *   *

RICHIE was delighted on visiting the studio to find the two women in tears as they finished their little scene.

"I didn't even know what I was doing finally," Annie said, hurling a hand mirror onto the sofa. "I've never been so sweaty, and grimy, and—ugly."

"Ugly you were not," Richie said, patting her shoulder. "I'm sure of that."

Kate set a martini on the dressing table before Annie. "Here. You know you need it."

Sigler's claim to be an experienced director was put in doubt, as Richie saw it, and he told his secretary to fly to the States and inquire further into the matter. "I wonder if he made that Florida film, for instance. You recall the story of the veterinarian who was chairman of a university music department for twenty-two years, Vorono . . ."

Three

RICHIE'S HOUSE was an ideal place for Sunday lunch, handsome and private, its acre of land completely walled round. Off the sitting room was a long terrace which could be canvas-covered or left open to the sunlight. Canopied at the moment, it looked out over a half-acre of lawn and flowering hedges, with raspberry rows and a cutting garden at the far corner. The house was served by a residential street, and by noon its curious neighbors saw a sight unusual even for this wealthy neighborhood: out front were a Rolls-Royce limousine and a Rolls-Royce convertible, both Richie's; three black Citroën limousines, one of them Kolisch's, one Annie's, the other Kate's; and behind them, just now pulling up to park on the sidewalk, a green, dusty Volkswagen.

Doug Sigler got out. He wore a pair of gaberdine pants, loafers, a blue work shirt and an Irish blue hat. Once admitted to the grounds by the Spanish butler, he stopped in the service yard to admire the sun dial, which was of stone and brass, and adjusted it carefully. Inside he put his hat on top of the marble bust of Napoleon and paused to consider the place, the munificence of an older, more fashionable France: marble figures of golden nymphs and leering satyrs, a tapestry of Pompeiian scenes, old and reserved portraits of lords and ladies. The plaster ceilings held reliefs of flowers, fairies, gods, goddesses, arabesques, curlicues. Here in the hallway was a full-figure painting of a king in chain mail wearing his crusader's sword; beside the painting a golden clock jutted from the wall and beneath the clock was a ceremonial chair covered with silk brocade.

The period furniture, the formal portraits, the Oriental rugs, the deep-colored draperies, everything was more intimidating than he could really endure. "I have come to bury Caesar, not to praise him," he said.

Through the open French doorway he could see Annie Logan, beautiful to a fault. She was wearing a tan hostess gown, and the sun was spilling, glistening, on it and her hair. His breath caught in his throat, as it had when he had first seen her. Within arm's length of her was Eddie Kolisch, dressed in a neat business suit, wearing a garish red necktie, politely listening to Richie tell a story. Richie's attire gave Sigler a start: a droopy, oversized, splotched costume, obviously that of King Louis XVI worn without its padding, so that the effect was clownish.

Sigler joined them, slid onto one corner of the chaise longue near Annie. Richie, in the midst of speech, stopped with a gasp and stared at Sigler.

"Sorry to be late," Sigler said in the offhand manner of a man who never cares about such things. "Your sun dial's wrong," he said to Richie.

Richie sat there studying him critically, openly astonished to find him here.

Sigler yawned, wiped his moist lips with his fat hand. Everyone turned from him to Richie, then to him again. Kolisch cleared his throat. "You still in a hotel, Sigler?" he said. "Annie has found a flat."

"I'm on the Left Bank, in an apartment," Sigler said.

"Small or large?" Kolisch said, warily watching Richie.

"L-L-L-Large," Sigler said. "Two rooms."

"Is that large?" Kolisch said.

"I like the Left Bank," Annie said suddenly. "Rather live on the Right Bank, but I like the Left Bank better."

Sigler turned to her, studied her noncommittally, unsure whether she meant to be amusing or not. "Nice place you have here, R-R-R-Richie," he said.

Richie instinctively started to blurt out a criticism in reply, if only to obstruct further familiarity, but he coughed into a spotless handkerchief instead, busied himself resetting his buffoon's costume. "I would buy it, but this fellow wants three hundred thousand dollars."

Everyone reflected respectfully on that healthy sum.

"Even so, if you want it, Richie," Kolisch said, "you have the money, and when a man gets as old as I am, he realizes—"

"Yes, I see," Richie said abruptly. "But old age will probably only make houses less important to me."

Sigler looked up, surprised by the comment, one more perceptive than he had expected.

Richie said, "I was born poor, Annie, in a city blighted by manufacturing, and I have ingrained habits about saving money." He was not looking at Sigler, had even partially turned away from him.

"If a man has three million pounds," Kolisch said, persisting, "what is three hundred thousand dollars, provided it satisfies a need he has?"

"Quite," Richie said. "But what if the man has the need to own three million pounds?"

Again Sigler started. The man was not a fool after all.

Happily Kate came out onto the porch, a pitcher full of Bloody Marys in her hand. "Whatever reason for?" she said to Richie. "Why need three million pounds?"

"To ensure respect from my wife in my old age," he said.

"You needn't expect any such bargain." Just then she saw Sigler and stopped dead in her tracks. Slowly she moved away from Richie.

Kolisch's dour secretary, Marge, came onto the porch from inside, bringing a tray of hors d'oeuvre. She also stopped in her tracks. Sigler took three or four of the hors d'oeuvre, and began to eat them one after another, ignoring her.

"I wouldn't take anything for the childhood I had, of course, though it was impoverished," Richie said. "My stepfather was a musician who spent most of his time looking for students of conducting, and my mother, who had married at the age of eighteen, was the daughter of a country gentleman who so hated my father that he disinherited her. I was brought up, Annie, on Bach and Handel and Michelangelo and Greek drama; my sense of beauty was so nurtured that I was scared to death of reality until into my thirties."

Annie laughed appreciatively.

Sigler asked her how it was to grow up in Ireland. "I've always wished I were Irish," he said.

"We dreamed," she said. "All the dreaming, the tortured dreaming. My father's imagination was as large as his gift of oratory."

"The Irish do have a fit with reality, don't they?" Richie said.

"Our household was every child for herself," Annie said. "It taught us to persevere patiently."

"With love, I imagine," Richie said.

"No, not really, not love, not hate. More—more than anything else, personality."

"Yes, of course," Richie said. "That's it, Annie. I can understand that."

Horace, Richie's big bulldog, appeared, put his

front paws on Richie's legs, his immense head in Richie's lap.

Richie rubbed him behind the ears, smiled self-consciously.

"Wish you'd do that to me," Kate said to him.

"You're looking particularly attractive today, Annie," Kolisch said.

"Yes, isn't she," Richie said. "The English have the prettiest women in the world just now."

"She's Irish," Kate said.

"Is there no swimming pool here, Kate?" Annie said, seeking to hide her embarrassment.

"No, I suppose not," Kate said hesitantly. "Is there no swimming pool here, Richie?"

"I don't know," he said. "Is there no pool here, really?"

"Richie has a huge pool in Beverly Hills, but he's filled it up with a marble stairway," Kate said.

"Nonsense," Richie said. "Last year when the skirts were short—or was it two or three years ago—the English had the most beautiful women . . ."

The Spanish couple had been putting food on a large table in the sitting room. About 1:30 Kate announced that lunch was served, and everyone finished his drink and went to see what it was, Richie coming along last. "I do mean to talk to you later, Kate," he said to her. "I expect to be asked about our guest lists."

Sliced turkey, sliced ham, boiled shrimp, fruit salad, tomatoes, lettuce, French bread, artichokes, celery . . .

"I think I'll eat a pickle," Richie said, rolling up the sleeves of his comic outfit.

. . . pickles, pâté . . .

With their plates filled—all except Richie, who had one pickle and three olives—they returned to their same chairs on the porch. The butler, Carlos, was waiting there with one bottle of red and one of white wine.

Carlos smiled and started to pour, and only then realized there were no glasses. He began to laugh. His wife came running out with the glasses, and at once he began scolding her dramatically, outrageously, and was still scolding her as they went back inside.

"Consider my own kingly costume, Kolisch," Richie said, munching on the edges of his pickle. "Made for a French barrel. Sigler likes it."

Everyone held his breath. Kolisch glanced uneasily at Sigler.

"I like it," Sigler said. "It's m-m-messy."

Kolisch laughed, as much at Richie's astonishment as at Sigler's effort at good humor.

"Too fat," Richie said. "I've always been thin in my films—"

"Needs more wine on it," Sigler said. "The costume, I mean."

Kate interrupted: "Richie wants to be knighted by the Queen, but he's been unable to live in England because of his taxes."

Laughter, Kolisch first, then the others, all except Richie, who waited for quiet, then turned on Kate and firmly said to her, "I want to discuss my film with Kolisch and—this—Sigler. Why *do* you interrupt?"

"Sorry," she said.

After a silent moment, Richie said simply, "It's a shame. Damn difficult to talk business here, Kolisch, but as you see, a film that's dependent on such costumes as this one—"

"Whenever I turn on television, Sigler," Kate said, "I can tell instantly whether real people are talking, or actors. Why is that?"

"Even without the sound on?" Sigler asked.

"Yes, even before I turn it up."

"But it's more obvious when you turn it up," Sigler said.

"Yes. Why is that?"

"Poor acting," Sigler said. "Old-fashioned."

"Since you asked me," Richie said bluntly, "I'll disagree. If acting is merely real life, there's no standard for acting any longer."

Sigler chewed lingeringly on a piece of turkey and tried to think that through. "Did you follow that, Kate?" he said.

"Now, let me return to the complaints I'm making," Richie began, leaning closer to Kolisch.

"Cheeses. Now we'll have cheeses," Kate said.

"Not another bite," Kolisch said. "Even cheesecake I couldn't eat."

"Everybody up for a stretch and some cheese," Kate said.

Everybody got up, Richie the last one, and though he gave Kate a withering look, he said nothing.

The French cheeses were white, ivory, brown, soft, semisoft, round, pyramidal, cylindrical, mild, zestful, full of flavor. "This one is an old goat," Kate said, "for Kolisch, in honor of the reputation producers have." There was a wheel of Roquefort, a big wedge of Gruyère. Sigler stationed himself squarely before the cheese-board, tasted a morsel of each cheese, interspersing cheeses with sips of wine, finally filling his wineglass to the brim with Montrachet. When Kate commented on his appetite, he withdrew to one corner of the sitting room and sat down on a stool, facing the wall.

"Oh, Lord," Richie moaned. "Oh, it is good, I know," he said, chewing a bite of Brie. "It really is exceptional. The French are fan-tas-tic."

"Sigler, you should be on your knees," Kate said. "Dumas said one should drink Montrachet on his knees, with head bowed."

Sigler slumped to his knees without comment, and drank.

Richie poured Montrachet into his own glass. "He does have a slight sense of humor, doesn't he?"

Coffee.

Then Cognac, Kolisch saying he liked Cognac "but it doesn't like me," Marge humming the theme song of *Kingstree Country,* one of Richie's films, which Annie was eager to recall, Annie humming with her, propped up on the sofa on the veranda, her beautiful hair, freed of hindrances, flowing over her shoulders.

More Cognac. More small talk.

"Those who have seen me act propose to endow me with a larger than average soul," Richie said, his tongue thick and his words languid, "but it's my observation that people like me, whatever our abilities or disabilities, have tiny souls. We understand all about souls and understand all the souls and faiths and about impulses and purposes and resolutions and good intentions and have no part of any of it, for we are able to be off a ways, observers, interpreters, wholly objective. For that reason we are thought of as being cold."

What he was saying nobody was quite sure of.

Marge said she thought the most appealing lover in all of movie history was Harpo Marx. "His beautiful, little sad face . . ."

Kolisch said what Lesher aspired to in life was a heavily padded *New York Times* obituary notice.

Kate said she didn't understand why a man, particularly a president, could not take libel action against himself.

More Cognac. More wine, too.

"Go to walk, take the dog to walk," Richie said. "Show off my baboon suit."

They all helped each other out into the street, Richie holding on to Annie, Sigler helping Kate, Marge helping Kolisch. They staggered past the sleepy, astounded chauffeurs, through a little group of autograph seekers. Richie got entangled in Horace's leash, Horace barked deeply, routinely at the strangers.

"He can't see well," Richie explained, "thinks they're monsters."

Down along the quiet street they tottered, several movie fans following, Richie's costume sweeping the ground. They went into a woods, a park. Kolisch and Marge stopped to count the circles on a tree stump, got confused. They came to a little stream, where Horace drank, then Annie knelt, drank from her cupped hand. Richie helped her to her feet, hugged her suddenly, impulsively, then released her, apologizing at once, trying to get his words in order. "Don't know literally what came over me." At which very moment Horace peed, mistaking Richie's leg for a post. Richie seemed not to mind.

Up the hill to the house they came, and to the playroom, where everybody lay down on the rug and on pillows as Kate flipped on the movie projector. "It's our friend Sophia Loren's latest," Kate said, as she went to sleep.

RICHIE sat on the veranda as dark settled in. Sigler came out, sank down on the steps. Richie decided to try again to approach the matter of the script, of the changes he wanted, but he couldn't quite remember what they were. "Even the first scene in my film needs further changing," he said aloud. "It has me lacking in appeal for my own wife."

Sigler murmured softly to himself, "Surprise, surprise."

"Inappropriate beginning," Richie said.

Kate came out. "It's finished. Thank God."

"Good," Richie said. "Kolisch like it?"

"He's gone," Sigler said. "I saw him moving off toward the gate."

"Oh. I'm surprised to hear that," Richie said.

"What's that truck stopping for?" Kate said. "The one there, with a man on top of it."

"Taking a picture of our house, I suspect," Richie said, disinterested. He turned his back to the road. "Rub my feet, will you, Kate?"

" 'Kiss me, Kate,' is how the line goes," she said.

"Understand you want to do an Irish film," Richie said to Sigler.

"*Storm in the North,*" Sigler said.

"Oh. Irish writer, is it?"

"Well, it was published in Ireland, so I suppose he is."

"You'll get an option, of course," Richie said.

"I suppose I've got some sort of commitment."

"Uh huh," Richie said, watching him thoughtfully.

Annie came onto the porch and stood near Kate, looking about sleepily. "You like to take me home yet?" Sigler asked her. "I can't drive."

She sat down, took her right shoe off and massaged her foot. She didn't even glance at him.

"You want a Reuben sandwich for supper, Annie?" Kate asked.

"I'd better go home sometime," she said.

"No hurry. Richie and Sigler can get to fighting while you're here," Kate said.

"Sigler and I will fight tomorrow," Richie said suddenly.

Sigler got up heavily. "You think it's worth it?" he said, and walked past him, into the house.

For supper they picked pieces of meat from the turkey, using only a fork and spoon because Kate said they might cut their hands off if they tried to use a knife. They drank great wines, and Kate set the cheeseboard up once more, this time in the kitchen.

"I love the Irish," Sigler said to Annie, with embarrassingly heavy emphasis.

"Want a beer, Sigler?" Kate said.

"If it's cold," Sigler said.

Richie looked in the refrigerator. Finally he straightened, mumbling, moaning. "There are no cold beers, Kate."

"Don't you shout at me," Kate said.

"There are no cold beers," Richie said more quietly.

"I told the Spanish couple you preferred your beer *cold*. They thought I was out of my mind."

"It's difficult for a Spaniard to understand about cold beer," Richie said, "but cooling beer is not difficult to do. If a butler has two holidays a week, every week, you can at the least see that he cools the beer during the five remaining days. Beers do stay cold."

Kate dragged half a case of beer from the pantry, pushed it over to the refrigerator and began putting bottles of beer on the shelves.

Richie said to Sigler, "She tends to overact."

That chore done, Kate went to the back stairs and called, literally howled, for Carlos, who did not respond because of either his slumbers or his fears.

"Please, Kate," Annie said, putting an arm around her. "Richie didn't mean—"

"I know what he means. He's been waiting all afternoon for his chance for revenge." She pulled away, moved to where Richie lounged against the refrigerator. "Tell me what you want to say, Mr. Sex of England and the U.S.A."

"Shut up," Richie said mildly.

Annie took Kate in her arms. "Please, darling. Don't."

"Good night, for God's sake," Kate said.

Annie helped her to reach the entrance hallway, but Kate fell on the stairs; Annie got her on her feet again, managed to get her up the steps. "He only mentioned the beers," Annie said.

"I know, he's a lamb, just a lamb," Kate said. She slumped down on the edge of the bed. "Wrong side of the bed. Story of my life." She sat there dejectedly studying her hands. "Drank too much, Annie."

"We all did," Annie said.

Kate stared at herself in the mirror across the room. "You old Scottish dog," she said.

"It has been a beautiful day, Kate."

"Yes." She leaned back into the pile of pillows. "Do you think he enjoyed it?"

"Oh, he did. We all did."

"There were a hundred things that went right. Even Sigler seemed halfway to fit in."

She took Kate into her arms. "Dear Kate, you worry more than you need to, I think."

"I get so scared," Kate said, pulling away suddenly. "It's all strange, being in his film."

"What do you mean?"

"I don't know yet, but I wish I could help him more." She patted Annie's arm. "I get so scared, Annie."

Annie held her, stroked her back and shoulders and the back of her neck, and rocked her comfortingly. "Dear, dear Kate," she said.

Four

AT 8:00 IN THE MORNING Richie was at the studio. At 8:15 was at his make-up table, yawning, frowning at his own face, still fretfully uncertain about his characterization. At 8:20 Kolisch himself wandered in, equipped with a pot of coffee and a jug of cream, and sat down in a chair across the room from him. "Have any coffee cups, Richie?" he asked.

Richie got out two cups, neither of them clean. He shook grounds out of them.

Kolisch poured the coffee. "I've been getting your royal breakfast delivered to the studio, ready for the first scene. I had Maxim's make what they termed 'a special effort.' They have a whole pheasant, a blue trout, four eggs with truffles, half a pound of cake with wild straw-berries . . ."

"The script doesn't specify all that," Richie said.

"Sigler's idea is to contrast the King's feasting with the bread lines of Paris, with a child waiting anxiously for a bowl of soup, and so forth."

"Now what—what will that do for us?" Richie said.

"How will it help—to establish me as an unfeeling glutton?"

"To present you as a human being—"

"A croissant with a demitasse could do that. It's bad enough that in the next scene I have to send for my young wife and say, 'Why don't you ever come to bed with me?' which you'd never get Burton to say to his wife on the screen."

"These are very human situations, Richie."

"People will have their heads wrenched if I appear both as a glutton and without sex appeal."

Kolisch sat back, rubbed his palms together to dry them. "I need this film, Richie, as much as you do. I've been in the backwash too long."

"What does that mean?" Richie said, seriously interested. When Kolisch turned away, began toying with the shade cord, Richie said, "I've played twenty-some different film heroes, and none of them was unattractive. It's not true, either, that they were all the same character. I've played bankers, doctors, the Prince of Denmark, one of the Richards, two or three ad executives, two Ivy League professors, and all have been characters the audience could identify with. They will not identify with a glutton stuffing his fat belly while his people famish."

Kolisch frowned. "It's in the histories, Richie. What makes you so surprised about a real-life situation?"

Richie slammed a wet towel against the wall. "I have always had to think for myself, make my own decisions, or I would have disappeared from public view a hundred years ago." He stopped, considered that, soon enough noticed the smile slowly widening on Kolisch's face. He turned back to the mirror. "Well, say something, damn you," he said.

"He never had a father," Kolisch said. "Sigler says he never had a father."

"Nonsense," Richie said. "*Who* never had a father?"

"Louis' father died young, and his grandfather was too busy with Madame Du Barry to think of him, so he was reared by Catholic tutors. He was an unhappy little fellow, never came to appreciate art or music; as king he rarely ever left the palace, except to hunt. He liked to make keys and to work in the gardens."

Richie, a big lipstick in hand, turned to stare at him. "Make *keys?*"

"He had a hideaway with chickens and goats and a cow. He liked to milk. Something about it for him."

"Nonsense," Richie said. He turned to concentrate on his image in the mirror. "I have always done my own make-up, Kolisch. I do it better than anybody else. I feel the character emerge on my face, take on its own eyes and lips, assume command of its own smiles. But the character I see here before me doesn't enjoy milking nearly as much as Sigler's does."

"He preferred a simple life. The fancy parties and plays and gambling that Marie Antoinette loved, he really didn't enjoy them."

"A pity."

"He was unaware of the revolution building up among his own people, because he had no contact with them, and even the notion of a republic was novel in his day."

"How do you film that?"

"But if you insist on playing him as you would Hamlet or Henry the Fifth—"

Richie turned on him, lipstick in hand. "Are you suggesting I would play Hamlet and Henry the Fifth the same way?"

"I mean with a polished air, a sense of attainment, then you will not give us the visual elements Sigler needs to explain him or the revolution."

Richie stared at him for a long while, then slowly turned again to the mirror, put shadow on his upper eyelid and smoothed it in with his little finger. He tilted his head in the light, studying the effect. "In that Sigler script I die one-third of the way from the end of the picture. Can you imagine? If the film is about *me,* and I *am* the only star in the film, what is the audience to do once I am dead? They're naturally going to assume the film is over. He doesn't know film-making, that's the point, now does he?"

"He's young yet, Richie." Kolisch watched him unhappily, frustrated in trying to find a way past his defenses and his defensiveness.

"And that scene in script four where I throw myself onto her bosom and weep and say I am unable to die and never see the bloody fields and flowers again and would she please forgive me, my pitiful life, which I never valued until it came into danger—"

"Which she cannot do—"

"That's got to be changed, too. How can I weep and have it shown in Texas? Have you ever been to Texas?"

"The New York critics, Richie, rather like—"

"Weeping is not done in Texas, Arkansas, Colorado—"

"On her lap, on your own wife's breast, I don't see anything—"

"On Kate's lap or breast, I'd get my ears boxed. She would heehaw. Muskie lost the presidency because his eyes got moist."

"Richie, you are going to give the greatest performance of your career."

"How do you know that?" Richie said, purring comfortably, acquainted from years past with that old chestnut. "Do you assume the target is so slight I can now do my best work because after thirty years I have you?"

"Richie, you are an accomplished actor, and you are now offered a challenging part, the greatest part of your career."

Richie coughed to hide his embarrassment. "Saint Paul instructed us to be a fool for Christ's sake, but I didn't hear Kolisch mentioned."

"Will you try to cooperate? I know Sigler's rough, but he's really good, Richie. He's got something new and all his own. We need him."

Richie, his eyes closed, his body taut, wearily said, "Afraid not, old chap."

"Will you try both ways?" Kolisch said. "Yours, then Sigler's?"

Richie thought about that. Almost inaudibly, he said, "No."

Kolisch waited. Richie said nothing else. Kolisch got up slowly; a pain seemed to be bothering his back. "I'm too old for these Paris mattresses, you know it?"

"You hurt your back?" Richie asked him, looking up, concerned.

"It's the mattresses, I believe."

"Better get a bed board."

"I know." Starting out, Kolisch said, "Richie, you're a big enough actor to try a young director's style. He's done two great films, Richie."

Richie frowned at himself in the mirror, his lips pressed together tightly. He began testing his expressions: frown, smile, frown.

"Very well. I'll let Sigler fight it out with you."

"I have director approval," Richie said.

"Yes, and you've accepted Sigler."

Richie still studied himself in the mirror. Smile, frown, smile, frown. He retouched his eye shadow with his little finger. He noticed, or appeared to notice, that Kolisch was still standing in the doorway. "I'll be down for my royal croissant in a few minutes. You can dismiss your phony pheasant and blue trout." He held up a warning finger. "And tell Sigler not to try to teach me how to act."

*   *   *

A TENSION spread outward from the sound stage, out into the courtyard and the other buildings. Houston came slowly along from the direction of the commissary, looking about warily. Inside the studio he plopped down on the dolly seat. "I could be in Italy this very minute," he told his French assistant.

Sigler came in, slumped in his canvas chair, which groaned and creaked under him. "Why did they hire me?" he said. "If they want an old-fashioned picture, why not hire an old-fashioned director?"

"You sorry you signed on with the studio, Sigler?" Houston said.

"The next film looks all right," Sigler said.

"Who's producing?"

"A man named Harry Something-or-other, or Peterman. I don't know that we've decided. I want to be in Ireland in three months."

"You think we'll be done here by then?" Houston said.

"Might be done here today," Sigler said.

Houston shrugged. "Yes. But then again you might not be done in three months. I saw Richie string a director up once, make him crawl. He can end your career, period."

"Bullshit," Sigler said. He was worried, however. Later he said, "I never should have got in bed with him. I knew that."

At 11:00 Annie arrived from her dressing room and sat down in her chair. At 11:30 Richie appeared, a fashionable, debonair king of France, slender and erudite, dramatically attired in white stockings, tight-fitting white pants, a reddish-brown formal coat, hair tied behind in a ribboned ponytail. His bulky, sweating dresser came bustling along behind, holding his train off the ground.

The crew at once came to life. An excited hum filled the studio area. Even Annie rose, stood waiting expectantly, respectfully. Sigler got up nervously and walked about among the canvas chairs, glowering at Annie, at Houston, at the set. The Maxim's waiter opened the warmers and proudly, affectionately, brought out the lavish breakfast Kolisch and Sigler had ordered for the King. Brilliant work lights were turned on, banks of floods. The magnificent king's room at Versailles shimmered with gold leaf around the mirrors and doors, even a gold balustrade near the bed, majestic portraits on the walls.

Richie, nodding, smiling in reply to the *"Bonjour, Monsieur Hall"* of the crewmen, took a turn about the set, evaluating it. "Camera's a bit too close here, Houston," he said, indicating the main dolly. "What say?"

"Roll it back," Houston ordered the crew, and a flurry of French commands ensued.

"Hope nobody minds my noticing," Richie said blandly, glancing at Sigler. "Now I assume I enter from here"—he took his place at the doorway, moved through it and into the grand room—"and come upon my breakfast from this direction, like this . . ."

"You're discovered seated at the table," Sigler said bluntly.

Richie turned slowly, frowning. He shaded his eyes to block the bright lights. "How's that, Sigler? Did you suggest something?"

"You're sitting at breakfast," Sigler said. "It's only a ninety-minute film."

Richie reflected on that, his head tilted to one side, his gaze on Sigler. "It's my first entrance and it might as well be done properly, as an entrance, shouldn't it? Suppose I enter here and rather quickly sit down." He turned at once, that matter decided, and came upon the wealth of food, the blue fish and all the other items of the banquet. "A croissant and cup of coffee will do," he told the Maxim's waiter.

The waiter's happy face crumpled, as if struck by a big fist. "Monsieur?"

Kolisch, grumbling like an engine, hurried forward. "We might need the food later on," he told the waiter.

The waiter threw both arms into the air. "It won't be—eatable later."

"Come back at three," Kolisch said frantically. "We've had an alteration."

The waiter, in a rush of words, began explaining the impossibility of Maxim's keeping food warm until three. Kolisch went away with him, comforting him, tipping him, getting him off the set.

"Now, I'll sit down here at the—where is the croissant?" Richie inquired of the world at large.

The confused propman appeared and stolidly received the order for a croissant and cup of coffee. He went scurrying off toward the commissary.

"The script does call for a breakfast," Sigler said tensely.

"Houston," Richie said, "the camera ought to be more to my left, shouldn't it? My left side is my strong side—my stronger side, you remember. I can turn slightly. How's that?"

"Fine with me, Mr. Hall," Houston said. "I don't know what your director thinks."

"Croissant," Richie called out.

As if fired from a cannon, the French propman came catapulting across the studio with a croissant in one hand and a paper cup of coffee in the other. Respectfully, he set them both on the table.

Richie, with immaculate detachment, with only a slight smile, looked down at the croissant, turned it with one manicured, bediamonded forefinger. He raised the coffee cup and sniffed at its paper rim. "Rather unusual service, don't you think, for an eighteenth-century king?"

Sigler through all this stood by his canvas chair, one hand rubbing the back of his neck to keep his head from trembling; the nerves in his neck sometimes had spasms when he became upset.

A proper cup was brought, and a dish.

"Why am I eating breakfast, Sigler?" Richie asked. "What is the dramatic motivation of this scene?"

"I thought it was intended to d-d-demonstrate your opulence," Sigler said.

"Shouldn't there be a plot reason for whatever I do?"

"There ought to be some reason," Sigler said.

Richie turned his most withering gaze on him, considered him as if from a bleak, long distance. "My greed was yours, wasn't it?"

The script girl said, "Mr. Hall, should I strike the written-in words 'pheasant and blue trout' and enter 'croissant and coffee' on the script?"

"Why not?" Richie said. "I say, is there more coffee? I'm afraid I've drunk this. Perhaps Sigler will get some."

Sigler sat down, plopped down in the chair, glowering at the famous actor, his own nerves distressed, too much so for him to offer any opposition just now. This was, he must admit, his first public humiliation.

"No, let Sigler fetch the coffee," Richie was saying. "Let everybody have a job."

Sigler rubbed the back of his neck, sat in the canvas chair, his eyes closed.

"Sigler," Richie called.

Sigler dared not move.

AT 12:35 the lighting was set to Richie's satisfaction and the first take was made. Richie himself called for the

second. He called for other retakes until 1:30, at which
time Antoinette was to make her entrance. Annie Logan
came on set, nervous, obviously confused—she had
never acted with Richie Hall, much less begun an assignment in the midst of a controversy. Sigler got to his feet
to direct her.

"Now you enter from there, my dear," Richie said,
moving in ahead of Sigler. "Yes, you enter from there,
come in on my left side. No, don't go between me and
the camera, which will be there."

"Do I say my line as I enter?" Annie asked him.

"Yes," Richie said, taking a sip of coffee. " 'You
never came to me last night,' I say."

Sigler said, "Line. What's the correct line?"

The script girl read from the script: " 'Yes. You
never come to me at night.' "

Richie stared at her, then at Sigler. "I changed the
line." To Annie he said, "Let's run through it, my dear."

Annie as Antoinette entered the brightly lighted
room, said her line. Richie gave his line just as he had
before, without Sigler's correction.

"It is your prerogative to send for me," Antoinette
said.

"It is a wife's prerogative to come to her husband."

"Ohhh, my lord, I've offended you," Antoinette
said.

"I know I am not sufficiently gifted at chatter to
compete with the young noblemen all around, and I
don't enjoy dances or gambling." He holds up a finger.
"I too often lose."

"Line," Sigler said.

"Damn it, I changed the line," Richie said to him.

"Who the hell are you to change it?" Sigler said,
rising from his chair.

"I am the one who must say it," Richie said. "Are
you going to say it?"

Kolisch touched Sigler's arm, whispered a warning

to him. Sigler glowered at Richie, then at Annie and Houston as they began rehearsing the scene once again. As their director, he was completely ignored.

AFTER Richie was satisfied with a shot's rehearsal, after every detail had been decided, most of them by himself, he at once fell into character, a magical, whimsical smile on his face, one he had used often in his career. He became a pleasant, erudite king of forty-five or fifty years. When a shot was made he became himself and began directing the next one.

"You make me unhappy because of your criticism," Antoinette says to him. Playfully she kneels at his feet. "You see, I am a servant of yours still, Louis. I am your footstool, Louis."

Louis lifts her to her feet as she laughs delightedly. "I can never be angry with you," he says gallantly. "You simply won't permit it. But I do hope for—for less of these all-night entertainments that do not include me." He smiles at her, then abruptly turns and moves away.

For a while, nobody broke the silence. Finally Kolisch said, "Is that what you want, Richie?"

"Well, what do you think?"

"I think it's what you want," Kolisch said.

"Jesus. It's 1920," Sigler said.

"We'll shoot close-ups now," Richie said. "What were the exact words I used on my second speech?" he asked the script girl.

"I don't know, my lord," she said. Realizing what she had done, she became quite flustered.

"Well, I must give the same lines. In the future, somebody write down my lines." To Annie he said, "I have to change every line in every scene."

"Apparently not always the same way," Annie said quietly.

Her criticism took him quite unaware and momentarily confused him; he had assumed her to be a mild and obedient woman.

A WORRIED Kate found Kolisch sitting in the commissary bar. "He wouldn't even try Sigler's way, would he?" she said, sitting down across the table from him.

"No," he said, not looking up. He was sipping his first bourbon on the rocks.

"He's doing the same character he did in his last movies, isn't he?"

Kolisch ordered a second drink from the waitress, and a martini for Kate. "A good character it is, too," he said.

She shrugged. "The world goes on, Eddie. Did you try to talk to him?"

"Yes."

"Good for you, Eddie."

"He didn't even let Sigler open his mouth. He gave him the harsh treatment."

"Did Sigler walk out on you?"

"No. He seems to be in a coma, that's all. He'll—he might accept it as a challenge, might win even yet."

"I hope so," Kate said.

Kolisch looked up at her, accepted that as a revealing admission. "He *is* a killer, you know. Everybody who has worked with Sigler tells me that."

Kate nodded, lost in her own thoughts. "Richie needs that."

The waitress brought the drinks. Kolisch tasted his, swished a bit of it through his teeth. He kept glancing at Kate, appraising her and her future usefulness. "Of course, Richie is not—not without his own killer instinct. There was a time six, seven years ago when nobody, nobody had more power in this business, or was more willing to use it."

"Lop their heads off, he did—directors, actors, staff. Cross him and he would make a slave of you, in public."

"What a difference a few years make. I want to get it back again, myself, Kate, my own confidence in film-making."

"Sigler might help you," Kate said.

RICHIE did another scene in the afternoon, the ceremony of the King's getting out of bed in the morning. Afterwards he reminisced with the American publicity girl, Helen, told her about the success of *Day of Gold*. "Two hundred million people have seen it thus far and every one has wept—even in Thailand." Whenever he was worried and felt insecure, he talked about past successes.

That evening he took Kate and Annie to the Palais Royale for dinner, and ordered extravagantly, whatever he saw that "might take my mind off this abominable situation you've got me into, Kate." After dinner he delivered an impassioned plea to Kate to "stay out of my business." He told her, "It has been known for centuries that it is most improper for a wife to interfere in her husband's work."

As he and Kate drove Annie home, even as they drove through the placid Paris streets, he was at fever pitch. "Are we to make our Henry the Fifths into Falstaffs?" he asked. "Our writers write comedies about healthy people, and serious plays about unhealthy people, just the opposite of the Greeks. No art anywhere today. Nothing lasting to any of it. Don't you agree, Annie?"

"I wish I could . . ." Annie said evasively. "It's my first such experience," she explained.

"My dear, are you a virgin?" he said, smiling suddenly.

"In films," she said quickly.

He took her hand and pressed it. "I should imagine *only*," he said. "Delicious. You are delicious." Turning to Kate, he said, "Tomorrow we do see the rushes, don't we? Isn't tomorrow the day?"

He and Kate went up with Annie to see her apartment. She lived in a fashionable building constructed after World War II, had leased a third-floor apartment, a walk-up. She produced a precious jar of fresh caviar, and Richie at once took charge of it, had Kate cut thin slices of dark bread—"Not too thick, damn it," he said. "Scots always overact," he said.

"All we've got left is bread, after English rule," she said.

"You've still got your charming revolutionary spirit," Richie said, licking a grain of caviar off his finger. "Excellent." He noticed Annie getting a lemon out of the refrigerator. "Oh no, dearest one, no. Let's not try to improve a glorious taste." He licked other morsels off his finger. "My favorite of all, Annie, is the Beluga; it has the largest grains. Connoisseurs have a tendency to veer toward Sevruga or Sterlet, which have small eggs, but as you'll notice connoisseurs often go astray following after delicacy until it disappears entirely. I prefer Burgundy to Bordeaux, for instance."

"Then why do you prefer the English to the Scots?" Kate said.

Richie considered that, a quaint frown on his face. Suddenly he smiled at Annie. "She's got me there." Abruptly, he bent over the pot of caviar, inhaled deeply. "Could you, could you, Kate, spread some on a toast for me?"

"You helpless ox," she said, smiling fondly at him. She fixed him a piece.

"Ahhh, to the stars, our rightful home," he said, offering the bit of toast and caviar for their full consideration. He took a nibbly bite, tasted it lingeringly, lovingly, then took the whole piece into his mouth with a sudden swipe, chewed slowly, concentrating on the taste, an expression of rich pleasure on his face. He swallowed. He closed his eyes. After a moment he said, "Bread's a bit thick, Kate."

ANNIE saw them off, and the moment their Rolls-Royce rounded the corner, she felt peculiarly alone, even deserted, standing on the empty sidewalk. They were a circus of excitement always, providing excitement by arguing if nothing else afforded it.

The hallway was cool; it always was. She looked in her mailbox. No letters.

She climbed the carpeted steps to her door, opened the door slowly, leaned against the doorjamb and looked at the dining room before her, with the little dish of caviar, still only half eaten, and two thin slices of bread remaining. He eats almost nothing yet makes such a production of it, she realized.

Had she been too—openly considerate of him? She was loyal to Kate, too loyal ever to hurt her even slightly, yet she did find it difficult not to respond to the warm, grateful smile he gave her in response to some word or gesture of consideration. He was a lonely man, she felt, extraordinarily vulnerable and insecure. If challenged he masked his insecurity with attacks, and protected himself behind old, familiar, well-tried techniques.

She wandered listlessly about her three-room apartment, the pretty home she had rented for herself. Most of the furniture was French Provincial, quite fine pieces for a sublet. Among the better ones were the antique dining table, three Louis Quinze chairs, and a buffet. There was no terrace, but the French doors in the sitting room opened onto a banister wall topped with window boxes full of flowers.

She drank half a bottle of Clos de Vougeot, a 1962, drank it down like water.

Wonder which restaurant Richie and Kate went to. Loneliness did creep into her very skin, into her flesh. She could not remember not being lonely. Even when she was with Kate, or making ready for a scene, she sensed the hurt of having been deserted.

She would phone him. Now and then, maybe once a month, she simply had to hear his voice. Hastily, before her own best reasoning could stop her, she dialed the overseas operator and placed the call.

While she waited for the operator to ring back, she made a cup of decaffeinated coffee and drank it, finished it, her hands trembling so that she sloshed much of it on the rug.

The phone rang. She snatched it up. His voice answered hers, his voice so very like hers after the twelve years they had lived together, even his accent English, or partly so, rather than Californian. "My dear, I was just about to phone you, my finger was on the dial, when the phone rang."

"Oh." Her breathing was erratic. Why couldn't she pretend, as he could, as he was.

"Been thinking about you every day. How are you and Richie getting on?"

"Fine. He's nice to me."

"Said the spider to the fly. And your old friend from Liverpool—what's her name—"

"How are you, Charles?"

"Me? Me? I'm fine, darling."

"Are you happy?"

"No, not any more than usual."

"Are you lonely?"

Pause. "No. I have several new clients, you know, and I'm trying to get them work. The film world is changing so fast—"

"Are you lonely at night?"

Pause. "No." Pause. "Annie, are you there?"

"Yes."

Pause. "Everybody's wondering how a demure, virtuous woman will do with this world powerhouse of an actor."

"He's really charming, Charles."

"Yes, so he's reputed to be. Is there a bit part for a client of mine, Annie?"

"How old is he?"

"Oh—she's seventeen. Arrived from Virginia."

"What—training, Charles?"

"None. None. That's the trouble."

"Charles, do you ever miss me, that's what I'm trying to find out."

"Every day in every way. I ask myself hourly how my dear Annie is getting on and if she ever thinks of me . . ."

On and on he talked, she listening, she silently considering the utterly false, contrived, ambitious, flawed man she had given her love to and could not find again, either him or the love. She would take either of them. She invited him to come see her in Paris, even that, then said goodbye.

She entwined her fingers and forced herself to sit there, still and quiet, until her heart stopped beating so fast. Why couldn't she simply toss him aside, a rag, worthless to her now. Why did she bother to call him anyway?

The phone rang. Probably Charles again. She let it ring six times. She answered it. It was—it must be Sigler. It was somebody who mumbled, anyway. Deep voice. "Do you want to see a movie?" he said.

"No," she said. Not even sure it was he. "I'm afraid to," she said, and hung up.

*   *   *

IN the bedroom she closed the thick window draperies and turned on the bedside table lamp. She undressed, watching herself in the mirrors, pleased with herself—tummy not quite flat enough, though. She had lost ten pounds but needed to lose more—how many more? Camera makes one look fatter. She turned sideways, patted her naked abdomen.

She tossed her bra into the corner. Her breasts were shaped like large pears. She touched their nipples and watched them enlarge themselves magically.

She lowered her body into the warm scented bath water and lapped it over her shoulders, let it run deliciously down her back. She rubbed soap into her armpits and with her hands lapped water to rinse with.

If the caller was Sigler, she really should have consented. At least she should not have insulted him. She ought to be more practical about the men she encouraged, anyway, less selective, for she really had no one. Maybe even Sigler needed a friend.

She knelt before the gilt-bird faucets and the phallic spout, flicked a drop of water off the spout with a delighted giggle. She turned the faucets on, held her hands beneath the rushing water to rinse them, then tried to press her breasts against the spout. She rubbed her tummy against the spout. She began gasping, giggling as her hands rubbed the rushing warm water into the wet hair of her body.

EVERYBODY gathered to see the rushes, maybe forty people. Among them Houston, the cameraman; Kolisch and Marge; the French publicity girl, Françoise, who preferred to be called Frances, clutching a pair of thick-lensed glasses in her hand, ready to put them on once the viewing room became dark; the Spanish location cameramen who had that week been helping Sigler sort through the Spanish rushes; the costume director, the chief propman, the script girl, the lighting director; the hairdresser, Alexandre, with two of his young assistants; Kate's dresser, Richie's Portuguese dresser, the chef who operated the commissary; an official named Brevoort, there to represent the City of Paris (later he would be needed to write out permits for location shooting, arrange to close off streets, assign police guards, that sort of thing). Kate sat beside Annie, hoarsely whispering, telling about not drinking as much here as in Beverly Hills. A young producer's assistant from Hollywood was there; he was in Paris to confer with Kolisch about release dates—a spy, Marge called him, "sent by Lesher to be sure Kolly's healthy." The company's still photographer was there. Six or seven chauffeurs sat side by side in the next to last row. Four actresses who played ladies-in-waiting were there, as were two actresses who had helped bathe Marie Antoinette. A young cameraman from Spain, Ernesto Barcelona, was there; he had been chief cinematographer of the Spanish footage and had flown from Spain that morning. Richie's male secretary, Vorono, in town for two days, was reading Stefan Sweig's biography of Marie Antoinette. Near him sat Richie's Hollywood agent, a hairy, round-eyed, pleasant gentleman. The general manager of the Studio Boulogne was there. The chief electrician assigned to the film, the chief grip assigned to the film. An actor from the Comédie Française who had been cast as a court jester, two elderly French actors who had been hired to play chess in Scene III-A-3. An official at the Louvre, which had rented the furniture for the Versailles scenes. A French actor who was to play Lafayette—red-haired, of course; the French actors who were to play Marat and Maillard, the revolutionaries.

Among the last Richie entered, coughed abjectly,

slid into the seat beside Kate, who pecked him on the cheek. At once Kolisch got up to introduce the screening. "... sorry to be a few minutes late in starting. We have some of the Spanish location footage. Then we have a few shots from the studio. If Mr. Sigler is here, we can begin—"

"He's not here," Houston said grumpily.

"No?" Kolisch said. "Well, let's begin anyway."

Sigler arrived just after the lights were turned off, stood at the back of the room.

In the dark Houston said, "Everybody keep his hands to himself," and laughed.

No response. The audience's attention was on the screen.

The first shot, a peasant woman's face, Madonna-like, touchingly tender. She is about thirty years of age, yet already her beauty is fading, and sadness has crept into the corners of her mouth and eyes. There is dignity in her face, and sadness, ever-present suffering even, as she smiles just now.

A man. He is talking as he works, using a mortar and pestle on some grain. He scratches himself through his dirty, worn shirt. On the shirt are sewn bits of blue, white and red thread, an insignia of the revolutionaries.

Another woman's face. Her teeth are none too clean, but her smile is warm, compassionate.

Peasant women are waiting in a line, standing like thin, harrowed scarecrows on a damp street. It is early morning of a rainy day. A cart passes, splattering water on one of them.

About all these shots is a calming naturalness, a relaxed, unforced realness, and also a beautiful pictorial quality.

Shots of hands: busy making a fire, sopping up gravy with bread, playfully poking a baby's tummy.

Then a few feet of black leader.

Faces again, but now angry, grotesque because of some fearful sight they are watching.

Shots of hands twisting, of children with blindfolded eyes, of a dog sneaking away, of two rough men with teeth showing, of boys climbing onto a wall to see better. A line of black-clothed women is watching like crows, the sky behind them gray, threatening.

Black leader.

Children playing, happy, peasant children. An old man with softness, hollowness in his gaze watches them.

The Palace at Versailles.

A pompous "Swiss guard" stands sleepily at a gate.

A long hallway, massive portraits on the wall, a wealthy clutter of furniture.

Queen Marie Antoinette, sweat on her face, her dress rumpled, is talking worriedly to the Princess de Lamballe; the scene is ruddy, calm, natural, and appears to be compatible with the Spanish shots.

The bath scene, the Queen's hair bundled on top of her head; again the scene is persuasive, realistic. A priest idly watches from the chair near the tub, a tableful of half-eaten food beside him. The audience whispers, titters with pleased excitement.

Black leader.

A night location shot: a huge carriage is waiting on a cobblestoned street. A man appears, a fat man, King Louis, perhaps, a stand-in playing the part. A little boy and girl wait inside the carriage. The driver sneezes as he quietly closes the door. The fat man leans forward, bows his head. Perhaps he's praying. There is a tenderness about the moment. Even the colors are subdued, as if faded, or seen through a glass darkly.

Then with a direct cut comes the contrast, the startling, mindshocking contrast of a brightly, flagrantly lighted Versailles room, as a slender, debonair King Louis, played by Richie and filmed in Paris, enters through a doorway. The nattily dressed, graceful King rather grandly moves to a table, seats himself, begins to examine a croissant. The situation is by contrast so theatrical, so artificial that the audience in the screening room titters.

Next on the screen is the King with Antoinette, his physical and verbal manner again polished, stylized, the lighting dazzling bright, the lines projected, ringing false, and again an embarrassed titter goes through the viewing room.

One after another, Richie's shots are shown, now intercut with some of the Spanish shots, so that Richie appears even more ludicrous, Sigler having made a sort of dance out of them, out of the lighting contrast and change of techniques, until the audience finally breaks into open laughter, helplessly stunned and amused.

Enraged, Richie stood, turned to face the glare of the projector bulb, faced Sigler. While his own images were being projected on his face, he slapped one hand into the open palm of the other, a sharp, hard slap. "Shut up," he told the confused audience, who were still convulsed, even as his characterization continued to be shown on the screen behind him, his pompous King contrasted with the lowly peasant faces.

WHEN at last it was over, when thank God the projector was turned off, Kolisch sat in a quiet stupor for a long while, munching pills and staring at the blank screen. Finally, slowly, he got up. He stopped at the back of the viewing room, where Sigler stood like an unconcerned stuffed animal. "That Spanish footage is *fan-tas-tic*," Kolisch said quietly to Sigler. "Can we redo the Richie shots to—to get a similar effect?"

Sigler said nothing. He appeared not to notice him, not even slightly to care. Kolisch, as in a daze, moved on.

Houston came by, glanced at Sigler uneasily. Sigler ignored him. Annie Logan came by. Sigler didn't move, and she only nodded to him. Kate followed, touching chairs along the aisle for guidance. As she went by, she barely murmured, "Jesus, mister."

Kolisch waited in the lobby. Even yet he appeared not to be certain just where he was. "No, Houston, we can't do the Spanish shots over," he said, only vaguely aware of Houston having made such a suggestion.

Houston, aggrieved, had not often been as frustrated as he was now. "What the hell—is this movie—am I to do?" His last words were softer than his first, trailed off as his question sought to avoid an answer. "I expect to do this bloody shooting," he said.

Sigler appeared. "You know where the projectionist got to?" he asked.

Nobody said a word, though every eye turned to him. Kolisch stopped him, caught his sleeve. "Can you do in Paris what you did in Spain, I asked you?"

Sigler gazed gloomily at the far wall.

"The Spanish shots are beautiful," Kolisch said.

"But the P-P-Paris shots aren't," Sigler said flatly, without concern.

"How can we get the quality uniform, Sigler?"

Sigler stared at Annie, who was across the room with Kate. "Pretty woman."

"What will help?" Kolisch asked. "What do you need?"

Sigler suddenly straightened, looked directly into Kolisch's eyes. "Less help," he said. He waited, reviewed that in his mind, approved it, then wandered away, apparently to find the projectionist.

Houston resigned as cameraman on the spot. He had been in this business for twenty years, he said, and could tell the score. His own comfort had nothing to do with life-and-death struggles, and this film was now a

life-and-death proposition. Kolisch didn't hesitate to accept it. He accepted in his gentle, courtly way, then went
to find Richie.

Richie was sitting alone in the front seat of his Rolls-
Royce limousine, his hands gripped together on his lap;
he was staring at the dashboard, his expression cold, set
as in a death mask; even his lips were drained of color.

"Richie, it's now or never," Kolisch said. He poked
his head inside the open window. "Only one man can
make this film, and it's going to have to be you or Sigler,
Richie. You hear?"

Richie nodded.

"You agree?" Kolisch said. "It's going to have to be
done Sigler's way."

Richie hesitated.

"I want him fat, Richie, and I want the scenes done
his way, you hear?"

No reply. Tight-lipped, gray of skin, the actor stared
at the veneered dashboard.

"Richie, you hear me?" Kolisch said.

"I hear you," Richie said, the merest whisper.

NEXT day Houston came out to Richie's house, sat on
the terrace. The two of them talked most of the afternoon about Houston's resentment of the young Turks,
as he called them, and about the old days in Hollywood,
"when cinematography was an art, not an accident."

Richie talked fondly about his estate in Beverly
Hills. "I would like to go there today," he said. He
thought about that pleasing notion, suddenly roused
himself. "At the very least I could sit in the sun."

"It's expensive," Houston said, "or I would buy a
country place in Italy."

"Well, there you are. Simplicity costs money these
days," Richie said. "Fishing villages, peasant farms,

they've all become terribly expensive."

"What do you do in Beverly Hills to—occupy your-self?" Houston said.

"I—I hibernate. I think of my acting life. Then I have a vineyard above the house—only fifty vines. Have you ever pruned vines?"

"They're all dead now, aren't they, the best ones?" Houston said.

"What?" Richie said.

"The stars, the great stars. Excepting you, Harrison, Brando, Olivier."

"Well—" Richie frowned in the direction of the raspberry canes. "From time to time, we all die."

Kate joined them on the terrace, stretched out on a chaise and began modestly, carefully joking about the idea of Richie's leaving the film, leaving Paris just now. Houston sat with his head resting on his hands, his arms propped on the arms of his chair, his gaze on her, then on him.

"You've bullied all the other directors, but maybe it'll be fun to work with this one," she told Richie.

"An ape with the beer-guzzling attributes of a Mafia king and the artistic taste of a tree stump?" Richie asked her.

"He has the most beautiful Spanish shots," she said.

He glared at her. Kate playfully stuck her tongue out at him and relaxed back into the chaise, smiling at him as if to apologize. Houston watched her, then Richie.

Slowly Richie stood, hovered over her. "I wonder about you, whose side you're on," he said. "I wonder why I ever fell in love with you," he said, the thought just coming to him, apparently, and surprising him so much he wandered on out into the garden.

A thousand thoughts tried all at once to crowd into her mind; Kate started after him, but hesitated at the garden steps, stood rigidly staring at the stiff-backed, slender man who was making his way through the maze of flowers, along the intricate paths, away from her.

VORONO came by for cocktails, reported interesting leads about Sigler's past. Richie told him to look particularly into the first film, to see who had helped him with it. "The film had a poetic quality this fellow could not have supplied. It's simply not inside him," Richie said.

"No one man makes a film, anyway," Vorono said. "Not alone."

"Perhaps not."

"Every director has had films taken away from him."

"Find out who did those scenes for him," Richie said. "And where he is. And go to Dublin on the way, find out about I.R.A. novels—old, new, all of them, especially *Storm in the North.*"

"Use your name?" Vorono asked.

"Only as the star being contemplated. I don't buy options in my own name, do I, Vorono?"

"We have an offer for one of the old ones, a Southern thing."

"Sell it, then. Who's name's it in?"

"Horace's."

"I'll sign it."

Richie was getting into the swing of film-making now, Vorono noticed. He had always been an avid participant in whatever he did. He owned several novels and plays; years ago, in his heyday, he had bought and sold properties often. "This fellow Sigler thinks he has some sort of commitment on that *Storm,* but you might find it's not as certain as it might be," he said.

Five

SIGLER'S DIRECTING in that first film had been noticed by most reviewers. He had combined camera techniques similar to those used by Robert Flaherty in *Man of Aran* and *Louisiana Story* with realistic, high-quality sound techniques, recently made possible by selective unidirectional microphones. In filming each scene he had used three cameras, two of them shooting close-ups and cutaways, the scene being filmed as a piece, without interruption. The lighting of many of the shots, therefore, lacked cinematographic excellence, but the sense of naturalness was if anything enhanced by this, and the audience did feel on viewing the motion picture that they were being allowed to watch actual lives being lived, actual lines said, and that the gestures, smiles, frowns, signs of tenderness, love, anger, fear were those expressed by human beings. Sigler had often observed, as Kate had mentioned, that a viewer of television could instantly tell if a scene was staged or actual, and he strove to do away with all artificiality, succeeding to a remarkable extent.

A few other observations about his style:

(1) There was more to see in his scenes than one could take in during a single viewing, because indiscriminantly Sigler would show a group of several characters reacting differently, naturally to a crisis before them, some tensely, others nonchalantly or evasively, never with the uniformity of response directors usually require.

(2) He was willing for each actor to develop his own characterization, so long as he settled into the realistic genre. He encouraged improvisation. Spontaneity was the gushing lifeblood of his scenes.

(3) He used very little music in the background, managed to leave occasional, long periods of silence.

(4) In editing, he eliminated weaker scenes and parts of scenes, much as Flaherty did, so the story line was random, lacked specific definition.

(5) The total film was a conglomerate of views, groping for and yet avoiding a theme. Sigler himself apparently tended to side with those in action, to view action as a desirable activity in itself, even violent action, regardless of purpose. In the first film, the sixteen-year-old son killed his parents supposedly in order to be able to live his own life in the isolated place where his family had for generations lived, privately knowing all the while that the action would make living there impossible.

(6) Sigler was embarrassed by anything he considered sham, and he considered pretensions sham. He was willing to destroy everything in order to destroy what was false or decaying. In most every sense he was nihilistic, yet his films conveyed deep emotional concerns and often rather basic, old-fashioned longings. In this new film, Louis XVI would escape one place after another, trying to find comfort and safety once again, only to end up each time in a more confining, tortured situation. Against him, on the other side, the revolutionaries would

adopt more and more heartless, desperate means to destroy nobility, finally killing without any except a madman's plan, seeking to destroy all the so-called superior citizens among them. In a sense they were the boy destroying his parents, and therefore themselves. Sigler, with his own hatred of pretentiousness, and with his own emotional lust for violence, was moving every day more devotedly into the vortex of the motion picture, and now was drawing it around him like a cloak.

IT would, of course, be necessary to stage Richie's next several shots with attention to his embarrassment, since the crew were aware of his failure during the past week, and so, for that matter, were their wives, children, neighbors and even certain members of the press, who had reported the matter as brief, pungent rumors to the effect that Richie Hall was having trouble getting inside the character of King Louis XVI: "Not the first time people have had difficulty getting inside our fat King Louis." The public report annoyed Richie, and to a significant extent frightened him. Apparently Sigler was prepared to move their contest into the open, where only Richie conceivably could be hurt by it.

Kolisch instructed Sigler to confer with him, in order to pick a scene with which to begin again. There was little apparent interest on Sigler's part in any such careful measurements of Richie's sensitivity, but he did come to Kolisch's office, as invited, did bring his copy of the script, did open it to the getting-up-out-of-bed scene Kolisch had selected, did listen with his customarily grieved indifference to Kolisch's proposal that the other main acting part in this particular scene be recast so that the rehearsals could be termed casting sessions.

"Recast Gottlieb?"

"Pretend," Kolisch said. "Cast Gottlieb finally. We

used to do this with Gable, have him audition the scene with different actors, until he began to find himself. You know—after a time he would hit on—on something."

Sigler bleakly considered the proposal, murmuring complaints about the loss of time. "The poor people will march soon," he told Kolisch, apparently consciously believing that their march might take place whether contrived or not, whether arranged by him or not, that the march was an actual prospect, unpredictable, imminent. "Need three cameramen," Sigler said. "French or Spanish."

"Yes, well—" Kolisch purposefully avoided that intrusion and busily began jotting down figures on a yellow pad. "Need a full day, I would guess, for casting this bedroom scene."

Sigler was staring out the window with the peculiar, rapt concentration that small boys often use in hateful school situations. "I need three other assistants," he said. "French."

"Sigler, I'm trying to talk about this one scene, the Richie Hall ice-breaker, and you're bargaining—"

"Two hundred dollars a week each," he said.

Kolisch stopped. A specific offer always caught his attention, a specific sum of money required a decision. Never want to miss a bargain. He wrote "200" down on the paper. "How long?"

"Th-th-th-th—"

"Three months? Thirteen weeks?" Kolisch multiplied by thirteen. "All right, done, provided we're settled on this ice-breaking scene."

"And two more researchers."

"I'll talk about that later," Kolisch said.

"Need to delete the storm," Sigler said.

"What storm?" Kolisch asked.

"Of the Bas-t-t-t-t—"

"Bastille? You can't eliminate *that*. The storming of

the Bastille was the start of the French Revolution."

"He wasn't in it."

"Who?"

"Fat Louis."

"Of course he wasn't in it, but it was *his* prison. They overthrew *his* prison."

Sigler shrugged. Gloomily, pensively he stared out the window. "Too much noise," he said, shaking his shoulders as if shaking himself free of the whole idea. "So I've cut it. The damned p-p-p-prison was empty anyway."

"Cut it?" Kolisch said, astonished.

"Need the money later," Sigler said, still staring at the window with an impish frown. "For my church scene."

Kolisch slowly shook his head in wonder. Now was the moment to check Sigler, to control his power, and he did not. And the reason was that he really didn't want to.

The scene selected for an ice-breaker involved reports about the Bastille, but did not show the attack. The scene had to do with King Louis getting up in the morning, a significant ritual indeed, written by the Hollywood team and rewritten by Sigler. One of the Versailles rooms in Studio A was selected for the wealthy King's bedchamber, and another, an adjoining room, was made into the bull's eye room, his office, and both were waxed to lend a somber, dull appearance, at Sigler's suggestion. Past the room of the red-cloaked Swiss guards, and across the staircased hallway, was the Queen's apartment, similar to the King's. The King's bed had a gold spread with royal steeds decorating it, the canopy had his lordly crescent emblazoned on it; the Queen's bed had a white spread with pansies strewn over it (Sigler changed it to gray), and the canopy matched it identically. In each bedroom was an ornate, graceful sofa, a small desk made of mahogany, a chair near the bed, where an attendant might dare sit down provided the royal person was asleep. On the wall, high near the ceiling, was a gold ornate clock. The draperies in the King's chamber were of woven threads of gold. The rug in each bedroom was brown, a suitable contrast to the light yellow of the moldings and the wooden frames of the beds and upholstered furniture.

On the day of the "casting session," Sigler had two nervous actors standing by to try out for the part of the Prime Minister. He was himself apprehensive. No information had leaked from the private dressing room area of the studio.

Richie appeared at the exact time of the call, Kolisch beside him, and his appearance was appropriately sloppy, gross. Kolisch obviously was pleased. Richie wore a robe, under it a nightgown, and under the gown a padded body stocking; even his upper legs were padded down to the knees, making his unpadded shins and feet appear ludicrously bony. His body was puffy with fat. His hair, actually a wig, was thin and receding. His face was plump, and his jowls sagged. His bleary eyes suggested a fair amount of royal dissipation. The overall effect, except for the shins and feet, was convincing; the King at thirty-eight years of age had lost his shape and had become slovenly and utterly comfortable and content.

Sigler was wary of such complete cooperation. With apparent indifference he introduced the first actor, a man named Foch, trying out for the Prime Minister. Foch was a veteran Paris stage character actor, just now frightened to be in Richie's presence. Sigler said to Foch, and incidentally to everyone, "We want to cast the Prime Minister, named Necker, though he was not the Prime Minister at this moment in history, for he had resigned, but he had been Prime Minister earlier and would be again." It was a long sentence for Sigler. "He is to be our one and only, anyway."

Foch, who understood nothing Sigler had said, looked blankly at him. Richie turned to him, smiled slightly, knowingly, then shrugged.

Sigler introduced another actor, Gottlieb, a German. He also was here to try out for the Prime Minister, Sigler said, but in this first run-through would be the Minister of Finance. Sigler supplied him with pages from his own tattered script. "One-line part," Sigler murmured, and pushed him into place. "In bed," Sigler said to Richie. "The King is a slob, but he's a royal slob." Sigler began going about among the actors, moving one person here, another there, the priest away from the bed, the historian nearer, the chief valet farther away, moving the covey of attendants into place. "Into bed, King," he said again, moving on, but Richie remained standing near the camera, observing the situation. At last Sigler stopped, turned to face him. "You're in bed, King."

"Sounds rather like a dog, doesn't it?" Richie said.

Sigler took an exasperated breath, but something in Richie's cool, aloof manner gave him pause. "What do you want?"

"Now the scene will open on me, will it? A close-up," Richie said.

"I will arrange the shots," Sigler said. "All you do, King, is wake up and follow that script."

"My acting changes depending on whether I'm in a close-up, medium shot, long shot, seen from the side," Richie said.

Sigler began to stutter. "You w-w-w-w—"

"Yes, I wake up," Richie said, still smiling at him. Of the two of them, here on the studio floor, Richie was in better control.

"W-W-Wake up," Sigler said.

Kolisch appeared beside Richie, took his arm. "Now let's do go to bed, King."

"I don't mean to be called King," Richie said.

"Your Majesty—are we to say Your Majesty?" Kolisch said. "Are Sigler and I to say Your Majesty?"

"Here, King, come, King. If I am to be a king, then I can't be a dog, now can I?" Richie said.

Kolisch whispered: "How reasonable."

"And that actor there looks too much like a queer to play a court attendant, Kolisch."

Kolisch turned to stare at the embarrassed young actor Richie had singled out. "I'll—I'll mention it later to Sigler," Kolisch whispered. "Now will you get into the bed?"

"My mother would stand at the back kitchen door and call, 'Here, King, here, King—'"

Once in the bed, Richie asked that his nightgown be drawn to its full length and straightened, which Sigler pointed out rather denied that he had been asleep, but never mind. Sigler himself, trembling visibly, straightened the bedcovers. Kolisch reminded Richie that this was, after all, only a casting session. "Let's get on with it."

Sigler finally surveyed the scene, a hangdog look on his face, a threatening anger lingering about him. Two of his new French assistants were present for the first time this morning; he bumped into one of them, a bright-eyed, shiny-skinned brunette named Charles, and shoved him away roughly. His French cameramen, three of them, were idly lounging in the King's office, smoking, the smoke rising in fans and billows into the work lights. No matter; there was to be no shooting just now. Kate sneaked in, tiptoed to a chair which she pulled behind a stand so Richie wouldn't see her. She peeked around the stand's columns, had a quiet laugh seeing Richie lying high on the feather pillows. She had herself reminded him last night of the stage make-up he had used for his characterization of Henry VIII in London years ago, when she first had seen him on the stage, she only a child then.

"Who's on set?" Kolisch asked. "When does this show get on the road?" he asked Sigler.

Sigler shook off his preoccupation, mangled a list of characters as he unfolded it. "Valet and two assistants," he called. "Are you here?"

The three actors held up their hands.

"Personal secretary. Two gentlemen-in-waiting. A barber. The doctor. The bootman. A priest. The historian. The Prime Minister. The Finance Minister. You two ministers are waiting over there near the window. Take your glasses off, doctor. Shut the window. Who opened the window? Now, this is the King, the God Almighty of the most powerful nation on earth, the stupid Supreme Majesty—listen, be quiet, will you? All right, wait for him to wake up. Don't disturb him. Everybody quiet." Sigler crouched near the main camera location, watching. All the attendants were in place, waiting for the royal eyes to open. Louis, on his back, slept on. He seemed to smell an unfamiliar odor; he sniffed significantly through his big Bourbon nose. A few anxious moments later he wet his lips. At last he opened his eyes, looked up into the faces of his covey of aides.

"All right, doctor," Sigler said, cuing the proper actor.

The doctor approaches. He bows as he takes hold of the King's wrist; he counts audibly the royal pulse beat.

The historian begins writing notes about the examination.

"What time is it?" Louis says.

"Half past seven, Your Majesty," the historian says.

"Whisper," Sigler says. "Don't speak out loud to the King, historian."

"Half past seven, Your Majesty," the historian whispers.

"What means the weather?" Louis says.

"Clear and warm," the historian whispers.

"I heard no clock strike," Louis says.

"Too loud, Louis," Sigler says.

"Too loud for what?"

"For waking up."

"Do you really think so? I do need to hear myself."

The doctor releases the King's wrist, feels his forehead even as he leans over his chest to peer into Louis' mouth. "Tongue clear, eyes clear," he murmurs to the historian. "No temperature. Pulse strong. The King is well."

The aides sigh, relieved, even if bored.

The doctor steps aside and another aide comes forward, lays one hand on the royal bedclothes. Slowly the covers are pulled back, revealing the royal person. Louis sits up. He belches and at once an aide hands him a pottery mug, from which he drinks coffee. He belches again, drinks from the mug, belches.

"Count the belches, historian," Sigler says, "count them, moving your lips, then write the total down."

Louis gets to his feet, accepts the aid of his bootman as he shuffles into two royal slippers. His valets bring him two royal robes. He chooses one, tries to tie the tasseled cord himself, even as an assistant valet tries to do so. The King slaps at the valet's hands irritably.

"Not bad, not bad," Sigler says. "Now move on, damn it."

Louis, taking his time, pads across the room, his stomach still bilious. He doesn't speak to the ministers. He tries to open the window, cannot do so. An aide springs forward and opens it for him. He stands in the open window breathing in the fresh air, a smile appearing on his face—the first smile of the morning, as the historian dutifully notes.

The Prime Minister, a small, puckered, stumpy man, cold, efficient, graceless, a blunt man full of statistical matters, approaches, clears his throat to introduce the fact of his presence.

"Yes?" Louis says, still looking out the window.

"There were but seven prisoners in the Bastille, Your Majesty. Four insane men for their own protection—"

"Where is my comb?" Louis says.

The barber slips forth from among the waiting attendants and begins to brush his hair.

"Another prisoner was there, having been found guilty of both incest and murder," the Prime Minister says.

"I'll not be shaved until after the hunt," Louis says and motions for the barber to scratch his back.

"I trust Your Majesty has decided to punish the offenders," the Prime Minister says.

"Rub his back, somebody," Sigler says. "Prime Minister, keep moving to stay in eye of him."

"What means 'eye of him'?" the Prime Minister asks.

"Look at him," Sigler says. "Keep turning, King."

Louis wistfully grimaces as his back is rubbed. Sigler motions to the head valet, who with two assistants approaches with Louis' clothes. "How many attackers were there?" Louis asks.

"Your Majesty, large crowds of people were on the streets yesterday, it being a holiday and very sunny weather, and a young man named Maillard was haranguing at the Hôtel de Ville—"

"How many?" Louis asks, trying to look over the heads of his busy valets, who are dressing the royal person.

"Soon, how soon I don't know, but soon, a mob was formed—"

"You don't know how many?" Louis asks.

"This mob decided to advance on the royal prison, the Bastille."

"How many in the mob?" Louis says, his head reappearing, disappearing.

"Perhaps ten thousand, sire."

Louis now wades free of the valets, emerges in riding togs, his belt undone, an unbuttoned silk shirt flapping, which he proceeds to button incorrectly. "I don't know how to punish *ten thousand people.*"

The Prime Minister continues: "They killed the guards, in cold blood, Your Majesty."

The King stops, seriously evaluates that. "Why?" Louis says.

"They were angry at—Your Majesty."

Louis' eyes are unwavering. He turns to stare at the Prime Minister. "Why?"

"I am sorry to say, Your Majesty, that some people hate the idea of you, of any nobility."

The idea is not an easy one for Louis to contemplate. A quizzical, annoyed frown contorts his face, a twitch annoys his right eye for a moment. He is on the verge of the decision, whether to punish the attackers or not, when he sees his little daughter, Charlotte, about eleven. At once he relaxes, smiles. "Oh, my sweet *chérie.*" He flops to his fat knees, holds out his hands, and the girl runs into his arms. Louis caresses her, moaning delightedly, covering her face with moist kisses. *"Bonjour, chérie, bonjour—"*

The Prime Minister throws up his hands, exasperated. One of the child's nurses, this one about fifty-five, enters, distraught. She sighs with relief on finding her charge, takes her from the reluctant King, leaves with the child, all of this in a flurry, which passes, leaving Louis on his knees.

"Look after her fondly," Sigler tells him.

"I am, damn it," Louis says irritably. "Can't you see me looking after her fondly?"

"Now, from outside you hear horses and go to the window," Sigler tells him.

Richie rises slowly, goes to the window, doing an

excellent fat man's walk. "Am I to see anything?" he asks Sigler.

"Hunting horses," Sigler says. "I'll insert them."

The Prime Minister approaches the King. "There are other insurrections, Your Majesty, like warts, popping out everywhere in France. Only if you take firm action now, Your Majesty, can you put an end to them."

"How do you stop a—wart?"

"Your Majesty, it is a revolution."

Louis' face freezes even as a flash of fire comes into his eyes. The word itself is abhorrent to him. Once more his mind seems to grapple with the tough decision being required of him, but gradually the sternness disappears and a friendly considerateness comes over him, his contented, natural bent returns. He begins to hum.

The Prime Minister says, "Release the army on these ten thousand, sire." When he receives no reply, he turns away, shaking his head helplessly.

The Minister of Finance approaches. "Your Majesty, we are near bankruptcy. It is my duty once more to remind you—"

"I wonder at my teachers," Louis says bluntly, "for in all my childhood they never once dared mention the words *bankruptcy* and *revolution.*"

Sigler moves the bootman forward, Louis' big riding boots in hand. The bootman proceeds to help him put them on, the King stomping, both men pushing, shoving manfully, with grunts and groans.

Sigler nods to an attendant, who brings Louis a selection of hunting knives, from which he takes one, puts it in the sheath on his belt.

"If you ever are left in the woods," he tells the ministers, "it is of no small importance to have a knife along." That said, he moves into his office.

"All right, take a break," Sigler said.

"Is that it?" Richie said.

"That's it. Be back in ten minutes."

"I mean is that your critical opinion?" Richie said. "I had expected to have an Olympian view."

"It's coming along," Sigler said.

"See here, about the queer one," Richie said to Kolisch. He saw Kate, stopped still. "Ahhhh, see me now, darling, with my royal belly." He was really quite pleased with the personality he had managed to portray, even on this first run-through. "Nobody will recognize me, will they?"

"Your feet are—absurd," she said, giggling. "And you're projecting too much."

"No, darling, I'm doing something foreign to you and Sigler—I'm acting."

That then was the strained but endurable atmosphere on the set as the real work of filming began, with the two chief male figures virtually isolated, estranged from each other and neither supported by anybody else —Kolisch in a conciliatory limbo, even Kate held in suspicion by her husband, nobody trusting anybody else— yet the scene working well, with a puffy, real King striving to emerge through Richie's body and voice.

The scene was rehearsed twice more, then there was rehearsal of a brief scene in the King's office, where he refused to sign an order to ferret out and punish the ten thousand.

After that Annie Logan came flouncing into the studio, dressed in the Queen's finery, and Sigler led her to the set, into her own bedroom, where a propman was serving out a feast. "Here, Queen, sit here," Sigler said. "Who is the hairdresser? Where are the ladies-in-waiting? Will everybody *shut up!*"

Three ladies-in-waiting presented themselves. The Queen moved to an elaborately served breakfast table, where her and Louis' chairs were placed. Sigler told her, "He's approaching. Offscreen you hear guards clicking their heels, doors opening and closing, then enter the King and his entourage."

A hush finally fell over the set as the rehearsal began.

Louis enters. "How did you sleep, 'Toinette?" he asks, walking up to her.

"I slept well. And you?"

"Well." He picks up a cooked pheasant from off the table and, after a moment's reflection, stuffs it into his hunting jacket pocket. In another pocket he stuffs half a loaf of bread. He bites off a large piece of cheese. "Cantal?" Louis asks. He tucks that into a pocket. "'Toinette, we must economize," he says, and at once turns and leaves.

As his footsteps fade away, as the doors close off-screen, Antoinette angrily strikes the table. She mimics him. " 'How did you sleep, 'Toinette?' " she says huskily. " 'We must economize.' " She picks up a platter of food and hurls it across the room at the door as her ladies-in-waiting scatter like quail.

"Now, see here, we're going to need that food when we rehearse again," Sigler tells her.

During the midday break Sigler busied himself with the three cameramen, deciding on placement, angles, lighting, and it was assumed he would proceed to the shooting. He wanted a pan shot of the faces of the aides as seen by the King when he wakes up. Also, he spent twenty minutes on a high-angle shot of the King as he and his bootman stomp the boots on, a sort of mad dance. Meanwhile Richie and Annie waited in the studio, trying to pass the time and remain calm.

"No, I didn't see your scene," Annie told Richie. They were resting in their captain's chairs. "But everyone says it went amazingly well."

"My dear, why amazingly?" he said, smiling kindly at her.

That smile again, so personal and intimate; it surprised and thrilled her.

After all their waiting about and all his perfunctory preparation, Sigler shot nothing, nor did he tell the actors when he planned to, on what day the scenes might be filmed. He did tell Gottlieb he had won the part of Prime Minister, and he chose the other actor, Foch, to be the Finance Minister. "This was only a casting session," he said to Kolisch, who had come forward to protest so wasteful and rude a maneuver. He dismissed the company and had started out when he seemed to notice Richie; he came back, stopped close to him. "We'll take the scenes later, when you've got hold of the part."

Richie blanched. "Son of a bitch," he murmured, surprised.

"And—King, enjoy the morning more, the air, whenever you get free of the worries, and we see this with your daughter, with your listening to the hounds, with the horses, the window, eager to throw it open and get a lungful of air, which any Frenchman—"

"Now, how do I—" Richie said, interrupting, "what do you mean *hounds?*"

Sigler was distracted by the interruption. "You do it then."

Richie looked helplessly after Sigler as he left, then at Kolisch, who in turn looked helplessly at him. "Hounds?" Richie said.

"His mind is on the big scenes," Kolisch said evasively.

Later in the courtyard, Sigler, who was talking with the new French assistants, stopped Richie as he was entering the Rolls-Royce. "I mean, we sense the open air and his indecisiveness."

With one foot inside the car Richie paused to think that over. He got on into the car, shut the door without comment, and rolled up the window in Sigler's face.

Six

ANNIE AND KATE were interviewed occasionally by reporters from French, Italian, English, American or some other country's newspapers or magazines.

Kate told the London *Times* reporter that Richie wanted to be knighted by the Queen but had an American image. That infuriated him.

"You said you didn't care whether you ever got knighted or not," she said.

"But then you tell them I do care—"

"Well, if you don't care, what do you care what I say to them?" she demanded of him.

"Not funny, not funny at all, Kate," he told her.

At the studio Annie was interviewed by a *New York Times* reporter, a weary young man who disliked Paris. "Everybody is so rude in Paris. In New York I expect it," he said.

Richie was interviewed as many times as his time and patience permitted, but he disliked anybody prying into his personal affairs and distrusted reporters. Often he contented himself and disappointed the interviewer by discussing his estate in California. "A small private vineyard, I make a delightful white dinner wine there. I can close my eyes and see the house: tile roof, terra cotta stucco walls, a central, tiled hallway, a view toward the south with the city dead below, the view to the north of my little vineyard in the sun—"

"About the film now being made, Mr. Hall," the reporter interrupted.

"Excellent film." Richie gave perfunctory answers to most all questions. If asked about his marriages: "Most happy." His childhood: "Extremely happy." His school: "Adored it."

"Adored school?"

"Well, I didn't like the studying part of it."

"What do you think of acting with your wife now?"

"I rarely think of it."

"Is there some other special part you would like to play with her?"

"You mean like Rhett Butler?"

"Yes."

"No."

"How do you feel about being Miss Logan's husband, Mr. Hall?"

"Am I her husband?"

"In the film."

"Oh?" Pause. "So?"

"How do you feel, Mr. Hall?"

"I feel very well, thank you."

"With Miss Logan?"

"No, I haven't seen her since yesterday afternoon."

"Why did Mr. Houston resign, Mr. Hall?"

"Has he?" Richie said. "Do I know him?"

"The cinematographer."

"Are you asking me?"

"Might he have been fired?"

"Did she fire him?"

Only occasionally was an interviewer able to disrupt Richie's customary restraints and refrains. A young Scot made one of the more serious efforts: "What is the purpose of art, Mr. Hall?"

"Of art?" Richie blurted out, startled to be asked anything meaningful. "Of art?"

"Of plays, for instance? Of films?"

"Well—they have been called our effort to re-create ourselves. Scotland has its art, Poland, Italy, et cetera."

"The film is the dramatic form we see today in Scotland, and the films aren't produced there."

"No. It is all international, isn't it?"

"And commercial. Is this healthy, to have all the world's peoples re-created by film-makers in commercial centers?"

Richie stared at him, quite considerate of the question. "I really never go into that."

"What do you think, for instance, of the new crop of films? Do you find that they have heart, mind? We have the genitals, but—"

"Well, if the people are to re-create themselves, perhaps the genitals will be . . ." He wound down slowly even as he talked. The subject was too important for jokes. He sat forlornly frowning at the Scot. "I understand what you're saying, of course; quite a serious consideration."

"What are your opinions about it?"

Richie turned to look at the view from his window, but he was not distracted; his mind was wrestling with the request. "Actors don't step out of their roles, you know, don't voice opinions. In the war they used to *sometimes;* at the end of a television comedy, they might appear on screen and say we must win the bloody fray."

"Will you give me your opinion?"

He was on the hook, all right, and was sternly attentive, but much like his characterization of Louis XVI, the sternness seemed to leak out of him after a few moments, and with a quick smile he broke free. "Row on row, golden in the sun, a little hillside covered with the vines, one golden crop a year, only one, all in an hour garnered in. I love Nature, don't you?"

Another incident having to do with the publicity department involved the government official who must approve location shooting. Monsieur Brevoort asked to read the script. Kolisch over the years had found that censorship could be a treacherous pit, indeed; however, he sent Frances, the French pub girl, off with a copy of the script and instructions to report back to him should the least trouble ensue.

She didn't return for three days. She brought with her a script with whole scenes slashed through, characters redefined, and the concepts of the film altered by a French patriot. "I thought you—if there was any trouble—" Poor Kolisch lapsed into silence, realizing that criticism of Frances wouldn't release him.

He humbly thanked her for her help. Blandly, he listened to her enthusiastic description of the new script, as apparently rewritten by her and Monsieur Brevoort. He admitted astonishment that such prodigious work could be done in three days and suggested that he send the revised script at once to Hollywood for their consideration.

Frances said Brevoort would not consent to any such delay. Apparently she knew his mind, or had confidence in her influence with him.

Later that day Kolisch told Marge he just might bring in a call girl from London, rent her an apartment near the center of town and give Brevoort the key. He phoned Brevoort, who was attracted to the idea, and who said the shooting could begin "as you please." Only Frances appeared to be undone.

*   *   *

A BIG sequence during these early weeks was the poor people's march on Versailles. Sigler had filmed much of it in Spain, where crowds could be hired cheaply, but a sizable amount of shooting remained, much of it requiring Louis and Antoinette, and Sigler put every minute, every thought on it. He spent several nights working all night, he and his Spanish and French assistants refusing to leave the studio, rehearsing the scenes over and over, shuttling bit-part actors about, redoing schedules, changing Richie's schedule often, rather capriciously.

Sigler decided to open the sequence with a bread line, using some of the Spanish footage. Babes in arms are crying. A man begins to criticize a soldier, and the soldier strikes him down. An old woman leaves the line, openly defies the soldier, and the soldier doesn't strike her. Given this encouragement, other women join her. Four soldiers come rushing up, but none will strike the women, so the women, congratulating each other, boisterously move on up the street. Other women join them from doorways, drop from first-floor windows, a "press" of dames, matrons, virgins, slim mantua-makers, housemaids with brooms, from every staircase they flow into the brook, increase its size, and lend their hissing, bubbly cries of jubilation.

The sequence then dissolves to an exterior of the Hôtel de Ville. Maillard, a handsome young revolutionary, the same one who led the mob against the Bastille, while beating a drum descends the porch steps of the building and enters into the mob of women, calling *"Allons, à Versailles!"* He reappears from the swarm, women following him now, all shouting "to Versailles," a happy group of people who tie red, white and blue ribbons to their hair.

On a dusty street, later the same morning, several women and Maillard, with his drum, lead the march, hundreds of dust-coated women trudging behind. One pretty teenage girl is beating on a warming pan; beside her a fair-skinned, serene Paris whore named Mademoiselle Théroïgue hoists a pike; her haughty eyes—one can see in this helmeted beauty an exquisite disdain for everyone else—her eyes see a cannon in front of a building and with a cry she goes running to it, mounts it, straddles it, calls for women to come drag it along, which several hurry to do.

On a country road later in the day, the women dusty, weary, walk steadily forward, the drums continuing. Some of the women have got clubs from the woods. Maillard leaps onto a wall, waves his hat in the air, laughing exultantly. "It goes forever," he calls. A flower jutting jauntily from one corner of his mouth, he returns to the front of the column.

Two cannon, attached to carts drawn by workhorses, roll past. A goat-drawn cart passes, a woman sitting in splendor on a bed of leaves.

Two old crones stop to tear down a road marker that says VERSAILLES 2. A woman far off, shouting from her perch on a tree limb, calls, *"Vive la Nation!"*

Other women shout, and wave clubs.

A troop of mounted soldiers watch unconcernedly, amusedly; one makes obscene gestures at the women, a few of whom gesture in reply.

Dusk. Light rain. The massive progression continues into the sun.

Dissolve to close-up of Louis in the innermost courtyard at Versailles. He has just returned from a hunt. Incredulously he listens to the hurried words of the Prime Minister. Behind him pass four great horses loaded with slain deer and pheasants. "Absurd," Louis says, speaking over the clatter of horses' hooves and the excited rushing about of guards. As he stalks upstairs and into his apartment, he tosses his crop to a groom, his hat to the valet, his jacket to an assistant valet, his hunting knife to an aide, coming at last to his bedroom where he stops.

The panting Prime Minister says, as he tries to keep up with him, "You must, you must, you must do *something*, Your Majesty."

The King says, "Call for General Lafayette to report here." He goes to the window, looks off at the place where the National Assembly is meeting, some of its members standing on the veranda in the rain, looking toward Paris. "Now the Assembly does have something to worry about," Louis says.

Cut to several assemblymen.

Two of them move inside the building, into the hollow, resounding chamber where the Assembly is meeting at the King's pleasure. Mirabeau climbs to the speaker's table, a Falstaff figure of a man with big belly, red nose, and foghorn voice so resonant that even his opposition likes to hear him.

MIRABEAU: "Paris is marching on us, I say."

A MEMBER: "What did you say?"

MIRABEAU: "Mounier, *Paris marche sur nous.*"

A MEMBER: "Not on us."

MIRABEAU: "Believe it or disbelieve it, that's not my concern, but Paris, I say, is marching on us."

The Assembly begins breaking up, many following the waddling Mirabeau, who walks much like a penguin.

The broad Avenue of Versailles is being swept by a misty rain. It is deserted except for several fleeing, scattering assemblymen. The rows of elms are bending in the rain and wind.

The Versailles guards, a contingent of army soldiers, wait at the palace gate, the men sulky in wet buckskins. Dismounted dragoons are being marched awkwardly into place behind them, and behind the dragoons are the smart red-coated Swiss guards, protectors of the royal family.

The King in his chamber is trying to get his boots off, his bootman helping, both grunting, going through their awkward dance, the King muttering, grunting.

The dour Prime Minister is watching bleakly. "I urge you and the Queen to—to flee the castle forthwith, Your Majesty."

"Flee a pack of women?" Louis says.

The women are entering the town even now; their carts and cannon and trappings fill the road. They are squalid, tired, dripping; they carry axes, rusty pikes, old muskets, ironshod clubs, *bâtons ferrés*, weapons which end in a knife or sword blade . . .

Mirabeau watches from behind a bush, a fervent prayer, full of astonishment, bubbling from his mouth.

The Queen in her apartment has several guests, a half-dozen noble ladies, among them the Princess de Lamballe. A harp is being played for them. The women are sipping tea, eating cakes. Every sudden noise, even of a door closing, causes them to start, to the Queen's amusement. The Queen is particularly assured.

Out at the Esplanade, women enter the palace grounds, dragging their cannons, coming up to face the guards, turning the cannon mouths toward them.

An officer of the guard says, "Mesdames, please," and moves to one side, out of a cannon's direct aim.

An officer gets up on the pedestal of a statue, holds to the statue's stone arm. "What—do—you—want?"

"Bread," a woman says. "Bread," they shout. "The King," some shout.

The officers tell a squad of men to go find food. To the mob an officer says, "Send forward twelve who are to see the King."

Maillard is one who at once leaps forward, stands

ready. Eleven women form a select dozen with him. The officers look Maillard over head to foot. "You named Marie?"

Maillard laughs. He is a handsome, playful, winsome fellow. "Annette," he says.

"He—overthrew the Bastille," a woman breathlessly says to the officer.

"Oh, well," the officer says, winking at one of his men. He waves the twelve on inside. Among them is Louison Chabray, a seventeen-year-old sculptress, quite beautiful.

Through a vast inner chamber, these twelve wet, tired, hungry people follow their military escort. Great tapestries look down on them, massive paintings observe their intrusion, the faces of marble saints and kings for centuries past watch them. The twelve draw into a tighter group.

The King in his room is being helped into a powdered wig and a long, purple robe. Both are slightly askew as the women are admitted by the Swiss guards. Louis tries to fasten on his sword, which problem baffles him, so he gives the sword to an aide. "Ahhh," he says, looking at the wet and withered company before him. "Who speaks for you?"

They all draw back, except the star-struck Louison Chabray, who has never in her life expected to see the King. She curtsies, then realizing she is expected to speak, faints.

Louis catches her, holds her in his arms. He smiles at the historian. "Makes it worthwhile," he says.

Maillard says, "We need bread, Your Majesty."

The King still holds the girl, vaguely amused by his predicament. He looks about for someone to give the young lady to. To the historian he says, "Don't record this."

The girl opens her eyes, leaps free, quite nearly faints again.

Louis tells her, "I said you made it worthwhile." He laughs at his little joke. "Now what do you want?" he says abruptly.

"Some millers won't grind," Maillard says.

"Grind they shall, or do worse, so long as their stones last," Louis says. "I direct that all grain circulate free as air, that all millers of France mill—"

A shot is heard outside. Everyone freezes in place. Slowly the King goes to the window, can't open it. "Go see," he tells a guard. "No more shooting," he calls after him. He returns to the twelve again. "I'm sorry you had to walk such a long way, and in the rain."

"If Your Majesty lived in Paris," a woman says, her voice quaking, "we would not worry so much about your forgetting us. We are afraid of starving there."

He shakes his head sympathetically. "Rest assured of my concern always, wherever I am." He motions for guards to lead them out, and as they leave, he goes back to the window, tries again to open it, cannot; he refuses help, bangs on it. "Why can't I open it?" he demands petulantly of the heavens.

The guard returns. "They shot a horse and are roasting it, Your Majesty. That's all."

He nods, goes back to banging on the window.

In the immense kitchen at Versailles, the chefs listen to the detail of soldiers. One chef says incredulously: "Enough food to feed three thousand people?"

"At once," an officer tells him.

"Oh, monsieur!" With a snort the chefs throw their hats onto a table and stalk out past the roasting pits.

Outside, Maillard, holding to the statue's arm, the statue that the King's officer had used earlier, shouts to the mob of women, which is spitting, seething like a stormy sea: "We have got the promises we wanted. Now go home, go home."

A shoe passes close to his head.

"Rather have your drawers, dearie," he says.

The King is still in his chamber. Before him stand three chefs, humble now, frightened. "You have endangered the Queen and my children by your refusal to feed the mob," Louis says.

"Your Highness, we had—the fires were out."

"Get to your kitchen and empty it of food, get it out to those people before they come in here to take it from us."

The chefs flee.

He says angrily to an aide, "They are good for nothing, except making crepes." He sees a bowl of fruit, and his fury slowly, visibly fades as he pauses to select an apple. He bites into it, crunches it appreciatively. He is a good judge of fruit.

Food is now being thrown by chefs into carts and onto wheelbarrows: stores of sausages, kegs of wine, big loaves of bread. Guards wheel the carts and barrows out through the gates and grates, which clang shut behind them.

The hungry women fall on the food, felling one another in their haste, tearing at each other's hair and clothes, as well as at the food, the guards shouting them on, laughing.

Newly arriving General Lafayette, young and handsome, though ungainly, rides carefully through the mob, a score of military aides with him. He sees the senior officer of the guard.

"Thank God, General," the officer says, saluting. Soldiers nearby snap to attention.

"It's bedlam," Lafayette says, laughing, as women around him fight for the food. Those who recognize him greet him by name; he is a favorite among the people.

"How many soldiers did you bring?" the officer of the guard asks.

"Enough," he says, and rides through the portals to report to the King. He dismounts in the Grand Court and is let through a gate into the Court of Marble, where anxious noblemen and their wives and servants gather about him, trying to find out the news.

The Queen in her chamber and the Princess de Lamballe are told Lafayette has arrived. "I would as soon die, if he's the one must save us," Antoinette says.

"He is awkward, it's true," the Princess says, "but we won't be dancing tonight."

The Queen laughs. "If I were the King, I would dismiss Lafayette. But the King's—not worth anything."

The Princess watches her guardedly, decides to say nothing, not even to acknowledge hearing this remark.

Louis in his office is listening to Lafayette, a likable, well-meaning pedant.

Lafayette says: "More provisions must be got for Paris. Second, I think the prisons should be emptied. Third, Your Majesty should live in Paris."

Louis frowns. "I agree to one and two. I don't like Paris."

"It would be wise to become visible, active there."

Louis shakes his head. "City of dogs." His mind turns elsewhere now, to the women outside who are shouting, *"Vive la Nation!"* in hollow, resounding calls into the rain. "What is it brings them here?"

"Fear of starvation. There are over one hundred thousand beggars for bread in Paris."

"They are fed now, yet are even more vociferous

than when hungry. My father contended that the people are a wild beast."

"Not true, Your Majesty," Lafayette says.

"No. Much that he believed was merely tyrannical. What is it that gives them confidence to come here?" He turns on Lafayette, anxious for an answer. "If they stand in the presence of one of us, they faint."

Lafayette watches him, aware that there are confused dimensions in the man, ones previously unnoticed, that at least Louis wants to understand. "If you would move to the palace in Paris, Your Majesty—"

Louis smiles at him. "How simple your solutions. And repetitive." Abruptly he says, "Keep your men close by but do not shoot those women. It is better to be gentle with women, I've found." He winks at the historian. "Don't write that down." As he turns to the window, he says, "Good night, General Lafayette."

Lafayette doesn't at first realize he has been dismissed. The historian looks up from his writing, nods toward the door, and Lafayette, bowing awkwardly, backs away. But even at the door he stops. "The farmers must bring their wheat to their lord's mill, their grapes to his wine press, must have their bread baked in his oven, must pay a fee to cross the river or to sell his products at the fair."

Louis has turned to look at him.

Lafayette says, "Then the church sets a tithe which takes most of what the farmers have left." For a minute longer he stands there facing the King. "Those are a few reasons, Your Majesty." He bows and backs out through the doorway. The door is closed.

Louis stares at the closed door, perturbed, thoughtful. "What am I to do about the ways of centuries?" he says. He motions irritably for the historian not to write that comment down and turns once more to the window. He stands there alone for a while. In a relaxed voice he says, "There is a rain cloud overhead, but you notice the sky is clear all around. It is only over us that the storm holds, I believe."

Lafayette and his officers ride through the inner courts. The grates are opened for them. Finally they ride out amongst the women, who are still eating and drinking, who jostle him, call his name, make crude overtures. He gets free of them, laughing, and rides off. A group of women begin to shake one of the grates, making a terrible clatter. "More wine," they shout.

"The King," some of them shout.

"The slut, the Queen," they shout, "show us the slut, the Queen."

The women at the back begin to chant, "The slut, the Queen," as they lunge forward, pushing the foremost women against the grate. Maillard, again up on the statue's pedestal, tells them to stop. They absorb his warnings, cheer him, but continue their lunges. The wave of women rises, falls repeatedly, with some individuals pressed painfully against the grates. Maillard's new pleas are more desperate, but the women press forward again and again, until the chain holding one of the grates begins to break. The women, shouting wildly now, push again, the grate yields, falls, and they trample each other in their haste. With tigress screams, wantonly, dangerously they move into the Grand Court. They capture an army guard, hurl him into the air, behead him even above their own heads, hoist his head on a pike. All their faces have open, screaming mouths. The statue Maillard stands on falls, he falling with it. The whirlwind now. One fleeing guard trips; the women hoist him, too, decapitate him, and his head also is raised. Torches throw golden light on the two guards' grotesque faces. The other guards, behind the far grates, fall back, terrified. The women force the next set of grates and enter the Court of Marble.

They flood into salons, breaking statues, tearing down tapestries and pictures and draperies, hurling furniture against windows, becoming cause and part of a holocaust of destruction.

Guards and nobles, their families with them, crowd into the third court. Horses, terrified, plunge, rear dangerously. The Swiss guards retreat into the inner buildings, swords flashing as the officers try at least to delay the murderous tide. One Swiss officer, backing up the Queen's stairway, slashes with his sword at the leading women of this tenacle of the pack, expertly delays them without killing anyone, finally retreats into the Queen's apartment. The door is bolted.

"Take her to the King's apartment," he says. "Where is the Prince?"

Swiss guards dash through the Queen's apartment, bundle the Princess de Lamballe and the Queen in quilts and carry them out the back way, even as the front doors are heard splintering. Other guards appear from a far chamber carrying the Prince and Princess. The guards retreat down a passage, shutting and locking doors.

The King, his hunter's instinct thrilled by the excitement, the noise all about him, waits in his chamber. He sees Antoinette carried in, approaches her. "It's hunger, they tell me," he says. "It's more than that, I believe."

There are a few gunshots now. Bugles sound in a massive disarray. The vicious cries of women are shrill and bellowing. The Princess de Lamballe, terrified, comes to the King, who takes her into his arms protectively. When he notices that his son is frightened, he says sternly, "Be a man; no fear, no fear. Your father is the sixty-sixth king in his line, and you will be the sixty-seventh."

Swiss guards, some of them lacerated, enter at the bedroom door, close it, lock it, push furniture against it. Swords and pistols are ready.

*   *   *

The plundering women are being distracted by the wealth they've found: some are stashing silver candlesticks inside their clothes, others are trying on dresses, hats, wigs, shoes, trying them on before gilded mirrors. One hag is sitting at a noble lady's dressing table applying rouge, obviously discouraged by the results. One trying on underthings is shivering from the cold touch of the silk.

In the stable women are freeing the royal horses from their stalls. Women mount them, the horses throw them routinely.

On Antoinette's bed, a rascally woman sitting in the middle among the piled up pillows is shouting insanely, "Cherries, cherries, six sous the basket."

Maillard outdoors is bleeding from lacerations on his face, is weeping, is helplessly decrying the demeaning assaults, the invasion, the thefts, the waste.

In the storerooms, women are taking hams, sausages, sides of mutton, bacon, beef, venison, armloads of pheasants hung in their feathers.

In the wine cellar, women already crazily drunk are crawling about trying to gulp more gushing wine as it shoots from the freed bungholes and jeroboams.

In the courtyard priests in black robes, a dozen of them, are on their knees, mock-praying to God, women parading around them snapping riding crops over their heads and now and then against their buttocks. The other priests have had their robes tied around their heads and are wandering about blindly, women running their hands over the men's bodies mischievously.

Nearby, ladies-in-waiting, surrounded by looters, are being required to strip off their clothes for the benefit of their captors.

The Queen and the Princess de Lamballe are waiting regally in the King's chamber. The King's hand comes to rest on the Princess's shoulder. "It's quieter now," he says simply. Indeed, the noise has changed its character, is subdued. He hears Lafayette's voice just outside and orders that his own door be opened. He steps into his office, where Lafayette hurriedly approaches him, many of his soldiers following, taking positions.
"Have they hurt many people?" Louis asks.
"Destruction is everywhere," Lafayette says.
The King goes aimlessly back inside his chamber. "A pity."
A buxom, heavy-muscled woman, her wig askew, is seen shyly walking across the courtyard in her new shoes. She finds them tricky.

The royal horses are still routinely throwing off the women who seek to mount them.

Carts loaded with grain are being driven out of the grain stores.

One of the blindfolded priests is seen falling over the staff of a pike.

No fewer than three women are splashing about in the Queen's bath.

Ladies-in-waiting, partially naked, their clothes robbed, file up a stairs, Lafayette's soldiers good-naturedly watching.

*   *   *

Soldiers at the gates are confiscating silver, gold, stolen clothes, and other loot and souvenirs from the women, putting the items on big piles.

Lafayette, on the balcony outside the King's apartment, is shouting to the noisy women below, asking them to disperse. They are calling for the King to appear. Lafayette finally can't be heard. The King stops beside him, looks about imperiously. Here and there women's rifles are raised, are aimed at him, but they are lowered again slowly by surprised marksmen, for the King is apparently fearless. The women become hushed, respectful, then one shouts *Vive le Roi!* and a mighty cheer goes up, covering all else: *Vive le Roi!*

Antoinette, standing just inside the King's chamber, says to the Princess de Lamballe, "Even if it costs me my life, I will appear." She steps out onto the balcony. Her appearance startles and almost silences the mob. Then one woman shouts, *"Vive la Reine!"* and that historic chant rises, too, an overwhelming acclamation. Pikes are raised, the heads of the decapitated guards are waved in tribute.

A woman, standing on the shoulders of another, holds up a hat to the King. Louis reaches down, accepts it, even though he surely sees on it red, white and blue ribbons. The crowd grows attentive. The guards watch expectantly. Lafayette is baffled. Calmly the King puts the hat on his head, and because of that simple act the women's cries are deafening, their gratitude for his gesture is overwhelming. Lafayette, with tears in his eyes, bows low before the King, then bows over and kisses the Queen's hand. The little Prince, just inside the King's chamber, has tears in his eyes as he looks at his triumphant royal parents, the King now waving, holding his hat aloft, the Queen waving, while the mob below them shouts their adoration.

"*À Paris!*" a lone woman in the crowd shouts, and the call is taken up. The King hesitates, then waves even to this.

Fade out.

Seven

KATE WAS DRUNK. She held to a closet door while she undressed: blouse, skirt, bra, panties. By the time Richie came out of the bathroom, she was naked except for her stockings and one shoe.

"Oh, come along, put something on, Kate," he said irritably.

"Remember when I made love to a closet door, Richie?"

"Oh, come, come, Kate," he said. "You're not that drunk, are you?"

"Sign your autograph on my stomach."

He cast a weary glance to heaven.

"You own me, Richie."

"Do I? Then I direct you to come to bed without hysterics, Kate."

She began moaning as she pressed against the edge of the door. "I need you tonight, do you know that?"

"Yes. But I am tired, Kate."

"Been working all day with Annie?"

"That's right, Kate."

"You prefer to watch, anyway, you told me," she said, still rubbing her abdomen against the edge of the door.

"Kate, I mentioned one occasion in my life—"

"Tell me again."

"Oh—" He slumped down on the edge of the bed. "Well, there was in Copenhagen a room where one could watch through a glass window, could see this other room to which women brought men off the street, men who didn't have any idea they were on display. In 1956 I spent five nights in that viewing room, the first five nights I was in Denmark. I kept refusing invitations to dinners, parties, receptions, in order to get back to that far-corner seat where I could be aroused. This was years ago, Kate."

"You love whores more than any of your wives, Richie."

"I—love my wives, Kate, have loved every one of them, but I distinctly dislike immodesty in them, and just now your door-rubbing is annoying."

"You want Annie Logan, I know that."

"Kate, I—first of all, Annie Logan is not a prostitute."

"You have an international reputation as a sex symbol, and you can't even get an erection unless you're in a dark seat in Copenhagen."

"Or in bed with a prostitute," he said. "Don't forget your own theories."

"Or in bed with Annie Logan," she said. "But meanwhile what am I to do, Richie?"

He turned the bedside lamp off and climbed into bed. "Lord knows, I've not been the least bit intimate with Annie."

"Why not? She's your wife. Is that why?"

As he lay there watching her naked body, he realized that she no longer attracted him. That was the truth of it. He might as well face up to it. He rather admired her vitality and her doglike affection for him, but she suddenly wearied him. He was now tired of her. He didn't even want to fight with her any longer.

"You'll never touch my body again," she said.

That caught him off guard, amused him, and he began to laugh. She flung herself on the bed and pinched his nose closed, then playfully stroked her fingers through the hair on his chest. "Fate worse than death, huh?" she said.

"Oh my, yes. Don't threaten me like that again."

She drew her knees up under her chin, lay watching him breathe and began imitating his breathing.

Suddenly he sat bolt upright. "I can't sleep with you staring at me. Now get out of bed, get dressed, turn the lights out, leave me alone, Kate."

She bounded out of bed, flipped off the light on her way to the bathroom and, blubbering complaints, slammed the door shut behind her.

KATE phoned Annie. She was drunk. This was only midafternoon, too. She said Richie was meeting whores.

"I don't believe—it's strange, Kate," Annie said, seeking a reasoning attitude. She suspected Kate was exaggerating, even fictionalizing, but she did want to comfort her.

"I told him he ought to be ashamed, giving whores syphilis."

"Kate, I don't believe for one minute—he's so much in love with you."

"Annie, shall we go to Yves St. Laurent's show together?"

"Of course, Kate."

"I do have to dress as Richie's wife, even if I'm not."

"Now, Kate, don't talk like that."

"Annie, help me, help me."

"All right, Kate. Of course, darling."

"If I can't hold him by myself, you take him, will you?"

Annie's hand trembled so much she had to press the phone hard against her ear to steady it. "Oh, hush. What do you mean?"

"Don't want to—lose him. Annie, *help* me."

"Yes, Kate, yes, darling," she said. "Where are you this minute?"

"At home."

"I'll come over now."

"And have a drink," Kate said.

She was asleep on the terrace, drugged unconscious, by the time Annie arrived. Annie and the maid prepared her dinner. Kate was too drugged to eat. Richie got home about eight, tired, worried about the film, irritated with Sigler yet impressed with the new scenes of his and Antoinette's arrival in Paris at the palace of the Tuileries. "Spooky, going from room to room in that old palace, the dust flying up from everything, you and I coughing."

Near them was their silent, sleeping companion, Kate, her face soft in the moonlight, her expression yielding. She looked rather pretty. Dear Kate, Annie thought.

"Some of the shots at Versailles must be cut," he said, "the more gruesome ones. I told Kolisch so. I said to him, 'Look here, that priest—I mean, that woman has hold of his genitals,' and he distractedly said, 'Yes, that's so.' " Richie somberly sank deeper into his chair, reflecting on the problems cast by such a callous reply. "Several shots will simply have to be deleted."

"Can you force them to?" Annie asked unconcernedly.

"Well—" He shrugged. "If no one else does, I will."

He closed his eyes, sighing. "Sigler says it's history, but if the film's truly historic, why did he eliminate one of my children? And the kitchen was in another—"

"I was so proud when you put that hat on," Annie said.

"Nice touch. It's in the histories. That's not Sigler's idea one bit."

"The horses throwing the women, is that in the histories?"

"Haven't seen it in any book yet. Must ask the new researchers." He stuffed a pillow behind his back. "You know, Kate has no children, Annie, and in that way she's unfulfilled. She has practically no home in any sense, but of most importance she has no children. Before you had your children, you were flighty, flirtatious, given to parties and coquetry, but when the children were born you became dependable. I've deprived Kate."

"Dear Kate. How pretty she is just now."

"She is rather pretty, isn't she, just now." He turned away from her, unwilling to be any longer impressed by Kate, and gazed out over the moonlit garden. "You were thoroughly flighty, unreliable; you never even slept in my bed for years, until your brother got word of it, came to Versailles, the Emperor of Austria on a love mission, and I talked straight sense to him, said you had taken fops as friends, gamblers and the like, that I went to bed at eleven, not six in the morning. And so did you for a while after that, came into my room each evening at eleven, prepared and scented. We sent the staff away, and I undressed you, caressed you, and soon—even if it was not love, even if you cared nothing for me, cared more for others—even so you bore a child and were fulfilled."

Idly, lingeringly she thought about that. "Do you really think so?" she said.

"Yes," he said, surprised at the question.

"How soundly she sleeps," Annie said.

"She's unfulfilled."

"She loves you so deeply." Shadows of a tree in the moonlight, barely, gently trembled on Kate's face, shadowed her eyes and the far side of the nose. Dear Kate.

They drank Cognac and talked some more, though he sometimes lapsed into long periods of worried silence. About ten he suggested he take her home. He held her hand on the way, and as the Rolls arrived at her flat, he kissed her gently, a proper, husbandly goodbye kiss, but then suddenly he embraced her and for a longer while he held her close, she consenting. He separated from her rather abruptly. "But see here, I don't mean to lose the movie to you," he said.

MOST all his scenes seemed to move along expeditiously now. For instance, consider this: Mirabeau and the Prime Minister are in the King's chamber at the Tuileries, Paris; the room is majestic, though somewhat bare of furniture. Mirabeau's foghorn voice is hushed as he waits for the King's decision.

Louis says, "The National Assembly was predictable at Versailles, but here in Paris it has got the reins in its teeth."

"Yes, as you say, Paris is a city of dogs. But I can hold the reins, Your Majesty," Mirabeau says.

"For what price?" Louis asks.

"One million sous," Mirabeau says, "payable when it's done, when the constitution is written, and you as King have an absolute veto."

The King considers, nods.

"To bring it all about, my suggestion is that you leave Paris, that you drive to the palace at St. Cloud, not Versailles, and call the better members of the National Assembly into a new session there. As a member I'll dictate the new constitution at once."

"I'm not certain I should appear to flee from here."

"Your Majesty, announce your departure, but not the time. Tell your guards to prepare the road. After all, it is the King's road."

"There are many among the people who wish me dead."

Mirabeau's deep voice growls, "Don't forget the people love you as well. They are children."

The King wanders off, his hands behind his back, his head bowed in worry.

Now that he is left with Mirabeau, the Prime Minister says softly, "The Queen is—more decisive."

Mirabeau considers that. "Will she see me?"

"No." He smiles, dismissing that idea.

"Will you ask her to see me?"

The Prime Minister considers. "No."

"I don't think she and the King should remain in Paris much longer. Do ask her."

"If you say nothing to anyone about it, even the King."

Mirabeau puts a fat forefinger over his lips.

THE short scene was filmed after two rehearsals, filmed all in a run, straight through. At the time of the screening, Sigler was able to introduce the scene with shots of Paris cemeteries, where dogs and rats and cats came to eat the corpses. When Mirabeau says to leave Paris, his words take on deep meaning, the advantage of leaving Paris is made emphatic.

AMBITION struck Kate. As a young actress she had never doubted she would be a success, a star someday; however, she had spent eight happy years doing all her acting at home for a limited audience of one. Now suddenly she was once more given an opportunity to break through.

From Marge, who had been an actress herself in silent films, she got the idea of having a bit of publicity released. One afternoon, after a few drinks, she phoned the only English photographer she knew, a matron named Edythe Rover, and invited her to Paris to do a fashion picture-story of her for a magazine, one to be chosen later. She suggested they use Richie's Rolls and dog and the autumn Paris fashion collections.

The photographer agreed, of course; she had never had an assignment in Paris.

Kate then phoned a salon and arranged seats for the next afternoon for her, her photographer, Richie, and Annie Logan. From among the exclusive names in Paris fashion—the firms of Givenchy, Dior, Ricci, Cardin, Grès, Heim, Chanel, Castillo, Lanvin, Balmain, and that of the Spaniard, Balenciaga—Yves St. Laurent was the one selected, and that company asked a publicity agent, whose name was Renée, to help with the arrangements. As on other such special occasions, a plush sofa was moved to the edge of the little arena where the cherished new fall collection was to be shown by the exquisite models. The sofa was for the use of the visitors.

To show the collection each day took about ninety minutes, and the showing began at 3:30.

Annie arrived at 3:25. She hadn't known what to wear so she had worn her very best, a suit she had bought at a shop in Beverly Hills just before leaving. Renée greeted her, said she recognized her from her films— most unlikely, Annie thought—showed her to a chair, then sat on a chair between Annie and the sofa. Before them was the small presentation arena, almost covered by an 8 x 10 rug, and around it were seated three rows of silent, waiting people, many of them tourists, some of them buyers; all of them seemed to Annie to be aware that she was overdressed.

The show was about to begin when a tall, willowy, tweedy man entered, stopped, retreated. It was Richie. Several members of the audience had recognized him and began whispering their news to others. Renée was off the sofa at once, the show was delayed by a wave of her hand. She got hold of Richie's arm, caught him at the top of the stairs and held on with professional tenacity.

"But she didn't say anyone else would be here," Richie explained as he was led by Renée, who had his left biceps, and a female secretary, who had his right, into the magical room, and to the golden sofa, where he was set down like a trophy. The audience surfaced from its lethargy and chattered, grinned, gawked.

The first model, thin as a rail, dressed in a black and blue suit, entered, took two or three strides, stopped, opened her jacket to show the tight blouse which clothed her flat chest, pivoted before Richie, exited as poor Richie gave an embarrassed side glance at Annie Logan. The second model, coldly professional, walking on spindle legs, entered. Renée whispered to Annie, "Did you like that one?"

"What?" Annie said, startled. "I don't know where she is; drinking, I'm afraid."

Renée sat back, coolly analyzing that possibility.

At 4:00 the photographer appeared at the doorway. Edythe turned out to be a hefty, butch woman in her fifties, just now loaded down with cameras, valises and gear, resembling a Japanese on tour. She strode across the arena to the sofa and plopped her big body down beside Richie, dropping leather bags on the floor all about her, oblivious of him and of others, breathing heavily as if she had been on a forced march. She was clothed in a mannish, square English tweed suit, the sort of goods that would do excellent service tramping through woods and streams anywhere in the Empire.

A pleasant, condescending ripple of laughter went through the audience.

Then Kate, pie-eyed, stopped at the doors, Richie's bulldog, Horace, on a leash beside her.

"My God, she's got a dog," Renée said aloud.

A secretary moved forward to stop Kate, but Kate, seeing her dear Richie, realizing that he had come if only to please her, moved directly toward the sofa, across the magic carpet, the big dog slobbering and waddling behind her. The audience snickered, then laughed, some of them deciding this simply must be comedy relief designed by a playful Yves St. Laurent.

Edythe from her sitting position, legs spread wide, snapped several pictures of Kate and the bulldog as they entered and as Kate found a seat on the sofa beside her husband.

The dog plopped down on the floor before them, even as a model entered from the wings, took three stalks, pivoted. She stopped, astonished, her cold aloofness shattered, for she had come upon a dog, a rather big bulldog. Everybody laughed except Annie and Richie, who managed a smile, yes, and Edythe and Kate, who were virtually unaware of everything going on. Renée did whisper to Kate, to ask if she liked a certain gown, and Kate emerged from her own thoughts long enough to say, "Darling, it's sweet; oh, I do want that one."

At 4:55 the show ended. Annie said she had an appointment at 5:00 and must run, but Kate said she would do no such thing and took her arm for support. "It'll only take ten minutes to buy my gowns."

"We'll be going now, Kate," Richie said somberly, firmly.

Kate tried to kiss his cheek, misjudged, almost fell over the dog.

"Are you a fashion photographer?" Annie asked Edythe, rather skeptically.

"Features," Edythe said. "Mostly travel," she said. "Egypt," she said, and waved her hand off toward the East.

With difficulty Kate, Edythe and the dog, with Annie and Richie stiffly following, halfway amused and halfway furious, approached the stairs that led up to the fitting room, Edythe taking the lead in order to get an upstairs position for pictures. Kate managed partway up the flight to entangle her feet in the dog's leash. Annie and Richie, below her, were transfixed, staring at the English photographer and Kate above them on the steps, arranging pictures, while two secretaries at the top of the stairs were watching, helpless.

Once the challenge of the staircase was behind them, Edythe told Annie confidentially, "I'll try to sell that one to the *Telegraph.*"

The gown Kate tried on first, made with lacy frills from floor to bosom, was so tight she couldn't get the snaps anywhere near closed. "If you have Kate turn so the gap is not toward the mirror . . ." Richie suggested to Edythe.

Edythe rose to her full height. "I won't take pictures if you try to instruct me."

"Where's Horace?" Kate said. "He's lost, Richie."

"We can make the dress larger here and there," a male secretary said. "Not indiscriminately, of course."

"I'll take it," Kate said.

"My Lord, Kate," Richie said irritably.

The male secretary recovered from his own surprise, nodded to the fitters, who at once proceeded to pull the dress over Kate's head.

"Horace, where are you?" Kate said.

Edythe was snapping pictures. Richie took Annie's hand, in need of company. "Incredible," he murmured over and over.

The dressers brought two other gowns.

"I'll take them," Kate said, apparently having difficulty remaining erect. "Miss Kate Holland," she said.

Annie took her arm. "Maybe tomorrow you can decide," she suggested.

"I'll take them," Kate said.

"Kate, Annie's right," Richie said.

"Do you prefer to pay in dollars, francs or pounds?" somebody said.

"It's my money," Kate said. She accidentally spilled the contents of her handbag on the floor. Horace began chewing on her change purse. Edythe for some reason was still taking pictures. Kate sat down on the floor and began writing out a check. "How much?"

"In pounds or dollars?"

"Pounds," Kate said.

"Thirty-five hundred pounds, Miss Holland."

Richie closed his eyes. "Incredible."

Kate wrote out the amount, but Annie knelt, gently took the checkbook away from her, even took the pen out of her hand. "We'll be going now," she said. "Maybe tomorrow," she said. She hung Kate's own dress loosely around her shoulders and helped her to the stairs, Horace and Edythe following along mournfully, Edythe still snapping pictures, Richie bringing up the tail, managing to assume an air of disdain and indifference. "Thank you," he said to Annie once they were in the car. He pressed her hand. Kate was asleep in one corner, the photographer was slumped over in the driver's seat up front, the dog was at Richie's feet chewing on one of his handmade English sandals. "We'll go home and have a drink," he said to Annie. "Admit you need one."

Eight

INSIDE THE TUILERIES in Paris, King Louis is sitting at a large table, sunlight spilling on it. He is working on his door locks, oiling, adjusting, prying. "I have averaged a lock a day," he says proudly.

The Queen, sitting nearby, finds the remark amusing, but hides her smile. "Fat Mirabeau is ill," she says.

The smile vanishes slowly from Louis' face. "Yes, I read of it."

"We ought to follow his advice and leave Paris."

He shrugs discontentedly.

"He told me himself he felt—that he *might* die, and then the—the forces he is holding back will overcome us."

He watches her thoughtfully. "You've conferred with him?"

"Didn't you know?"

He glances away, then at her several times, wondering how he ought to reply. He begins to open and close a lock. He sets the lock aside. "There is a revolt at Nancy," he says simply, with characteristically vague concerns. "There are riots at Aix, Douai, Usez, Perpignan, Avignon. Here and there the soldiers and even the sailors mutiny. It is not only Paris that is upset."

"Even so, I will breathe more freely out of this city."

"Go to St. Cloud, is it?"

"Mirabeau tells me General Bouille can protect us better than General Lafayette."

"But why do you trust Mirabeau? What if we are on the road and a mob overcomes us, kills us or holds us for ransom?"

She waits calmly. "He tells me you promised a million sous," she says.

He shrugs and goes back to his locks. "Why wasn't I born a locksmith, instead of—of this other? A king has no trade at all, seems to me."

"Our friends are going to other countries, Louis," she says. "Even the priests are fleeing."

"I told Cardinal Rohan that soon no priests will be left to cleanse us mortals of our sins. The Cardinal's own sins are fascinating, I'm told." He discovers he has the wrong key in a lock, changes it. " 'Erect eight hundred gibbets in rows and proceed to hoisting,' editor Marat writes in his Paris newspaper. Meaning all of us, two hundred and sixty thousand human bodies would be hoisted. That's real work."

"I feel he should not be allowed to print such remarks."

He puts a drop of oil on a lock. "He says he is the friend of the people."

"Not my friend, not my people."

"No, he would agree." He shudders. "Where is my dear Princess Lamballe?"

The Queen forces a smile, perhaps a bit too quickly. "I think she should be sent to England, Louis."

He looks up slowly. "She is a joy to have around," he says. "It's a dull place here."

"I am here."

"But you said it was dull."

"She can go to England when we go to St. Cloud. You can find someone else at St. Cloud to entertain you."

He absorbs that thrust, then says gently, "For her own safety, is it?"

"Mirabeau suggests you announce that you are going to visit St. Cloud this week."

"You are concerned about her safety, is that why you would deprive me of the one person—"

"Lafayette says he will protect us on the way. I have ordered the two best chefs of Versailles to move to St. Cloud and to prepare our dinner on the eighth."

He absorbs all this, too, his lips once more shaped in a silent whistle.

"The royal announcement might be as simple as this one." She pushes a piece of paper across the table to him.

He glances at the writing on it, silently whistling all the while, leaning his head first to right, then to left.

"Your son was attacked in his own garden day before yesterday by a dozen men. Your Queen cannot go in or out of her gate without having hurled at her scandalous accusations. Even whenever you appear, I hear few welcomes. This palace is dull, the furniture is shabby and inadequate, and only my friend the Princess de Lamballe seems to interest you."

He seems rather to admire her anger. "I've not seen you excited in a long while," he says and smiles briefly.

She seeks to ignore his remarks.

"I have seen you excited only on those few times when you did decide to—bear children for the State. They do belong to the State, you told me once."

"So they do, Louis."

"An official assignment, was it? Yet it seemed in

those moments your excitement became a personal matter. That was years ago, 'Toinette."

She is still bitingly piqued by his references to the Princess de Lamballe and turns from him.

He accepts his defeat. Patiently he glances over the paper she has written, takes up a pen and signs it. He hums to himself. "I admit all I do here in Paris is as good as simply nothing."

The Princess de Lamballe, in a corridor, a bare passageway, is listening to Louis, who is speaking softly, urgently to her. "I don't want you to go to England. What will I do without you?" Lovingly he touches her face.

"Not now, Your Majesty."

"You're my pet, my pet, aren't you?"

"She is my dearest friend."

"And *mine*. And that's about all, too. Are all Austrians cold?"

"Does Your Majesty tell the Queen you love her?"

"Tell her yourself for me, if you please."

"Shall I say that you happened to mention it to me this afternoon in the passage?" She has to smile at the notion.

"Oh, say I said it in my sleep." Suddenly he grabs her roughly in his arms and kisses her.

She permits it, lingers with the kiss for a while, then firmly pushes him away. She moves several feet down the corridor, stops, confused. She gathers her strength. "I will go to St. Cloud, as you direct."

He laughs softly. "My dear."

She comes to him, kisses him on the cheek, playfully avoids his pinching her, goes on out the far door, stopping at the door momentarily to straighten her clothes and wipe her mouth.

Fade out.

*   *   *

" 'Y O U bastard," Kate said to Richie, flouncing her skirt at him. "Even in the corridors you're unfaithful to your wife."

"My dear, it's only a film," Richie said defensively. Kate kicked him. "Make passes even at your wife's best friend."

Richie grabbed her, playfully shook her. "Just wait till I get you on the soft grass at St. Cloud."

FADE IN the King's carriage, an immense Berline with eight black horses. Around it are a dozen soldiers, four of them mounted, including Lafayette. "What is the delay?" he demands. The Berline is standing outside the main door of the Tuileries, in its courtyard.

Citizens have begun to run over the drawbridge, toward it. A nearby church bell is ringing an alarm.

"Keep them back," Lafayette orders. "You, go stop that bell." The soldiers all seem to resent his brusqueness, but they try to obey. On the whole the National Guard is a sultry, undisciplined outfit.

The King comes out of the palace, the Princess de Lamballe on his arm. She enters the coach. The King's two children enter the coach, and at once an old toothless woman calls out, "Don't go, don't go, God's warning."

Louis stops, considers that. He takes a coin from his pocket and gives it to her. "Pray for me."

Lafayette, mounted, intervenes, pushes her back, his horse shoving her.

Several citizens denounce him angrily.

"Where is the Queen?" he calls to Louis.

Louis, much quieter than the manic general, tells a valet to go find the Queen. Other carriages have pulled up behind his, and aides and even the Prime Minister and Finance Minister now are boarding them.

At last the Queen appears, along with four guards buried under luggage. They begin to load the luggage on the carriage roof, strap it there. Louis fretfully waits, mentions the need for haste, speaks to a child in the crowd, even as throngs of other citizens swarm across the drawbridge. Finally Antoinette gets aboard. "Do we need always to take so much with us?" Louis asks her petulantly.

By now the crowd blocks the Place du Carrousel. Lafayette shouts to the carriage drivers to drive straight ahead anyway. Recklessly, they try to do so, but citizens seize the horses' bridles, stop them. Whips crack, the horses rear, the carriage rocks, the drivers curse, the Queen frets, Lafayette harangues, the citizens remain, the King patiently waits. Citizens by now have not only clogged the road but have filled the courtyard as well, and even dare to begin rocking the carriage.

They stop when the King opens the carriage door, steps down. The people back away from his royal person. Calmly he helps the Queen down, then the Princess, then his children, and leads the way into the palace, leaving Lafayette to shout, acclaim, order and fume helplessly.

Just inside, Antoinette turns on him, her pretty mouth contorted, her eyes close to tears, and says angrily, "Well, couldn't you have done—something?" She turns and haughtily leaves him.

The Princess de Lamballe watches her leave, then smiles at Louis kindly. " 'My lord,' " she says. "She forgot to say 'my lord'!" She takes the two children's hands and follows Antoinette.

The hands of the King's clock are at 8:00, and off somewhere in the palace a clock is resonantly sounding the hour.

The King is sitting in a dim chamber, a single candle burning by which he reads a stack of newspapers. The Queen is knitting. The King groans as he reads. "A magnificent funeral. It saved me a million sous." He flips through the papers. "I never trusted him, Antoinette."

"Do you—*have* plans to try again to leave here, Louis?"

After a moment he answers, speaking slowly. "If I could trust someone. I need someone, for instance, to bring a carriage to the street outside on a certain night at bedtime and drive us to a place near the frontier where General Bouillé will be waiting."

She has paused in place, listening. The candle is flickering its yellow light on her face. "When?"

Louis pours Calvados from a flask, sniffs its delicious bouquet. "As soon as a carriage can be arranged, a swift one, a not large or noticeable one."

"Who?" she whispers tensely.

He drinks a sip of the Calvados, licks his lips. "I trust one man more than any other. He will not betray us."

She is most anxious, but keeps her voice hushed. "Who, Louis?"

"The man who loves you," he says.

Her gaze doesn't waver. She even leans slightly toward him, as if better to see his face.

"The one who has a visitor's permit to enter this palace day or night, which you arranged with Lafayette."

She sits back, stunned. "Cruel," she says. "Cruel, Louis."

"Oh, I've known all along. So, my dear . . ." He pauses, looks straight into her eyes. "When Count Fersen visits you tonight or tomorrow night—"

She cries out from her pain, a lonely, soft cry, a mangled sound.

"Don't cry," he says, suddenly sympathetic. He waits until she is quiet. "Ask Count Fersen to bring a convenient-sized coach to the Rue de l'Échelle, very near the outgate of the palace, opposite Ronsin's."

"Ronsin's?"

"The saddler's shop. He need only tell us which night."

She lowers her head into her hands and is silent for a while.

"He's Swedish, so there's not so much danger to him personally, 'Toinette." He drains his small glass of Calvados, replenishes it. "If I meant harm to him, I would have harmed him long ago."

She rises, her hands folded at her belly, her gaze averted. "Anything else?"

He smiles. "That you pardon me."

"For what?"

"For having told you that I know."

She turns away, unable to reply or even to look at him.

"'Toinette, the two children are—are mine?"

She waits for a moment, nods. "Yes."

"Yes, of course," he says, the merest whisper.

She leaves him, without replying further.

He rises slowly, wearily goes to the window and tries to open it, manages to do so after a hitch. He looks out at the night. "On the King's head sits a Swedish cock," he whispers. "A count. A cock. A count." He laughs softly. "A count, a cock, a count."

Fade out.

Fade in a glass coach, actually a huge, ornate carriage, this one drawn by eleven horses. It is opposite the door of the saddler's shop.

A hooded woman with two hooded children pass through Villegouier's door of the palace, where the sentry is on the outside, and into the Court of Princes, then

into the Carrousel, then into the Rue de l'Échelle, where
the coachman admits them to the coach.

A thickset individual wearing round hat and peruke,
arm in arm with a servant, passes through Villegouier's
door. The thickset one starts a shoebuckle as he passes
a sentry, stoops down to clasp it again, moves on.

The coachman drops to the ground, opens the carriage door for the children, closes the door after them,
only to have to open it for the thickset one, Louis.

Meanwhile, a lady shaded in broad gypsy hat, leaning on the arm of a courier, passes through the gate,
stops near the arch of the Carrousel, even as a brightly
lighted carriage draws up, Lafayette in it. The lady
touches the carriage with her *badine,* a little magic rod
women often carry.

"The royalty has retired for the night," a guard
reports to Lafayette.

The lady and her servant go through the arch, into
the Carrousel.

Dissolve to shots of the ornate coach swiftly moving
through Paris streets, night.

Dissolve to the coach entering the sleeping hamlet of
Bondy, dawn, where a chaise full of ladies-in-waiting is
drawn up, as is a chaise full of guards. There are happy
greetings all around. Count Fersen approaches the
Queen, shyly murmurs adieu. Louis clasps him on the
shoulder. *"Merci, merci,"* he says jubilantly. He busily
shoos his children, the Prince and Princess, into the glass
coach. When he sees his wife kissing Fersen, he stops,
watches them with unshaded agony. When the kiss is
done, he says simply, "Into the coach, madame." She
enters it. Still he stands there, bleakly, blankly looking at
Fersen, then follows her forlornly.

Dissolve to the royal convoy moving along a French

road, tall poplars on either side, day. They cross a country bridge, roll through a village. A man is almost hit by the coach, and even as he leaps back, he looks up into the startled face of a passenger, one whom he seems to recognize. In the fan of dust left by the coach, he tries to recall just who it is. "Someone I know from somewhere," he murmurs.

Dissolve to the royal procession entering the village of Sainte-Menehould, dusk. The coaches stop, the coachmen go into a tavern while their horses are tended to. A few villagers are curious, among them Jean-Baptiste Drouet, an acrid, choleric man, who is the postmaster and is waiting for the post, which is late. "Have you seen the post coach?" he asks a guard, who ignores him. He goes closer, peers into the big carriage. "Seen the post?" he says into its shaded interior.

"No," a voice, the King's, replies.

Drouet turns toward the tavern, says hello to an acquaintance. "Post is not in as yet," he says.

At this moment Louis leans forward in his seat, and Drouet momentarily sees him quite clearly. At once he takes his acquaintance by the sleeve, leads him into the post office, unlocks a drawer. "There he is," he says, indicating a postage stamp, "the man in the coach."

Outside, the King's coachman is trying to get his coach around the yellow guards' coach, which is not ready to leave. Several townspeople are loitering about now. Drouet comes out of the post office, moves closer, tries to see inside the coach again. He is unable to do so. He watches as the whips crack and the coaches, all three of them, roll away. Abruptly belching an adieu to his acquaintance, he hurries to his stable next to the post office, pats his horse's neck to calm her. "For this one night I've lived my life," he says.

Dissolve to the three coaches rolling along the road, dusk.

Cut to Drouet, mounted, riding swiftly on a country road, dusk.

Cut to the three coaches rolling ponderously through Clermont, dusk.

Cut to Drouet on a trail, riding through a woods, dusk.

Cut to the King, his face silhouetted by the moonlit countryside. "We would have been there three hours ago, except we have this ungainly big coach, loaded with luggage. I said I wanted a common coach, 'Toinette—"

"Can a Queen sneak away in a cart?"

Cut to the horseman, night.

Cut to the three coaches, night.

Cut to the King. "No man is more often ignored than the King of France."

Fade out.

R I C H I E did the bits for this sequence sitting in a mock-up carriage in Studio B, Annie Logan beside him, rear-screen projection equipment behind them, a crewman rocking the mock-up to simulate the movement of the carriage, Sigler looking on, wondering aloud if Annie, that is if Antoinette should reply to Louis' criticism of the coach. "Is she too worried about Fersen?" he said. "What do you think?"

"Louis is only thinking out loud," Annie said.

"Therefore, you don't feel called upon to reply?" Sigler said.

"I'm only following what's in script number four," she said.

"A tragedy really," Richie said. "That big carriage went only sixty-nine miles in twenty-two hours. I can *walk* faster than that."

Annie said defensively, "Count Fersen did what he thought was best."

"But I told you, I told you to tell him—"

"Which I did, I'm sure, but he had his own ideas of what is suitable for me."

Sigler said, "Annie, do you feel like replying to Louis or not?"

"Yes," she said, with a disdainful toss of her head. "I must."

Sigler said to an assistant, "It was very dark on this particular night, the researchers say, so keep it dark. And bob your head less, King. Do you have them both in the frame?" he asked the cameraman.

"The coach is too big, too slow," the King said petulantly. "We would have been there hours ago, except we have this big coach loaded with luggage—"

"Line," Sigler said. "You left out 'ungainly,' Louis."

"Oh hell, did I? Well, it's tricky to say."

"You'll be in Germany before we get this right," Sigler told him irritably.

FADE IN the village of Varennes, a very dark night. It's an unlevel village shaped like an inverse saddle. The Bras d'Or Tavern, across the sloping marketplace, is open, and a shine of light comes through its dirty window, as do the voices of drunk drovers.

In the interior of the Bras d'Or, Boniface Le Blanc, a huge, happy man in white apron, is serving the drovers. Into the place comes the postmaster, Drouet, dead tired. He waits for Boniface to acknowledge him. "Are you a good patriot?" Drouet asks.

"*Si, je suis,*" answers Boniface emphatically.

"In that case," whispers Drouet, "I have a mission for you."

Dissolve to a furniture wagon being pushed onto a bridge by the drovers. Boniface is shouting instructions now. Barrels are rolled onto the bridge, as well as barrows, tumbrils. Helping are perhaps a dozen men in all, most of them drunk.

They hear the carriages and take up places under the archway, muskets in the hands of three leaders. Drouet says, "I'm not sure it's he, you understand."

The carriages, careening, come to a dusty stop, the horses rearing. Lanterns flash out from under coat shirts, bridles are caught by the drovers, the muskets are leveled through the doors of the big coach.

We see the King's face, his eyes mere slits, his mouth open in surprise.

"Step down," Boniface says respectfully.

A moment later the carriage door opens and the King gets out. Then the Queen. The two royal children follow. Boniface motions them into his tavern.

Inside, the King moves to a table off by itself; he and his family stand about, baffled, confused.

Antoinette whispers huskily, "My God, Louis, do *something.*"

The ladies-in-waiting file inside, select tables, sit prim and frightened. The royal guards unarmed come in, take tables. The drovers come in, glancing at the ladies approvingly.

Boniface appears before the King, good-naturedly puts a huge tray of bread and cheese and wine on the table before him. Antoinette shakes her head irritably. The King's stomach growls. She, hearing it, turns away from him. "Please, for God's sake, Louis, think of your family."

The two children watch their father as he surveys the food, his resistance crumbling almost visibly. He tries a tiny bite of cheese. He tastes another. He likes it, he approves. He is conscious of Antoinette's displeasure, but tears off a piece of bread. He begins to eat, trying to ignore her anger. He pours wine in a glass, sniffs its bouquet, is favorably impressed, sips it, lets it flutter over his tongue and palate with a raspy noise, one particularly offensive to her; in effect, he breathes inward through the wine, through his mouth, in the French cellarman's method. "As good a Burgundy as I've ever had," he says.

Nine

SIGLER'S MEMORY became the computer for the thousands of shots filmed in Spain, in the Paris studio and on location in France, as they were edited into the rough cut of the motion picture. In one sequence showing the tension of the royal family when they were put back in the Tuileries under house arrest, he used shots of an empty corridor and of the long, tall, sheer side of the palace with the garden below, a shot he had made himself from the Louvre, and interspersed shots of a stairway back of Studio C and shots of a beetle in a bowl, shots of Antoinette's face as she listened to guards walk past her door, the face of her young son with his flaxen hair and ruddy complexion, listening apprehensively, the face of a lady-in-waiting, of a guard, actually one of Lafayette's soldiers, of the long hallway again, a shot of the Tuileries garden from high up, then the beetle once more, so that the Paris palace and its grounds became an oppressive, stifling prison, the sequence closing with a shot of Antoinette standing proudly before Lafayette and tossing into his hat her chain full of keys.

No sequence was ever finished. When Kolisch proudly wanted to show the women's march on Versailles to a visitor, an American banker, he discovered the work print had been disassembled. Later, when it was spliced back together, he found new inserts. In one of them the affable Maillard spit into a handkerchief; Kolisch and the banker caught the merest glimpse of red blood as Maillard stuffed the handkerchief away. "My God, he's dying," the banker said aloud.

"I think perhaps," Kolisch told Marge later, "I think perhaps it's going to be a masterpiece. They say they happen this way, arise out of the work itself, unexpectedly, can't be contrived or imposed. I can taste it, Marge. It's the only medicine I really need."

THE favorable impression of the film was reported in the trade magazines in the United States, as Annie's husband told her when he phoned. He was drunk. At least, he was giddy. He was embarrassed, certainly, for, as he told her, he now realized he missed her. Reading about her success had apparently made his fondness grow.

She pulled her feet up into the big chair in her living room and listened, let him make his confession. How peculiar it was for her to hear him even express affection. His dear wife was becoming a star, a leading lady, and he was ill-prepared to sustain such loss.

"So I've booked a Pan Am plane for Friday night, if that's agreeable with you, Annie. I'll fly over the Pole and be there Saturday at—I believe it's three P.M." Pause. "It's Orly, of course."

She didn't know quite what to say to him. Shouldn't she ask somebody? How was she to tell Louis about him? She was content just now being the character of Louis' wife in the film, and this appeared to be a brash intrusion.

"Will you meet me?"

"Don't come, Charlie," she said suddenly.

Pause. "How's that, Annie?" His voice was tense, annoyed.

"I won't meet you."

"Why?"

"I don't know."

"You invited me to come."

"That was earlier," she said.

Pause. "Another man?"

"No, not exactly."

"Well, either another man or not another man—what do you mean not exactly?"

"I'm not the same person myself, Charles."

Pause. "What the hell?" His voice, his surprise said he couldn't imagine her changing; his tame, complacent wife couldn't become any person other than the one he had year after year known, made love to, ignored, dismissed. "Are you well, Annie?"

She held the phone over the cradle, waited, listening to his voice as he continued to talk. Slowly she lowered it into place, the click of the phone silencing him, neatly cutting off dear Charlie's head.

THE Princess de Lamballe was sent to England, Antoinette deciding this matter, as most others, which Kate resented. She was temporarily not on call at the studio, and, of course, Annie and Richie were on call often, so one of her problems just now was the empty hours. At first she would go to the studio and spend them in the bar, but when Kolisch, ever aware of certain dangers that had marred previous films, asked her to gain no more weight, she found the bar intolerable and went out to see Paris, having her driver take her to Montmartre or some other tourist spot, where she would walk from street to street, her car following like a black pet dog. Why they hadn't sent it along with the Princess de Lamballe she didn't know: she kept thinking that thought and chuckling over it.

She walked through jewelry districts buying inexpensive jewelry, hat districts trying on hats, fur districts, where she bought a beautiful leopard coat. She walked through the district where the young women of Paris bought their clothes, and another where the old women bought their suits. She climbed one morning to the top of Notre Dame, which she decided was the most foolish action of her life.

"Three hundred eighty-seven steps," she told Richie. He and she were standing in the courtyard among the limousines, waiting for Kolisch to finish with a phone call to New York.

"Could you see all of Paris from there?" he asked her, not really caring.

"I don't recall," she said. "I spotted a dear little bar on the street alongside Notre Dame. I think it's my favorite place in Paris."

She valiantly tried to amuse herself with such tourist activity, but each day she had begun drinking heavily before cocktail hour. She was lonely and bored, that also was part of it, and of course she felt neglected, rejected by Richie.

Her favorite day was Sunday. Sundays were always fun. Usually she spent the morning walking with Richie and Annie through the open-air market near Annie's apartment. The market consisted of stalls selling pork or fish or meats or poultry or cheeses or pâtés or flowers or kitchen equipment or fruit or—something else. When the three of them were together, she felt safer. They would move along the sidewalk rows and examine the wares, Richie complaining about the English and American societies, envious of the French for maintaining a way of life more opulent than theirs, less the product of factories.

Annie and Kate always bought large quantities of goods, so much that he and the driver had to help carry the stuffed, overflowing shopping bags. They would go to Annie's for a glass or two of good Burgundy before sallying forth about 2:00 for lunch, usually at a restaurant, often the dining room of a small hotel, where they would order broiled fish, a Chablis, fresh green salad, cheeses and coffee. On one Sunday Richie ordered not only a Chablis but a red Bordeaux. He invited Annie and Kate to try some of both with the fish. "Now which is acid and which is full and complementary to the fish?"

They all agreed that the Bordeaux went better with the fish, which pleased him, yet Annie noticed that the next Sunday he ordered a Chablis, and she asked him about it.

"There's ever so much to say for tradition being the most satisfying of all," he told her. "A red wine actually is better with fish, a white with cheese, but we are taught to do it the other way around, aren't we?"

How amusing he was about his own English habits, she thought. He was curious about alternatives, was free to make his own decisions, but, as she saw it, was not free to change his course of action.

After brandy and Richie's ceremony of tipping the various waiters, they would move into the park, where the stamp collectors offered their beautiful collections— he was curious about that, as about most everything— and would wander past the Comédie Francaise, Richie setting a swift pace in order to discourage interference from passers-by. They would gaily parade down the incredibly broad sidewalks of the Champs Élysées, heads turning as Richie went by, as people stopped to stare at the tall gentleman in the tweed sporty clothes and tweed hat with a woman clinging to each arm: "Someone I know from somewhere, not sure where." Richie would finally purchase a London *Times* and an *Observer*, then signal his car and off they would go to the Ritz for a drink in the bar, which was dark and cool and virtually deserted on Sunday afternoons, and where the two bartenders were eager to wait on them: they remembered Kate for her lavish tips.

Richie's manner was mild and generous; he was a warm, friendly human being on these Sunday afternoons. He never criticized Kate, no matter how drunk she got. He could even talk candidly with Annie about business matters. "Never know what one's next work will be. I do *wonder*. Not a long line of producers at my door these days, Annie, did you know that?"

They often rode together in the Rolls to Richie's house for supper, which consisted always of whatever the refrigerator provided. Annie and Kate served what was there, and the three of them would sit in the dining room, drinking great wines, eating cold meats, talking leisurely, virtually putting themselves to sleep.

Then Annie would slip into the Rolls for the ride home, Kate and Richie usually coming along with her, both holding her hands, both doting over her affectionately, both admitting a separate need for her just now, she doting on them, too. She loved them, loved them both, was most alive when she was able to be with them, which was the strangest sort of relationship she had known in her whole life.

It was on one of these Sunday nights that a first call came through from Vorono somewhere in Florida, and she noticed a delighted excitement in Richie. He could scarcely contain himself. "They've found the lad," he told her and Kate later. "For a while he was in a home, one of those crack-up places. Left there in June. It's been devilishly difficult to track him down, let me tell you."

"Who?" Kate said.

"A real mess, he is, Annie, even for an actor."

"I think you've been drinking brandy, Richie," Kate said. "Look at him, Annie."

He did have a fantastic gleam in his eyes, a knowing, happy smile on his face.

"Anyway, we don't know yet that he'll want to visit us," Richie said.

RICHIE'S portrayal of Louis hinted at the grossness Sigler kept pestering him for, more than it supplied proof of it. Deftly he ducked in and out among Louis' diverse, perverse qualities, remaining a gentleman through it all, leaning toward becoming the Fat Louis in Sigler's mind, a dull dullard of a fellow, but avoiding the immersion. For instance, he was not really fat. Or, as he said to Sigler when Sigler complained about his characterization, "I'm fat, but not *too* fat."

"Every week you're less fat, is what I'm saying," Sigler told him.

Which was true, and only when Kolisch suggested he use more padding did he do so.

His Louis, in spite of, or maybe because of the compromises with Sigler, was vigorous and alive. He was wondrously indecisive, had an all-consuming physical appetite, was passionately in need of affection from Antoinette, who was bored by him. And he was likable. Now there was the rub, there was an aspect of the genius of Richie Hall: he was likable. He was a person one would like to have a drink with at the Ritz bar, or the Savoy, or at a proper pub on Shaftesbury Avenue. Whenever Louis XVI, as created by Richard Hall, was on the screen, he was the person the audience identified with, in spite of his awkwardness, cumbersomeness, helplessness and physical deficiencies. "He is simply dear, like a cuddly bear," Marge said.

Not much of this was due to Sigler's direction.

About all Sigler had done was submit to it. He even had to permit Richie to take as much time as he pleased with a line or a bit of business; he encouraged everybody to go through their lines expeditiously, but Richie ignored him, and the consequence was that Richie, that is Louis, seemed all the more hesitant. In final shooting, Richie often deleted the last part of a line he had slavishly delivered in every rehearsal; thus Louis would be reaching toward a decision, then would delete the line, replacing it with the mannerisms of indecision, which were beautiful visual moments in themselves, distinctly cinematic. These bits Richie left as evidence of the King's ineffectuality, but also they made the character a unique, as well as believable human being.

"It's not what I had in mind," Sigler grudgingly told Kolisch, "but it has—something."

The ones who became most perturbed by Richie's portrayal were the French members of the crew, who had read in school about Louis XVI, but only as an historic oddity. Here for the first time they were jolted into realizing that Louis was an actual person, and some of them resented the idea. "Which side is the bastard on?" a grip asked Kolisch.

"Who?" he said.

"That Louis," the grip said.

"Why, he's on his own side," he said.

Of course he was. And that admittedly was confusing to the unhappy grip, who had begun to like Louis and not want him to be executed. The death of Louis XVI was no longer the uncomplicated triumph of a free government, which the grip had believed it to be.

Yet did the King have a right to a side? Did this American film company have the right to show his side? Who the hell are they, anyway? Are we sending Frenchmen to America to humanize their kings, or whatever they've got?

This was no short-lived argument, not in the minds

of the French grips as over their bottles of luncheon wine —actually a bottle each was their usual ration—they huddled, trying to get their minds rearranged, to accommodate Louis XVI as a likable person.

"After all, we had to kill him, didn't we, or we'd have had no place for Napoleon?"

"What do you think Napoleon was, but a king?"

"He wasn't a king."

"His entire family was, every member."

Silence. Uncomfortable silence as each wondered about the mysteries of French history.

"How long after Louis, how long before Napoleon?"

Nobody knew.

Too much sympathy annoys, twists a man's well-ordered, schooled mind, makes him ask questions that ask other questions, which jumble all together like a mincemeat pie, the questions finally coming to this: Should the French Revolution be shown naked, without its usual red, white and blue clothes on?

A grip said, "Did you see him this morning, Fat Louis? He wakes up as usual, but now there's only one valet, one Prime Minister, and one historian, and the historian was only there to resign. So Louis brushed his own hair, tried to put on his own boots, found he couldn't, so he wore slippers instead."

"You see what I mean?" another grip said, hinting darkly at a conspiracy. "They're at it again."

THE palace of the Tuileries is gone now. The gardens are there, but the palace was destroyed. Annie went there, to the place it had been, and she regretted deeply not being able to walk the rooms Antoinette had used, to see her bed, her mirrors, the chest containing her perfumes, one of the vital accessories she had insisted be taken on that abortive ride to freedom.

Coming back to Paris from that ride, citizens were waiting in the villages to shout at her: "Austrian whore, trying to go home to Austria, were you?" Or, "Going to go get your brother's army?" It was a long ride through streets lined with soldiers, guns ready, and behind the soldiers she could see the closed faces of baffled citizens wondering what one did with a French queen who tried to flee France.

The gardens, they remained. At least gardens remained, the paths, benches, fountains, yes, the river alongside the gardens, the pleasing maze of paths and flower and shrub and tree places. Did Antoinette, lonely as she was, as Annie was lonely, come to them for solace? Did she dare expose herself here in this very garden after those days of her ignominious return—was ever a queen less supreme than she, entering Paris that day amid the stifling cloud of sullen attitudes?

And in her room: Who are you, why are you standing behind the screen? Are you a soldier? I demand to know if you actually mean to remain in my bedroom. Speak to me.

"I'll sit by your bed, if you prefer."

She slapped him, then at once fell back from him, from the fact of having struck him, flung herself into a chair and wept.

Later, the Queen again, she proceeded to undress for bed, one lady-in-waiting only to help her, trying to hide herself from him, the soldier behind the four-foot screen, who would be there in one face or another day and night, night and day, because General Lafayette claimed his own life was at stake should she escape. Perhaps she dared not leave that hateful apartment, even to come to this path, maybe this stone bench, to look at the green and white and purple living things, or on a day of dampness and rain to see the drops fall on the river.

Proud Queen, with the soldier watching you over the four-foot screen as you sleep, as you dream of the postmaster riding on a nighttime trail, as your maid brushes your beautiful Austrian hair, Empress Maria Theresa's daughter, consort of Louis XVI, mother of the dauphin and dauphine, guarded "for your own safety," Lafayette says.

The man behind the four-foot screen will protect you even from yourself. And watch over you.

He will, for instance, come to see my loneliness.

Dear, poor dear woman, Annie thought, do I play you well enough? Can I play you well enough? How for a while can I come close enough to be you?

Dreams she had, daydreams in that not-alone room. Fersen, talking to her in his thick accent, lying beside her in her bed, whispering into her pillow instructions about a style of love-making he said was at least quite common in Sweden, she replying, "Yes, it is common enough, certainly."

Another: Louis riding on a thundering royal black, his royal greyhounds racing with him, a score of horsemen behind him vainly trying to keep up, he laughing suddenly, shouting out triumphantly, happy, happy, absolutely free. She admired him only when he was proud, like that.

Another: The drawbridge full of people, the courtyard clogged, the carriage couldn't move forward, St. Cloud only in her mind, the drivers shouting, Lafayette haranguing, Louis at last firmly stepping down, closing the door, walking forward toward the citizens who held his royal horses' reins and with a motion of his hand dismissing them, so that they fell back. See how he walks ahead of the carriage, and it proceeds, rolls between walls of startled citizens, the crowd itself giving way before him, before royalty that knows itself, the people behind the carriage even whispering, *"Vive le Roi!"*

Another: Louis, dismounting angrily from the carriage. "Clear the bridge. It is the King's bridge. By what authority do you dare aim a musket at me? Do you possibly mean, can you intend, to kill a king? Don't be absurd. Guards, clear the bridge."

Daydreams of nonreality.

Also of reality. Fersen laughing. They were in her little theater: a masterpiece, her theater, which Louis had given her. Fersen was applauding her as she delivered an Austrian poem she as a child had learned, ending with a curtsy to him. He finds it charming to have her curtsy. She comes quickly to him. "My dear, I want to kiss you," she says. And she does. "I don't even care if we're seen," she says. Nor does she. "My dear, I will curtsy to you every single night of my life," she says. "You are the only mirror in which I find myself."

Louis standing at the table in the tavern, munching cheese and bread they have given him, one of their muskets aimed even then at his blubbery belly, he tasting their wine, gurgling it, then royally proclaiming: "As good a Burgundy as I have ever had."

Next day, his words to Lafayette, his own royal statement rising from his royal mind: "Well, now you have me." He is chatty, conversational, ignores the scornful stare of his wife. "I do assure you, Lafayette, I did not mean to pass the frontiers."

A comico-tragedy. The King talkative, hungry, the miserablest *flebile ludibrium* of a pickled-herring tragedy.

The King concerned when he hears the National Assembly would have executed Lafayette if the escape had succeeded.

"You can imagine my relief on finding you," Lafayette says.

The King nodding sagely. "I would have assured them you were not involved."

"Who did help you, Your Majesty?"

"Oh, one you've often befriended."

"That tells me but little."

The King enjoys the game. Silly game. Boyish game. "I shouldn't say, really."

The idle dreams, daydreams, sitting in her room, or on a stone bench, or wandering about, and when no guards watched or even when one did—after all, she was the Queen—picking a flower.

Too soft, Annie thought, too fragile. The thoughts were not tough enough, not for Marie Antoinette.

Why did you crush the flower, Antoinette?

Tough. Angry. Bitchy. Behind her flashing eyes, a far more flashing mind than the simpering woman giggling with Fersen. She would use Fersen as a necessary instrument, use the Princess de Lamballe as a foil, tantalize Fat Louis enough to get a million, ten million, twenty million, to fill up her royal belly with French money, stuff her royal bosom with French jewelry, enlarge her royal womb with his heirs; the only payment she made to that royal steed, her husband, was flippancy.

"How many horses do you have in the stable, Antoinette?" he had asked her once.

"Three hundred, Louis," she had said.

"Three hundred horses?" he said.

"I find the number a convenient one to remember."

And do you, Annie Logan, can you still imagine her whimpering in Count Fersen's arms?

Stronger. Harder. Tougher. Meaner. It is a crime only a playful God would commit, to put such devilish qualities in a princess as beautiful to see, to touch, to kiss, my dear, as you.

"WHAT do you mean tougher?" Sigler said, looking up from his beer and luncheon prawns; he was standing alone at the bar, or had been before she stopped opposite him.

"Tougher," Annie said bluntly.

"You see," he said, his face scrunched up in the agony of trying to express himself, "you see, she is—she insists on b-b-being admired for b-b-being."

"For being what?"

"A woman, for God's sake. She *is* a woman who *must* be, *insists* on being—"

"Being what?"

"Admired. Frivolous woman, of course."

So I don't admire her, he said without saying that. So clear he was, in the glaring silence as he chewed prawns and drank beer, having forgotten that she was even standing there.

She slapped him. She slapped him smartly, too, turned at once and returned to Kate's table. Kate, having heard the slap, was watching her, astonished, as were Richie and Kolisch.

"He's going to have to learn just who I am," Annie told them, realizing in that instant that she had entered the skin, the beautiful skin, so attractive to see though cold to touch, of Antoinette.

FADE IN the sinister, sneering faces of working-class men, gimlet-eyed, standing in packs of six or more, lounging against shops along the street near the Tuileries. An alarm bell is tolling from a church.

Inside the palace the King is being shaved, white foamy soap covering his face. His barber is a huge sweaty fellow who uses a long, straight razor. Louis holds under his chin, firm against his chest, a half-moon-shaped pottery vessel to receive the lather.

The Prime Minister and the valet are present also.

Louis, angrily: "And he receives them, welcomes them to Paris, so I want to see him, here, today, to answer to me for it." Up and down his head bobs, as he decides to look at the Prime Minister, and the barber has to be adroit.

"Well—" the Prime Minister says helplessly.

Louis, pointing a finger toward the Prime Minister, says emphatically, " 'Six hundred men who know how to die,' that was slogan number one. The other was 'March, strike down the tyrant.' That's me, isn't it?"

"Yes, it is," the Prime Minister admits.

"Walked all the way from Marseilles, wharf rats, galley slaves, butchers come to kill me."

"Your Majesty, I will require Mayor Pétion to appear here this very morning to explain his welcome of these traitors. Then, I must, I simply must ask you to accept my resignation."

Louis rests back in the chair once more, ignores him.

The Prime Minister unfolds a paper, to read from it. "A bill to permit priests to marry has been passed by the National Assembly—"

"Veto," Louis says. "Let them have mistresses, as always. How many Swiss guards have I here?"

"One thousand, Your Majesty."

"I don't know what protection I'll get from the army. How many assassins are on the way?"

"Over ten thousand have so far announced themselves, Your Majesty."

"Are you done?" Louis asks the barber.

"Almost, Your Majesty."

"Keep all the Swiss guards on duty. Did you know that one of them, a chap named Berne, has a team of dancing dogs?" He smiles quite boyishly, pleased about this. "Funniest act you ever saw. Dance on their hind legs." When nobody appears to be impressed, he says, "It really is funny."

Outside, a number of carriages are waiting to enter the palace grounds, as well as, interestingly enough, twenty old men dressed in black waistcoats, a delegation of some sort. The Swiss guards open the grates and the visitors are let in. When the grates are closed, two officers of the National Guard interrogate the visitors. When two of the Swiss guards on duty help a lady down from her carriage, these army officers chastise them. The Swiss guards wave the criticism aside and escort the lady toward the palace door. One of the army officers stops her, rudely turns her to face him, and so comes face to face with the Princess de Lamballe.

He starts to bow, stops confused, turns away awkwardly, begins fussing at the Swiss guards, who laugh at him.

The black-waistcoated old men begin taking weapons out of carriages—blunderbusses, rapiers, poniards—and distributing them among their number, while the army officers and Swiss guards watch, amused.

A shout rises from a blustery giant outside the gate. He wants somebody to fight him. The army officers ignore him. Up on the walls the cannoneers call down to him, joking with him.

Louis and Antoinette both fondly welcome the Princess de Lamballe, both tell her she should not have returned. "You were so utterly safe in England and are so precarious here," the King says.

"And every day is more dangerous," Antoinette says.

"She left England to come join us," he says happily, trying to kiss her. "My ministers resign, my noblemen flee, my army is mutinous, the church is disintegrating, and one friend have we!" He smothers her with hugs and kisses, even as the Queen stands back, jealously watching. Coldly she straightens her dress and waits.

The town hall bell is bronze. It turns on its pivot, its clapper raising a great racket. Marat pulls the rope; he's an ugly man covered with sores, an ill, infested, yes, a stinking creature. Those passing nearby must hold their nose, so awful is the odor of his pus. A gnome, a pained devil, he pulls the warning sounds denoting imminent dangers, smiling grotesquely all the while.

The aged leader of the twenty old men is on his knees before Louis XVI, who is embarrassed because he can't ignore the Princess de Lamballe's teasing smiles nor the Queen's critical gaze.

The aged leader: "I have come to save your life, Your Majesty, and have brought a number of officers who served in the army under me, and we have sent out word far and wide to loyal-hearted men to repair here, dressed even as we, to serve with us, to save our monarchy."

"Poor dear," the Princess de Lamballe says, crouching beside him, putting her arms around him. "You may, indeed, be the one who saves us."

He is irritated to be so intimately dealt with by her. The Princess, acknowledging his rebuff, withdraws, flustered. He testily straightens his black waistcoat, once again focuses his rheumy eyes on Louis. "My men are on the roads, Your Majesty, and so, I warn Your Majesty, is every sort of assassin, saying they know how to die. Your Majesty, I am here to give them their opportunity."

The Queen watches him disdainfully, but Louis affectionately, if awkwardly, pats his shoulder.

A number of soldiers sitting on the wall watch the parading of the ruffians outside, some of whom have made fires and set about cooking. The soldiers toss food down to them. More carriages wait at the drawbridge, as does another group of black-waistcoated old men. Drums have begun to beat off in the distance.

Marat still pulls the rope at the town hall.

*   *   *

A frightened gentleman sits in secretive consultation with Antoinette. "We have everything arranged at Rouen," he says. "We have Swiss guards to protect you and the King. We can provide for your use the Castle of Gaillon, which is impregnable. We have great horses, my lady, and we know back roads, so that not even a stir of dust will give away the journey."

"What price?" Antoinette says.

"My lady, no price. If the monarchy falls, we all fall, every child born of a nobleman. It's my family's life. I hear my family's fate in those drums."

"The King will never flee," she says. "He simply will not flee."

The nobleman's face clouds with disappointment. "In that case, I must go, Your Majesty, to try to protect my family."

Soldiers on the wall are still throwing food to the ruffians below. "You willing to fire on them?" one of them asks another.

His comrade considers this, shakes his head. Down the line of soldiers, one by one the gunners remove the linstocks of their cannons and toss them into the street.

The old general passes down a column of old men. Now and then he tugs a man's waistcoat straight, examines a blunderbuss. He takes hold of a fire shovel one old man carries, tosses it aside with an oath, then proceeds. He has by now a sizable force, over fifty men.

More bells are ringing. Drums far off are beating, perhaps for the masses of men marching elsewhere, approaching.

The national guardsmen are drawn up for review. None other than Louis XVI is reviewing them. He stops when men in one of the nearby ranks quietly chant, *"Vive la Nation."* They stop the chant when he turns to them. Another rank then replies, *"Vive la Liberté."* Louis waits a moment longer, the wind tousling his wig, before he moves along the ranks, just as before, as if nothing had been noticed.

Inside the palace enclosure, a soldier chews meat off a big bone. He wipes the grease from his face, onto his clothes. "I'll not be killed for him." He spits near where a Swiss guard walks.

The Swiss guard moves on, methodically standing his post.

"What I don't understand is why you welcome them to Paris." Louis is in the garden.

Pétion, the mayor of Paris, is with him, a frightened, anxious man just now.

"If treason is to be welcomed in the city," Louis says, "why should not the city be overthrown?"

"Your Majesty—let me explain—" The mayor has no excuses at hand, cannot think of one. "I'm terribly apologetic. It never occurred to me . . ." Realizing this argument to be absurd, he chokes his other words back. "I don't know when I've felt so baffled."

"My order is this: You are to remain here with my family."

"Stay *here?*"

"Oh, yes."

The mayor obviously is scared. "Here?" he blurts.

By now, afternoon, well over one hundred black-waistcoated gentlemen have arrived, and outside the walls are assembled the rabble of Marseilles and Paris, making ready through wine and brandy to assault the palace and die. Some of the rabble are singing "Richard, O My King." Some of the more muscular members are moving cannon forward into place opposite the grates, and the cannoneers are stripping off their shirts.

Inside, three dogs are dancing on their hind feet, apparently in a cellar chamber. For a minute or so Louis' chuckling is heard. "See, Princess, I told you they were delightful," he says.

In the garden a group of about twenty army soldiers sneak to the wall along the street and help one another to climb it, to desert the palace.

Louis is allowing Antoinette and the Princess de Lamballe to put on him a quilted cuirass, a chest protector which Antoinette has had made. "It will turn a bullet, a pistol bullet," she tells him.

"Oh, turn it where?" he asks, delighted with the spiffy gift.

He signals his valet, who hurries forward and helps him put on his waistcoat.

The Prime Minister worriedly comes in, sees Antoinette and the Princess de Lamballe, bows. "As to my resignation, Your Majesty—"

"See here, it'll turn a pistol bullet," Louis says, showing off his vest to him. "Antoinette has had two made. I suppose the Princess must entrust her bosom to poor marksmanship."

"Your Majesty, I wonder you should stay here. There's a terrible mob assembling."

The Queen shakes her head fiercely. "We will not give them the slightest satisfaction."

"Go to the National Assembly," the Prime Minister says, "where you will be protected."

"We will not," Antoinette says.

"The mob might not attack, saving much bloodshed," the Prime Minister says.

Louis sits down wearily, considers the complicated

matter as best he can. "Why must there be so many problems in my life?"

"You could go out through the garden," the Prime Minister says, continuing with his argument. "They meet close by."

Louis's eyelids flutter from indecision. His breathing grows more ponderous.

"He will not leave," Antoinette says.

Bell ropes are being pulled, bells turn all over Paris, clapping their warnings in brash tones. In all parts of the city drums are being beaten.

A very young officer of the guard, noticing that the linstock is gone from a cannon, is shown where it is and is told what he can do about it. He stands with hands on hips looking down at the thronged street, where the grizzly Marseilles patriots roar for him to come get them, laughing at him. Abruptly, quickly, the officer moves along the wall, urgently examining the other cannon.

The dogs dance on their hind legs.

The red Swiss guards look at their priming, take their places, stand at parade rest. The common soldiers look on disdainfully.

The old men in black draw their rapiers.

The "King" is hanging in effigy in the street outside the grates.

The dancing dogs dance faster.

Louis sits in his room, the Queen and Princess with him, his children nearby, listening to the bells and drums. Suddenly there is a cannon's voice, which trembles through the air, blends with the other sounds of the calamity. "All I've ever required," Louis says, "is that matters go back to being what they were."

The Princess de Lamballe, frightened, says to him, "Will they kill us?" She says softly to the Queen, "It's only just there. You can see where the Assembly is meeting."

Another boom of cannon shakes the room.

The Queen turns slowly, regally, looks out the window. "The King will never ask any help from them."

The King studies her, then the Princess. He rises, pulls his chest protector into place. He takes the Princess's arm. Another cannon booms nearby. "It will save many lives, I believe, for us to leave here."

THERE were to be camera shots taken in the garden of their flight; Sigler said not to worry about it. Also he would delete the Assembly's debate, he said. "To hell with politics," he said. He seemed to be pleased with the scene in the palace, however.

Kolisch wandered about, trying to find some use for his authority. Finally he sank into his canvas chair.

Sigler crossed the studio and entered the *loge des logographes,* a chamber ten feet square used usually by editors, just off the Assembly's meeting hall, where the royal family sat in squalid dejection. As he enters, a cannon's blast shakes the air, then a whole battery of cannon speak, and agony sweeps into the King's face. As this noise shatters, the Swiss guards reply, the Swiss rolling-fire crackling like a whiplash. "Turn off the damn sound track," Sigler shouts.

The King whispers to Antoinette, "It is all a dream only." He pats her hand, wanting to comfort her, wanting to be comforted, but she is aloof, arrogant, a flinty woman even yet.

Sigler sat down on the edge of the table, shoving a

dish of chicken out of the way. "Now—you are not to be concerned, Louis."

"My God!" Louis said. "My palace is destroyed, my guards slaughtered."

"Suspending our crowns was an insult," Antoinette said sullenly, hatred in her eyes.

"Louis *wants* his crown gone," Sigler said. "Historically, he even smiled when—"

"Oh, nonsense," Louis said.

"He doesn't '*Oh, nonsense,*' " Sigler said angrily. "He would rather go deer hunting than rule anything."

Kolisch, rising from his studio chair, moved onto the set. "What is it you want, Sigler?"

"The King—is—is not to be offended," Sigler said. "He must smile when they suspend the monarchy."

Louis to Antoinette: "What the hell does he mean?" To Sigler: "As sixty-seventh king in my line—"

"Those people have been suffering for sixty-seven generations," Sigler said adamantly.

"Sixty-six," the Princess de Lamballe said.

"After fourteen centuries, I am not going to bicker," Louis said. "If those animals out there *can* be excused, *can* be I say, on the basis of heredity, then why do you believe heredity has had no influence on *me?*"

"I see it hasn't," Sigler said.

"I would never try to excuse them," Antoinette began, "if I were you, Sigler."

"Heredity in Sigler's view only works when it debases people," Richie said.

Sigler moved angrily away, Kolisch wearily moving after him. "Now what?" Kolisch said.

"Struck close to home, Louis," Antoinette said approvingly. "I only wish you had spoken up long ago."

Louis glowered at her. "Maybe that's what he's trying to tell me, that I'm a bit too much myself. I do sometimes respond as I would myself, don't I?"

She fanned herself, lost in conflicting emotions. "What do you mean?"

"But I can't be only a fool, after fourteen centuries, can I?"

The Princess de Lamballe began wiping sweat from his brow, dabbed it off so as not to smear his make-up. "Poor Louis," she said.

He puts his arm affectionately around her. He whispers, "When you were in England, was there no one to capture you and take you into the green grass?"

"My lord," she says, embarrassed, glancing nervously at Antoinette.

"Any king would have," he whispers.

Sigler and Kolisch have come back, Sigler carrying a mug of coffee; he considers the royal family. "To hell with it," he says, suddenly. To his cameramen he says, "Get a cover shot of the Princess eating the chicken leg? Where's the chicken leg?"

"I ate it," the Princess admits.

"Where's the damned bone?"

"I ate it too. I mean, I chewed on it. I always do," she tells Louis.

"Anybody know where the other chicken leg is?" Sigler asks.

Louis belches.

"Is that a royal confession?" Marie Antoinette asks him.

"How we going to do this film without a chicken bone?" Sigler says.

Louis imperiously turns to Antoinette. "He has lost his mind."

"I can use a wing," Princess Lamballe suggests.

Sigler turns to Kolisch. "I can't proceed. Don't you see that?"

"They're merely being the royal family," Kolisch says.

"But they're not the royal family," Sigler says. "That has all just been suspended by the Assembly."

Louis glares at him. Antoinette rises slowly, regally. "Oh, shut up," she says.

"I will not shut up," Sigler says to her, turning on her, his face white as a ghost, "until I've killed every damn one of you."

LOUIS, sitting with the Princess de Lamballe in his Rolls as they approached their house, stirred from his reverie, cleared his throat. "He's on their side, darling. Did you realize that?"

"You've always said we didn't know whom to trust."

"He's an animal, just as they are. He has shown his colors, right enough." He put his arm around her protectively, kissed her forehead, then gently kissed her on the mouth, laughed as if he had stolen the kiss.

That evening, which happened to be a night in August, he made love to her, his dear mistress, there just beyond the terrace on the grass.

Ten

SUNDAY MORNING three of the larger Paris
newspapers had articles about the new film, speculating
about whether it was going to insult France. As a consequence Kolisch received two calls from London; that
afternoon he received calls from New York City, and
before dinner he had talked with the West Coast, with
Lesher himself. All this activity, even on a Sunday.

Since the articles were similar, virtually identical,
Kolisch suspected a single inspiration for them, and
when he talked the next day with his publicity staff, he
decided Frances was herself the source. For one's own
publicity officer to become destructive was particularly
reprehensible, but it was not Kolisch's method to con-
front anyone, or even to make his suspicions known.

Next morning another newspaper took up the question, giving the same particulars: the beastly characterization of Marat, the shallowness of Maillard, the sympathetic portrayal of Louis XVI and Marie Antoinette, the
dearth of French actors in the cast. The last complaint
had, interestingly enough, often been mentioned by
Frances in conversation.

To dismiss Frances would, Kolisch decided, only give her free rein, as well as a more hateful motivation. Better to use a tactic that would put her under his control. He discussed the matter with Marge at dinner—they sometimes walked to a small family-type restaurant just off the Avenue de la Grande Armée. He said that appealing to the child's ambitions was the easiest way to handle her. "Obviously she's self-assured, has a thirst for power. There is no way to embarrass her, no way to buy her off."

"What are you going to do, Eddie?"

"Murder is often justified," he said. "An underestimated crime, murder." He tore off a hunk of French bread, coated it with butter and salt, though his doctor had forbidden him both, and devoured it. "You want to kill her for me, Marge?"

"Oh, hush. The waiters will report you."

"Or offer her a part in an Orson Wells film?"

It really did strike Marge as funny, his eating one bite of bread after another, when he never ate bread because of his protein diet, tearing the hunks off the loaf as if the loaf were the body of the publicity girl, belching, for indeed his surprised digestion wasn't able to adjust to such innovations, even talking mean, when he rarely talked mean, rarely even criticized anyone.

"What you laughing at, Marge?" he said.

"You're such a fussy one tonight."

"Think she'd prefer murder?"

"You don't usually eat bread, Eddie."

"Put her on a Greek ship alone."

Marge laughed. It was all wondrously astonishing, this film business. There was never an end to the problems, but Kolly always did keep his sense of humor, even with phone calls flooding in. "What *are* you going to do?"

Kolisch put the loaf of bread aside. "I'm going to cast her in the film. She's to kill Marat in the tub. Sound like type casting?"

To enhance his plan, he managed to plant a story in several Paris newspapers to the effect that Frances had been discovered. As he said, "We were testing several French actresses and she was merely looking on; suddenly she took up the knife. She was magnificent. She was dynamic, most appealing, another beautiful *French* person." Next day he released information about Frances' life, some of it actual, much of it fictitious—the standard bit about the orphanage, for instance. The day after that he released hints about his studio's plans for her, closing with the confession that his own personal ambition was someday to produce a *Joan of Arc.*

He had, meanwhile, made appointments for her at Alexandre, at Dior ("Just don't buy anything," Marge told her), and with the best singing, diction and dance instructors. During the next week he confessed to the press his joy at "the beautiful prospects of her stardom." For Sunday's papers, he released a dramatic still of Frances stabbing Marat in the bathtub, a shot staged over Sigler's protests, and *Paris-Match,* which had earlier been highly critical, printed it below a five-point caption: A STAR IS BORN.

From one appointment to another, Frances was driven in a Citroën, all at Kolisch's expense; kindness radiated from him, only compliments of her came from his lips. Of course, Frances recognized the signs of a purchase, suspected that she was the item being purchased, but she didn't know at what price or for what reason, nor what was going to be demanded of her.

"She's such a frightened child," Kate told Kolisch. "She's always in my room, asking me how *I* was discovered. You are going to let her do Joan of Arc, aren't you?"

THE newspapers' criticisms had stirred M. Brevoort to life. He said he was concerned about losing his job, should the film be unpatriotic. He also happened to mention that he didn't see the English call girl any longer due to a spat.

"We'll have another one there by tomorrow night, with a gift," Kolisch told him, and indeed he had Marge arrange the transfer. However, two mornings later, about 9:00, Brevoort phoned Kolisch. "Which apartment is she in?" he asked. "I rang the bell for half an hour."

Kolisch sensed the man's embarrassment. "Let me inquire," he said. He wasn't able to get an answer from the new call girl until 11:40.

"Why, I've been out with 'im all evenin', Captain," she told him.

Kolisch was unprepared for that. "There's a mistake, then, that's all," he said. "Describe him."

"Reddish-colored 'air, he 'as, and 'e pinches."

"How old?"

"Oh, 'ow do I know? I never noticed. Thirty?"

"Too young."

Pause. "Was it the wrong man, are you telling me?"

"Yes."

"He was most appreciative, I must say."

"Did you give him the gift?"

"What do you call it?"

"The watch."

"Oh, the watch."

"Did you?"

"Yes, but he said he never accepted gifts from a la-dy. Who do you suppose he was?"

"I don't know."

Pause. "Whoever he was, he went round the world twice."

KATE'S attitude toward Richie had become ever more agreeable; she was flagrantly consenting, conciliatory, attentive, now that he was loving toward her. Every day she rode back to the house in his Rolls, nestling close to him, her own car following along behind. She refused guest invitations. She and Richie spent each evening alone, talking until late bedtime, mostly about what they had learned in books and imagined about the Princess de Lamballe and Louis XVI, lingering over those aspects which enhanced their own personal relationship.

They talked a great deal about Versailles, the old days there. "You know you slept with Antoinette off and on for years, and never made love to her."

"Oh, I find that hard to believe," he said uncomfortably.

"She would invite you to spend the night with her, this beautiful little girl, and you would climb in bed, but you were impotent. No wonder afterward she was—unfaithful to you."

"Both of us scared, I imagine. Each on a side of the bed, now and then touching. France and Austria, two empires."

"She was a beautiful girl."

"Girl, indeed. She was only fourteen."

"Then fifteen, then sixteen."

"You always come up with the most innervating statistics, Kate."

"She never did get over it, she told me."

"Well, I needed your instruction, I must say. It is true that when you took this matter in hand, so to speak—"

"I had been married and—so—being young and widowed, I did have a languishing ability."

"My father must—I suppose my grandfather thought you knew something about it, the positions and all that."

"Why do you try to bring your grandfather into it?" she said.

"The Austrian Empire, that was the fleshy part, of course."

For a while they reflected silently on that, he smelling the brandy snifter in which he now and again twirled his Cognac. "Did my grandfather—ever—make you a proposition for himself?"

"I'm not able to say. You know that."

"He thought of himself as a magnificent lover. He *was* a successful seducer of court ladies."

"Oh my, I'll agree to that, certainly."

"He wanted Antoinette, I'll wager on it, but I suspect he never dared touch her, for reasons of foreign affairs. He always respected world politics and geography."

"Surely you don't mean to suggest that your grandfather and Antoinette would dare."

"Either one of them would dare, darling." He lapsed into silence. "It would make my son my uncle, wouldn't it?"

She considered that moodily.

"Did I make love to you in that room off the back stairway, the gold one?"

"I imagine so."

"Oh, a nice place that, with my own lock on the door and a view of the garden. Even Antoinette came to love that room."

"She never loved it or you, darling."

He sniffed the Cognac. "Would that your dead husband could have seen you there. You squirmed deliciously."

"Wouldn't any woman? My husband had virtually kept me on a leash, as an exhibit, that was all, his young bride, pure, virginal, while he plied his way with others."

He took a sip of the brandy, decided not to swallow it; he let it roll from his mouth back into the glass.

"Don't do that," she said.

He glanced at her apologetically. "Sorry." He sniffed the brandy. "Then for years afterward not a consent from you, not one, is that what the researchers tell you?"

"She became my closest friend, Louis. I was spoken for by the two of you, at the same time."

He considered that for a moment. "What do you mean 'spoken for'?"

"She needed me. Only that."

"Don't tell me you have come back from England to see *her*?" he said irritably.

"No. I won't tell you that."

"I can easier believe you had your own Count Fersen waiting on the quay, or that some young duke had decided to crash the doors of your gold room—"

"No, I have known only two men in my life. I am a person of strong loyalty."

He poked a pillow down behind his back, smothered a belch with his hand. "Annoying trait in a woman, that."

"I suppose in heaven God will judge me disloyal to Antoinette, even for those two nights, but at that time—"

"The Lord has more to do, considering the state of my grandfather's court. Oh, he was a lecher, that man. But let him be alive today, and he would entwine my enemies about his fingers so charmingly that they would begin to defeat each other."

"And you are not—as clever."

"No, apparently not."

"Does it frighten you?"

"What?"

"Your death."

"Yes, though I hope to be able to do what is expected of me. It is being king that annoys me."

"What is that, what is now expected?"

"To persevere nobly. My father could not have done

that, not under adverse circumstance. Antoinette could
not."

"You are a marshmallow, dear."

"Not in bed, not those two nights with you. Not the
last few nights on the lawn out there, either. Nor was I
on those nights when I finally got around to Antoinette."

"Tell me about them."

"I entered her through Vienna, as I recall."

Hour by hour, strangely they talked, confiding in
each other, exciting one another with word games, until
they went upstairs together, or fell into an embrace on
the terrace itself, and each lost his identity as actor-king,
actress-princess in the other, confused by old times and
the present, he petting her, comforting her, husband and
prince, making her part of his smile and pleasure, and
she rubbing, touching, clutching, begging, giggling with
happiness. Never before had he been more anxious to
love her; there had been nothing to surpass these firm
embraces as they claimed each other, strangers once
again.

THE tower was an ugly mass of stone, thick-walled, a
hundred feet high, square at the base, with a turret at
each corner. It was virtually impregnable, and that was
why the royal family was housed there, to protect them.
The ground floor was assigned to guards. The Princess
de Lamballe and Antoinette and her children were to go
on one floor, Louis on another. The Princess said she
preferred to be on the same floor with the King, which
annoyed Antoinette.

Sigler, noticing this, said that the King and his valet
were to sleep on the third floor, the women on the second, and that was that.

Kate, that is the Princess, refused to consent.

The interior of each of the floors was 35 x 35 and

was divided into four rooms. Also, there was useful space in the turrets, only one of which was occupied as the stairway.

The guards were cast by Sigler to represent in appearance the vilest, the lowliest men conceivable. Richie voiced a strong complaint indeed, but since the National Assembly had no guards of its own, Sigler explained, the City of Paris was providing them, and this meant Marat and other Paris super-patriots helped determine their selection. They chose guards who had no respect for the royal family.

"Even a small room near him," Kate begged Sigler. "And a scene can be added, Sigler, to show me and Louis making love. I need it, damn you. I need it at home."

Annie went into a pout because the Princess de Lamballe was being considered for special privileges with Louis, her husband. That demeaned her and her part, she decided, and also hurt her feelings personally. She discussed the affair with Sigler, who said he rather liked the idea of a love scene between Louis and the Princess. "After all, they're married in real life."

Annie appealed to Richie, who turned that down emphatically. He suggested a casual love scene, an amusing encounter on the stairway. "I don't intend to display myself before hundreds of millions of people in Asia, sitting in their dark little seats—" he told Kate.

Kate persisted. But Annie's and Richie's objecting resulted in her getting only the modest scene in the stairwell.

"You oaf, you're supposed to hold me in your arms," she stormed out at Richie during its filming session.

"I wasn't through," Richie said defensively.

"Try it again," Kate said. "Sigler, shoot it again."

Richie finally called it quits and Kolisch took Kate, wrapped in a dressing gown, into the bar for a drink.

"He can't *act* in a love scene," she told him, speaking across the table in her most decisive, adamant, Scottish manner. "He's really a sexual *oaf.* If Richie *would* let himself act, he would be one of the *greatest actors* in the *world.*"

In the dressing rooms Richie sought to comfort Antoinette, who remained despondent about there having been a love scene of any sort. "Oh listen, darling, it's only a temporary phase, until we can get the Princess off to La Force Prison, don't you know. She's only going to be here with us for a few more days. The researchers and Sigler will assure you of that."

Eleven

IN THE TOWER there was only one servant, Cléry. He waited on the King, rolled up his hair at night, closed his bed curtains, served food to the royal family, helped make the beds and look after the Prince. In fact, he had for years been valet to the Prince, Charles, aged seven. He had been deserted at the Tuileries when the royal family evacuated it, but he had escaped by wearing old clothes and mingling with the mob. He was closely attached to the royal family.

Marat knew this. That is, the actor playing Marat in the film knew it and detested the actor playing Cléry. Also, the actor playing the part of Maillard knew it, and was cautious about associating with him. The actor playing Robespierre was a bit more friendly, but it was interesting that at lunch in the commissary none of them would be seated near him.

Of the royal family only Kate would associate with the revolutionary leaders. She did so out of a sense of longing for preserving her life which was pathetic. Of course, she knew these three would not now save her, but she hated to think what losses her death on the screen would cause her actual day-by-day relationship with Richie; it might end their sex life, she knew, and might also enhance Antoinette's prospects with him. For those reasons, as the dreary days crept by in the tower, she argued for still more time.

Sigler let her stay in the tower for several extra days, solely for her personal benefit, rescheduling the shooting. Finally, when he did order her to go and let him get on with the motion picture, she became a tigress, even there on the tower set in Studio B, demanded that he take dozens of additional shots of her dressing the children, making the beds, being coquettish with Fat Louis. Exasperated, Sigler told the guards to carry her out of there, and so they did, four big, hocking, brutish, callous, snickering men, she kicking, screaming, biting; they carried her, clothing askew, away from the horrified royal family, and put her, held her in her dressing room until she consented to be reasonable.

ANTOINETTE and Louis and the two children were now alone, living in a stone fortress which was furnished as an apartment, without many adornments or luxuries, but with comfortable beds, a sizable library, and those personal possessions that they requested. As there was but the one servant to wait on them, the family waited on itself and began to discover a more affectionate, intimate relationship. Even Antoinette began to awaken to stirrings of affection.

In the tower, at 6:00 A.M. each day, Cléry pulled aside the King's bed curtains. The King shaved, doing the razor work himself, while Cléry made the bed. He combed and brushed his own hair while Cléry laid out his clothes. He dressed himself, then went into his private turret room which he had designated as his study, knelt there and prayed for about five minutes. He then read until 9:00.

At 9:00 the Queen, the two children and the King met in the Queen's bedroom where they had breakfast seated at a square wooden table near one of the grated windows. Guards watched from the antechamber. Louis served the plates himself, and he and Antoinette encouraged the Prince and his older sister to eat.

At 10:00 the royal family, with Cléry's help, made the Queen's and children's beds. Louis then busied himself with the education of the Prince, had him recite brief passages from Corneille and Racine, gave him lessons in geography, showed him how to make maps. The Queen showed her daughter how to sew, to knit, to weave tapestries, none of which, unhappily, the Queen was expert at herself.

At 1:00, when the weather was fair, the royal family went into the garden, which required permission each time of the Commune Committee, the committee in charge of protecting them, which met in all-day session on the first floor. The arrangements usually took only half an hour to make.

From rooftops and windows of nearby houses, citizens could watch the royal family in the garden, four somber people in a walled cage, one fat, the others lean. And Louis was quite much fatter than usual, for he had had virtually no exercise for many days.

At 2:00, Cléry served the midday meal at the Queen's table. Normally during this meal, General Lafayette (actually Santerre was commander of the National Guard in Paris now that Lafayette had stepped across the frontier, but Sigler preferred to maintain continuity in his cast) would inspect the tower with two aides-de-camp. He was polite, circumspect, ill-at-ease. "All we do is merely for your protection," he assured them.

"Yet I notice we cannot leave," Antoinette told him.

"That is a temporary matter, Your Majesty."

After dinner the royal family played a game of either backgammon or piquet.

At 4:00 Louis rested on the Queen's bed, and the others, seated nearby, read their books while he slept.

At 5:00 he gave writing lessons to the Prince; usually he had him copy from works of Montesquieu.

At 6:00 there were indoor games, battledore and shuttlecock, for instance.

About 7:00 a crier would stop near the tower and cry out news of what had happened at the new political convention, at the Commune of Paris, and in the army that day. Most of the news was despairing, since the government of France was helplessly, hopelessly in disarray.

Soon after 7:00, the family would sit around the table, and the Queen would read aloud from a play.

Supper was served the children in one of their bedrooms by Cléry. Louis might sit with them, amusing them with riddles taken from a collection of *Mercures de France,* which he would peek into from time to time to refresh his memory.

After supper, the children dressed themselves for bed. Antoinette came to their bedsides, heard their prayers, and it was her idea to insist on special ones for the Princess de Lamballe in La Force Prison.

At 9:00 Louis and Antoinette had their supper in the Queen's room, the door closed. At these sessions he and she politely admitted their worries, and even their weariness with one another. Whenever she would start a conversation, he would very likely be deep in thought and might not even hear her, or whenever he would initiate a conversation, she, staring off into space, would rarely reply.

The food was varied and plentiful, sometimes with three soups and four entrées, always with plenty of wines; it really consisted of whatever the King requested. Each week, however, brought a tightening of the menu, just as it also brought an increase in the insolence of the guards and a longer wait to get permission to walk out into the garden.

Among the guards, at least for the first few weeks, was a man named Turgy, who for years had been a waiter to the King at Versailles. It was he who brought the food from a distant kitchen. Sometimes he would also bring newspapers, sneaking them in to Cléry. The other guards, those who remained after several weeks, were simple-minded, loathsome fellows. One, named Léon, would sit in the turret study each morning, close beside Louis, and whenever Louis objected to his presence would proceed to criticize the King for reading foreign literature. Another guard, Simon, a huge cobbler who apparently resented cleanliness and courtesy, a gruff, gross man, his hair matted, pimples on his filthy neck and face, came by every morning and slouched about in the King's company. "If you want anything, Monsieur Capet," he said, using the family name recently assigned to the King, "tell me now, so that I will not be put to the trouble of coming up again."

"I am in need of nothing," Louis invariably replied.

It was this Simon who objected to the use of a multiplication table; he interpreted it as Louis' effort to teach the Prince "to speak by means of figures." He also objected to the Queen's weaving, claiming her work likely contained hieroglyphics. He said she might be requesting help from her brother, the Emperor of Austria.

Another guard, a dolorous fellow named Turlot, despised the monarchy and wrote on the King's door these words: "The guillotine is permanent and waits for the tyrant, Louis XVI." Cléry asked permission to erase the words, but Louis replied, "Leave them there; we must learn to bear anything." Turlot also wrote obscene words and drew vulgar pictures on the stairway walls, where Antoinette and the children must necessarily see them, and when these brought no reaction from Louis, he painted a sketch of the King dangling from a rope, which he captioned, "Louis taking the air."

Louis' reaction was a modest consenting. "Conserve yourself for what you can do," he advised Antoinette.

"Louis, I have never been a coward," she told him, suggesting he was.

"My dear, there is nothing to be gained by burning our own souls."

Antoinette was not able to comply. Her whole being wanted to cry out against the torments of this prison, the barbarity of the guards, the debasing status just now imposed on them, the royal family. She avidly resented Louis' calmness, his royal *bétail*, his being like a sheep who was submissively going along to the slaughter; even so she was also intrigued, and even covetous. She could tell that Louis was not simply vacillating, venal; he was in some mystic way a secure man. Even as her own sense of insecurity increased, in large part because her position became more precarious, his confidence in himself grew. Their strained partnership was complicated by her astonishing thought that she had never known him, that he was supplied with strengthening resources she knew nothing of and which were denied her.

RICHIE decided to try to locate his son. He wasn't sure why the odd notion kept appealing to him and he had not the slightest idea where in Greece his son might be. Vorono would know, but he was somewhere in the wilds of Florida with the lad who starred in Sigler's first film. Richie phoned the headmaster of the Connecticut prep school his son had attended.

"He graduated eight, nine years ago, sir," the headmaster, a Mr. Seymour, said.

"Yes, of course, but I thought you might have an alumni directory."

Pause. "I suppose we should, actually."

"Yes. I've been alienated from him, and being put in close quarters with my other son and my daughter—"

"Do you have other children?"

Pause. "He was in Greece, last I knew."

"I never knew you had but the one boy."

"Yes. Well, that's true," Richie said. "It's all rather complicated, actually."

Pause. "I'll certainly not mention it from here, sir. One thing we learn early on in my profession is to be discreet."

ON September 21 at 4:00 P.M., the guards accompany a Monsieur Lubin and two soldiers to the Queen's room while the royal family is studying. In a stentorian voice Lubin proclaims that the new convention has today formally declared an end to monarchy.

The guards watch Louis with perfidious smiles, to record his expression in order later to report his despair publicly. Louis manages to permit not even a hint of disappointment to alter his expression. As soon as the reverberations of Lubin's voice are gone, he calmly returns to his reading, and the Queen and the children do so, too.

Lubin clears his throat. "Did you hear me, Capet?"

"That is not my name," Louis says gently.

"Did you hear my pronouncement, Capet?"

"Why, they heard you blocks away," Louis says quietly, a tiny smile showing through. "You are veritably a trumpet. God has given you a voice that surely will find a great need for itself elsewhere."

Lubin frowns at him, almost certain that the King is making fun of him, not quite sure. "You will," he says, turning to Cléry, "tell monsieur to take another title."

"Tell him yourself, monsieur. I am not your servant," Cléry says.

Lubin absorbs that sullen retort, turns from Cléry to address the room itself. "And I am to have all paper, ink, pens, pencils, both from the persons of the prisoners and from their rooms, also from yourself, Cléry."

"The *prisoners?*" Antoinette says, looking up slowly to meet his gaze.

"Why, Madame Capet, what else?" he says, holding his hands up to indicate the room, the guards.

The King rises, removes a pen and pencil from his pocket, lays them on the table. Each child lays a pen on the table, as well. Cléry places his pencil there. The two soldiers then go away to search the rooms.

Lubin once more approaches Louis. "The enemy army has entered Champagne. The King of Prussia is marching on Châlons. The Spanish are moving to the frontier. The Sardinians are arming themselves. All this is because of you."

"I?" Louis says, surprised. "I have no power over any such armies. You can testify that I am a prisoner here."

Lubin continues adamantly: "We know that we and our wives and children will perish, but we will be avenged; you will die before we do."

"Now, monsieur," Louis says calmly, "to kill a king is a crime that requires punishment for three generations. You will want to save your own descendants from any such curse."

Lubin stands before him, impressed. "Is that a threat, sir?"

Louis smiles. "Would either of us have reason to threaten the other?"

Lubin is plainly baffled. The King is not the buffoon he has been told about. Rather, he is considerate, and seems to have a reserve of strength, quite admirable in these circumstances. Lubin turns to Cléry. "Careful what you do here," he says. He turns once more to Louis. "There's a mob out there would come in and kill you, if we weren't here to protect you."

"How grateful we are, you must only imagine," Louis says. He returns to his reading. The children and Antoinette do so, also, and nobody even asks Lubin to leave. At the door he says fretfully to Simon, "If the tribunal won't guillotine this family, I'm of a mind to do it myself."

When Simon and Lubin have gone, Antoinette, who is distraught, lays aside her book, rises, goes to the window; only by firmly holding her face in her clenched hands does she manage not to scream.

The Prince, without moving his head, says, "You must do like Papa."

She swings around, her eyes flashing as she faces the boy. "You instruct me?" When he patiently ignores her, she slowly relents, regains control. She returns to her chair, takes up her reading as before. Now and then she glances at Louis, conscious that the children are impressed by his imperturbability, which gives him at least the appearance of moral stature.

Twelve

AUGUST HAD BEEN a month of vacationing for Parisians. Paris traditionally rests in that month; even many doctors' offices and shops are closed. For years, each year, the government has pleaded for Parisians to vacation anytime except August. Each year, regardless of the pleas, the marvelous August exodus is renewed, escaping citizens driving autos stacked full of tents and books and clothes; like lemurs they spread out to the east and south, their autos skittering, stalling, stalking, fuming, jamming Europe, and every August 30 home they come, exhausted, famished for Paris, their mother and their jewel.

So now, in September, they were back on the sidewalks again, parading up and down, hiring chairs in the sidewalk cafés for the price of a cup of strong French coffee or a *citron pressé* or a glass of wine, talking, explaining, complaining about the government, about their own lack of funds, about the languishing quality of French opera, theater, music, painting, literature, philosophy . . .

Annie loved to creep into a seat at a sidewalk café three blocks from her flat and listen to the flow of their words—not all of which she could understand, admittedly, but she could share the speakers' enthusiasms. She also could watch the parade along the sidewalk: proud poodles, men dressed in cuddly sweaters and tight pants, young lovers stopping near a streetlight to kiss lingeringly, lonely female prostitutes swinging their black bags, a certain wigged gentleman who would retrace his steps past the café time after time, as if hoping for someone to notice him, just now striking his leg with his rolled up newspaper, literally exasperated by frustration.

When out on the streets this way, Annie wore a shapeless tweed suit, black-rimmed glasses with clear glass lenses, and a square hat set squarely on her head, so that nobody would recognize her. Recently the studio publicists had been releasing her picture, along with Richie's, and Paris newspapers and magazines had printed a few. Also, she carried a shopping bag, which a hustler would not do. By means of these various infringements, she was privileged to be left alone.

The light at the café was not bright enough to permit reading; all she could do was watch strangers, listen to the rise and lilt and fall of conversations, and think about herself, enveloped, protected by precious loneliness, her conventional cloak these days. She would sit there sometimes for an hour, trying to read the headlines of a neighbor's newspaper, being polite to the bitchy waiters, looking at her wrist watch, the time passing languidly in five-minute scenes and bits of scenes. One night a young woman from the West Coast plopped down beside her, talkative in English, glad, so glad to find "another American," wishing she could move to a cheaper hotel, fussing about the devaluations, even about the American Express office.

A bore, but at least she was alive, and that night

Annie was able to sit there for two hours.

On another evening, walking home alone, a young man of about twenty, Latin, handsome, nicely dressed, spoke to her in French, fell in step beside her, laughed gently as he uttered flattering comments, walked all the way to her house, she not speaking, he waiting as she unlocked the street door, she waiting also, unable to say to him or herself what she had decided, would decide.

He started past her.

"No," she said, wishing he had not moved.

He stopped, his expression strained grotesquely by disappointment, and she went quickly into the apartment house and slammed the door in his face.

KOLISCH hinted to Sigler that his best avenue for moving the film into a still more realistic vein was Kate, which never would have occurred to him. Sigler even approached the suggestion suspiciously and hesitantly. To use a man's wife to influence him seemed unnatural, just as apparently it appeared to Kolisch to be the most natural ploy in the world. It seemed illicit to Sigler and demeaning. He knew she and Richie were now at odds again. There was no secret about that or any other of her personal relationships, for she had no secrets, she openly told all she knew to everybody. He also knew she was susceptible to flattery about her acting, or her over-acting as Sigler thought of it. She had got over her early fright of the camera and now literally fed her soul on every chance to perform, and, to give Kate her due, in no case was a performance stilted or uninteresting, nor was it merely a mimic of some earlier one she had seen some-body do, or had herself done.

"Aren't there scenes in your version, particularly in the last half, which might use her?" Kolisch asked Sigler one evening, speaking nonchalantly, without any stress at all.

He had invited Sigler to a night club to see a comic Kolisch had heard about, a scouting assignment for the studio. Anyway, that ostensibly was the reason. "Didn't you have a Princess de Lamballe death scene in your version?"

He had indeed.

"And your church scene, doesn't it have a woman in command?"

"What if Richie refuses?"

"But if his wife is the one who—insists."

"Cast her as two characters?" Sigler asked.

"Not all at once," Kolisch said simply.

To approach the matter with Kate, Sigler took her to a bird shop he knew about, located near his apartment. Many of the birds were artificially colored, he suspected, and their first bath would wash the brilliance away, but he allowed Kate to buy the ones she wanted, regardless of their garishness, and a large brass cage to house them in. All the while he hopelessly tried to find a way to praise her past performances and to discuss the possibility of a death scene for her. As it turned out, his bashfulness made him particularly incoherent when he sought to praise her, and the tortured notion of using her to influence Richie made him inept with the latter half of his self-assignment, as well.

Driving in his Volkswagen back to the studio, she driving at his request, he holding the big birdcage with its overpopulation of chirping citizens, he read his new version of the death scene aloud to her, his dull voice quaking awkwardly as he rushed on faster and faster, slurring over the lurid details of the incredible murder, finishing just as Kate stopped, actually swayed to the curb, jarring both of them and sending the birds into a noisy scramble. "I simply have to do it, Sigler," she told him. "Why isn't it in the script?"

So. So, very well, it was done, another downward step in his career.

"Sigler, it's the greatest scene in the film," she said.

"Maybe that's why R-R-R-R—your husband will veto it."

"He can't. He simply can't."

"You could be—magnificent in it," Sigler whispered.

"Please, Sigler."

"Yes, but what will R-R-R—will he say?"

"I don't see why he ought to say anything about *my* scene."

After that, preparations went quietly along for the scene, Kolisch ignoring them, yet consenting, refusing even to read the new scene. Sigler kept changing it, anyway, enlarging it, meeting most every day with Kate to tantalize her with new material. The bit parts were cast. The call was posted late and without reference to the scene by name, and on the day of shooting everybody involved was in place, except, as it turned out, Sigler.

He had, of course, hoped to be present early on this very special occasion, but unfortunately when he finally reached the studio, about 10:00 A.M., he didn't appear even then to be able to direct anything. His skin and clothes were grubby, his hair was uncombed, his eyes had the deep-set, dark-socketed look of a man who is retching inside. He went at once to Studio B, where the film crew and two-score actors were waiting, had been waiting for hours, made his shaky way to his chair, sat on the edge of it, moaning, and refused to acknowledge any salutation. Kolisch also had a desperate look on his face, Sigler noticed, and on his lap, as Sigler saw, was a xeroxed copy, the newest version of the death scene, into which Sigler had put what he chose to call "the mustache," as well as others of the more explicit details provided by history.

The reason for his own illness was this: He had a week or so earlier gone to a mannequin maker and ordered that a lifelike corpse be made, the Princess de Lamballe's corpse with her measurements and coloring. It was to have breasts, heart and vagina, must be able to bleed, and must have hair. He had been particularly specific about the pubic hair. He had perfunctorily put in the order. Yesterday afternoon, as agreed, he had gone to the little factory to get the corpse, and the police were there waiting for him and arrested him.

They hauled him to the neighborhood station house where for nine hours, well into the night, they questioned him, he not speaking or understanding French, they misunderstanding English, their interpreter antagonistic to him, everybody sure he was hiding evil, criminal intent.

He was finally put into a cell, one which he decided must have been built five hundred years ago, in which he could hear the echoes of the tortured long since dead.

In the morning he had been allowed to use the phone. He called Frances, who knew French and English. Half an hour later she arrived in a limousine, came storming inside, literally stomped the floor—until she saw the white, clammy corpse, nude, complete with arms, legs, torso, black hair, Kate's facial features, stretched out on the precinct station table. Frances began to simper. "What you going to do with that?" she asked Sigler. "You—going—to use *that*?"

"Can I go?" Sigler asked her, rising to his full height. "Can I go?" he asked the chief.

"For such an artist," the chief said in English, bowing, indicating the door.

The cell, the wretched conditions, had made him ill, and now that he was here, scarcely able to begin, he saw Richie approach him from the Studio B doorway, holding in his outstretched hand the freshly mimeographed pages of the Princess de Lamballe death scene, advance directly across the studio, one of his world-famous expressions on his face, this one connoting revulsion. With everybody watching, Richie stopped before Sigler, waved the script's pages in Sigler's face. *"What* is *this?"*

Sigler didn't intend to say. Indeed, by now the entire episode was torturous.

"It is *not,* repeat *not,* going to be included in my motion picture," Richie said. "I'll tell Kolisch that, and if necessary the Coast."

Sigler accepted a cup of coffee from an assistant. "You got any pastry?" he said to him. He was having trouble keeping his stomach settled. "We'll have to shoot it or she *will* die," he said to Richie.

"Who will die?"

"Your wife." Sigler shrugged. "Simply have to shoot it."

Richie hurled the pages onto the floor. "My wife will not, repeat, will not be in *that.*"

"Tell her, not me." The shooting was to begin at once, and soon messages began reaching Sigler saying that Kate was on the way. Whether she would or not arrive was anybody's guess, he supposed. He rehearsed the other actors, Frances doing Kate's part, and at noon broke for lunch.

At 2:00 Kate, followed by a sullen, really hateful, but silent Richie, came into the studio. While Richie was being consoled by Kolisch, Sigler confronted the cast. "Now, we've got a lot—listen here, we've got a lot to do," he said. "I d-d-don't want anybody to think we d-don't have a lot to do." He stopped, seemed to be concentrating on an itch on the inside of his right thigh. "What the hell are you doing, anyway?"

Kate was praying, was kneeling on the set, her eyes closed, preparing for her death.

Sigler asked, "Now, who has the script?" He glanced over the script girl's shoulder. "I want visitors to be put out of the studio."

Nobody was listening to him, certainly not Richie and Kolisch, who were in agitated conference.

"Pray out loud, Princess," Sigler said. "Pray for me."

One of her eyes opened.

"Test the mike for me," he said to her. " 'Mary had a little lamb—' "

" 'Mary had a little lamb,' " she said.

"Now we might as well have a shot or two of this praying. We maybe can start with it. Then the guards come for you."

Kate continued praying.

"You get talked into the most ridiculous things," Richie abruptly shouted at Kolisch. "What is my wife doing in this awful scene?"

Kate, on her knees, looked up at Sigler, an angelic smile on her face.

"You ready to rehearse it, Princess?" he asked.

"Well, you don't need my permission to shoot whatever you damn please," Richie shouted, "but you sure as hell won't use it." He continued to argue during the guards' entrance and exit, but quieted down for the tribunal scene. The judges were meeting in a street-floor passageway, Maillard one of the eight members, and Marat also, who was heard murmuring *"À un autre."*

First off, a prisoner of seventy is brought before the Committee, two guards holding him by his hands, a third by the collar of his coat. His pretty, rather frail granddaughter, nineteen, is nearby.

From just outside the room comes the hissing voice of many people.

"Your name, your profession?" says the chairman.

Another judge says casually, "The smallest lie ruins you."

"My name is Jourgniac Méard. I have served as an officer forty-one years."

"Do you know why you were arrested?" the chairman says. He can't seem to find the man's records on the table.

The man, trembling, has difficulty replying. "I do know what was told me, what a neighbor said that I had said, but this was not so—"

"Where there's smoke there's fire," a member says.

In the background the Princess de Lamballe is brought in, her guards holding her. She looks about the cluttered room, bravely returns the stare of the filthy Marat.

"He was not plotting to overthrow anything," the old man's granddaughter says firmly.

The chairman says to her, "Who are you?"

"He is my grandfather." A guard pushes her away, but she returns. "I love him," she says. The word *love* is like a foreign bell clanging in this room. The judges recover their composure, each one returns to his stony attitude. The girl moves to the table. "Never has he lifted his hand once against anybody. The neighbor was a spiteful man who had argued with him over a garden plot."

The members consider. They are affected by her courage. "Let him go free," Maillard suggests, and most of the other judges appear to agree.

"Let her go outside and talk to the people, and if she convinces them—" Marat says. "We are only the friends of the people."

The other members, clearly intimidated by him, murmur unhappily, but they comply, all except Maillard and the chairman.

The guards wait for instructions; none occur, so they take the old man to the door, open it. In the street outside a mob of brute men and hags of women are waiting, armed with pikes and clubs and knives. "This girl has got a plea to make," a guard tells them, even as the door is closed and the tribunal turns its attention to the next prisoner. *"À un autre,"* Marat grumbles.

The Princess de Lamballe is brought forward, her guards holding her roughly; one of them pulls her dress tight to show her body to the tribunal. "Your name and profession?" says the chairman.

"The smallest lie ruins you," says a member.

"Princess de Lamballe, head of the Queen's household."

The three members who have been dozing look up; everyone's attention is on her now.

"Too loud, Princess," Sigler, from off set, says, "too assertive."

"Do you know why you were arrested?" the chairman asks.

"No," she replies, as loud as before.

"Princess, he's only right there," Sigler says to her.

The chairman again can't find his proper papers, which irritates him. "Do you willingly take an oath, madame, to abhor royalty and the so-called royal family?" the chairman asks.

She hesitates. "If you ask me to take an oath condemning my husband, the Prince de Lamballe, I will do so."

"Princess, will you please stick to the script," Sigler says.

The chairman says, "Do you abhor the royal family?"

"Surely the two children are without blame," the Princess says. "I have helped rear them from babies."

"She's padding every line," Sigler says helplessly.

The chairman says, "Will you swear to abhor royalty as a cult, and the King and Queen as individuals?"

She closes her eyes tightly. "What possible good will such an oath do? My saying that to save—"

Maillard says, "Madame, don't seek to understand

the matter from our point of view—"

"I wasn't through," the Princess says.

"My script says you were," Maillard says. "Sorry."

The chairman, warily watching her, says to her, "Simply take the oath against royalty and the King and Queen, madame."

"I do so swear," she says, but without conviction.

"Very well," the chairman says.

The Princess is bothered by her oath, her deception, but she takes some comfort in Maillard's reassuring smile.

"Surely you don't mean," Marat says in his bitter voice, "that she should take the oath as a subterfuge?"

The chairman sits back wearily, accustomed to Marat's interruptions. "No, of course not."

Marat says, "Madame, do you in your heart abhor Louis Capet and his wife, here often erroneously referred to even by my colleague as King and Queen and royal family, *which they are not.*" The last is said viciously, and he leaves the words hanging with fire in them. "In your heart, madame. I inquire."

"I've forgot my line," the Princess says.

Maillard murmurs, "Marat thinks a woman knows her own heart."

Marat is not amused by that. "Shall we be serious?" he says to Maillard. "Madame, it is generally known that you and the Austrian whore were friends, even to the extent of making love one to another."

"No," the Princess says, gasping with surprise.

"It is generally known to be true," Marat says.

"Where there's smoke there's fire," a member says.

"It is untrue," the Princess says.

"We will have the full truth, madame," Marat says. "It is generally known that the Austrian is a whore, and you one of her lovers."

"Why no, monsieur . . ." the Princess says.

Marat is interrupted by a hunchback guard who enters from outside and whispers to him.

"Leave the door open," Marat says to him.

The chairman, trying to proceed, says, "Madame, did you ever on the Queen's behalf communicate with any foreign rulers?"

"No," she says.

Through the door to the outside now can be seen the old man of seventy on his knees, his pretty granddaughter standing beside him. A rough-hewn citizen, actually a butcher, dips up blood from the street and extends the full tankard to her. "This is blood of aristocrats," he says. "Drink it."

Maillard gasps. "That is abhorrent."

Marat says, "It is their court, not ours."

The granddaughter accepts the tankard, appears to teeter on the edge of fainting. She takes a sip.

"More," the butcher says.

She takes another sip.

"What in God's name are you filming this for?" Richie, off set, says to Kolisch.

"More," Marat murmurs intensely. "More."

The girl offers to return the cup to the butcher.

"More," Marat shouts out. He sits there, enveloped in his sickness, his cancerous malevolence, and watches the girl drain the cup.

"My God," Richie says off set.

The butcher himself suddenly shouts, "She is innocent!" and as the old man embraces his daughter, there are shouts of celebration. *Vive la Nation! Vive la République!*

Inside the courtroom a thick horror has settled, and a greater darkness as the door is pushed shut by a guard.

The chairman, trembling with suppressed emotion, says, "Madame, did you ever know the Queen to seek military intervention from Austria?"

The Princess, deeply shaken by having witnessed the scene outside, only stares at him. "Monsieur?"

"They will all lie," Marat says. "How else are we to account for the military invasions taking place? Let all nobles be executed and the guilty will be among them."

"Hundreds of thousands of human beings," the chairman says, "cannot be slaughtered—"

"There are twenty million commoners such as I," Marat says.

"Not quite like you, Marat," Maillard says. "They lack your subtlety." He smiles at him.

Marat sees some humor in that and laughs. "Madame, I subtly vote to transfer you to another prison," he says.

"What does that mean?" she asks.

The chairman says, "I think a person of her standing must be protected—"

"Of her standing?" Marat shouts, rising. "We have done away with that. Is it possible that members of this tribunal don't know our purposes?"

"She might later give us evidence against the royal family—" the chairman begins.

"I want no evidence against their august asses. Let her and them be transferred through the streets, let the people judge what majesty means. I will no longer sweep off my hat and bow to anybody. I am myself the—"

"The sun god," Maillard suggests, smiling.

This time there is no laughter. Marat approaches him angrily. "I have only one vote, and I cast it to send her through the streets." He turns and, as he goes back to his chair, says, "Let the rest of you look to your heads."

After a moment, the chairman says, "Those who vote to save the lady will please—"

"The vote is to be recorded," Marat says, sitting down.

Those judges who have been about to raise their hands hesitate, caught in various poses.

The chairman murmurs an oath, leafs through his papers. "Very well. In order of seating."

Marat says, "I vote to send her to another prison through the streets."

The member next to him nods, so do they all except Maillard and the chairman, neither of whom votes.

Marat says, "Record Maillard's vote as contrary, negative."

The chairman does so.

"And how do you vote?" Marat says to him.

"I do not vote."

"On a matter of such consequence, you should record a vote."

The chairman sadly looks up and into the face of the Princess. "It is foolish for me to vote for anything other than—to send you to another prison."

Maillard sits back in his chair, deep pain on his face.

"What does that mean?" the Princess asks again.

"We will have guards walk you to another prison, madame," the chairman says.

"Through the streets?" she asks.

"Well—how else?"

"Will the guards protect me?"

"As best they can, madame." He does not look at her.

"Of what am I found guilty?"

"There is no sentence, no charge. We are merely sending you to another prison." His voice is hushed, husky, his manner evasive. "We have that authority."

A guard at once opens the door and bright sunlight floods the room. The terrified Princess is turned to face it. Guards push her toward the door, even as outdoors the butcher and his cohorts pick up their pikes, axes, knives . . .

"Follow her through the doorway," Sigler off set says to a cameraman. "Can you, Camera One?"

Her guards desert her at once, move off to one side out of danger. The butcher approaches her. Beside him a smaller, neater human being, in real life a barber named Charlet, unfolds a razor. Two men and two women start toward her from either side.

"I have done nothing," she says softly, whimpering, choking on the words. "I have done nothing, except be born—"

The butcher strikes her with his pike, knocking her bonnet off. The barber with one swipe of his razor opens her clothes down the front. The women rip her clothes off, and the barber moves in to split her body open.

"My God," Richie says.

"Where is the corpse?" Sigler says. "Get the corpse."

Kate staggers off the set, sinks to the floor and begins throwing up.

"Now, see here," Sigler says to the butcher, "you're to pull out her heart—it's in there. You hold it up for the crowd to see."

"He licks it," the barber says.

"You toss it to that guard who runs it onto his sword," Sigler says.

Richie, off set, says to Kolisch, "Why do you film this?"

"Barber, get on your knees beside the corpse," Sigler says. "Split her open and pull her genitals out."

"My God," Richie says.

"Then cut off her pubic hair, turn to the crowd, and plaster the hair on your lip as a mustache," Sigler says. "At which point you members of the crowd will roar, applaud, and you two women go into a sort of orgasm, as we rehearsed."

The butcher holds his cleaver over the corpse. "I cut her open from the neck, is it?"

"Yes, when the cameras are rolling, take out her heart and lick it."

"I mean the head."

"Oh yes, cut off her head. Hold it by the hair, hold it up to the people, and you people have deliriums, clutch each other, pull at your own clothes, necks, faces, whatever. Put the head on a pike."

"Show it to the Queen," one woman says, and the crowd cheers.

"Careful you don't bang the head on that light," Sigler says. "We'll need it at the tower when you show it to the Queen."

"Sigler," Kolisch begins, approaching him guardedly, "this is—gruesome beyond—I mean even in a new day—"

"You two drag the body along. Pull her by the legs. You carry the wad of guts, monsieur."

The barber says, "When do I make my mustache?"

"As there's time," Sigler says.

Richie stalked out onto the set. "I—don't know how else to react." He stops beside Kate, who is still sitting on the floor. "My God, darling—" he says.

"Is it over?" she asks him through her tears.

Thirteen

RICHIE WAS UNWILLING for the death scene to be entered into the work print, in spite of Kate's pleading, and finally her downright, outright attacks. He would, he said, be the only one who was to die in this motion picture. Like a rock he stood on that. But she like a tigress attacked unrelentingly, so in one weak moment or another he gave her some hope of the scene's qualifying eventually in a tightly censored version. Her pleadings about the matter had become absurdly personal. He had never had a professional decision brought into his bedroom by his wife, never before, not in any marriage. Also, as each day passed, he noticed that Sigler and often Kolisch phoned Kate, apparently to tell her how magnificently she had done the bloody thing, what a fabulous actress she was, what other character parts were in prospect—something about a church.

The scene was totally abhorrent to him, an unartistic exploitation of an audience, and of course was all the more hateful because of his wife's cooperation, the shameless exploitation of herself. The scene so clawingly annoyed him that it further reduced his willingness to make allowances for her.

She realized this, of course, and began to impose herself on him all the more. Pathetically she bought gifts for him, and even gifts for Annie to give him.

Contributing to her frustration was the fact of her death in the film. In a sense she was now unemployed, even unwanted at the studio as actress or visitor. Richie and Annie were on call daily. Sigler showed her the church scene he hoped to maneuver into the script, and the part he suggested for her was perhaps the most dramatic and tearful bit part she had ever seen, but he tantalized her with it only as a possibility, forbidden her by Richie. So, idle, rejected, she started drinking a bit earlier each day. Kolisch reminded her of her career, of abstention being a wise policy. Sigler mentioned her drinking to her, tried to convince her she might be in his Irish film if she could get control of herself. She spent exhausting afternoons in the bar near Notre Dame, regardless, telling the waiters and American tourists just who she was and what dangers lurked in the hearts of her husband and her best friend. "I know. Don't I know?" she told a young couple from Wisconsin. "Two times I've slept with *her* husband."

During one of these sessions, a reporter heard enough to write a soupy gossip item about Richie and Annie Logan. His story appeared only in one of the smaller Paris newspapers, but it was seen by everybody at the studio and created many speculations.

"Frances," Kolisch murmured, attributing the story to her. "We do need to make more use of that girl, Sigler. Can't you promise her something?"

Annie's husband phoned from Hollywood. He had heard the rumor. Was there anything at all to it? In some mystic way he perhaps would have found his own history with her enhanced if she were now with Richie. She was aware that emotionally he was a long way off from her now; she was more conscious of his remoteness than his claims of interest in her. She didn't even need to hang up on him now.

THE story of an affair seemed to Kate to confirm her suspicions, and momentarily calm came over her; a martyred, fateful attitude replaced her customary tempestuousness. She was even irritated by Richie's denials.

It was all terribly embarrassing for him, of course. He dropped by to see Annie one evening on his way home, to apologize. "Brought you a bag of apples," he said. "Suitably delicious ones, of course." He said he couldn't stay, must hurry, but she tugged him into the apartment. "Don't want to interfere with your plans," he said.

"Where did you get *those?*" she said.

"Frances. You know Frances. Well, she brought me about a bushel."

"The idea of the giver makes the gift less sweet," Annie said.

"Terribly accommodating girl, actually—or does one use the word 'girl' any longer?"

"I do," Annie said, "in her case."

He took off his topcoat. She would hang it in the bedroom closet, she said, for there was no other. He followed along to get a book out of the pocket. So, that done, they found themselves standing in the bedroom, beside the bed, quite alone. "Nothing more fitting in the world than a pretty woman near a bed," he said.

She took the book out of his hands. "What you reading?"

"Oh, yes—well, it was written long ago by the valet in the tower, Cléry. He tells what you and I did up there."

"What clothes we wore, you mean."

"Yes, that too."

"Nothing more personal, I suppose."

"No, no. He was a proper servant. Exemplary."

She pretended to read its title page as she walked past him, necessarily close to him, and out of the room.

He found her in the sitting room, looking through the small, brittle volume, distinctly aware of his presence, "Richie, where did you get such an old book, and in English, too?"

"Vorono, my secretary, has arrived from Dublin and Florida—have you met him?"

"Look at you in this picture. Look at the fat belly on you here."

"No exercise," he said, sitting down beside her on the couch. "At Versailles I hunted, worked the forge, helped the gardeners—"

"And look at me," she said, surprised. "Louis, am I turning gray?"

"It happens so gradually, one doesn't notice."

"How old am I here?"

"Let's see—you were born in Vienna in November, 1755, and this picture is in the tower, September, 1792."

"September? Yes, it is—the September massacre is when the Princess was killed . . ."

"So your thirty-seventh birthday is soon."

She smiled at him. "It's to be celebrated in such luxury, too."

"No leg of lamb for us. No haunch of venison."

"I don't care about that, if only we could be out of there."

He rested his head back against the sofa. "You were which of how many children? Was it ten?"

"My poor, fat darling, look at you here. There's the guillotine. There's your head, Louis."

"I might very well have married a sister of yours instead, and saved you the pain of—living with me. I didn't need, didn't deserve the most—the prettiest and most vigorous princess in Europe. I was a—clout."

"Now, now," she said softly.

"My grandfather picked you from a batch of pictures." Richie took her hand, kissed it. "The most charming princess in the world." He kissed her hand again. "Though a frivolous one."

She took her hand away and turned a page in the book. "I will never forgive you for those—those nights," she said to him.

He stood, annoyed, walked to the window, called down to his driver, "Won't be long."

"No wonder I was frivolous, being ignored on my honeymoon," she said.

"It is a painful subject with me," he said. "It is rather like you to find one string that vibrates my complete being, then to strum it." He returned to the sofa, picked up the Cléry book from beside her. "Shall I leave this?"

"Please," she said.

"It's—interesting." He dropped it onto a pillow.

"I'm sorry I was so outspoken," she said.

"No, you're not, really."

"But I am."

"I don't think you can be. You were born of that— that Austrian empress, who was as much a man as a woman."

"My mama?" she said, astonished. "My mum?"

"Your mum was able to breed standing up, and naturally you expected your own husband—"

"My mother was the most gracious, loving, generous—"

"I said she could breed standing up."

"You utter bastard."

"So you also have a string to be plucked, you see. Don't you?"

"Just leave me alone. As usual."

"You leave me alone, then," he said and went into the bedroom, came out with his coat in hand. "Well," he said, "a kingly good night."

"I am not a rug for you, anyway."

"I am going home."

She was sorry. Her anger wilted, even as she heard his car pull away. She was utterly sorry and humiliated and surprised.

Later, while undressing for bed, she saw his hat on the bed. It was unlike Richie to forget anything like that, any part of his costume. He must have been quite distracted. Mustn't refer again to his impotence. Must control myself, she decided. And how silly he was to charge Maria Theresa with masculine traits when—well, when Mirabeau himself had said the only man around the King is the Queen.

She laughed softly, climbed into bed naked, let the cold sheets delightfully sting her breasts and tummy and thighs. She put his hat over her face and laughed into it.

Once the phone rang, rang and rang, oh perhaps twenty rings; it was bound to be Kate, agitated, pitiful, wanting to know if Annie by any chance knew where Richie was. She called most every night of late.

"No, darling, he's not here, sorry to say," she said into the hat.

RICHIE offered next day to drive her home. She consented. He wanted to apologize, or so he said, but actually he talked only about acting. Rex Harrison was now in Paris, he and Elizabeth, and something he had said that afternoon had launched Richie into a sea of theory. "On the stage one lives a part, but rarely if ever in a movie," he said to her. "A movie usually is in bits and pieces, isn't it? I mean, if it has a dozen scenes in the park, they're shot all at one time, when the crew and cast do the park shots, regardless of where they fall in the story. But this Sigler film doesn't do that, for we don't have scenes at Versailles except in the Versailles sequence, and so at the Tuileries, and in the tower, or whatever. It's startling, the difference."

They crossed the Pont de la Concorde and turned left into the Boulevard St. Germain, where a policeman directed traffic, his white-gloved hands slashing the air precisely. "Would you tell me where we are going, Richie?" Annie asked.

"Well," he said, "Rex and Elizabeth invited Kate and me to have dinner with them, and I thought about our little argument and thought how silly, how silly."

"I agree," she said quietly. "But where are we going, Richie?"

"Kate's drunk, of course. So—well, if you and I are going to be blamed for having an affair, I thought we might at *the very least* go to dinner."

They stopped at an intersection.

"Do I have a choice?" she said.

The question surprised him. "Yes."

Her impulse was to get out of the car, flag a taxi and go home, but she did nothing. She didn't want to. All the arguments about loyalty couldn't send her away from herself just then; even her guilt was dear.

"Sorry," he said. He patted her hand affectionately. "I'm not always rude. I'm simply worried about Kate, you know. She has sleeping pills, I'm sure, somewhere."

Annie didn't focus at once on what he meant. "What, Richie?"

"The sleeping pills," he said. He took her hand and held it tightly in his own. "Don't ask again."

"I love Kate," she said, whispering, as if issuing a reminder to herself.

"We're to play backgammon in the tower, I believe, aren't we," he said. "Do you know how?"

"Except for her I might be counting pills by now."

"We hear the raucous shouting of a mob approaching. Simon tells us the mob wants to show us something. 'Hold it higher, stand in a cart,' he shouts, and we, poor blighters, leave the game—"

"What game is it, Richie?"

"I told you. Backgammon."

"I can't hear *everything*."

"We go to the window and there we see it, in the torch light, the head on the pike, the flaxen hair blowing in the wind, her eyes open, looking at me, at you, whom she loved."

"She loved me," Annie said softly. "Poor Kate."

"It's really the best part Kate's ever had."

ANOTHER evening they went to dinner at the Plaza Athénée. He wanted to ask her about Kate, he said, and he did mention Kate's drinking, but he talked more about Sigler, on whom he had got a report from America, which he unfolded. "He is a most unhappy fellow, as we know. Even his mother is a recluse." Richie was reading off the typed front sheet.

"Where did you get that, Richie?" she said, annoyed. "Do you have a report on *me?*"

"His father's gone off somewhere. Left when Sigler was in elementary school. Good school, it says here. He bit a teacher, ninth grade. Resents authority passionately. Attended NYU Communication Arts School. He certainly didn't learn to converse, did he?"

"Richie, I'm amazed at you. Really!"

"Yale one year. Fell in league with a man named Flip Roma. How do you like that name? A cinematographer. Roma helped him learn pictures. Killed himself in Florida. Age fifty-three at the time." He looked up at her. "He's the one who really did that first film."

"Sigler's film?"

"Star of the film was a sixteen-year-old boy, a sort of swamp natural, and Sigler took him in, signed him to a contract personally, drove the boy into a nervous breakdown, released the film with his name as director and the boy's name fictionalized."

Annie resented the pleasure in his voice.

He was now scanning the second page. She noticed that the first page had no heading, no address, no salutation. Even Sigler's name was abbreviated.

"I'll ask Sigler about Flip Roma," he said, "and the boy actor. It's time we all knew the truth."

"You wouldn't dare," she said.

"Why not? When he attacked me in that viewing room, I marked him then for a similar experience."

"Richie, you will only demean yourself."

That argument seemed to intrigue him. He stared at her, a kindly, worried frown on his face. "I've done far worse in years past, believe me."

"Men don't have to be brutal. Don't tell me they do."

He folded the report, returned it to his pocket. "You chilly in here, darling?" he said. "You're shivering, I noticed."

"What else does it say, Richie?"

"His mother was named Conley," he recited blandly, "and she spelled it three different ways, so we judge she was illiterate. He won his first writing prize at age sixteen. Had one year at Yale Drama School. Did I say that? Left in a huff. The important thing is Roma's death and the swamp lad. Vorono has found him, of course."

"Please, Richie, hush. It's indiscreet to inquire into a person's personal life."

"You care about him, do you?"

"I care about you. I don't want you to hurt him."

"Why?"

"Because it is demeaning. You are a gentleman."

He watched her carefully, trying to determine how serious she was. Suddenly the smile, the million-dollar smile unfolded. He took the report out, fondly looked over it, sighing, then returned it to his pocket. "There's a woman's way and a man's way, you know, quite different. I've heard that if you take a baby duck away from its mother for one of its first three days of life, it won't fly south in the winter and won't breed with other ducks."

Annie looked over at him speculatively, her mouth open in surprise. "What sort of absurdity—"

"So mothers do have a way with them." In a while he smiled again. "With these nursery schools in America —you know, the mothers working and all—do you suppose Americans will stop going south in the winter?"

She had to laugh. She doubled over laughing, the question was such a surprise. "I was trying to warn you, Richie," she said.

"Did I change the subject?" he said.

KATE phoned Annie. "Richie is almost never home. Did you know Richie is working at the studio at night now?"

"Yes, you told me yesterday, Kate," Annie said.

"The press wants to preview the film in December here in Paris, did you know that?"

"You told me, Kate. How are you, dear?"

"Ohhhhh, I'm—I'm mostly left by myself. I invited my mother over to visit, but she's terrified all the time. You know. There are fourteen French doors. 'How can you lock all those doors?' she says."

"Yes, and with your jewels and furs—"

"Jewels! I have nothing. Richie never gave me anything." After a deep breath, "Did you see him yesterday?"

"Yes. At the studio."

"Did you see him last night?"

After a deep breath. "Yes, Kate."

"At dinner?" Kate asked.

"Yes, Kate. We ate at Joseph's. We had worked late, Kate, on our scene."

"Which one?"

"It's a love scene. The one. The only one."

"Where you screw him after all those years?"

"Yes. That one. But it's not explicit. I mean we don't really."

"What did you have? I tell you a better idea, you and I will meet for lunch at Joseph's, and you can tell me."

"Oh, now, Kate, that sounds—honestly, incestuous, as if Richie and I—"

"Two o'clock."

"No, I won't do that."

"Annie, I brought you to Paris—"

"Not to act in a restaurant."

"You were acting in a restaurant last night." Hard, brittle she was now. "Two o'clock," she said, and hung up.

So—lunch at Joseph's. Two o'clock. An intimate, street-level, white-tablecloth place with sparkling crystal glasses, immaculate waiters, exquisite food, a tall, gray gentlemanly *patron,* green vines forming the south wall, the sun shining through and around their leaves.

Kate had been drinking, of course. She brought along her mum, a white-haired, wrinkled Scot, in clothes and manner pleasantly unsophisticated. "Annie's my only friend," Kate said, introducing her. "My closest, dearest friend."

Mum looked at Annie out of sleepy eyes. Sensing a sympathetic listener, she began to complain, saying that Kate wouldn't let her sleep because of thieves, and wouldn't let her be abstentious. "I tell her I don't drink, but she won't listen."

"Drink up, Mum," Kate said. "Waiter, bring my

mum a bottle of that red wine my husband likes so much
—what is it, Annie?"

"I don't know, Kate."

"What did he order last night?"

"A Château Margaux."

"That's it," Kate said, not knowing, not caring. "For
my mum, Château Margaux."

"She won't let me be an old woman," Mum said.

"Did you sleep with Richie last night?" Kate said to
Annie.

Mum choked on a bite of bread and butter.

"Of course not," Annie said.

"Kate," her mother said critically. To Annie she
said, "She's the only child I've got that talks like that. She
has no modesty. When she was sixteen—"

"Drink up, Mum. Waiter, where's my mum's Margaux?"

Her mother's eyes filled with tears. "Since my husband died," she explained to Annie, "Kate's been supporting me."

"Richie screwed me in a broom closet once," Kate
said to Annie. "Papa ever screw you in a broom closet,
Mum?"

The old lady closed her eyes tightly.

"I have hundreds of other fond memories of my
marriage," Kate said. "But it's been going to hell in a
basket just lately."

The wine arrived. The usual ceremony was per-
formed: opening it, Kate smelling its cork, tasting it. The
waiter poured each glass slightly less than half full.

"Drink up, Mum. My dear little mum. Wouldn't ever
let me be alone with a boyfriend. Hid in the closet.
Wanted to watch. She and Richie are watchers. Like to
play games."

Her mother moaned. "Kate never was one to keep
her clothes on."

"I had to run away, in order to undress."

Kate was acting, was overacting, going to the limits of what her tiny audience would accept as credible, seeking some ever more dramatic situation or thought to put upon the immaculate white tablecloth of Joseph's. "Typecasting, I tell Sigler. He phones me every day. I wonder what he's after, anyway. Says he wants me to tear open a corpse in his church scene. I said, 'Sigler, they're going to lock you in the loony bin before this is over.'"

"Maybe you can tear my corpse apart," Annie said, watching her.

Kate considered that, not revealing any animosity. "Or his, that fat king that has come between us."

For a long while Annie watched her steadily. "What did you say?" She had heard clearly enough, but she was not quite sure of the meaning.

"What did Richie eat last night, before he got around to you?" Kate said, turning to a new topic, her eyes sharp now, her mouth open, saliva in the corners of her lips.

"I—don't recall. Pâté, I think, to start," Annie said.

"What else? Let's *us* have pâté."

"Lobster."

"Ah. Let's *us* have lobster."

"Your mum's falling asleep," Annie said.

"What else did he have?"

"Kate, I think Richie had *veau*, but he ate almost none of it."

"He never eats veal. You know why he orders it?"

"Why?"

"So he won't eat it. He dislikes it."

"Why does he order it?"

"He has to order something, don't you see? He never eats anything."

"I—understand what you're saying, but surely—"

"Everything he does is acting."

"Kate, what an unflattering comment to make about the man you love."

"Love?" The word was explosive, startled others elsewhere in the restaurant, contorted Kate's face with anguish. She stared at Annie for a long moment, then slowly sat back, finally managed an apologetic smile. "I've always loved him, you know that, Annie," she said.

They ordered lavishly but ate almost nothing. Kate ordered two bottles of the wine, and they did drink most of those. Each course, the waiter brought exquisite food and, after a discreet wait, took each course away and brought the next one.

"All men are cheats, Annie," Kate said. "Wake up, Mum. You'll have to take care of me, Annie, you know that. If you take Richie, you'll have me on your hands the rest of your life."

"How you talk, Kate," Annie said. "I won't take Richie. I have my own soul to worry about."

"I need a man—wake up, Mum. Don't let life pass you by, Mum."

AT the studio Kate lavished praise on Annie, often in Richie's presence. She would come drunkenly to his dressing room with Annie in tow. "Why don't you take Annie to bed, Richie?" she asked. "She's got no one."

Richie was genial, considerate, even appeared to enjoy the spectacle of his wife's voluptuous emotions. Only when he realized Annie was embarrassed would he petulantly demand that Kate hush. "We'll talk at home, Kate."

"You don't come home."

"My dear, you fall asleep before I get there. Last night you were asleep on the stairs."

"I wanted you to have to wake me."

"Snoring on the stairs. Not a stitch on."

"While you were out seducing all my friends," she said.

"No, no," he said.

"You got any gin in here, Richie?"

"Of course, darling," he said at once. He poured a water glass half full and handed it to her—no vermouth, no ice, no onions or olives, no adornments. "Down the hatch, dearest one," he said calmly.

IT was perhaps to strike back, to flail him that she invited the Duke and Duchess to lunch, as well as Burton, who had recently divorced Elizabeth and had just begun shooting scenes for a new film elsewhere in Paris. Maybe it was to help Richie get a title, for the Duke was a powerful figure socially and definitely had the Queen's ear in matters of protocol. Maybe it was simply out of desperation. Kate, if cornered, would fight back, whether intelligently or not, and she felt rejected by Richie, unfairly, coldly, cruelly. In any event, she did invite this languid, sixty-year-old, fatuous duke to lunch, along with his garrulous lady, yes, and Annie and Burton. The place of the feast was to be the Versailles set in Studio A, a corner of which she asked to be lighted for dramatic effect. The food was to be catered by the George V, Maxim's refusing to entrust its food to Studio A again, and for this particular lunch Kate had even promised Burton she would provide entertainment. "After lunch I have a treat for you," she told him. "Don't want either of us to miss *that.*"

Of course, each special guest was late, which gave Richie further opportunity to become critical of Kate, to find fault with the idea, with Kate for suggesting it, and even with the set. "Annie and I are to film a major scene this afternoon, aren't we, Annie, our love scene, and here we are dillydallying with nobility. I expect to have some trouble with this afternoon's scene, Annie, I warn you now."

"Which scene is it?" Kate asked innocently.

"I am to throw myself on Annie's bosom and boo-hoo about my lost kingdom," Richie said. "I am to seek my wife's sympathy and try to seduce her at the same time. The truth is that I've not had any sympathy from my wives in so many years—"

Messages were brought that the Duke and Duchess's car had arrived outside.

Richie fixed a second martini for himself. "Astonishingly bad idea, this, Kate." He never drank two cocktails on a filming day, but he needed this extra boost to get through lunch.

The Duke and Duchess entered at exactly 2:15, she making exuberant comments about "A wonderful location, this," and Richie instantly became a generous, considerate host, armed with his most gracious smile, soliciting orders for cocktails.

"Let me have anything, so long as it's gin," the Duke said.

Burton arrived wearing a dressing gown. "Been doing a scene," he explained. He greeted everyone, took Annie's hand and whispered pleasantly a few compliments, then with a whoop gave Kate a bear hug.

Finally everyone had a drink in hand, and at that point the conversation collapsed. The longer the pause lasted, the more difficult it became to terminate it. The Duchess at last seemed to settle on something appropriate. "I understand he is simply magnificent." She nodded to Kate, cuing her to reply.

"Who?" Kate said obediently.

"What is his name, darling?" the Duchess asked the Duke.

The Duke grunted, shook his martini gently to mix it thoroughly.

"Isn't he the film's director?" the Duchess asked cautiously.

"Sigler?" Richie blurted out, surprised.

"So," she said, relieved, as if that name had got her across a fearful chasm. "Is he *really* immense?"

"Immense?" Richie said.

"Richie simply adores him," Kate said coolly.

"In body?" Richie asked. "He *is* fat."

Kate said, "One might call him immense."

"I hear marvelous praise of him in—uh—where was it, darling?"

The Duke sniffed, shook his martini. "Cannes, was it?" he suggested.

"Yes. From—near there. Somebody said—"

"Stevens," the Duke said.

"Yes. It was Stevens, wasn't it?"

"Which Stevens?" Richie said, flagrantly jealous of Sigler's notoriety.

The Duchess lapsed into silence. The Duke grunted and tasted his martini, the merest sip, suspiciously. From his grimace, one might suppose that it was not yet quite to his liking.

"Too warm, is it too warm?" Richie asked him.

The Duke smiled. "It is a bit chilly. If the doors were closed—"

"I meant the martini," Richie said.

"It is a bit chilly as yet," the Duke said unhappily. "Has more of an American temperature as yet."

"Too long in the shaker, I expect," Richie said.

Silence. Kate calmly surveyed the scene. "Richie wants to be knighted," she said.

Had Richie been struck with a soppy cold towel he could not have shown more astonishment.

The Duke, startled, splattered martini from his mouth. In his experience a matter of possible royal favor was mentioned only with discretion. On the other hand, the Duchess for some reason took the matter as a perfectly natural, everyday progression of conversation. "And so he should be," she said. "England's greatest actor—" She stopped, considered that, her gaze coming to rest on Burton. "One of them," she said.

"Lord Olivier," the Duke said, recovering, coughing.

"One of England's greatest actors," she said. "Of all time."

"Kean," the Duke said.

"Even so. One of them, I said."

Kate, ignoring the woeful, bleary eyes of her husband, said, "Sir John Gielgud has been knighted, Sir Ralph Richardson, Sir John Clements."

"Of course," the Duchess said firmly. "Darling, you must mention this," she told the Duke.

The Duke gave his martini another little shake and taste-try. He let the harsh brew flit over his tongue, warm his mouth. He swallowed it, accepting it into his noble person. "You do pay taxes in England, do you?" he said to Richie.

Richie twisted uncomfortably. "Not at this moment."

Burton also was noticeably scrunching down in his seat.

"When did you last?" asked the Duke.

Richie cast Kate a withering glance. "Some years ago," he said.

The Duke nodded. After a while he said, "We had a pleasant time in Cannes. Our hotel was not on the sea. One does get satiated visiting so many places on the sea."

"Yes, quite," Richie said, pleased to be launched on a different subject, even this one. He rose to pour himself another drink.

"How relieved I was to look out and not see the sea," the Duke said.

The Duchess said to Annie, "Supposedly an immense director."

"Oh, is he?" Annie said.

Richie said, "Shall I fix you another one, Your Grace?"

The Duke was lost in his own considerations. "One isn't really conscious of the sea in England, is one?"

"No," Kate said.

"It's so stark and clear in—uh—the South of France. Every day is clear," the Duke said, as if commenting on one of life's more playful absurdities.

"Astonishing," Kate said.

"Bermuda must be the sunniest place on earth," the Duke said unhappily. "And the Bahamas. Brutally sunny there."

"The Mediterranean," the Duchess said, "is sunny."

"Quite," he said, and directed his attention once more to the little drink in his hand. "I said Mediterranean earlier."

Silence.

"Well, he is a genius, and Richie adores him," Kate said.

The Duke looked at her, speculating about what she might mean. He shook his head, as if a taste of the martini were troubling some spot in his mouth or throat.

"You and His Grace must stay after lunch to see Sigler at work," Kate said to the Duchess.

"No, no," Richie said quickly. "They would not be interested."

"Can we all stay?" Burton said, a devilish smile on his face.

"After all, the scene is to be shot nearby in Studio B," Kate said.

"I assure you—" Richie began.

"I would like to," the Duchess said. She waited for confirmation from her husband. "Let's." No sign came out of him, however. "Let's."

"I would, yes," he said finally.

Richie stared in horror at him. "Oh, my Lord," he uttered. On seeing the Duke react, he quickly added, "in heaven."

The food was not more successful than the martinis had been. Their waiter was adroit, but the soup, a consommé, was "too salty," the Duke said.

The fish was not hot. It was warm, but it was decidedly not hot. The crust on the fish was soggy. The Duke didn't say why he ate only the flesh, but perhaps this was the reason. The *canard à l'orange* was not crisp. It had been a poor choice, since duck must be hot to be crisp. The Duke removed the skin of his duck, obviously unhappy about the surgical operation. The salad was soggy, even though the chef had only just put the dressing on it a moment earlier. It had too much oil, the Duke said. The wines were not authentic Clarets, had been diluted, he said. "How much English income tax have you paid?" he asked Richie abruptly.

Richie floundered. "I have paid—uh—" He glanced at Burton self-consciously. "Well over a million pounds."

The Duke, who had been chewing a lettuce leaf, stopped still, his mouth slightly open, so respectful was he of that staggering sum. He resumed chewing most thoughtfully.

Richie slowly, uncomfortably changed positions on his chair. The wine had made him drowsy—the three martinis and the wine and his apprehensions about the Duke had combined to drug his spirit.

"Not to be sneezed at," the Duchess said.

The Duke, for some reason, found that amusing. He had to hold his napkin over his mouth while he chuckled, repeatedly casting glances at her.

At last the dessert, a *crème plombières pralinée* was served, and was delicious. Even the waiter was relieved.

Coffee.

Silence.

Cognac.

Silence.

The Duchess sat in a pleased stupor. Unlike the Duke, she had drunk and eaten everything served her except the fish's tail, and she was stuffed. The Duke fastidiously laid his napkin on the table. Annie did as much. Burton glanced at his watch. Kate was regally content, still the observer, still waiting. Richie began to explain something, lost his way, changed to a few comments about his favorite barber.

A number of times a bell sounded, signifying that shooting was soon to begin in Studio B, but nobody on the Versailles set moved. Vaguely Richie knew he and Annie were expected, were being awaited. He was unable to think through the entire matter, however. He was safer here. "The Americans have the right idea, in a way," he said.

Everybody turned to him, curious about the next phase of so astonishing an introduction.

"Steak and potatoes," he said.

The Duke once more began to chuckle behind his napkin, casting appraising glances at his companions.

"That's all they eat in restaurants," Richie said, forming the words carefully, trying to avoid slurring.

"And toasted bread," Burton said.

The Duke ventured into speech. "The three main dishes in an American restaurant," he said, and paused to consider the deliciousness of his remark, "are rare, medium rare and medium."

Burton burst into laughter. Annie could not help but join him. Even Richie laughed. The Duke chortled into his napkin. Kate, with a big smile, looked on appreciatively. At last, the lunch was successful.

*   *   *

A WHILE later, on the Studio B set, Antoinette was propped up drunk in the bed, dressed in a flimsy gown. Near the bed sat the contented, bemused Burton and Kate. Between them sat the Duke and Duchess. The awed crew was respectfully silent, and even moved about the set circumspectly. Sigler came on set, concentrating on an agonizing conversation he was having with a French assistant cameraman about Marat and the French Revolution. "The bastards were assassinated because they claimed to be nobility," he said adamantly.

The Duke and Duchess looked up, startled.

"It was because of their vanity that the people killed the sons of bitches," Sigler said. Belatedly he recognized that there were visitors present, and for a long while he stood staring at the Duke, whom he vaguely recognized.

"This is our young genius," Kate said.

"Quite so," the Duke said, not bothering to rise.

Louis XVI at this moment appeared on set, stood erect as best he could at the bedroom door. He was clothed in a long white cotton gown and had a silly nightcap on. He also was staring at the line-up of visitors. A crewman helped him across the set to the bed. There, too, Richie stood as if transfixed, staring at the Duke and Duchess and at Burton alternately. Marie Antoinette was moving about in bed, wiggling, trying to stay awake, her head nodding sleepily.

"All right, let's begin," Sigler said.

No response from the King.

"Antoinette?" Sigler said.

A studio warning bell rang, all instantly was quiet. The slate was clapped.

No response. Louis XVI stood by the Queen's bed, staring at the Duke.

"Cue," Sigler said.

The script girl softly gave the cue line to Richie: " 'Antoinette, the dogs are barking at our heels.' "

216 : John Ehle

"Antoinette," he said and stopped. He was mummified by alcohol and apprehensions.

" 'The dogs—' " the script girl said.

"Antoinette, the dogs," he said.

"Come to bed, my lord," Antoinette said, her head bobbing.

No response.

She turned the covers down for him. "My lord, you are still the King."

The Duchess glanced apprehensively at the Duke.

"They have come out of the dogs," Louis XVI said.

"They have what?" Sigler said. "Cut."

The cameras were switched off.

Sigler slowly approached Louis XVI. "The dogs have come out of the woods," he said. "What went with your characterization, Louis?"

"Huh?" the King said.

Sigler, realizing he was onto an unusual and potentially delightful experience, stepped back out of the way.

"Shot 331, take 2," the slate boy said, and clapped the slate.

" 'Toinette," Louis XVI said.

"Come to bed, Louis. You are still the King," she said listlessly.

"The dogs have come out of the woodwork."

"Here, lie with me tonight," she said dreamily.

Louis stood transfixed, staring at her breasts.

Marie drew a sheet over herself. "My lord," she said, patting the bed beside her.

Louis plopped down on the bed, his legs failing him. His back unhappily was to the camera. Antoinette took hold of him, tried to turn him, only managed to topple him. He lay there, panting, a drunken sot on her heaving chest.

Burton and Kate were contorted, were close to breaking out in open laughter. So was Sigler.

"Once I knew you only as a queen," Louis XVI said ponderously. "There was always between us the crown, so that you and I were never able to be man and woman."

The Duke stared as if transfixed. The Duchess began to fidget nervously.

"You were unapproachable," Louis said.

"Queens are now commoners," Antoinette said sleepily, caressing his head, running her fingers through his disheveled hair, pulling his wig loose by mistake.

"I am so happy now," he said. He turned his face into her bosom and wept.

The Duke stirred uncomfortably.

"Cut," Sigler said finally. "Now that's the strangest interpretation," he said. "King," he called as Louis XVI made his way across the set toward his dressing room, in full flight. "King—"

A COLD shower and two cups of black coffee later, Richie was able to discuss the matter and would discuss nothing else. "I want to know when she invited them, what day," he shouted at Vorono. "The very minute will be the minute she knew the shooting schedule of that scene." He threw back his head and roared toward the hallway. "Kate, you've not heard the last of this!" To his secretary: "I suspected a trick but didn't know, couldn't work it out. She said nothing at lunch. When a woman like Kate doesn't talk, you know she's planning to kill you." He stormed about the room. "She was engaged in her favorite new sport," he shouted, "destroying her husband!" He pounded the wall that separated his dressing room from the hallway. "Do you want my blood as well? What's your price for a divorce, you Scottish witch?"

He did not go home. He went directly to Annie's apartment. His Rolls was parked all night outside. He had expected to stay only long enough to tell her he was sorry about the afternoon, to say he knew he had been the intended target, not she, but he ate the caviar she presented to him and drank the wine, and, of course, got even more drunk. He went to sleep in her apartment.

Sometime in the night he awoke. He was in bed flat on his back and she was in the bed beside him. At first he had no idea what bed he was in. He could see her face, her eyes closed in sleep. He was still drunk, of course, but even so he realized he must have got her there. How this passionate, compassionate woman had been persuaded to favor him, he didn't know, but it was all most exquisite, actually, to awake in this beautiful, sweet-scented place beside her.

And how reassuring to find his own body responding properly; he was not any longer in the seven years' impotence of Louis XVI, certainly. He lay there, considering the miracle of his own erection, the filling with lifeblood—or so he had read, that blood was the means Nature used; he preferred to see life more poetically, ordinarily, so that it was affection which flowed into his penis and increased it into a useful, delightful, large, firm living creature with a head and body and desire of its own.

He turned his head so he could look at her, even as he contemplated the breaking of the veils between them, the ones that separated him from the actress who had splashed in his pool and from the Austrian wife who had cuckolded him with a Swedish count. In a minute or so more she would lie in his arms, would respond to his fat hands. Yes, and he would choose the proper moment to enter her. No doubt her royal Hapsburg muscles would respond the same way as a slave's—no difference between hers and a London urchin's, except hers were perhaps less exercised, more tender, even more anxious to be massaged and tested.

He touched her right breast, touched its nipple through her nightgown, and it sprang to life. He leaned over it and let the clothed nipple slip into his mouth. She slept on, moaning contentedly. His right hand slid up along her stomach, over the skin of the Austrian princess, and came to rest on her other breast, which swelled invitingly. He gently pulled the nightgown free of it and changed over, sucked the bare nipple of the princess, sucked his own mistress's nipple, his eagerness growing with each pulsing rush of blood; affection, blood, lust and love were filling him, love for the exclusive princess who was awake now, who at first instant gasped in fright, then rested her head back into the pillow, her eyes tightly closed, her body tense as a spring, even as his right hand moved toward her face to comfort her. He lingered at her neck. His thumb massaged her lips, which suddenly richly kissed his hand. His thumb entered her mouth and met her tongue. " 'Toinette," he whispered to her, his queen and mistress for the night, "where have we been?"

Fourteen

ANNIE WAS DREADFULLY embarrassed next morning, got up before he awoke, dressed, and went out for breakfast, had to wait for the café to open. At that dawn hour, the waiters obviously thought she was a prostitute. Well, she rather thought so, too. If only Kate had not given her the very opportunity she was exploiting. It was very like Kate in her present mood to set up a dam and then create the waves which crashed against it, a sort of Scottish perversity seizing her, an anxiety should life be less than catastrophic now that it was no longer ordinary.

She drank her coffee and ate her expensive eggs and bacon, and went home, determined to apologize to Richie and ask him to leave her apartment and please to leave her alone. She found he was gone; no note, no forgotten hat. At least she was spared the problem of seeing him. She made the bed, longingly, hatefully.

When she got to the studio, he was singing in his dressing room, his dressing room door open, and he waved to her jauntily, only that, and smiled kindly, warmly. It was as if nothing out of the way had happened.

Maybe, please God, he had been so drunk he didn't recall, she thought.

He came to her flat next night after they rehearsed an entirely new love scene all day. He had a cooked turkey in his arms. "I was on my way home and came upon this," he said.

She was chagrined, confused, yet so relieved to see him that she had to laugh, if only at the turkey, and wave him on inside.

He ate a few slivers of the great bird, she ate a great many. Neither of them mentioned the evening until finally he said, "Do you regret it?"

The question was so simply asked it served to calm her. "You do recall?" she said.

"Did you think I would not?"

"I was ashamed, really. This morning, I mean. And I hoped you would not."

"Really?" He appeared to be surprised. "Well, in fact I can pretend to be vague, if that pleases you."

"Men are more—objective, perhaps. I can't believe Kate doesn't matter."

"Yes, there's always Kate, isn't there?" He nodded finally, thoughtfully.

There was nothing about him just now to suggest power or even glamour, she noticed. Across the table was an aged actor worried about his wife and his reluctant mistress. This lonely man here must be what Richie really was beneath the glossy veneer, a character quite different from the world connoisseur.

"My dear, it seems a long time ago now when she and I were in love," he said.

Was she to discourage him with Kate, or encourage him? What was her fair role? "I think she only needs your love, and she would be well again."

"Actually, darling, I don't simply *love* my wives.

That's a common enough experience. I adore them, I idolize them. So . . ." He looked up at her helplessly. "I am eventually disappointed in them and come to ignore them."

After a while she said, "I wish I could be—as objective about it as you."

He reflected on that, nodded. "She has invited me to dinner. That's her latest maneuver. She mailed me a formal invitation with an R.S.V.P. telephone number. My own home's, as Vorono discovered."

Annie laughed softly. "She is dear."

"Innovative, anyway. Invigorating, if not exciting. Her dinner is to be for two and is to be at the Tour d'Argent, on Wednesday next."

"Are you going?"

He shrugged. "I guess I'd *better,* don't you?"

He was sweet, Annie thought. If she had not herself helped to seduce him, the memories of the seduction would not embarrass her quite so much. She couldn't claim she had been overcome, overwhelmed by him. Forces inside herself, having to do with her own loneliness, her own husband's rejection of her, her own association as Louis' consort, had been responsible, she supposed, and Kate's making a wide road to the compromise. "We must call an end to it, Richie," she said abruptly. "You know that."

"No, my dear, I'm quite certain I cannot do anything of the kind." He spoke at once, as if expecting her declaration, as if this were by no means the first affair of his life.

THEIR love scene was to be a climax of the tower sequence, the coming together of Antoinette and Louis. The love scene as written in draft four was rewritten, but even then Annie and Richie kept breaking down laughing. Sigler introduced a love scene from his own script, which Richie at once set to modifying extensively, which so unsettled Sigler that he stormed away from the studio.

That night Annie and Richie celebrated Sigler's fury and the old scene's passing with a gracious dinner together at the Ritz dining room, and a leisurely discussion afterward. She was particularly lovely this evening, he thought, at this very moment, with candlelight on her face, her chin propped up resting on her arms, her eyes admiring him. He had been lecturing about the arts, their recent debasement, and he realized he would bore a saint. There was not the slightest indication of boredom on her pretty face, however. "I tell myself the film medium is possibly in the early stages of something better," he said, "the childhood, as it were, and that it will eventually arrive. Even a great wine is unpromising when it is quite young. So we must wait. But I don't see how incoherence and grunting can produce understanding, how irritations will eventually enrapture an audience, how crudity will result in grace, how the body will be enhanced by nudity, how silence will become eloquent, how profanity will give us forcefulness in language equal to the voice of a Shakespeare, Sophocles, or even a Racine or Chekov."

"If for the rest of your life you could choose only Romanée-Conti or Clos de Vougeot, which would you choose?" she asked, sipping the Romanée-Conti in her glass.

"I would take—you," he said.

"How dear," she said. "Take care. You'll make me cry."

"What a pleasant vintage that is. I choose the tears. Would they be too painful?"

"Not for me."

"Oh, I meant for me, my darling. A man thinks only of himself. Didn't Kate tell you?"

"How is Kate?"

"Kate is playing golf every afternoon, so as not to drink so much. She has a pro named Dockery. At first she had difficulty believing he was serious about her batting that little white ball about in a garden, as she calls the links, but he persisted, insisted, encouraged, cajoled, and she has taken him on of late. I have my own views about what happens once the ball goes into the woods."

"You can't believe that of your wife."

"Well, can you believe Kate actually tries to swat a tiny white ball over a two-hundred-yard field into a cup?"

"No. Well, perhaps not. Is she drinking less?"

"One bottle of gin a day—it's her self-imposed limit. She started out with twenty-ounce bottles, sneaked into quart sizes, and now is onto magnums."

"She'll kill herself, Richie."

He watched the elderly couple sitting at a nearby table, who had been openly staring at him.

"Did you hear me, Richie?"

"Oh yes, darling," he said.

Tonight he seemed particularly callous toward Kate, yet affectionate toward her; he was a mixture of hardness and gentleness, coldness and warmth. He appeared to be less artificial than usual, too, and the naturalness of their conversation suggested to Annie that they might design a love scene for the film in this same mode. She mentioned this to him. They would use the outline of Sigler's scene. They would not memorize lines, would simply talk, and film everything they said; later, Sigler would edit it. Richie was skeptical, of course, as he always was when faced with any new idea, but Annie was able to lead him along.

The scene as first tried out didn't go well. That first take opened with Louis trying to embrace her. Squirming free, she says, "I wish I had had such attention from you when I was first married. Whenever I think of that wedding night—"

"Not all that again, Antoinette," Louis replies unhappily.

"The Cardinal sprinkled holy water on the sheets, and that was all the mussing up our bed got," she says.

"Let me simply say I found you cold, madame," he declares.

"You never found me at all. I lay awake all night, wondering where you were."

"Must you always talk about sex when I am trying to seduce you?"

The line proved to be funnier than she was prepared to accept. She laughed, so did Richie, and the scene came to a helpless halt.

Next try, the scene ended in another argument, this one virtually a fight, she repeatedly striking the startled Louis' face. He kept saying, "Here now, that won't do." When Sigler at last interceded, Richie angrily told him to stay off the set—"and out of my life and my wife's life."

"Yes, we've had enough interference from you," Antoinette told Sigler, waving one royal hand at him, dismissing him.

"They are absolutely mad," he said later to Kolisch.

That night at Annie's apartment, Antoinette and Louis talked over the various topics they might discuss in the tower, and next day the try went better. The scene was slow, admittedly, and it ended on what Sigler termed a "no-reward" note. "I mean, she has to go to bed with you," he told Louis.

"I do not," Antoinette told him.

"She ought to forgive me, I agree," Louis said. "Or what's the scene for?"

"Exactly," Sigler said.

"Do we agree?" Richie asked him uneasily.

"I am not a toy, to be taken into your arms after twenty years of callous treatment—" Antoinette said.

"Let bygones be bygones," Louis said grandly.

"Oh, it's easy for you to say, but—*I'm* not a saint, Louis."

"That's just as well, is preferable in a woman. But I do think every mortal must forgive her enemies."

Slowly she looks up at him. "Forgive them? What enemies have I, except you flatter them, what friends except you loathe them, what lovers except you endanger them, what enemies do I need with you as my protector?"

"I say, dear, that's not in the cards at all, is it? What's the matter with you, dearest one?"

"They break down our doors and you feed them, they insult us and you discuss the weather with them, they paint crude pictures on the wall and you evaluate their worth, you eat their food, you never once command, much less retaliate, and then you have the—the indecency to think I'll lie squirming under that mass of fat while you slobber on me."

"My dear girl, that's a terribly unattractive way to put it."

"I'm not going to consent, Louis."

"Well, don't then. But don't think you're snow-pure. Who are you, anyway? A frigid Austrian bauble my grandfather picked out for me and I never wanted."

"Because you're a freak."

"Showed me your picture one night after supper, he did, proceeded to explain to me how to sleep with a woman and how to ally France with Austria, all at the same time. He even had a map of Austria."

"So let's call it quits, the lot, I mean. I'll be in my room." She started for the studio exit.

"This is your room. Antoinette, this is your room."

"Where's she going?" Sigler said from off set.

" 'Toinette, come back here."

The studio door slammed after her.

"Sometimes I think she hates me," Louis said helplessly to Sigler.

*   *   *

BY next day Sigler had developed several new ideas for the scene, and he discussed these with Richie and Annie separately. Also, he put in a call for a few more actors, the two children, Prince Charles and Princess Charlotte, among them. The postmaster of Sainte-Menehould, Drouet, was another.

When Sigler arrived on set, he sent the royal family, the four of them, into the Queen's bedroom. "Now, you, Prince, sit in that chair," he said. "Where's a book for Prince? And you, Princess, the chair next to your mommy, and you're making a tapestry, Antoinette. Now, hopefully you two adults will eventually get into bed."

"With the children present?" Antoinette said indignantly.

"Out they go, just before your dinner. Now build up to the dinner, as I told you, talk about a Versailles menu, then when a sorry little chicken is served, send the two kids away, eat the chicken and screw."

Richie slapped the table top. "Please, dear sir, how can any man make love to a woman of quality, a queen, when he's told to screw her?"

Sigler wandered on over to the main camera. "You two pick-up cameras ready?"

"He obviously knows nothing about it," Richie said to Annie. He patted the Princess's knee. "Don't you listen to him, sweetheart."

"Must I?" Antoinette said.

"What?" he said.

"Screw?"

"I hope so, Antoinette. I really do. How long has it been?"

"Oh—not long enough."

"I've read that men facing death become quite insistent, want to propagate themselves."

She frowned at the little girl. "Don't ever marry, darling."

Sigler bumped into Kolisch, apologized. "Lights. Turn the fan off. Camera ready? Damn it, shut up, everybody."

The lights suddenly cut on, blinding the family.

"Muss the Princess's hair up," Sigler said.

Charlotte mussed up her own hair.

"Now, as I say, talk among the family, then let's insert a visit of the postmaster, a brief visit, and I imagine you'll d-d-disdain him, Queen. Then what's next?"

"Are you explaining something?" Richie asked him. "He's exasperatingly vague. Somebody said he was the director."

"Build up to dinner. Speculate. Then eat the chicken. Is that it?"

"He forgot part four," Richie said to Antoinette.

"Yes. Screw," she said.

"Now, let's just explore it," Sigler said. "Where should it start?"

Nobody suggested a place.

"Are the cameras ready? Might as well film it, might use it for cutaways, anyway."

"Cutaways, anyway," Richie murmured appreciatively.

A slate boy slated the scene, confusion continuing in the studio.

"Be quiet," Sigler called. "Now notice it, Queen."

"Notice it?"

"Well, you've got to start somewhere. The hair. Tell her to fix her hair."

Antoinette continues weaving. There is no sign she even heard him. Finally, casually, after the noises have died out, she says, "Your hair's mussed up, Charlotte."

The Princess feels her hair.

"Can't you brush it?" Antoinette asks.

The Princess only looks at her, nonplused. "I?"

"Yes, you. Do you want mummy to show you?"

"Yes." Primly the child consents and silently endures her mother's effort.

"Cléry, I'm having trouble," Antoinette admits, wielding the clogged hair brush inefficiently. The child's hair is in worse disarray than before. "Where is Cléry?" she says. "Cléry," she calls sharply.

"What would we do without him," Louis says kindly, gently. In a way he is reprimanding her.

"But where is he when I need him?" she says fretfully.

Cléry comes in.

"Show this helpless child how to do her hair. Really, she *is* helpless, Louis."

"I don't remember my mother ever being impatient," Louis says suddenly. "I'm wondering if you will take after her, dear," he says to the child.

"Your papa had no family," Antoinette tells her. "He simply grew."

"How?" the girl says. "Like a flower?"

Louis laughs. "Very like a flower. Except I rarely bloom."

The child laughs.

"This tower is not quite the ideal atmosphere," he says slowly. For a moment he is gloomy, but only for a moment, then rather zestfully he says, "Do you know why a flower blooms?"

Charlotte's lips form a kiss as she tries to think it through. "Because their parents will them to."

He is about to deny that theory and to go on to a more scientific one, but he nods instead, turns to where his son is engaged in the book. "Hear that, Charles? I think she's correct." To the girl he says, "It's also a relationship of soil and sunlight and water."

"Nonsense," Antoinette says.

Taken aback, he turns to her. "What is nonsense?"

"When I was seven I tried to ride a certain horse named Patty and was thrown. Each morning for a week I got up at dawn in order not to be seen by my mother and the court and tried to ride that horse, a most obstinate, beautiful horse, a gift from my brother. Every morning I mounted and was thrown. Then in the third week I mounted and rode him, and after that I rode him every day, to the delight of my family." She looks about at them all, alight with the pride of an adult who recalls the marvels of childhood victories. "Why was I able to ride the horse?" she asks Louis.

"You were—the horse was, through experience— that is, your reflexes and his reflexes became trained."

"Nonsense."

"Well," he says helplessly, turning once more to glance at his son. "What then?"

"It was a miracle," she says.

Louis, surprised blurts out a laugh. "A *mir-a-cle?*"

"For which I was most grateful."

Louis peers about like a cock marveling at his roost. "Is everything one learns from experience to be called a miracle?"

"No."

"How are you able to know?"

"I am so thoroughly grateful for those that are."

He rests back in his chair, lips pursed, eyes partly closed. "Of course," he says.

The scene was going well. It had a fragility, and a languid sweetness that caused Kolisch to sit on the edge of his chair, apprehensive should somebody cough or make an interrupting sound. He was walking along a beautiful path that led through a woods he would not be able to find again; every moment to Louis and Antoinette was a jewel, for they would not come this way again either.

The door is opened and in pops the postmaster, he of the nightride and subsequent detainment at the bridge. Why the fellow thinks the royal family will want to see him, only he knows, but there he stands, interrupting the family's conversation. Antoinette's reception is icy, Louis tries to be polite; at least he smiles at him. The intense little man sits down at the family's table, nodding like an old friend. "Good to see your handsome family again, Louis," he says.

"I was wondering if my daughter has my mother's manner," Louis says absent-mindedly.

"Oh?"

"I have nothing left, except my family, so that's all the more dear."

"My daughters favor me."

"I can scarcely imagine it," Louis says, so sincerely that the postmaster does not even suspect ridicule.

Antoinette laughs, can't help it, tries to make the laugh appear to be a cough.

"I'm now a member of the Convention, Louis," the postmaster says proudly.

"Really?" Louis says.

"It's not as simple as handing out parcels, let me tell you. With hundreds of other delegates in the room, I'm known to no one, yet am known to everyone as the—the —the—"

"As the nightrider, I imagine," Louis says.

Antoinette coughs again.

Louis smiles kindly at him. "I suppose if you were to address them from horseback—" he says.

The postmaster laughs uneasily, glances at the others. The Princess bends double in silent laughter.

"How go the wars?" Louis asks.

"Don't you know?" the postmaster says.

"Only what a certain crier tells me. We are not allowed newspapers."

"The Prussians occupy Champagne but can't get through the mountain passes of the Argonne."

"There are only three passes in that chain," Louis says.

"Four."

"I think you'll find there are but three. Who holds them?"

"General Polymetis."

"I'll pray for him," Louis says simply.

The postmaster looks up at him, surprised. "Better for you, Capet, if the Prussians overcome Paris and free you."

"Once King of France, always a Frenchman," Louis says.

"Yes. Whether King or not," the postmaster says, chuckling.

"Whether King or not," Louis says. "A king has no feeling, anyway. Do you know I have never bled one drop of king's blood, of all the drops of blood I've bled?"

The postmaster most seriously thinks about that. "Whose blood was it, then?"

"Why, my own."

"Ahhh," the postmaster says, baffled. He pulls his coat closer about himself. "Suppose your father did, though."

Louis shrugs. "I never saw him bleed. He died when I was a small boy."

The postmaster, unable to follow the conversation, turns to the Queen. "Too bad you didn't reach Prussia on your flight, madame."

"We weren't going there," she says.

"Austria then."

"We weren't leaving France."

"No?" he says. "Why not?"

"The King wouldn't hear of it."

"Don't ask me why," Louis says. "I've been asking

myself all this while, Should a king not put off his royal
robes once they begin to fade into a shroud?" He sits
with mouth open, considering that; soon he shakes his
head, as if trying to free it from the thought. "Now, I'm
sorry to admit we are no longer provided here with Calvados or brandy."

"I have no need," the postmaster says, comfortably
crossing his legs, preparing for a stay.

Louis scratches an itch on his face. "I bid you good
night, sir," he says.

"Oh?" the postmaster says, belatedly realizing what
has been said. He rises.

"Give our regards to the tavern keeper," Louis says.
"Tell him he runs a good house." When the postmaster
lingers, Louis says, "What more is there to say?"

"Yes, sir," the postmaster says. "Shall I go now?"

"We will not detain you," Louis says.

At the door the postmaster bows, and the guard
Simon cuffs him, takes his coat collar and swings him
about, pushes him down the stairs. "What are you bowing for? And you in the Convention!"

The Prince, without a word being said, goes to the
door, quietly shuts it, returns to his chair, which he draws
up to the table.

"You go to bed," Antoinette says, not even looking
up from her work. "Both of you."

"I don't want to go to bed," the boy says.

"Go to your room then."

He sits there still, apprehensively watches her and
his father.

She looks up. "Louis, tell them to go to bed."

"Go to bed," he says obediently, patiently.

"Louis, *order* them," she says.

Louis, mildly: "I order you to go to bed." He smiles
at his little joke.

Antoinette lays her tapestry work aside. "Louis, to order is to make it mandatory."

He frowns discontentedly. "It is *your* order, Antoinette."

"Let the children go, so we can have our supper and —close down this—this desperateness," she says.

Louis, trying to revitalize the conversation, says, "What do you want for supper, 'Toinette?"

She doesn't hear him, or she hears him but doesn't reply. She is quite depressed, lost in the world of her own mind's terrors. Perhaps she sees the Princess de Lamballe again, her head on the pike outside that window, the one just there, her eyes looking at them, while on the ground her mutilated body and even her guts were on display. The crowd was chanting: "Come kiss her."

Louis says, "You children, you can imagine how your mother and I feast each night after you are in bed, with what an infinite variety of foods, served steaming hot, except of course for the sorbets."

The Princess smiles at him, knowingly winks.

"Tonight, as you lie sleeping, your father will dine on *amuse-gueules au Roquefort,* followed by *potage crème d'Orseille.* Your mother as usual will begin with *soupe à l'oignon.* Then we will have *coquilles St. Jacques à la Parisienne—*"

"No, no. Let's have nothing *à la Parisienne,*" Antoinette says.

"No? We'll have *moules* tonight, Antoinette. We have not had *moules* in weeks."

She had been watching him, moodily distracted; now a smile begins to tickle her mouth. "Anything but *poulet rôti.* We have had that quite often enough."

"It's inexpensive, of course," Louis says. "But that need not concern us. Why, Charles, your mother alone has three hundred horses in my—in our stables at Versailles." He pauses for Antoinette to reply. She has always had a reply to any criticism of those horses, but she only watches him, half amused. "My kingdom for a *gigot*, 'Toinette," he says. "Let's have a whole leg and eat it all."

She laughs. "A glutton, Louis."

He pats his belly, grandly satisfied with it.

"I would prefer *veau poêle.*"

"Really? A *casserole?*"

"Not as fattening."

"Lamb has virtually no fat on it."

"But the sauces do, Louis. You bury everything under the richest sauces."

He licks his lips anxiously, his nose tweaks with pleasure.

"I need not tell you that most of the darning I have done here has been to the seams of your clothes."

He is smacking his lips happily. "I had a sauce in Versailles, made for pork out of mustard and cream—"

"*Sauce moutarde à la Normande,*" she says, smiling fondly at its mention.

"I put it one night on lamb," he says.

"He did, he did," she admits.

"And ate fully a pint of it."

"A quart," she says.

The children laugh.

"I had a terrible cold when I sat down to dinner, and got up cured."

The Prince rolls his head, laughing.

Louis, beaming, says kindly, "So tonight your mother and I will have that sauce again."

Antoinette smiles at him, tears in her eyes.

They are startled by the abrupt noise of guards approaching. The door is flung open, Simon enters, a platter in his hand. He advances to the table, plops the platter down with a bang, turns and leaves, slamming the door behind him.

On the platter is one skinny roasted chicken and one baked potato.

Louis, after a long and serious contemplation of the event, begins to chuckle, then so do the others. All four begin finally laughing uproariously, holding to one another.

At last they grow quiet. There is a friendly, warm sensation among them, this tiny family group holding to one another around the table. Louis looks down at Antoinette's hand in his own. They linger in the comfort of the moment until Antoinette withdraws her hand.

ONE of the cameramen ran out of film, so Sigler had to call a break. It distressed him to do so, for they were deep in the material now, were sniping at each other just enough and were now and then revealing the horrors in their minds without fawning. Of course, the scene was long and talky, indeed was more a stage scene than a film scene, but it was genuine, and he could make cuts.

Marge walked on set, began talking with Annie. Sigler called her back, suggested she not interrupt.

"But you *have* interrupted," she said.

"More than I want to." Sigler paced the floor near the delinquent camera, watched disgruntledly as a fresh magazine was brought and attached. "That wasn't bad," he said to Richie in passing. "Need more grit, once you get to the clutch with her."

"More grit?" Richie said.

"I mean, when you grab her," Sigler said.

"Well—" Richie sighed. "We'll see. Grab her?"

"It's not a musical; you'll want to send the kids to bed and get on with it," Sigler said, taking his seat. "Somebody slate it."

Richie, with the mildness, sadness of Fat Louis, sat at the table staring at Sigler, his own resentment mellowed, mellowing. Sigler was a big, shabby dog and Richie had learned to tolerate him—or at least Louis had, and might even come one day to understand what his instructions meant. "Go to bed now, dears," Louis says quietly to his children.

The children hesitate, but when he says nothing more they go to their mother and kiss her, then approach their father; the Princess Charlotte kisses him, throws her arms around him and hugs him. Next Charles kisses his mother. He approaches his father, hesitates, seems to be debating whether to kiss him or not.

"You're getting to be quite a man," Louis says, and holds out his hand.

The boy takes it in both of his, shakes it warmly, goes on out, softly closing the door.

Louis, close to tears: "They're going to be quite acceptable."

Antoinette bites her lip, looks away from him to hide her tears.

He picks up the knife. "Now then, my dear, white or dark?"

"White."

He whacks the chicken up rather crudely. He serves Antoinette's portion on a plate. He picks up a thigh, leg attached, in his fingers. She says nothing all this while, nor does he.

She uses the carving knife to try to cut the meat from the breastbone. "Your daughter already writes a better letter than I do," she says.

"Oh?" he says, stopping in the process of chewing.

"And Charles reads all the time, Louis."

"So did I, and here I am, vastly unsuccessful."

"What?" She is intrigued by the comment.

"Please study in me the improper tutoring of a prince. I read everything but never was put on my mettle, pushed into decisions, made into a man of action. A prince needs athletics, soldiering, games of all kinds, speeches, riding, hunting, even writing. But not an exclusive diet of reading."

"Why, Louis?"

"Because I cannot act," he says.

"Oh, don't. It makes no sense to blame that on—"

"I am a person who, like the reader of a book, observes, feels, senses, laughs, is carried along, but is not able to affect. I cannot act."

She shakes her head, amused at his logic.

He resents her amusement. "You can act. You never read a damn book in your life."

"I have read books," she says indignantly.

"Never finished one."

"That's untrue."

With his mouth full of chicken, he says, "You are willing to decide anything, anytime, but you don't know what you're doing."

"Louis!" she says, stunned.

"And I, equipped with the wisdom of Greece, Rome, England, Spain, Germany, France, *can't act!*" He tosses a spent bone onto the platter, annoyed with himself. Only then is he fully aware of her own anger. He wilts apologetically under her stare, his shoulders even stoop. When his obeisance doesn't placate her, he dismisses the problem with a wave of his hand. "But let Charles read what he pleases. He'll not be King, anyway. Let him enjoy his life."

She is perplexed, as well as offended, but she is also hungry and begins with her fingers daintily to pull at the chicken meat.

"Workman here today, installing locks on the outside of the door of my room. The workman was inefficient, so Charles and I drilled the holes for him."

"You put the locks on your own door?"

"Very grateful he was, too. Said I was skilled. And

Charles was impressed. I took one lock apart and showed him—took the plate off—showed him how it closed its metal jaws." He flexes his own jaw. "Like France."

She pushes her plate aside, sits dejectedly looking at the empty, damp circle on the table the plate has left. "Pass the crepes," she says.

He chuckles. "There is one potato here, if you want it."

"No bread?"

"He must have forgot the bread." He licks his fingers, stops doing so when he realizes it annoys her. "And he forgot the salad. And the wine. And the cheeses. And the dessert."

"It's time for bed," she says. "Good night."

He licks one more finger. "I'll go, unless you prefer otherwise," he says.

She rubs her eyes sleepily. Her hands stop, she allows one eye to look at him.

"We might discover a more interesting arrangement." He sucks at a tooth.

"Louis, is that really you?"

"Give me a chance to find out what's under those petticoats." He glances at her speculatively.

Slowly she lowers her hands from her face. "I've never known you even to be curious."

"Oh? I've never before seen you every day, as here, bending over, working."

"I—how—bending over?"

"Living together like this does have its—having you close by all day—"

"Please don't go on," she says. "It's unnerving."

"I suppose having me about doesn't have a similar effect."

"I suppose not," she says.

"Not a poignant sight, certainly. Though some women prefer fat men."

"Who?"

"I'm told of it." He accepts her skepticism with good nature, breaks off a bite of the potato, sops the potato skin in the gravy. He chews on the delicious morsel. He even removes the potato skin from his mouth, sops up more gravy and returns it.

She closes her eyes, to spare herself.

"I love romanticism," he says. "A woman, or a man without it is—is as bushes. I mean, wood, sticks, twigs, logs."

"What are you saying, Louis?"

"But there are places and times when romanticism is—is not the only suitable climate."

"Are you proposing something?"

"I'm saying you might as well be practical."

She still is confused. "Do you suggest yourself as a practical alternative to twigs?"

"I suggest in this place, at this time in our lives, particularly in this place, that you can't do any better than me."

She slowly, thoughtfully sits back in her chair, sweetly bemused, helplessly intrigued.

"We are left with each other," he says. "The fancier nobles have fled, the servants are gone; no longer can we whistle and have even a dog come to us. What we have left is—ourselves. I have you, and to be plainly honest, you have only me."

She watches him, impressed.

He waits. He picks up the chicken carcass and chews some meat off the back of it. He has the misfortune to belch.

"Louis, is your stomach overfilled again?"

"With that little bird?" he says incredulously.

"I judge it is upset."

"Would I could die of nothing more."

She turns away in order not to need to watch him eat.

"What say you, madame?" he says, pausing, chicken carcass in hand.

"It might be interesting."

Surprised and pleased, he puts the carcass down, wipes his mouth with the sleeve of his shirt. "I thought you would turn me down."

"Why? We are married."

He rises, goes to the bed, hangs his waistcoat on a hook. He feels the bed to test its softness, then sits back on it to judge its bounce and to see if it is secure enough. He then plops his full weight on it, to give it the final test.

Antoinette, her eyes wide with astonishment, watches him.

He untangles himself from the counterpane, gets to his feet. "It'll do," he says. Then, wagging his finger at her, "But it's not like the bed I had in my gold room."

She smiles. "I'm not that woman, either."

"Ah?" He stops before her, touches her graying hair. He sits down in what had been the Princess's chair, a big, haggard, kindly man. Gently he takes her hand.

"I no longer dare look in a mirror," she says.

"I wager your body's the same," he says confidently.

She smiles at him. "What do you mean?"

"Women's faces and hair change first; they often have firm bodies into old age."

She studies him with a fresh puzzlement.

"Their breasts rise, just like a young woman's—if anything, are even more eager to express a welcome. My observations from my own—" He stops, a baffled frown gradually replacing his look of confidence.

She waits. She allows him fully to evaluate his predicament.

"Not that I know," he admits firmly. "I mean to say that in reading the Latin scholars—" His voice falters. "The Italian women—" he says, faltering once more. He looks at her directly, helplessly.

"I'm pleased your knowledge of Latin has prepared

you for the night's pleasures; however, it is unnerving to entrust myself to literature after your recent criticism of it. Have you had no practical experience?"

"None," he says at once.

"No other king in history, Louis, can make that claim."

He is about to rise to his own defense, decides in favor of humility. "I'm different in other ways, as well."

She smiles warmly at him. "Why not tell me the truth, Louis. We are able here to have the truth."

He seriously considers accepting the challenge. He sighs and moans as he wrestles with the decision.

She waits. "Which woman, Louis?"

He hesitates. "The Countess d'Orléans," he says hoarsely.

Antoinette gasps, utterly surprised. She controls herself with severe difficulty. "She's—not as ugly as I had hoped for. Nor as old."

"She had gray about her ears."

"Not over thirty-five."

"The Countess de Marseilles was older."

"Her, too?"

"Rather too chatty."

She reflects on that. "What did she chat about?"

"I mean in the bed, when excited—she could go on and on about her excitement. Though—" He smiles, remembering. "A man has ways to stop that."

"And are there other elderly—mounts that you want to trot out before us?"

"The Duchess of Bordeaux."

"Louis, did you have a—I assumed you had suffered an indiscretion, but you seem to have had a stable of old mares."

He shrugs, not without pride, however. They sit close together, glancing at one another, she suspiciously, he with a satisfaction he cannot conceal. "The Marquise de Tours had—uh—multiple reactions, don't you know?" he says.

Her frown vanishes and a serious interest replaces it. "Multiple?"

"One after another. Amazing to watch. Every minute, off she goes again." He beams at her.

"Every minute?"

"More or less."

"Never would have thought so at court."

"You will recall there was speculation at the time as to why the Marquis had married her, a commoner." He clears his throat, pauses contentedly.

"And you found out."

"Madame Lafayette was more reserved."

"Madame *Lafayette!*"

"But she had a time staying in the bed, she did. Let out a scream once that raised the hairs on the back of my head."

Antoinette is finding it difficult to control her anger.

He chuckles to himself, a contented, friendly fellow as he thinks about his pleasure.

Antoinette casts a prayerful look toward heaven. "So it wasn't all hunting for deer, was it?"

"Nooo. A cup of coffee and brandy on a cold day at the nearest castle keeps the chills away."

"Especially if the lord also is away."

"Well, he can be detailed, can't he? Military or diplomatic or civil or personal or financial."

"You've used them all?"

"No," he says honestly. "I was only—was but mildly occupied."

"With Madame Lafayette's wiggling and the Marquise de Tour's minute-by-minute eruptions and the Countess d'Orléans' special pleadings and the Countess de Marseilles' chattering." She rises indignantly, rubs the chicken carcass in gravy, and hands it to him.

He sits there, the chicken in his two cupped hands dripping sauce, looking up at her with boyish astonishment.

"And now you'll try me, is that it?"

"Oh, that's not fair," he says.

"Did you think I would line up?"

"You asked me to tell you."

"If it had been a better list—"

"What others do you want?"

"Are you prepared to add to it?"

He realizes doing so won't get him anywhere.

"If I had them in my court again, I would tan their bare bottoms. They would eat grass on their hands and knees in a pasture. They would beg me for more whippings. To think they connived their way into my court and there seduced my pitiful husband—" She takes the combs out of her hair as she paces. "I would insist on their standing naked on tiptoes, old women that they are, in the four corners of my bedroom." She unbuttons her jacket, throws it aside. "I would have them expose themselves to the cold winds of January, to see if there is still life in them." She takes her dress off, throws it into a corner of the room. "I would see Madame Lafayette naked riding one of her husband's horses through Versailles at noon. I would like for the Marquise to erupt, as you call it, in my presence, minute by minute." She turns out an oil lamp. "I would—" She stops, her anger having lost its voluptuousness. She is now wearing only a chemise. She busies herself turning the bedclothes down, apparently not even aware of Louis. She comes to the table, takes the candle, places it near the bed. Even as he watches, she slides into bed, and with a thoroughly impish, attractive smile, says, "You must do the rest, Louis," and blows the candle out.

*　　　*　　　*

IN the studio nobody said a word or made a sound. After quite a long moment, Richie sighed.

Kolisch came forward, stumbling over cables, kissed Annie's hand. "Beautiful."

"Of course, it *is* terribly long," Richie said, hoping for reassurance.

"Astonishing," Kolisch said. "You *are* the King and Queen."

A deep contentment came to Richie at that moment, a satisfaction that quelled his insecurity. He was, he decided, the master of his characterization of Louis XVI; not since his early appearances on the West End had he felt as close to his character. He was inside the mind and body of the King.

He helped Antoinette from the bed, pulling the robe around her. He kissed her forehead, then her cheek. "My dear, I have missed you," he said to her.

THERE were two other brief scenes on the day's schedule, involving the Prince and Princess only, but Sigler canceled them. In one of the canceled scenes, the Prince was to try to wash off the drawing of his father hanging from a rope; that failing, the Princess was to draw under her father's dangling feet a rock on which he could stand. It was a simple shot to make, but Sigler would not just now even consider it.

At his apartment he plopped on the bed, lay in a partial coma for perhaps an hour, trying to forget the scene, forget her in the scene, forget her loving, being in love with Louis in the scene, forget most of all the gentility of the scene, which was the weakness of the scene, the old-fashioned, 1950 stamp, the obsolescence. The scene was beautiful, but was overly romantic, overly clever. It was a sort of marvel, but would not supply much grit.

When his youngest assistant, a Frenchman named
Charles, came in from the coffeehouse next-door, Sigler
began complaining about the film. "Why weren't you
there?" he demanded. "1940, 1950 come to life. Get this
place cleaned up."

The apartment consisted of a sitting room with a
mohair sofa and a chair with one leg missing; the chair
was propped on an upside-down wastecan. Twenty or so
books were piled on a plank shelf. On the wall were three
film posters Sigler had found in a closet at the studio. He
had stuck them up with Band-Aids. Off the sitting room
was the kitchen, a closet uncleanable because of the maze
of plumbing, gas pipes, wires, sockets, toaster, posted
instructions in French and English about disposing of
coffee grounds and garbage and defrosting the refrigerator and putting out roach powder. The third room was
the bedroom, the largest room in the apartment. There
was no closet, but there was a wooden chifforobe,
crammed full of dirty clothes and unpressed suits, its
doors open; it resembled a giant beetle that had been
skewered to the wall. The bed was brass, tarnished, and
had a decrepit mattress and springs, tending to sag even
from their own weight toward the middle.

Also off the sitting room was the bath, which obviously had been installed after the apartment had been
built and was located in the entrance hallway. Getting
into or out of the apartment required stepping around
the commode and skirting the bidet, in which Sigler
soaked his dirty underclothes.

Sigler got up from the sofa. "They played it like a
church play," he told Charles. He went into the bath,
filled the tub about a quarter full. "We left that behind
years ago." Heavily, wearily he brought boiling water in
a spaghetti pot from the kitchen and dumped it in. He
stripped naked, quickly wrung out the underwear that
was soaking in the bidet, then plopped today's in its

place. He slid down into the tepid water and settled back to reflect on the unfriendly, jealous, confused, complicated sensations in his mind. She and Richie had developed their characterizations, and whatever he thought of them, the two no longer needed him as director or adviser. That was part of his discontent right there. He couldn't and shouldn't change their charmed, doomed faces, even though both of them were too soft, too companionable, too romantic to give the film the harsh, gutsy cry it needed, that in real life these two bloody bastards must have had.

At hand was a pasteboard tube of bath salts. He twisted it in two and poured the lot between his legs, making a foamy pond about his crotch. This bath was at least an honest bath, while the film would be another Richie-polite sensation unless the scenes in Sigler's own script could be used. Most of the best ones followed Louis' death. The church scene alone would give Sigler a chance to make the film a contemporary statement.

Charles returned from the garbage cans, banged the door against the tub, didn't shut it properly, thereby leaving Sigler exposed to the main hallway.

He slammed the door shut. Too young, that boy, too bloody sure of himself.

Charles came back, asked if he had left the door open again.

Sigler grunted, handed him the brush. The boy grumpily set to work scrubbing his master's back and shoulders. "I wasn't there because you did not invite me," he said, speaking in precise English.

"You missed the longest scene in film history." Sigler splashed water over the floor as he dragged himself from the tub. Charles dried him, rubbing him harshly with a big towel, from which finally Sigler stepped. "And the talkiest." He made his heavy, lumbering way to his bedroom, plopped his full weight on the bed, lying on his stomach. "He didn't once take hold of her."

Charles crept alongside and began to rub his back and thighs.

"Get away," Sigler ordered. "Where's Frances?"

"Not here, certainly," Charles said.

"Phone her."

Charles hesitated. "You going to take her to Ireland?"

"Yeah. You, too, if you get her over here."

"What if I don't get her over here?"

"Then close the hall door on your way out."

Charles wearily went to the phone. "Why are you so polite?" he asked. Even with his hand on the phone, he hesitated. "Rather have Richie come over?" he said.

Sigler looked up. He stared at the boy for perhaps a minute. Slowly he got up. He advanced on him menacingly, but the boy only braced himself. The phone was still in his hand when Sigler struck him beside the head. The boy crumpled at the knees, and Sigler's knee jarred forward into his head. "You crawl out of here and find her," Sigler said.

Charles crawled, tried to rise.

"No crying, you hear," Sigler said.

The boy made his way, felt his way through the bathroom. Sigler, naked, had to go slam the hall door. Too young, too bloody young.

The phone was off the hook. He picked it up off the floor to put it back on, and it was in that instant he decided to phone Kate. That was the first moment the idea came into his consciousness.

He rummaged through the bits of paper on his bureau, found her number. What if Richie answers, he wondered. Hang up.

She answered. She was slurring her words. "Sigler, what you want?" she said.

"I'll explain," he said. "Richie there?"

"No. Where is he, do you know?"

"I'll explain," he said, "when I get there. Kate, I've thought of a way we can make Richie do most anything we want."

Fifteen

SUNLIGHT WAS SPILLING in through her windows, which were sparkling clean, which intrigued Sigler—how the hell do you keep French windows clean? Wash them all the time? Have slaves? What am I doing here in her clean bed?

He had been awakened a moment before by a maid standing beside him, a tray in her hands. "You want his coffee, señor?" she had said in Spanish. He lay there in this room of glass-sparkling sunlight in Paris, wondering if the maid should have said, "You want his coffee, too, señor?"

He was sitting up in bed proudly drinking Richie Hall's coffee with thick cream, wondering if he had played the fool. He knew, had all along known Kate was one of God's creations deprived of the powers to keep a secret. This particular secret ought to be kept, however, until just the proper moment. He was playing with a dangerous fire, indeed, as he knew.

Even so, regardless of the dangers or his own purposes, he was aware that he would not have it any other way, that this woman and this room had fed him a rich food he had needed, one Richie Hall's wife and bed could best provide. He might even view himself as being in danger of falling into a painful addiction, for pain was involved, all right, the twisting of muscles and emotions. "Jesus," he said aloud, moaning contentedly.

"What you say, Richie?" she murmured. When he didn't answer, she turned over groggily and opened her eyes. She permitted herself a variety of facial expressions, including incredulousness. "You are *here*, Sigler?"

He shrugged. "That's a rhetorical question, Kate."

"Don't you think you better get out of Richie's bed?"

"Speaking of the devil, Kate, I would as soon he didn't know of my having been here at all, at least until the ideal moment."

"Let's talk in the garden," she said, clambering out of bed. She began pulling open dresser drawers, rummaging for panties and bra. "Lord, what have I done now?"

"I recall we were using a laburnum tree as a maypole, doing an Indian dance. Pushing me into the raspberry patch was unkind, Kate."

She pulled on her slip backwards, found a knit sweater, pulled it on. With a swipe or two of her brush, she dismissed her hair. "Now, I want you to sneak downstairs and go out, then ring the bell at the gate, so the Spaniard can come let you in."

"Kate, I have something to say to you."

"Love at first sight?" she asked, pausing at the doorway.

"I really d-d-don't want Richie to know about this until the proper time."

She watched him speculatively, a wry little frown on her face. "What time?"

"I'll tell you."

She calmly watched him. "You're sweet," she said, and bolted for the stairs.

She served him coffee and croissants on the terrace, and he had to admit she looked rather pretty and inviting, with her white sweater cuddling her neck, her brown hair fuzzy, her hair needing to have his hands run into it to hold her head still and to make her look at him. "Raspy raspberry patch," he said, scratching his buttocks.

"You hit me, I push you," she said.

"Did I hit you? Not on the face, was it?"

"No, no," she said.

"Don't hit an actor or actress in the face—I've learned that. Kate, you got any eggs?"

"You ever—feel like life is a cloud you're moving through, can't see what's about you? In a cloud, going, going, going, then bang."

He drained his cup of coffee. "You got any eggs, Kate?"

"Inevitable, predictable, undeniable, unalterable, unseeable."

"What?"

"Bang."

"Uh-huh," he grunted. "Kate—"

"You rarely think of it because it's impossible to see it coming at you. It has an odor, a musky, dusty odor, they say, leaves an acrid taste on the tip of the tongue. It says 'later,' or it says 'soon,' or it says 'now.' But it never says 'never.'"

"Not even any berries on them this time of year."

"And what makes it so surprising is that it never should be a surprise at all."

"That's surprising, is it?"

"Not to me," she said. "Not any longer. Not after this."

"What's that butler's name? Juan, Manuel?"

"Carlos."

He shouted the name, then sat contentedly relaxing in the warm sun, considering how fortunate he was. "Two fried with four bacons, on the double," he told Carlos.

While Carlos fixed breakfast, she suggested they walk down to the laburnum tree. She said she wanted to see if their dancing last night had damaged the lawn. "You are so huge, Sigler," she said.

"I think I'll cut the trial scene," he said.

"You will over Richie's dead body."

"Interesting idea."

"Richie has to be tried," she said. "He deserves it." They walked slowly, languidly to the little laburnum and she knelt at the ravaged spot of lawn.

"I need that time for the church sequence at the end."

"Going through a cloud," she said, still kneeling on the grass, "with Richie gone. Where is he, Sigler?"

"He's an actor. Who knows?"

"So?"

"He acts," he said.

"He'll never hear the sound at all."

"Won't he? What sound?"

"He'll hit it, that's all, and then he might say, 'Oh, this can't be right.' Kneel down, Sigler."

"I'm not much of a kneeler, Kate." He sank heavily to his knees.

"See?" she said.

He looked about, nonplused.

"Do you see it yet?" she said.

"No, not yet."

Carlos appeared far off, on the terrace. Not favored of God, Carlos, not benevolently endowed with brains. Carrying the tray, he descended the steps and approached across the lawn. Sigler watched, fascinated. He couldn't help but think of Carlos as one of God's more dour messengers sent to fetch Kate, or himself, or them both, without muss or bother.

Carlos set the breakfast platter on the lawn and returned to the house, as little nettled as if he had each morning for years given this particular service.

"He scrambled them," Sigler said, frowning at the platter.

Kate began tucking the bits of torn turf back into place, murmuring apologies to the injured lawn. "My mother will be getting out of bed soon." She looked toward the house. "Hers is the other set of windows on the second floor."

"See us?" he asked, his mouth full of toast.

"Don't think she's awake yet."

"Last night?" he asked.

"Oh, I hope not," Kate said. "Last night never was, Sigler, except for this grass. That's what I think."

"Thought it was," he said, winking at her.

"Actually, for him to die wouldn't mean *anything*," she said.

"Carlos, you mean?"

"*Carlos?* Who would ever think *Carlos* would die?"

"You ought to be a poet, Kate. I don't understand a word you say."

"Don't poets have to rhyme?"

"Naw. Not any longer. We're all free now."

"Then what we kneeling on the grass for?" she said.

DEATH was the motif of the remainder of the film, the death of hundreds of members of the nobility and of Fat Louis, the living death of Antoinette, and finally the abrupt assassination and execution of the revolution's leaders, which ended the Reign of Terror. Also involved in Sigler's version of the script was the so-called church scene, showing the people's pillaging of the Church at St. Denis, the historic burial place of French kings and their families. In history, the Convention decreed that all these sepulchers of royalty should be destroyed, and on the appointed day, anxious to eradicate even the memory of nobility, the populace broke open the crypts and debased themselves with the skulls and corpses. The scene represented to Sigler the culmination of the spirit that had come to dominate the people's revolution. The sequence could be a major one of film history, he felt, and even with his disjointed, stuttering arguments, he had convinced Kolisch that this just might be. Also, Sigler assured Kolisch that Kate would indeed be in it—a second part for her—and she would help take care of Richie.

Neither of them quite dared to beard Richie in his den about it, nevertheless. Kolisch wasn't certain how much power Richie had at the studio. He did suggest that the matter not be broached until after Louis' death. Obviously it was better to have Richie's main scenes on film before taking the risk of losing his full cooperation.

KATE was curious about Richie's attitude toward his own approaching execution. She prodded him about it. Challenged in this way, he refused to reveal to her the slightest apprehension, denied her any satisfaction, and angrily denounced her study as an intrusion on his privacy. Actually, as death approached, he was experiencing three tidal changes within himself. He was more acutely aware of his own physical senses: sight, sound, the feeling of heat, the nip of a wind, the blue of the gas fire in Annie Logan's flat, the self-conscious smile of a young lady who sold newspapers near the studio, the warmth of Annie Logan's hand—the warmth of her as a human body near him, near his. The second had to do with God. He had been a communicant of the Church of England all his life, but the power of the Church, the feast of security which it had always offered, had not appealed to him until now. He read in Cléry's book about the religious fervor that Louis attained in the tower, and Richie empathized with him so closely that he was attracted to the Church with similar devotion. Finally, there was a stronger compulsion to be loved. Day by day he and Antoinette shared the rehearsals of the execution scenes, and night by night he continued to seek Annie's company. Often he stayed the night with her, pleading exhaustion with the depressing day's work, fell asleep in her arms. Usually he roused himself before dawn and forced himself to go home.

One morning in Kate's room, as he was groggily getting out of bed, feeling for his slippers with his naked feet, Kate appeared before him in her negligee. "Do you know how many suits you have, Richie?" she said.

He paused in his search, one slipper on and the other not yet located.

"One hundred four," she said. "You have forty-seven pairs of shoes. You have thirty-three hats, eighty ties—"

"What is all this, Kate?"

"But you have only eight undershirts and nine drawers, so we have to wash every week."

"I'm finding the subject offensive, Kate."

"Where were you last night? With your dying Antoinette?"

"She's not to die. Her execution was deleted months ago."

"I want her to die."

He considered that. "Indeed?"

"Richie, we saw your car."

He looked up slowly, watched her, waiting to determine if there was a new danger here, or merely a reoccurring irritation.

"We were in your Rolls convertible."

He was stunned by that, actually. "I have—given no one permission to drive my Rolls drophead, Kate."

"Filled it up with suits, all your suits and shirts—I think you've got a hundred forty-two shirts."

He sprang toward the closet, threw it open. Empty. He pulled open drawers, all empty, turned on her, grabbed her and shook her fiercely. "Where are my clothes?"

"In the drophead, drophead."

He threw her into a chair, pulled on the wrinkled pants that were hanging on the closet doorknob, pulled on yesterday's shirt. "I want you to know that I do not give *anybody* permission to drive my car, especially drunks."

"Oh, we were drunk, all right, all right."

"My car, my car is the dearest possession—I gave myself as a gift when I finished the Metro film, and nobody drives it without permission."

"What about your wife, Richie?"

"She cannot drive it, either."

She screamed up at him, "What about your wife, God damn you? Don't you even care who drove *me?*"

He stared down at her, startled, his fury abating, draining away, as embarrassment crept in. "Yes," he said simply.

"Oh, shit," she said, and hurled a shoe at his belly. "Go on out of here. I wish we'd left it over there on the street at her place, I do, but he wouldn't. He's got no nerve. I think he's scared of you."

Richie went into the bathroom and proceeded to brush his teeth. Kate's other shoe plopped against the wall nearby. Calmly he rinsed his mouth out. He tied his tie as he came back into the bedroom. He noticed Kate was sobbing. "Then after the shock, you understand, after the announcement of my death-to-be, I talked with Maillard, who had opened my wall safe, the safe I had hid behind the wood paneling of my Versailles bedroom; I even made the locks myself. The boogers found it and in it were secret letters and notes and accounts, among them a few notes implicating Mirabeau. Also, letters to the Emperor in Vienna, Annie's brother, a few other rather revealing compromises. So, they decided to kill me, Kate."

She had been sobbing all this while. "Good."

"So I—talked with him, about Mirabeau mostly, and it—it came about that—I mean, if Mirabeau had lived, Maillard thinks I would not now have to die."

"Well, bully for Maillard."

"And I tell you something else—I think so, too. That little quirk of fate—"

"Well, I'll tell you something, King the Sixteenth: you're full of shit."

"Vulgar. In a woman, even a Scottish woman—"

"You're *vulgar,*" she said huskily. "You're so filthy vulgar you make me puke."

"Now, listen here, lady—"

"I'll take the smirk out of your face. Ask me. Ask me?"

"Ask you *what?*"

"Who drove your drophead."

He waited for a long moment, then calmly said, "Who drove my drophead, Kate?"

She hesitated. Her courage deserted her at the brittle moment. "Oh, God knows," she said, moaning.

He left her, damn tired of her histrionics, went downstairs, said good morning to Carlos, ordered him to bring his clothes back into the house. He was chatty, cheerful, as Kate could hear, was talking blithely away, and she, hands clenched—even with her clenched hands she struck against her ears, trying to drive away the agony of hearing him.

"Nobody, but nobody is to drive my Rolls drophead . . ."

*   *   *

HIS preliminary-to-death scenes went well, with a naturalness that even Sigler was pleased about. In one scene Antoinette and Louis try to decide which of his worn suits he should wear tomorrow, at his execution. After they decide, she, almost overcome with grief and horror, goes alone into her room and takes her own three worn dresses from their hooks and one by one holds them up before herself.

The effect left even the stagehands gasping.

And how precious were the final scenes with the children! At the rehearsal of the lunch scene, Louis put his watch on the table so he could watch the precious time pass. "I will not see this exact time again, will I, Charles?" He looks up suddenly. "Did you hear the tower strike eleven?"

"I—I didn't notice," the Prince says, lost in desperate worry.

Louis shakes his watch and listens to it. He taps it on his open palm. "I think it might be in error."

A bell begins to sound the hour outside.

"There. This is not a day one wants a watch to go *fast,*" he tells the watch. He sits back in his chair, endeavors to compose himself. "It is the last round for me, Charles, but it can be borne. It is well to know it can be borne."

Less successful was a scene Richie requested himself, one having to do with his religious beliefs. On his own he rehearsed it with Antoinette and Cléry, then sprang it on Sigler, who complied rather meekly to hear at least a rehearsal of it. In the scene Louis and Antoinette are alone, she fitful, nervous, all sorts of awful fears finding niggling ways past her defenses, but Louis is immaculately competent, more so now than ever before. The elements bothering his life have been simplified, their number reduced; he is the master of the few of them remaining, has accommodated himself to them, wretched as they are. Antoinette's resentfulness does not even ruffle him. When she expresses her fitful prayer that her brother will send his army, Louis, smiling kindly, warmly, says, "God is not going to answer a war prayer. He's conciliatory by nature, will avoid violence. He uses compassion rather than might, whispers rather than shouts."

"What—does he whisper?" Antoinette asks, whispering.

"Oh, it's in Latin usually." He considers that fondly. He folds his hands contentedly. "Or French."

Antoinette has to smile at the thoroughness of his patriotism. "What . . . words, Louis?"

"Sustinuit anima mea in verbo ejus, speravit anima mea in Domino, A custodia matutina usque ad noctem."

"What is it? What does it mean?"

"I look for the Lord, for in Him is my hope and trusting, my soul doth wait for the Lord, God, the God of truth, more than they that await the morning long before its dawning." He is bashful, boyishly modest about his achievement.

"My soul doth wait for the Lord," she asks, "more than they that await the morning?"

"Excellent those old Jews, David and that lot. More poetry in them than the current crop of writers."

"Ask God in Latin never to forgive them, Louis."

He says nothing in reply, for he sees her attitude is hopeless. He smiles kindly at her. "Would you care to write out my will for me?"

"I can't. Please."

"Where is Cléry then?"

She calls for him, and Cléry enters at once.

Louis says, "They gave me paper and a pen, so that I can write my will."

Sadly Cléry sits down, puts the paper in place, takes up the pen.

"Let it begin, In the name of the Most Holy Trinity, I, Louis XVI, King of France, leave my soul to God. I pray him not to judge it on its merits, but rather by those of Jesus Christ who offered Himself as a sacrifice to God His Father for us men, however unworthy we may be, and me most unworthy of all."

Sigler, off set, groans. "Where did you find the Jesus Christ commercial, Richie?"

"Yes. Well, it's in his will, Sigler."

"It dates the film," Sigler says.

"I thought you were after historic accuracy," Richie says.

"We can't include everything."

"Well, if a man is dying, his religious views deserve review."

"We only have ninety minutes. Maybe one hundred at the outside."

"We have plenty of time apparently for everything except what you are insensitive to."

"That's what I can't stand, the hypocrisy—"

"Are you addressing me?"

"All a façade—"

"Are we now discussing architecture, or this dying man?"

"I'll cut the scene out in the editing room," Sigler said.

"Then you won't need me any further," Richie said, and at once stalked off to his dressing room. "No, I won't return until I have the assurance that Jesus and the will remain," he later told Kolisch.

Kolisch promised. "My God, do you need it in writing?" he asked.

This was the most abrupt studio confrontation between Richie and Sigler in several weeks, and in it Richie got what he wanted. In all, about an hour was lost before he returned and immaculately became Louis XVI once more. He took up where he had left off, with the will and its Christian entreaties, even while Sigler moaned.

"With all my heart I do pardon those who have made themselves my enemies."

"No, no, Louis," Antoinette says, "you can't mean that."

"I recommend my children to my wife; I have never doubted her maternal tenderness for them. I beg my wife to forgive me for all the evils which she has suffered on my account—"

"Too fast, Louis," Sigler says. "This part is more interesting."

"—just as she may be sure that I forgive her for anything of which she may—have reason to reproach herself."

She sits there staring at him, her lips parted as if to speak a thought not yet formed. Her eyes fill with tears. "Louis, I don't ask to be forgiven."

"I forgive you anyway."

"Not in a will, Louis."

"I enjoin upon my son, should he be so unfortunate as to become King—"

Cléry looks up, surprised.

"Louis, too much," Antoinette says.

"Too damn wordy," Sigler says. "We really should delete the will."

Louis says, "It's part of dying. It was part of his dying."

"It's not moving me," Sigler says.

"I will not delete it," Richie says from the table. "I am writing this will here in this tower—"

"Don't tell me my business, and I'll not tell you yours," Sigler tells him.

"It is *my* will," Louis says. "What do you mean *your* business?"

"It's my decision," Sigler says. "Cut the will. Cut the Jesus commercial, too."

Richie, exasperated, shouts, "He was a Christian, and he is a Christian king dying, and the will will remain!"

"Break. Call a break," Kolisch says to Sigler. "Break, please."

But the damage was done. Even Kolisch in the firebrand heat of the moment could see the suspicion in Richie's eyes. Richie was a survivor of decades in this film business. He realized Kolisch was capitulating or was in collusion with Sigler. No longer was he even pretending to be the one making such critical decisions as this one. Sigler was taking over command.

Later Kolisch asked Sigler what in the world he had thought to gain? The confrontation had been needless. Sigler was too confused even to reply. It occurred to Kolisch that as the film neared the point when Richie no longer would be involved in day-to-day shooting, Sigler instinctively sought to test his strength against him.

As Kolisch feared, Richie for his part was taking no more chances. Certainly he was not going to entrust this film or his career to this new director. He phoned the Coast that afternoon, told his agent what situation he was up against. He told him to get the word promptly to Mr. Lesher that Sigler must be replaced. "Well, why are you taking a percentage of my income if you can't discreetly get word to Mr. Lesher about this problem with the Paris film?"

The agent asked if Richie realized what complications this might cause for Kolisch.

"Of course I do, and I like Kolisch, I've liked Kolisch for years," Richie said, "but my work comes first, old boy. Did you think it didn't?"

He did regret having to move in on Kolisch this way, and when next he saw him, he made friendly conversation with him, said he and Kate would like to have a cast party at their house on Sunday week, to celebrate his death and the end of the shooting. What did Kolisch think of that? They even went off to lunch together, had two cocktails together.

Annie joined them. Kate, surprisingly enough, arrived sober, though under the poetic cloud of death that comforted her these days.

Kolisch laughed appreciatively, in a friendly, warm way at all of Richie's jokes, relieved to sense that they would not have a confrontation. He admitted he was in "fine fiddle" these days. His film was going to be a "fantastic success." It was over budget, true, but he had personally covered part of that added expense, enough of it, he felt, to keep the studio's wolves from eating him alive, and he had managed to get his volatile cast past the dangerous pits and asides which awaited every film's cast. He said he had even begun to wonder about his next film. "Who is to do the Irish film? Does anybody know?" he asked his luncheon companions.

"Sigler," Kate said.

"Yes, of course," Kolisch said. "He directs. But who is to produce?" Nobody knew. Kolisch made a note to himself to inquire. Making the note was intended to indicate to them that the matter was of such casual importance to him that he might forget it otherwise. "This one will be such a success—"

Kate said, "If you were to die tomorrow, Kolisch, what would you be thinking now?"

Kolisch stopped chewing on a bite of calves' liver, stared at her critically, measuring her impertinence.

"I had a week to prepare for my death," Kate said. "No one will ever know how rich and painful it was."

Richie turned to her. "But you *didn't* know, darling."

"I knew very well," she said.

"You as Kate knew, but the Princess wasn't told until the minute she died. Louis knew for a day and night."

"What's the difference?" Kate said, rising firmly to the debate.

"My dear, I know *and* Louis knows, and he has twenty hours to examine the situation."

"What did Louis actually do in the history books?" Kolisch said.

"Why do you want to take that away from me?" Kate asked Richie.

"He made his will and requested a priest," Richie said to Kolisch.

"Richie—" Kate said.

"My dear, I didn't take anything away from you."

"I found the world so much more intense and beautiful than before," she said. "I went to bed every night thinking to myself: Remember every moment of sleep, for even that is precious."

"The Scots often exaggerate," Richie said to Kolisch.

"The green of the grass, have you noticed it, Kolisch?" Kate asked.

"Huh?" he said.

"The shapes of little things, like leaves," Kate said.

"No, not recently," he said. Marge brought him a note, went out again. He unfolded it, glanced at it, closed his eyes in pain. "Have to call the Coast at three," he explained. He belched; nervousness seemed instantly to affect his digestive system. "Now what could he want with me?"

"Call whom?" Richie said.

"Lesher." He pushed his food aside.

Kate said to Annie, "Everything in nature is rounded, except oak leaves."

"That's not true, is it?" Richie said.

"I kept examining the different forms of roundness," Kate said.

"What about the Matterhorn?" Richie asked.

"Richie, hush," Annie said.

"Don't tell my husband to hush," Kate said, a brittle crackle in her voice.

"Sorry," Annie murmured.

"You see, I've never given my death a thought," Richie said. "I am Church of England, and maybe as such I would send for some—uh—whatever—saint—"

"Priest, Richie," Kate corrected him.

"And say my confession, or whatever it is."

"What would I do?" Kolisch said helplessly, "if I had twenty hours and needed to confess?"

"Phone Golda Meir," Richie suggested.

Kolisch laughed.

Kate said, "Even the thorns became my friends."

"Rounded thorns, were they?" Richie asked.

"The clouds are round," Kate said, ignoring him. "The sun, the moon."

"My clothes," Richie said suddenly. "We've got a little scene about what suit to wear. Why can't we flash back to see how many suits I once had?"

"One hundred four," Kate said.

"We need to do something in the tower to strike the contrast with my previous life, to emphasize my poverty."

Kolisch took the note out of his pocket once more and read it, his expression bleak. "He's such an abrupt man—decides it here and now, bang."

"Bang is what it's going to be," Kate said, "for each one of us. You, too, Annie."

"I can imagine a scene in the fields," Richie said, "maybe hunting, to relieve the tower's oppressiveness. In that tower room I must somehow reflect my past splendor, must contrast—"

Kolisch said, "I'll ask him, simply ask him."

Richie looked up. "What?"

"About the Irish film."

"Yes, do tell me about the Irish film," Richie said.

"Do you want it?" Annie said to Kolisch.

"I dunno. It's appropriate timing. Big Irish population in America."

"I heard the studio doesn't own the option," Richie said vaguely.

"Nonsense," Kolisch said. "Surely not."

"There are so many new novels coming out about the I.R.A.—"

Kate said, "Annie, do you care?"

"About Ireland, darling?" Annie asked.

"About *me*," Kate said.

It was so direct a question that all conversation came to a stop, and Richie, irritated by Kate's overly emphatic method of gaining attention, said, "We all do, Kate, you know that."

"I do," Annie said sincerely.

Kate watched her for a long moment. "I think you do."

Nobody knew quite what to make of it. Of course, Kate was always temperamental anyway.

"Has a priest come to see you yet?" Annie asked Richie.

"The Committee has to vote on that," he said. "It seems the revolution is against both Church and King."

"Ever so many are," Kolisch said. His hands were gripped tightly together on the table; his knuckles were absolutely white.

"Of course, if a person had the early novel, and rights to the new ones, too—" Richie said.

"He leaps to a decision, clomps down like a tiger," Kolisch said.

"I've made quite a neat penny in the past, buying up options," Richie said, as if the matter were an incidental one. "Using one name or another, but using me as the offered star. Didn't cost much, if they thought I would do it, you see."

Kate had begun humming, but so quietly she seemed merely to be amusing herself.

"You haven't eaten *anything*," Annie said to Richie.

"No, but I—I might get a little something in the tower. Yes, then maybe later in the day we can think of something, some—flower or other device to dramatize—"

"Maybe a horse can come into the garden," Annie said.

"Why not?" Richie said. "I can visually drool over the idea of riding over the hills and fields and streams."

"Then bang," Kate said.

"Anything visual will do," Richie said, "but the trouble is that visual items do not have much soul to them. It's through words we come closest to our own souls, and Sigler is antagonistic to words, just as he's scared of romanticism, alarmed by modesty—"

"Are you modest, Richie?" Kate said.

"I don't parade naked, if that's what you mean."

"You come home naked," she said.

"I undress in the hallway, in the dark. Don't *irritate* me, Kate."

"I can't help it," she said softly, "you're so dear."

"Kate, darling, you seem depressed today," Annie said.

"Don't you worry about it."

"Let's not any of us," Richie said.

Kate laughed softly; she seemed to be trying to keep her lonely self company. "Let's go back to Beverly Hills, Richie," she said.

"It is a sign of our times, that there is no visual symbol which continues to merit respect," Richie said.

"Not even a dollar bill," Kolisch said grumpily.

"Words only have power," Richie said.

Annie said, "I have loved you better than my soul for all my words."

"Oh?" Richie said, pleased. "Irish truth, is it?"

" 'Where got I that truth?' " Annie said. " 'Out of a medium's mouth, out of nothing it came, out of the forest loam, out of dark night where lay the Crowns of Nineveh.' "

"Don't stop," Kate whispered.

"I'm afraid I'm unable to remember what's next," Annie said.

"I know one, too," Kate said to Annie. " 'I had a beautiful friend and dreamed that the old despair would end in love in the end: I looked in her heart one day and saw his image there.' "

Annie stared at her, dumbfounded. "That's—that's pretty, Kate," she said.

Kate smiled. "It's my own Scottish version of Yeats."

"Oh, are we doing Yeats? I simply love Yeats," Richie said, delighted. He recited stridently: " 'Now that we're almost settled in our house, I'll name the friends that cannot sup with us beside a fire of turf in the ancient tower, and having talked to some late hour climb up the narrow winding stairs to bed: Discoverers of forgotten truth or mere companions of my youth, all, all, are in my thoughts tonight being dead.' "

Annie and Kate clapped. Others in the restaurant turned to look, and Richie beamed at them.

"I simply love Yeats," Richie repeated. "Does the imagination turn the most on a woman won or a woman lost?"

Sigler called from the door to Richie. "Time to go."

"Our master's voice," Richie said. "Well, Annie, Kate, I will see you later. You're due in an hour, Annie."

"Yes, later," Kate said. "Much later."

"Sigler," Richie said as he moved to join him, " 'endure what life God gives and ask no longer span; cease to remember the delights of youth, travel-wearied aged man—' " He put his hand on Sigler's shoulder as they went out. " 'Delight becomes death-longing if all longing else be vain.' "

Kolisch wiped his mouth, then carefully wiped his fingers with his napkin. He rose and wandered off without a word.

"You are so sad, Kate, I worry about you," Annie said.

"Thank you, but it's not possible," she said.

"It is, Kate."

"I don't want you to waste my time." It was too curt, too abrupt; she shrugged apologetically, dismissing her own annoyance. "I sent my mother home. Did I tell you?"

"Oh?"

"Last evening. I was expecting a friend, a lover—"

"Kate, that isn't discreet to say—"

"Oh, you and I are friends, that's the point. So I told Mum to get out."

"Last night?"

"Put her in Richie's drophead, but the Spaniard couldn't find the key, so I had a taxi take her to Orly. Told her to say hello to Glasgow for me. How's that for a parting?"

"Not—not a song, Kate."

"Then I told the two Spaniards to leave after Richie's cast party."

"Why? Aren't they proving out?"

"Richie and I are to have dinner Wednesday. Did he tell you? I've invited him to the Tour d'Argent."

"The duck place?"

"It's very high up."

"Expensive?"

"The seventh floor, I believe, though I've never been good at math."

Annie laughed. "You are dear."

"My mother doesn't agree with you. I don't either."

"Oh?"

"You keep saying 'oh.' "

Annie shrugged.

"I am tired of your saying 'oh,' Annie."

"Oh, darling—"

"You said it again. If you say it one more time I'm going to throw up on Eddie's liver. You and I have much to talk about, and you keep saying 'oh.' Hold my hand, Annie."

Annie willingly took the hand Kate offered.

"Hold it tightly. Tightly."

"Yes, darling."

"Don't let me go, Annie."

"No."

"Tell me an Irish poem."

"I don't remember many. I grew up on poems and songs, but Hollywood is so unlike Ireland—"

"Tighter. A song then."

" 'I went out alone,' " she sang softly, " 'to sing a song or two, my fancy on a man—and you know who.' "

"Tighter."

" 'And that was all my song—when everything is told; saw I an old man young or young man old?' "

Sixteen

MARGE PLACED the overseas call to Lesher. Kolisch, waiting, opened the one drawer of his desk, pulled it against his belly, poured a few pills from a vial so they lay loose in the drawer. He laid a yellow pad and a freshly sharpened pencil on the desk top.

When Marge said, "Hold for Mr. Kolisch," and handed him the phone, he took it at once and with full cheerfulness said, "Hello, hello—" A big smile was fixed in place, but his eyes were grim and his body tense.

"Having fun in your work, Kolly?" the distant, smooth, deep voice said.

"Yes, we're enjoying being here," Kolisch said, perhaps too buoyantly.

"That's only fair after all your work. I've heard a few complaints about your director, Kolly."

Marge watched Kolisch as his right hand sought out a pill in the open drawer, plopped it into his mouth. "I don't know what they could be, Lesher."

Marge pulled up a chair and sat down as close to him as she could, close enough to hear the overtones of the velvety voice from Hollywood.

"Have we seen all the takes here?" Lesher asked.

"Yes, we've sent all the rushes to you, of course," Kolisch said, "except for the Princess's death scene, which we're debating using."

"Who's death?"

"The Princess's."

"What's that?"

"Richie's wife's."

"Richie doesn't trust the director."

Kolisch pressed his head against the back of his chair. "The film means a great deal to Richie," he said, his buoyancy more forced now even than before, "and I can't believe he would want Sigler—out of it."

"Lack of confidence in the director, that's Richie's problem, I imagine."

"We—we are almost done with Richie—"

"What about the publicity for the film?"

"We don't have to have him," Kolisch said. His eyes were tightly closed, his jaw was almost shut entirely, his face was red as a beet. "I think it is a masterpiece."

"How do you know?" Lesher said.

"I don't know how I know."

"In choosing between Richie and a director, do you mean to say—"

"I would try not to choose."

"Richie has asked for the choice."

"Not of me," Kolisch said.

Pause.

"Maybe I should come over there for a day or two."

"Well, you are welcome, of course, if you think I can't make the decisions."

"I can fly over this weekend, overnight Friday."

"Yes, you could, of course. However, Lesher—"

"Meet me, Kolly?" he asked casually.

"Oh, certainly. We will arrange for all you'll require . . ."

When he was done, Marge tried to take the phone

from his hand, but he gripped it so tightly she couldn't free it. He returned it finally to its cradle himself, and his hand sought out another pill and lifted it to his mouth. "I'll be all right, Marge," he said.

Later he sought the sunlight in the courtyard. Marge made him wear his hat and she turned up his topcoat collar. "You're especially vulnerable to pneumonia when you're like this," she told him.

He was still in the courtyard when Annie came out, on her way to Studio B. Dear Annie: how much sweeter she seemed now to him, in the light of his present danger. Dear Annie Logan from old Ireland. Beautiful Annie Logan, what poems have been written about you?

"Did you ask the Coast about the Irish film?" she said, stopping before him.

He smiled kindly at her. "No. I forgot all about it."

"Silly you," she said.

He took her hand suddenly and squeezed it. "Silly me," he said.

When Kate came outside, he led her aside and confidentially told her about the phone call, and what it might mean in terms of her own success, the use of her death scene, for instance, and of the proposed church scene in which she would star, and of the proposed Irish film Sigler planned. "Now, Kate, we are coming to the place where we must help Richie, if we can."

"What do you want me to do?" she asked him.

It was, of course, the attitude he had come to expect of her, and counted on.

ANNIE had no idea that the "lad actor" was due to arrive in Paris. She didn't know why she had come to the airport in a rented limousine with a contented, quiet Richie beside her.

It was almost 11:00 P.M. when they arrived, and he

pulled up his raincoat collar and put on dark glasses. He was too excited to remain in the car, he said. They paced the lobby until Vorono came through Customs. He was drunk, but that was not unusual—Annie had seen him drunk even at the studio. He said nothing to her at all.

Richie was suddenly wary. "Is he with you?"

Vorono cast a prayerful glance toward heaven. "Jesus help us," he said.

"Where is he?" Richie said.

Vorono nodded toward a young man waiting at a Customs desk, shifting uneasily, shrugging at the questions of the Customs officer, a shy youth with scraggly beard, long hair.

"They're going to search him for dope," Vorono said.

"My Lord," Richie murmured and stepped back out of the young man's line of sight, adjusted his dark glasses more securely on his nose. "He certainly is a dramatic-looking fellow, isn't he?"

"They don't believe he's clean," Vorono said.

Richie found a back out-of-the-way bench in the lobby for himself and Annie. Vorono appeared from time to time to report to them. There was no crowd in the lobby; only a few people were about at this hour, now that the plane's passengers were scattering into the taxis and buses outside.

Annie said, "Mind telling me what you're doing, Richie?"

He smiled at her. "I really don't know, dear girl. I suppose I don't really."

She noticed a teenage girl squinting curiously at Richie and mentioned this to him.

"Yes, darling," he said and took her hand. "Maybe we'd better go to the car."

They sat in the dark in the back seat. The windshield wiper was going because of a slight drizzle. The driver had the radio on low, listening to a French music station.

"You want to tell me about it?" Annie said.

"Yes, of course," Richie said, but for a minute he said nothing. "Vorono went back to Florida and told the lad Hollywood wanted him for a part in a film in Paris. He didn't dare mention Sigler to him."

She wished the driver would turn the radio off. She rather liked to watch the wipers move on the windshield, but not to hear the music. "He was in Sigler's first film, the—"

"Yes, except Sigler never really did that film. When his friend died—suicide probably—Sigler took over and finished it, but all that beautiful footage in the first two-thirds of it, Annie, where the water and trees and animals are shown, the natural life of this family, well, that was the other man's work."

"I see," she said dully, unimpressed. Back and forth, back and forth, with the sound of squishing, swishing. The driver was nodding, almost asleep.

"This boy became dependent on Sigler, lived with him while the film was being finished, then was dropped, couldn't even get him on the telephone, was given screen credit only under a name Sigler made up; the boy had given up his family and friends, never got a cent out of it."

"It's a long time ago," she said softly.

"Of course, Sigler doesn't want him known, nor the truth known."

Back and forth. Swish. Back and forth. Swish. Nodding a bit deeper now. Vorono coming outside, finding them in the limousine, going back inside.

"So we've got a film test arranged for tomorrow. I asked Kolisch, I said would you do me a favor, old man, and he said anything, anything; he's quite worried at the moment about me, actually. So I said there was this young man who wanted to win a bit part, that was all."

Richie smiled, but it faded. "Was all."

Annie could imagine the scene in the studio when Sigler came in, when he and the boy saw each other after a year, two years, however long. Swish. Chilly night in September, late September, almost October, wasn't it— the year has gone swish, squish through its seasons. All the years of her life—except that in Southern California there are no distinct seasons. "What part did you have in mind?" she asked.

"Oh, I've not decided yet," Richie said. "I haven't met the boy, and Vorono has been quite guarded about bringing me into the matter. The lad only knows it's to be a film I'm the star of."

"Yes."

"I thought I would look him over and see."

"Yes," she whispered.

"The main purpose was not the screen test, you understand, but the confrontation."

"Yes." She tried to think of some way to say what she really felt, without alienating him. She could so easily antagonize him, she knew him well enough to know that, for he couldn't abide criticism. Now he was arguing with himself, and that was really the only argument she could expect to win tonight.

Just then the lad came out of the door, Vorono with him, holding his arm to guide him. He was about eighteen, was incredibly beautiful, Annie thought; his shoulder-length blond hair was glistening, angelically one might say. Vorono held his arm tightly, led him to the big car and guided him into the jump seat facing Richie. Vorono hurried around the car and took the jump seat opposite Annie. Nobody said anything, no introductions. Finally Vorono said, "That rain gets to your skin, you know it."

"Ahhh," the boy whispered. He had been staring at Richie since getting into the limousine. "Hello," he said, choking on the word. He extended his hand. "Pleased to meet you."

Richie took his hand, shook it, was unable to get his hand back at once.

"I've saw you in films since I was this high," the lad said.

"I've admired your film, too," Richie said, retrieving his hand, wiping the palm on his crisp shirt. "We hope we can do something to help you."

"Yes, sir. Yes, sir," the lad said happily. The car turned a corner and almost threw him against the door. Annie instinctively reached out to grab him, but Richie sat as if mesmerized by him.

"You saw my film?" the boy asked Richie.

"Yes," Richie said.

"We all scattered then. All of us went off alone, strange as dogs that eat their own, so I don't know where I was. I had fallen into sin. The Bible says, 'Ye are a chosen generation, a royal priesthood, an holy nation.' "

"Yes," Richie said, staring at him in his most aloof, perplexed manner.

" 'A peculiar people,' it says, 'that ye should show forth the praises of him who hath called us out of darkness into his marvelous light.' "

"Uh-huh," Richie said, glancing at Vorono.

" 'A *peculiar* people.' Well, we were ever bit of that in making that film, I'll tell you."

Vorono laughed. He was tense and tired and the remark struck him as being funny.

"I tried living in the woods again," the young man said, "but without the others, after the other, it's—not a way of life. The Bible says, 'Take no thought for your life, what ye shall eat, or what ye shall put on,' but where does it tell you to live in the woods?"

"You remember a man named Sigler?" Richie asked.

The beneficent smile on the lad's face slowly crumpled, leaving a deep frown. "Yeah," he said.

"He's a film director," Richie said.

The boy leaned closer to Richie, stared with his hateful eyes into his. "Where is he?"

"Has developed quite a reputation."

"Where he is?"

"I—could inquire," Richie said.

The boy stared at him for a moment more, then sat back, slowly relaxed. " 'Precious in the sight of the Lord is the death of his saints,' " he whispered.

They were on the highway now, which was virtually deserted at this late hour. When the French go indoors early, Annie thought, do they go to sleep? Does anybody ever get invited to visit in their homes? "Did you have a good flight?" she said to the lad.

He nodded, but still he would not look at her.

"Have you flown across the ocean before?" she asked him.

He shook his head and said something that sounded like "Nommm."

"What is your name?" she asked.

"Joel."

"That's a musical name, isn't it?" she said.

"Yes'm."

"Look at me, Joel."

He did not. He looked instead out the window, watched the buildings flash by as they sped along.

"Why not look at me?" she asked him gently.

He turned to her briefly and smiled, a friendly, warm smile. " 'Whosoever looketh on a woman to lust after her hath committed adultery with her in his heart,' Matthew says." As he finished the declaration, he turned once more to the window.

Richie laughed softly, surprised as much as amused. He took Annie's hand and lifted it to his lips and kissed it. The lad did not notice; he was in his own world, whatever that might be, with signs posted in the form of

Bible verses and with dense woods and long expanses of wonder. Richie reached forward and tapped the boy's shoulder, which caused him to start in fright. "You've got a wit about you," Richie said.

The lad smiled. A calm was still on him. He said nothing for a while, then he said to Richie, "I hope you find out where I can find him."

"Oh? Oh, yes," Richie said easily.

"Maybe I should ask you not to, but as Job says, 'Man is born into trouble as the sparks fly upward.'"

"I understand," Richie said.

"'Man that is born of a woman is of few days and full of trouble. He cometh forth like a flower and is cut down; he fleeth also as a shadow and continueth not.'"

"Were you as religious when you lived with Sigler?" Richie asked.

The brooding gaze swept over him. "No."

"When did you—uh—"

"After. It was awful, mister, being beat on, dogged."

"Dogged?"

"Yes, sir. After the devil came the washing in the blood."

Swish, squish, swish. The radio wasn't playing now. Someday she would look back on this drive into a wet, shiny, nighttime Paris and believe it had all been a dream, nothing but a dream, or at the least a dream more than anything else.

"I don't know what I'd do if I met him again," the boy said to Richie. "I've not planned to meet him."

"It would upset you, would it?" Annie said.

"Can one go on hot coals, and his feet not be burned? The Bible tells us no, you can't, and it was like coals to my feet, and after I left, when I was saved, all I could do was make myself kneel down whenever the hate swelled, wherever I was, and I don't know what would have happened to me, ma'am, if I hadn't become so sweet on Jesus."

Sweet on Jesus, swish, sweet on Jesus, swish. How sweet a boy he is, Annie thought.

The limousine stopped at the Hôtel de Trémoille, where Vorono and the lad had reservations. The lad shook Richie's hand feverishly, told him he was pleased to meet him after all these years and hoped to do well at the film test tomorrow. Vorono paused for a moment at the limousine door, waiting for any last-minute instructions, but Richie didn't even glance at him. "I'll phone you here," he said. "We'll take Miss Logan home now," he told the driver.

"What time is he due tomorrow?" Vorono asked, but the limousine pulled away.

Annie said nothing. She rested her head against Richie's shoulder, then took his hand and held it. She knew he was debating what to do. The driver had the radio on again; admittedly he kept it low, but why Richie let him play it at all she didn't know. Maybe he told him to, in order to cover up the sound of conversation from the back seat. "I like him, Richie," she said.

"He's a strange fellow, isn't he?" Richie said, and laughed uncomfortably. "Is he a Jesus freak of some sort?"

"He's hopped up on something; I agree with Customs on that."

"Confusing personality. Did you hear him say he was sweet on Jesus?"

She laughed softly. "How dear."

" 'I don't know what would have happened to me if I hadn't become so sweet on Jesus,' he said."

She laughed.

"As a boy I knew a thousand people who were sweet on Jesus, but I never thought to come upon one here tonight, in Paris," he said.

"No," she said. "Hold my hand tighter, Louis," she said. "It is a damp night, isn't it?"

"City of dogs. You know that was because the dogs

had a habit of digging up the bodies in the cemeteries. They ate them, you know."

"Yes, I know."

"Well, there wasn't grave room, was there, not for everybody who died in Paris. Especially when the executions were going on, thousands of heads lopped off, so that the stain will never be washed off the hands of the people."

"No. And let it stay to haunt them, I say."

"Forgive them you really must, Antoinette, or it will corrode your own heart."

Swish, squish, swish. Music playing. "Are you going to pardon Sigler, Louis?"

For several minutes he said nothing. He held her hand and said nothing. "Oh, I must decide, mustn't I?" he said. "I'm not the sort of man who can strike down his enemies. That's my shortcoming, 'Toinette, and I realize it. I can't be someone other than the man I am."

"I hope you'll free them," she said.

"Yes. I can send the lad and Vorono to Spain. There's a film being shot there somewhere, always is, and I can get my agents to place him in it. He can change his name. I'll help him get a part."

She kissed his hand. "You are kind, Louis. Too kind, I realize, for your own good."

"I could do that, but I have the stutterer dead to rights, you know I have him. I can twist him now."

"Yes, Louis, but you are not that man."

"Are you sure you know me, dear?" He waited. "Would that I were," he said.

At her apartment building they went upstairs together. They held to one another, their arms around each other, and stopped to kiss before they even reached her door.

Next morning Richie phoned Vorono, told him to escort the young man to Spain and to find him employment. He asked Vorono also for his own son's address in Greece, and before leaving for the studio he put in a call to him. His voice was trembling like a tense child's, and his hand was shaking as he waited. At last he heard Larry's voice.

"This—this is—Richie," he said. Lord only knows what the boy would call him.

"Who?"

"Richie. You know. Richie. I'm in Paris, Larry, and I thought we should get together."

"Who the hell is this?"

"It's your father, damn it."

No answer. Both men were breathing heavily; there was no other sound for a while.

"Are you married, Larry?"

"No."

"I didn't think so. Vorono never mentioned it."

"Who?"

"Larry, I'm calling to say—to admit I do hope to see you—I mean, it has been a long time, hasn't it, and will you think about it and phone me? I'll give you my phone number, Larry."

No response.

"Larry . . ."

No response. The line went dead.

Richie phoned Vorono at the hotel. "Perhaps he will talk with you," he said. "Phone him from Spain, find out how he is, will you?"

The conversation confused him. What had he intended? Why had he phoned him? After all these years he had made this . . . insipid overture. Most unreasonable, really.

THE last night, the one before Louis' execution, the royal family is seated at the dining table, Antoinette to Louis' left, his son Charles to his right, his daugh-

ter across from him. Simon and three other guards
are standing close by to stop any attempt at suicide.
On the table are a small roast of beef and a loaf of
bread.

"I have no carving knife," Louis says to Simon.

Simon says, "You are not allowed a knife tonight."

Louis turns to stare at him. "Ridiculous."

"I will cut it for you." Simon takes out his own knife.

Louis shakes his head. "Thank you, no." He tears
the roast with his fingers and a spoon, a messy operation
which causes the guards some mirth, and serves it.
"Bring us a little water and four glasses, Simon," he says.

The guards smile knowingly at one another. Nobody obeys.

The Queen begins to weep, and Louis says, "Darling, please. They mean no harm, any more than a dog
would." He picks up a piece of meat in his fingers and
eats it, glancing uncritically at Simon. "It's not bad
beef."

Cléry comes in.

"Some water, Cléry," Louis says.

Cléry goes out, a guard shoving him at the doorway.
Louis ignores this too.

Antoinette says, "I had so many thoughts to tell you,
but they have all slipped away. So many fears for us,
Louis."

He reaches out his left hand toward her, even as with
his right he takes another piece of beef.

She squeezes his hand in both of hers, most affectionately. "You still have your appetite, my dear sir."

"Till morning," he says grimly.

Cléry returns with glasses and water, which he
serves as if it were a rare wine.

"God's wine," Louis says to his son.

The boy smiles. "Yes, sir."

Louis sniffs the wine. "I fear God has neglected its
bouquet."

"If I could take your place," the boy whispers. "Papa—"

"But you will not, cannot," Louis says quickly.

"Must they be here?" the boy says, looking at the guards.

Louis shrugs. "Even a cat can look at a king, Charles."

Simon says, "We were a dog before."

The other guards mumble annoyances, but Louis ignores them. To Cléry he says, "You may go to bed."

"I can't sleep, Your Majesty."

"Your Majesty," Simon mimics him, snickering.

"Your Majesty," another guard says, purring like a cat.

"Your Majesty," another guard says, laughing softly.

The guards purr like cats, bark like dogs, until there is a babble of such sound.

Antoinette, rising: "Be quiet!"

All sound stops. Bitter smiles come on the guards' faces, but they say nothing.

She sinks back into her chair, takes her husband's hand in both of hers, presses it hard. "I never believed men could be so cruel."

"Oh, there is no limit as to that," he says quietly, with simple conviction. "If they see a way to make cruelty effective."

"I don't know how I will sustain myself, Louis."

"Pray. Ask God," he says. "I have done well, for it seems my tutors prepared me to suffer rather than to rule." To Simon he says, "How many others have been executed today?"

Simon shrugs. "All day, all day," he says.

Outside a cart creaks by, stacked full of naked corpses. It is on its way to a cemetery, and the stiff arms and legs jut upward here and there, askew, as if even yet pleading. On top of the pile is a line of severed heads, some with eyes closed, others with eyes open, some with fear, agony, solemnity. Dogs follow the cart, driven by hunger, excited by the prospect of food.

Louis climbs into his green bed. Cléry pulls the bed curtains closed, hangs up Louis' clothes. Antoinette, carrying a candle, enters, carefully shuts the door. As Cléry leaves quietly, she approaches the bed, puts the candle on a stand. She pulls the bed curtain aside and is about to climb inside when she notices that Louis is in a seizure. His eyes, staring at the sights yet to be seen, are white balls with tiny pupils, his breath is now rasping through his soon-to-be-severed throat. She cries out, a gasp, a sob, and her legs go weak under her. She holds to his bedclothing as she sinks down.

Her face is near his now. She kisses the bedclothes near his face and begins to sob. There is no evidence that he hears her.

Fade out.

Fade in the sunlighted bed curtain as Cléry pulls it open. The King wakes at once, but the Queen does not. Louis rises quietly, stands shivering in the cold beside the bed. Cléry closes the curtain. "Has five o'clock struck?" Louis whispers.

"It has on several outside clocks, sire, but not on yours."

Louis stands patiently, sadly by the bed. He touches its curtain, as if admiring for a last time the texture of tapestry.

"I lit the fire. It is bitter cold," Cléry says.

"I will not get out of that bed again, Cléry." He pauses to reflect on that. "Did a priest arrive?"

"Yes."

"Where is he?"

"Asleep on my bed."

"And you, where did you sleep?"

"On a chair."

"I am sorry."

"Ah, sire, can I think of myself at this moment?"

Cléry leaves, closing the door. The King at once pulls back the curtains beside Antoinette, who is asleep. He leans over her, kisses her, adjusts the covers over her. He wanders to the far side of the room, inhales deeply, seems to have trouble getting enough breath.

Still in his nightgown, he removes his watch from the white waistcoat he wore yesterday, listens to it tick, removes his seal from it and places the seal in the waistcoat, puts the watch on the mantelpiece. He takes a ring from his finger, looks at it several times rather fitfully; he puts it in the same pocket where he has put the seal. He draws out his wallet, lays it on the mantel.

Cléry returns, carrying a clean shirt. Louis dresses himself, putting on the pants and white waistcoat from yesterday. "If we shove that bureau to the middle of the room, we'll use it as our altar," he says. "Can you serve Mass?"

"I—don't know the responses by heart, Your Majesty."

Louis, his shirt unbuttoned, fetches a book from near the bed, finds the proper place in it, hands it to Cléry. Together they move the bureau into place. Louis covers the bureau with a cloth and puts a hair pillow before it. Cléry brings an armchair and sets it just behind the pillow. Antoinette is awakened by the noise and watches much of this from the bed.

Louis sees her. "Come, my dear, we will have Mass." He hands her the robe as she rises.

Cléry admits the priest, who enters carrying a flask, a book, a cross. Four guards enter. The priest is perhaps forty, a fey but competent man just now frightened almost to the point of helplessness.

"Wait outside the door," Louis says to the guards.

They hesitate.

"This is to be a place of God," Louis explains to them.

The guards uneasily withdraw, but stand just beyond the open doorway.

Louis assigns Antoinette to the hair pillow. He kneels on the bare floor beside her. Cléry takes his place, the open book in his trembling hands. The priest takes his place at the altar, arranges his implements. At last the sacred service is begun, the priest's voice trembling, his manner halting, the Queen scarcely attentive, Louis alone in a pious state of meditation; about him is the noblest attitude.

The guards watch with various expressions of cynicism. Simon becomes so annoyed he blurts out angrily at the others, "Soon I'll see him beg." He goes bunglingly into the Prince's room, finds him kneeling in prayer, withdraws to the anteroom once more, frustrated. "It's a most holy family."

Drums begin to roll outdoors, the beating of "the general," announcing the approaching execution. Simon nods in tempo with the sound. "I'll see him beg today," he whispers feverishly.

Outdoors, soldiers are taking their places in long, straight rows, their muskets ready.

Indoors, Louis and Antoinette drink the wine of the sacrament.

Citizens in the street beneath the tower listen to the clatter of hooves, the dragging of cannon. Maillard is here, just now harried, worried, the gloom of tragedy having fallen over him. General Lafayette moves to the tower door. Maillard and the other officials follow. The doorman unlocks the metal door with a loud, resounding bang which causes Maillard to start.

Lafayette says to him, "You are even more nervous than I."

They enter and ten gendarmes follow.

They walk up the stone steps.

There is scarcely room for everybody in the ante-room upstairs. Louis sticks his head out of his bedroom doorway. "You have come for me?" he asks simply.

"Yes," Lafayette says.

"Wait a minute." Louis turns back into the room, where Antoinette waits. He shuts the door, holds out his hands and she comes to him. He embraces her. "Ask God to sustain me." He kisses her. "If I go a coward." He kisses her tears. "A pity."

"Goodbye, my funny lord."

"I hope not to abandon whatever remains of—of my tattered nobility." He gives her his ring. "The smallest gift of jewelry I've ever given you," he says. "The dearest." He kisses her, holds her tightly, then turns to the priest. "Come with me."

The priest hesitates, then nods, consenting.

"Stay with my wife, Cléry," Louis says, "and my children." He pauses before the closed door. Suddenly a frightened boy, he turns once more to Antoinette. Abruptly he straightens. "My love is like a flower," he says.

"My love is like a flower," she whispers, smiling through her tears.

He opens the door, sways in the doorway as he faces the men waiting for him. He seems to falter, but abruptly he steps forward. He takes a folded paper from his pocket, offers it to an official, actually in name Jacques Roux. "Kindly give this to the Commune."

"That does not concern me," Roux says, drawing away, frightened.

Louis offers it then to another official, Gobeau, who accepts it.

Roux says, explaining, "I am here only to conduct you to the scaffold."

Louis, ignoring him, turns to Cléry. "I don't need a coat, Cléry. My hat only." He puts on his hat. "Gentlemen, I would like that Cléry remain with my family, who are accustomed to his care." When there is no reply, he turns to General Lafayette. "Let us go."

The guards scrutinize every flicker of his expression, watch for any break in his composure. There is none. At the head of the stairway Louis notices Simon and stops. Everybody becomes quiet. "I was somewhat sharp with you yesterday; do not be angry with me."

Simon does not reply. He even withdraws, as if the possibility of the man's touch might cause him illness.

Louis, Lafayette and the priest, with gendarmes before and following, go down the stairs. Only Simon and Cléry remain in the room, Cléry in tears, Simon frustrated, resentful. The noise of the iron door downstairs startles both of them. They hear the bugles announce that the King has left the tower. With particular ominousness the drums roll now.

Cléry sees the Queen appear at the doorway. He goes to her at once and catches her as she collapses.

Two rough gendarmes hold the carriage door open. As the King appears, one of them enters it and takes his seat in the front. Louis enters, the priest following; they sit in the back. The other gendarme enters and closes the door. Through the window can be seen mounted soldiers, as well as civilians armed with pikes. The carriage jolts forward.

Louis' breathing is deep, his eyes glazed. Once more, abruptly, he shakes free of fear. "Would I had a carriage of this small size once upon a time," he says. He feels the window frame, the roof. "It's light, you see, but it's solidly made." He bounces once or twice on the seat. "Springs are excellent." He closes the shade, testing it. "Good workmanship all around."

The guards, surprised by his attitude, glance uneasily at one another.

Once out of the courtyard, the drums are less oppressive; Louis peeks out of the window, sees a double line of soldiers holding back rows of silent citizens.

The priest puts his breviary into Louis' hand. Louis examines it, seems pleased to have it. "What psalm is best for me in my—situation?" he asks.

The priest helps him find a place, and Louis begins to read in Latin, murmuring the words.

When the sudden angry shouting of a mob is heard just outside, Louis cracks the shade, peeks out. He sees a mob of men and women, armed with axes, shovels and pikes; they are being thrown back by the soldiers, who close in about the carriage to protect him. "Some of the people can't wait for my death," Louis tells the priest. "I suppose they don't feel fraternal until I am gone."

The carriage lurches forward, and as the cries fade away in the distance Louis relaxes once more. "Fraternity is part of their motto," he says, "but of all men they are the least fraternal."

"And liberty," the priest says.

Louis shrugs. "I don't *feel* free."

One of the guards sharply says, "Do not talk so, you."

Louis smiles at him, a rather boyish smile, completely disarming and self-effacing. "And equality," he whispers.

The guards remain baffled by him. "Did you think as you gorged yourself that hungry people would forgive you?" one asks him.

"If I had eaten half a fish, would I be half as guilty?" Louis says.

When the guards say nothing more, Louis returns to the breviary. " '*Si iniquitates observaveris Domine, Domine, quis sustenibit?*' " he murmurs.

The priest translates, " 'If you measure iniquities, God—then, God, who may live?' "

" '*Quia pud te propitiatio est, Et propter legem tuam sustinui te Domine,*' " Louis reads.

The priest translates, " 'For that there is mercy, even pity with thee, and for thy mercy shall thou be feared much, O Lord our God.' "

Louis looks up, ponders that. "For his mercy he shall be feared much?" he asks the priest.

"That is what it says, sire."

Louis shakes his head. "That's not the way it is in government."

"I only know what it says here, sire."

Louis studies the words again. "It is yet another difference between heaven and France," he says.

The sound of the drums stops, startling him. One of the guards nudges the other one. Louis cautiously looks out the edge of his shade, then sits back in the seat suddenly. He lifts one hand and touches his lips, as if afraid he might cry out. "*Et propter legem tuam sustinui te Domine,*" he whispers.

"What are you saying?" a guard demands.

"I said, if I ate half a fish . . ."

The guard says, "To hell with that."

Louis smiles suddenly. "Would I be half as guilty?"

The carriage is still. His door is opened. Two executioners, both of them black-hooded, stand there. One says, "Step down, brother."

Louis stares at the hooded figures. He pats the priest's hand, as if to reassure him. He steps down and the executioners move to try to take off his waistcoat. He pulls free, takes off his own coat and drops it on the ground.

The executioners move to him in order to bind his hands behind him, but Louis again frees himself. "No, I will not consent to that. You must give up that project."

"We are going to bind you," one says in a louder voice. They move toward him, but Louis with an emphatic, angry gesture of his hand stops them.

"Guards," one of the executioners calls.

Several gendarmes move closer.

Louis says to the priest, "You see how they treat me."

"It is their last outrage. It will only bring yours closer to Christ's own death," the priest says.

Louis considers that. "It is such an insult." To the executioners, he says, "I have decided to drain the cup."

They bind his hands behind him, shove him toward the wooden steps that steeply lead to the platform. Awkwardly he climbs them, the priest on the steps above him helping him along. Louis reaches the top and pauses to look out over the multitude of citizens.

His hat is knocked off by an executioner. The wind ruffles through his hair. Suddenly he strides to the edge of the scaffold and imposes silence by a nod of his head at the drummers. He stands alone, looking out over the great crowd of upturned faces. When he speaks, his voice is so strong it must carry as far as the Pont-tournant, and each word is distinct. "I die innocent of all the crimes imputed to me. I pardon the authors of my death. I pray God that the blood which you are going to spill will never fall on France."

Silence. The mass of humanity below him is attentive. For a while longer he stands in silence, then comes back to the guillotine. He kneels. The chief executioner throws a rope over him, in a single motion lashing him to the machine. The executioners confer briefly, then one trips the knife, and the big knife falls with a loud, singing, vigorous metallic swish.

The chief executioner picks up the head by the hair. He appears before the crowd and holds it aloft; it turns in the air, its gaze looks out over the crowd of stunned human beings. Then a cheer tentatively rises, but only from a few: *Vive la Liberté.* The crowd is strangely intimidated and hesitant. The bugles and the drums begin again as the bloody head turns.

Seventeen

SIGLER'S OWN TREATMENT of Richie after the death scene was typically complicated. He did not admit to liking it, but he seemed prepared to accept it. The lines about nobility were Richie's unexpected additions and were there merely to annoy him, he felt, and Louis' noble mien at the end was much more soulful than Sigler had wanted. Whether an audience would accept it or not, he didn't know. It did go gently to its purpose, was of an English type, delivered from an aloof perspective, rather than American, with a welcome of direct action and commitment. "I think we got it on film," Sigler said grudgingly. "But the film needs more guts, somehow, somewhere."

"Yes," Richie said, pretending he was not the least bit disturbed by Sigler's attitude. "I would *like* to do *all* of it over, of course, preferably in the nude. Isn't that more your style?"

Sigler stood there stolidly, frowning at the impertinent actor. The remark merely annoyed him, that was about all, but for some buried reason, suddenly with a shove of his hip he moved against Richie, sent him stumbling backwards across a few light cables and against a main wall of the tower set. Richie fell through the flat, ending up supported in a partially reclining position by its corner braces. He lay there in the arms of the flat, gasping with anger and surprise. "See here," he said in a high voice that might have carried to the courtyard. He pushed himself to his feet and with a dancer's precision moved to Sigler and with his right fist clipped him smartly on the jaw.

The giant growled, that was all.

Richie clipped him again.

At which second sting Sigler turned away bashfully, even ashamedly, and walked away from him.

"That's quite enough," Kolisch said shrilly, finding his voice. "*Enough!*" he shouted, an emphatic, definitive bark that nobody could ignore. He took Richie's arm, led the dazed man toward the courtyard. "Never in my experience," Kolisch said.

It had all taken but half a minute. It came about so unexpectedly that few of the witnesses had been able to move or speak. Sigler's exploding feelings seemed to have left him as dazed as everybody else. He walked about the little arena of the set, massaging his jaw, moved among the booms and dollies, shaking his craggy head, confused by his own erupting emotions.

Kolisch suddenly appeared before him. "I want you to hold your temper, sir. We are almost done with him."

That was, of course, the very pin on which the hammer had swung.

Richie climbed into the back seat of his Rolls sedan, rested back in one comfortable corner. At a time of insecurity, sitting in one's Rolls offered a sense of confidence, he had always found. He felt his jaw, ran his forefinger along his teeth, checking to be absolutely sure not any feature of his famous face was marred. He wig-

gled his nose between his fingers. He gently massaged
his lips.

Annie climbed in beside him. Kate was leaning over
the back of the front seat, trying to put a car rug over his
knees.

"I do not want to see him again. When I have the
party Sunday for the cast and crew—isn't that this coming Sunday?—I don't want him to be there. Did you hear
me, Kate?"

"Please lie back, Richie," Annie said.

"That compress I was using in the tower, Annie,
would you be good enough to get it? And, Kate, some
hot water—but not too hot. I do think he's rather like a
trailer truck that's going out of control."

O N C E years before Kate had formally invited Richie to
a special dinner, one just for the two of them. This had
been at San Blas, a remote Mexican resort generally
visited only by Mexicans, located on the Pacific north of
Acapulco. They had eaten shrimp, oysters and a large
flounder, and had drunk two liters of cheap wine. The
result was a headache, that was about all. They had
talked about their honeymoon trip, their decision not to
have children, their affection for one another. The dinner had served to bring them closer together.

The Paris dinner with Richie was to be a similar
experience, she decided. At least its original purpose was
to probe into their relationship, seeking some way to
save her marriage, or some reason to save it beyond the
obvious advantages to her of wealth, position in society,
better attention in restaurants and from room service.
She loved him, as in the years before, but not so simply
now; her life was complicated by the potential of her own
career, and by the sting of his rejection of her.

Sigler had decided the dinner ought to serve a more

direct purpose, and had told her to tell Richie about their affair. The suggestion so shocked her she couldn't fathom the purpose of it. She refused. She told him she was displeased even to have the suggestion put in her mind.

It was in her mind, however, and began to make its own way. Each hour spent in anger at him or pity for herself added to its strength.

How common, she thought. How utterly despicable. Yet wasn't it for his own good, to bring him back to reality, and to force him to deal with her, maybe on her terms.

She came to enjoy the prospect of telling him. It was a dear secret, certainly. She tasted the deliciousness of seeing his reaction when the words struck home. She wanted suddenly to tell Annie, too, to tell her first, and watch her face, maybe even hear her plead for Richie to be spared, but on Wednesday afternoon when she arrived at the studio, this matter on her mind, Annie was on set, deeply involved in one of her own last big scenes, and Richie, dressed in a gray business suit, was calmly sitting close by at the edge of the lighted set, lending her his advice and support.

Kolisch was sitting beside him. Sigler was lounging near the main dolly camera, a bottle of beer in his hand, watching Maillard and Antoinette speculatively, obviously dissatisfied, disgruntled. "It ought to fall in three blows," he said.

"Here we go," Richie murmured to Kolisch. "Gaul has three parts."

"First you tell her the fact of the boy's leaving, Maillard," Sigler said.

Maillard was sitting on set in a chair at the dining table, his legs stretched out before him. "Yes," he said.

"Then secondly, you tell her where he'll be."

"Yes."

Kate selected a chair behind Richie and Kolisch, and sat down quietly.

"Then thirdly, tell her she'll not see him again. Antoinette, you want to know what I just said, or do you care?"

"I heard it."

"It ought to come to something different, that's the problem," he said. "This film is too much of a waltz. Nobody goes to dances any more."

"She seems to be doing quite well," Richie said kindly.

"She ought to go to pieces," Sigler said.

She looked up slowly, focused her gaze serenely on him. "I don't feel that way about it," she said.

"Well, you're given every reason to," Sigler said. "In actual history she did beg—"

"I hope she won't, old boy," Richie said simply.

"Oh, for God's sake, shut up," Sigler said.

"Simply an observation from—"

Kolisch said, "Richie, please—"

"One who has lived in films for—"

"Shut up," Sigler said.

"And knows film audiences. The torture of a kitten in a box is not as interesting to most people as it might be to you."

Silence. A long quiet, nobody moving. Richie calmly crossed his legs, sat contentedly looking about, with the same attitude as he might have while relaxing on the first-class deck of an ocean liner. "Tragedy requires characters strong enough to accept tragic shocks. Always has," he said.

There was no chance for Kate to talk with Antoinette. Kate had to go finally, and saw only one rehearsal of the scene.

"You saw your son at breakfast, I believe," Maillard was saying to her on set.

"Yes. He's in his room reading."

"No, madame, he is not."

Antoinette rises, surprised.

"He has been taken away to be educated," Maillard says.

"Where is he?" Antoinette says, in little more than a whisper.

"You can see him each day at noon from that window; he will walk in the garden."

"Where is he?" she asks, louder.

"But you cannot speak to him."

"Where is he?" she says, shouting.

Maillard after a moment says, "The Convention at first felt that the tutor should be Condorcet, the philosopher and mathematician, secretary of the Academy of the Sciences, but the vote—that is—Simon was appointed and has him in his charge."

A whisper, "Simon who?"

Maillard nods toward the guard, who is standing near the doorway. Slowly Antoinette turns to him, and slowly the horror comes to her.

Maillard, personally rebelling, yet with administrative callousness, says, "To save the boy's life, madame, it was felt necessary to be agreeable—"

She screams, a single, loud, piercing scream, and crumples into a chair.

Maillard turns away, crushed by his own emotions. Simon approaches the woman. He quietly says, "Can you hear me, Widow Capet?" When there is no reply, he winks at the two other guards. "She cannot hear me," he says, smiling. He snaps his fingers, to indicate the breaking of her mind.

She looks up slowly, stares into his face. "Yes, I can hear you, Simon."

"I thought perhaps your mind had gone, as sometimes happens, you know, in the tower." He snaps his fingers again, to show how the mind goes.

"No, Simon," she says. "But you are thoughtful to inquire." She watches him for a while longer, then rises slowly. About her is the same dignified mien Louis had developed in the tower, his solemnity. "When will I be with him again?"

"From the window—" Maillard begins.

"To touch him. To talk to him."

Maillard shakes his head. "Never, madame."

The anguish rises inside her once more, almost forces another scream of anguish from her, but she controls herself.

"It worries me, I admit, to find more cruelty on my side than ever was on yours," Maillard says. He notices Simon watching him and sets aside any further confession. "Good day, Madame Capet," he says. "We are all, it is all in ruins, madame," he says quietly.

Simon leaves, too, shuts the door, and Antoinette lowers her head into her hand.

''WELL, it comes to nothing," Sigler said. "Cut," he said.

"I thought it was immaculate," Richie said. "You must be desperately tired, darling," he said to Annie.

"I am, I am."

"Is that it for today?" Richie asked. "I am having dinner with my wife."

"Well, go to dinner then," Sigler said, "but it's not all for the day."

AT 8:00 Richie arrived at the Tour d'Argent. Kate wasn't yet there, but he was expected and was at once shown to the central table by the windows. A hum of excitement began stirring the air of the restaurant, a comforting, reassuring sound to him. Many stars no longer were even recognized, he realized. He contented himself with the view of the river, where barges were passing under the bridge below.

At 8:15 Kate joined him and they enjoyed the view together. Notre Dame was to their left, Sacré Coeur off in the distance, hundreds of chimney pots off to the southeast. They could enjoy the vista, but were close enough to make out the fishermen along the quay. "This *is* a civilized place, Paris, isn't it?" Richie said.

"How is she?" Kate said finally. "How does she look in the morning?"

"How quaint of you to ask," he said.

"This morning, for instance."

He hesitated, considered actually answering her, decided not to. He ordered a bottle of Dom Pérignon from the headwaiter, a gray-haired man—not old, but old enough to know his trade and to know to smile, Richie thought.

"Are you going to deny being with her?"

"You know I wouldn't make any claim at all, darling, concerning a lady."

They watched the other diners for a while, neither speaking, Kate deliciously sensitive to the news she had for him. "What do you want for lunch on Sunday, at the cast party?"

"Anything you choose. Caviar, certainly, and smoked salmon and a Stilton."

"I suppose you'll be going to the South of France, to our house soon," she said, looking off at the view.

"My dear, it is *my* house," he said.

"*Our* house."

"It was my first wife's and my house, then my second wife's and my—"

"And now it's—"

"So I made it clear when I married you that it was

my house, that it wasn't any longer even listed in my own name—"

"I do wish he would come with the Champagne. If you're going to be adamant about everything, we can't really talk, can we?"

"Waiter," Richie said. A flurry of activity ensued at once, and the cool green bottle and two cool glasses were brought forth. "It's a terribly public restaurant, Kate, this. Do you like it, really?"

"Whose name's it in?" she asked.

He ignored the question, seemed to be concentrating on a tug towing a barge down the Seine.

"What are your retakes?" she asked.

"None have been mentioned. Usual thing, I suppose. Back of my head so they can cut away—"

"I wish Sigler would do all my big scenes over and actually kill me next time."

He looked up at her, waited to see if a smile appeared. None did. "That *is* throwing oneself into a part, isn't it?"

"Maybe I'll go home after dinner and do it myself."

He continued to watch her. "Yes, let's do wait a while." Indeed, she appeared to be serious, but she had often threatened suicide, three or four times anyway, and had made a few vague passes at it. "Waiter, it's the duck, isn't it, that you're known for?" he said, looking over the menu, glancing now and again at Kate. She appeared to be in a hypersensitive state, maybe on some sort of pep pill. "We—we—we will try the pressed duck for one, and a roasted duck with peaches for the other, and maybe we'll serve—serve part to each, depending on whether we're both still alive by then. And tell the wine waiter to bring a Corton '64, preferably a Louis Chapuis."

The waiter left. Another waiter arrived, quietly, unobtrusively poured more Champagne.

"Where will you work next, Richie?" Kate said.

"I—wonder. Burton tells me Paramount has a property, and they've asked *him* about *my* health. Can you imagine?"

"How old a part?"

"Oh, forty-eight, I imagine. They all are, aren't they?"

"Where will it be shot?"

"Yugoslavia, but it's about a Sicilian outlaw of some sort, Guilliano, is it? Not my—life-wish, exactly."

"Am I expected to come with you?"

"My dear, but a few minutes ago you were going to die. You claim such deep unhappiness, I don't know what to expect." The bridge had two twelve-foot sidewalks, he noticed, and not many pedestrians were likely to cross here. How French. How beautifully French. A coal barge was moving under the bridge now. "There's no other skin as ripply and ever-changing as a river's, is there, Kate?" he said.

"I think Sigler will give me a part in Ireland."

He was annoyed, irritated by the idea. "He doesn't know much about the making of films, does he, about options and the like."

"You won't be jealous if I get a part?"

"Not much. No, not much. Of him, you mean?"

Kate watched him for a moment, then turned to the scenery outside. The toy cars were skittering across the bridge just below. "What did Annie wear this morning?" she asked.

He hesitated, as before, then quietly said, "I can imagine her in a pink robe with blue bunting. Please try to be mature, Kate."

"Did you and she—get on well last night?"

He nervously, testily tasted his champagne. "I think there will soon be work of some sort for me, but how do I know? My life is getting to be such a wigwag."

"A wigwag?" She laughed and gazed at him fondly. "How dear."

"Where do you *want* to go next, Kate, assuming there is no Irish film."

"I don't know, Richie. Can we go to Beverly Hills and be what we were?"

"You have friends all over the world, you know."

"As your wife."

"Well, you *are* my wife."

"In name only."

"What else is there for a name, except to be a name only?"

"It would be kinder to kill me with an ax."

He shook his head irritably. "Please don't be crude. I have no animosity toward you."

"It would be less painful."

"I—do you suppose we'll have to have many of these unhappy conversations? Really, Kate, dinner is not enhanced by controversy, darling."

"You sound so far away, even now, Richie. Shall I try to reach you, your heart, shall I?"

"No," he said at once. "Even the image of your groping about for my heart is disenchanting."

"I haven't been able to reach you for a long while, Richie. I remember years ago in your flat in London, one night we fought and I fled, and you ran after me up the street in your slippers and robe, calling, 'Wait, Laura, wait Margaret, wait Jane . . .' You couldn't even think of my name."

He began to laugh. "We had been out dancing, hadn't we? What ever happened to dancing, Kate?"

"It's not done any longer," Sigler says.

"No profit in it for management, perhaps," he said.

"We danced most of every night back then."

"Yes. It's all like a far-off dream now. Something ethereal, out of a Bogart film of the thirties."

"I got drunk last night, Richie. Sigler and I."

He was caught off guard momentarily. He looked

away, pretended to be attracted by a boat moving up the Seine. *"Sigler* and you?"

"While you and Annie were getting drunk, and around to each other. You'll never know how marvelous it was, Richie, for me."

He absorbed that comment, his face reddening.

"He had not been by for several nights. I had begun to worry."

The waiters interrupted. They brought the entrée and poured the wine. Richie nervously kept glancing at Kate while the bothersome carving and serving proceeded. On a dais nearby he saw three waiters working away, operating the silvered duck presses, turning the screws tighter, the juice of the duck dripping into silver bowls.

"Harry James, Dorsey, Kyser—where are they?" Kate said. She tasted the crisp skin of her duck. "Isn't he dead?"

"Who?"

"One of them."

"Probably." Barbaric practice, actually. He tentatively tasted his food, laid his fork aside. "About last night—what do you mean?" he said.

"The Spanish couple, they know the holiday's all over, so yesterday he went out, bought a big color television to take back to Spain with him, and I said, 'Do you think a French color television will work in Spain?' The poor darling had never even thought of that. So I phoned the British embassy to inquire."

"Sigler?" he asked, staring at her.

"And the Embassy said no, no, it's different electricity there. It's Spanish electricity."

"Kate, I don't care about Spanish electricity."

"So Raphaela began to cry, and Carlos said they would take it to Spain anyway, that nobody else in their village had a color TV set, not even one that doesn't work." Kate finished with a delighted snicker.

"About Sigler," he said, his voice loud enough to attract attention at nearby tables.

The headwaiter appeared at his side, asked if everything was properly prepared, poured some more of the Corton in Kate's glass. By the time he was gone, Richie had got control of himself.

"Richie, if I'm asked about our present—relationship—" Kate began.

"What about it?"

"Since you're not with me often, who shall I say I am? I'm not your wife, now am I?"

"My dear, nobody could possibly know what you will say in any circumstance, you have taken on so many different personalities."

"Are we separated?"

"No. When would we have become separated?"

"Are you planning a divorce?"

"Let's not be silly, Kate. Nobody can plan a divorce. Might as well plan one's own dying."

"How would I know?" she said. "You're the one with all the experience." She watched him sadly, her eyes moist and loving. "I'm sorry I've been such a sot, Richie."

"It's not your, not anybody's fault about that. My father drank too much."

"Maybe if I go to the Beverly Clinic again—"

"My position concerning our marriage is this: Shouldn't I do what I want? If I want to take a trip alone, well, at my age, if to deny myself deprives me of the last such pleasures for me on this earth—"

"They liked me there."

"At my age—not many years left—"

"Take Carlos' color set with me."

"I think I have the duty to use my own life, to enjoy it."

The waiter removed their plates. Neither of them had eaten much of anything. Richie ordered coffee for them both. "Incredible place, actually, sit here in warm comfort, looking out over Paris while the waiters press ducks under a few thousand pounds of pressure. A serene, immaculate, cruel place, with these bloody, smiling waiters. Some people probably come here every year to —you know—on the same day and all that."

"It's like in the films, Richie."

"Is it? Which one?"

"All your films. I sit in the cinema and see the crevices of your mouth, the pimple on your forehead, the smile, see you clearly, your famous face, yet can't reach you."

"No, of course not. I'm merely images projected on a screen."

She smiled fondly. "So you are, Richie," she said.

He got the point, of course, a blunt, heavy-handed stab it was, too. A twitch began to trouble his mouth. "Not kind, Kate."

"Did that reach you, Richie?"

The coffee was hot and strong. "I needed this," he said. "Let's not talk any more, Kate."

After a while she said, "The headwaiter will remember the day *and* the table, if you will but sign his menu for him with your famous name."

"Don't be rude, Kate."

"Inscribed as he completes *his* new picture in Paris, using his wife's best friend as his mistress."

"About Sigler," he said impatiently.

"Yes, I did want to tell you about Sigler," she said. "Didn't I?"

"Nothing offensive I trust, Kate," he said.

"He made love to me last night."

At first his face revealed absolutely no change. It served as a mask only. Then slowly the mask reddened.

At the same time his breathing noticeably began increasing.

She watched him all the while. "He's very good, Richie," she said. "Rough, enjoys pain, but very good. Lord knows, his women will all have orgasms."

"Is he?" he said huskily, in a voice as lifeless as the mask.

"At least I have every time, and that's not usual for me, you know."

"Of course," he whispered.

"I wanted you to be the first to know. You and Annie."

He was having difficulty maintaining his bearings. He wiped his mouth with his napkin. He was an old man now, a red-skinned old man with a blob of slobber at the corner of his mouth. She had wounded him, all right, had torn open a veil inside him.

"Have I hurt you?" she asked.

"To—be honest—"

"What?"

"Yes, you have," he said.

"So you can be reached, after all, even your bloody heart, Richie. You're not quite dead yet, Richie."

"I suppose not," he whispered. He wouldn't, couldn't look at her any longer. He sat staring at the silvered presses and the immaculate waiters using them. "Shall we for a minute or so not say anything else?" he said.

She rather gloated on the sight of the old man, her husband. She watched him for that long minute as he tried to regain control of his own countenance and voice, he the supreme master of both on most every occasion.

DOWNSTAIRS, waiting for him at the elevator door were a dozen fans, most of them women who wanted him to sign their autograph books or napkins or the scraps of paper they held out to him. Automatically, perfunctorily he signed them, having no alternative, really. He was not smiling, not speaking; slowly, steadily he made his way to the street.

There he stopped, dazed by the sunlight. The fans gathered around him again.

"You'll be coming to lunch Sunday, Richie, the cast luncheon?" Kate asked.

"Oh yes," he replied out of a haze that closed him in. He had forgotten she was still there.

"I really must invite Sigler, Richie. You understand that."

He said nothing.

"Do you have your car, Richie?"

"Yes. Somewhere. The driver parked it somewhere."

"I'll take a taxi. Will you flag me a taxi, Richie?"

"The doorman," he muttered and started off across the street toward the river, walking slowly, tottering slightly, unwell apparently, a covey of fans following behind whispering to one another about him, about their luck on seeing him.

Eighteen

ON SUNDAY KATE SELECTED a new word for the day. This was a self-improvement program recommended to her years ago by Peter Finch which had fallen into daily disuse, but was revived for special party days, like this one, when the cast and even Lesher were coming to her house—and it was her house now, she felt; she had managed to get that much of herself back from Richie. Lesher would be the guest of honor. His word could launch a motion picture or shelve it, could launch a career or enhance it.

The word was *evanescence*. It had all the requirements she had imposed on herself: (1) it was a stranger to her, and (2) it was pretty. She found it in the house library in a translation into English of Ionesco's *Notes et contre-notes*, which had, except for *evanescence*, rather depressed her. She wasn't certain what the word meant, but since Ionesco's translator had used it, chances were that it had to do with a diminutive measurement.

It was a disgrace, she decided, that the house library, which had two copies of *Who's Who in America*, one of

Burke's Peerage, several old copies of *Social Registers,* even one of Washington, D.C., had no English dictionary. If Richie were here, she would ask him. He might know, actually. One section of his mind was made up of thousands of nooks into which he stuffed little bits of information, no nook having much to do with another.

One never could be sure what lay waiting there.

Evanescence.

But he wasn't here, and he wasn't at Annie Logan's flat—at least, Sigler said his car wasn't there. At Kate's request Sigler had sent one of his assistants to find out, for he was busy showing scenes to Lesher, Sigler himself out of sight at Kolisch's specific instruction, crammed into a cranny in the editing room unseen by the mellow-voiced, noncommittal executive producer who never blinked, or so Sigler told Kate, never gave even that much of a clue as to what he thought about any shot, sequence, idea, question, utterance of Kolisch's, as hour after hour he watched the work print and the unused shots and scenes.

"Evanescence," she told Carlos, who with his wife was to take tomorrow's train for Barcelona, but he had no mind for any details except those of cardboard boxes. He had arrived with two, the best Kate could recall, and was leaving with eighteen.

She walked out onto the lawn, gravitated toward the little laburnum tree. There she could enjoy the evanescence of the place where she and Sigler had first fallen to the ground, where they had enjoyed each the other's evanescence, and from there she could see the whole front of the house she had made her own, the place where she and Richie had spent many dull, dreary hours together, and many happy ones full of assorted longings, wishes, arguments. Relaxed, contented it appeared to be just now, with the evanescent sunlight reaching the front terrace, where Raphaela was rolling the awning up, preparing for the visit of His Majesty, the King of France, and his Queen, and their charming children, and the Princess de Lamballe, some of them but recently arrived from visits to Paris' newest attraction, the guillotine, about which perhaps they could be persuaded to tell others, a little something about its *ambience*—a word she had learned in Italy on Anna Magnani's birthday. Nobody there had even dreamed Anna ever had a birthday, she was so mature, it simply never had occurred to anyone about Anna's birthdays at all.

Richie had been deeply hurt, she knew that. He hadn't even dared to come to the studio since. His wings have been clipped, Sigler told her, which worried her simply because she didn't know what that meant. She rarely got a glimpse of Richie. He had dropped by sometime during last night, then had sneaked out again. She knew, because yesterday's suit and shirt and underclothes were on the bedroom floor, and a towel, sopping wet, was on the bathroom floor. She had been meaning once more to count his suits, to determine if he had taken any to another apartment. To count his suits, however, was quite a wearying task, involving a more consistent mathematical ability than hers. She could count as high as she pleased, but not if along the way she found a suit which reminded her of a special occasion with him; emotions were likely to complicate whatever her mind was doing.

She rather preferred life that way. Too many people today were afraid of their emotions. She had met men in Beverly Hills who jogged five, six miles a day who never exercised their emotions. It never occurred to them. Just their legs. Richie was somebody who needed more emotional exercise. He had been burned to a husk by his own popularity and publicity and exposure. He had adroitly survived the battles in the film world, and the cost had been the shriveling of his heart, particularly toward his own wife. She had found it, touched it Wednesday at dinner at the Tour d'Argent on the seventh floor overlooking the Seine; would she had grabbed it out and put it in her pocket, to take out now and then and pinch, squeeze, exercise, so he couldn't, wouldn't continue to ignore her. That haughty way he had of ignoring even her most abrasive irritants simply irritated her to distraction. The control knobs of his heart were put on wrong, obviously.

Have it repaired. Take it to a shop. She could hand it over through the window slot. Its tuning is all wrong. Please fix its knobs, unless that means he will not have any feeling for his loved ones. For me, for instance. I'm a loved one. Does a new set of knobs mean a new heart? It matters a great deal to me. You see, he's the only one in the world I love.

The Spaniards were still finding additional boxes. They had gone through the house debating what should stay and what should go along with them, being fair, of course, not taking more than half the things they really wanted, making their decisions out in the open where Kate, who was intrigued, could verify the scope of their sacrifices. He couldn't wear Richie's suits, alas. She would gladly give him twenty. Some morning she and Richie might have the happy occasion breakfasting somewhere in the world to open the paper and find Carlos listed as one of the ten best-dressed men. "Discovered walking ahead of his wife and donkey on the road to Barcelona was an immaculately attired gentleman. His suit was English tweed, hand-sewn, narrow waisted, the coat single-vented in the back, natural shoulder line, three buttons with, of course, only the middle button fastened, the pants low at the hips, slash pocketed, tight behind and at the crotch, without cuffs. His wife, looking out from under the two hundred pounds of Paris loot she carried, told us his heart had recently shrunk to the size of a knob on a French television set. 'I don't know what's pumping him,' " she said.

R I C H I E had arrived. It was 11:00. From upstairs she heard his high-pitched voice wafting about in the entrance hallway. Why was it that all film actors were tenors? She put his heart in her pocket and glided downstairs, feeling rather like Hedy Lamar this morning.

"Vorono has found in a book that what was wrong with me sexually was that I needed a minor operation," he was declaring to poor Carlos, who understood only every other word, "and he says Sigler has known it all along but preferred the psychological discomfort—"

"They're due at twelve," she told him. "Sigler sent you your court costume."

"I do not mean to wear it," he said flatly.

"All the others of us are to wear ours. Please, Richie."

"Did you invite Sigler?"

"Yes, of course."

"Good," he said emphatically. "Incidentally, Lesher has seen the film," he said, his voice steady, his gaze resting serenely on her. "He asked Kolisch why was I *disguised.*" He marched out onto the terrace, took a chair full in the sun, sat down.

She followed obediently, sat down nearby, on the foot of the chaise. "And . . ."

"He said I was not Richie Hall at all."

"And . . ."

"He said unattractive fat men are a dime a dozen, not half a million dollars apiece. He said Annie was emerging as a voluptuous star but needed to keep her chin up while on camera."

"What about me?"

"I don't recall."

"Richie, please—"

"He said the film was likely to be nominated for various awards in America and other places, but needed more slash to it, something that could be denounced or announced."

"Slash?"

"His very word, or so Kolisch said. Poor dear man, he's more confused than ever. I fear his days in films are numbered."

"What does 'slash' mean?"

"My very question to Kolisch, who only nodded vaguely. He becomes more like Sigler every day." Richie took an envelope from his jacket pocket. "Speaking of Sigler, I have a reference report on him, which you ought to read."

She grabbed it. She knew about Richie's reports. Perhaps a dozen times he had shown her reports on individuals, usually somebody threatening to sue him. She read it through, gobbling the information about Sigler's childhood, poor mother, lackadaisical schooling, the entire welter of information about his erratic life, unstable finances, unsatisfying friendships, theft of credit for the Florida film . . . Finally Kate folded the report.

"Thirty years old," Richie said, "and that's his track record."

"He's perfect," Kate said.

"He's a very unhappy fellow, I would say."

She threw the envelope into his lap. "He's more than *that*. He's one of the *most unhappy people in the world.*"

INVITED was everybody in the cast who would receive screen credit, quite a large number actually, perhaps forty. The names of all the prospective guests had been given to the press, except in Lesher's case; his name never appeared anywhere, even on films his studio made.

A number of cars were circling the block at noon, guests who didn't want to be first to arrive. Also, a polite crowd of fans had gathered at the gate. Lesher, who didn't need to worry about protocol, was first to reach the house, and Richie greeted him formally, pleasantly, helped him off with his coat. "A cheery day, but a bit too windy for the terrace," Richie said.

"Let's try it and see," Lesher suggested brusquely.

He was small physically, about five-seven, was in his early sixties, walked and moved rapidly, probably played squash well, had gentlemanly manners, appeared to be consistently wary of his adversaries, those present and distant, known and unknown, all abounding. He had once taught at a college, or so Mankiewicz had told Richie last year when Lesher began to emerge as the next choice of the studio's board. He was married, had three children, lived in a one-story house near the studio lot, usually drove his own car. He was balding. He knew more about the financing of films than about their substance or structure, but he had opinions on all matters, refused to be intimidated by the greater experience or abilities of others. He made decisions promptly. He had a phenomenal memory, one possible reason for his recent election to power as head of the studio.

A camera truck was passing by on the street as he and Richie selected chairs on the terrace, each moving his chair slightly so as not to have the sun in his eyes. "Got word you were concerned," Lesher said as he sat down. He smiled at Richie. "You're an old favorite of mine, you know, and of my wife and daughters."

"Old favorite?" Richie asked mildly.

"So I came at once. Here I am."

Richie cleared his throat, annoyed to be openly implicated in a plot against Kolisch. "I had nothing to do with it."

Lesher's smile faded slowly.

"But—so—so you are here," Richie said simply.

Silently Lesher tried to evaluate Richie's denial, or his evasion. Abruptly he said, "And I have seen the work print and other scenes, those up to your death, have got copies of the various versions of the scenes to read, including Sigler's old script, have talked with Kolisch at length."

"Yes," Richie said simply. "My death should be the final scene of the film. Sigler's script had additional scenes, was unacceptable for that reason, as well as because of the depravity inherent in them. If we lose our own sense of nobility, which is the very disease the French contracted—"

"Kolisch is sick, of course," Lesher said, interrupting calmly, "and sees this as his last shot at the target, but I said to him, 'Why don't you go ahead and do another film, too, Kolly, since you're in Europe and know Sigler, and nobody else seems to know him." He had spoken simply, directly, and now was quiet.

Richie tried to figure out what that interjection signified, if anything. It had come about as a type of gentle digression. "Perhaps an Irish film," he said. "Annie Logan's Irish, and my great-grandmother—"

"Annie Logan's superb, as you say."

Richie's long, thin forefinger scratched his cheek. He studied Lesher speculatively. "What do you think of *my* characterization?"

Lesher cleared his throat. "I respect it," he said. "Of course, I realize it's art."

Not a compliment, not really, as best Richie could tell, not the reply one would hope for from a money-conscious producer. "I have confidence in an Irish film. I happen to know—"

Kate descended on them, cocktails in hand, one for each of them. Lesher stood, accepted his drink from her promptly, stiffly. "My dear, you were quite effective in this film."

"Did you like me?" Kate said.

"Loved you. And Richie as the King, well, he is the King, you know, has been the King in the film world for years."

Frances, the French publicity girl, arrived with a tight-suited French boyfriend. Count Fersen arrived alone. Maillard arrived, dressed in a costume replete with red, white and blue ribbons. Mirabeau waddled in, dressed as a seventeenth-century count; he didn't know who Lesher was, asked him his profession. "I'm in films," Lesher said simply. A number of other costumed players arrived and glided for the whiskey table.

Richie found himself in the living room, Scotch and soda in hand, his second highball, or maybe his third— Lesher's aloofness had put him in special need. He began explaining to sleek, handsome Lafayette why years ago he hadn't liked a certain film actress. "I asked her once what sort of summer she had had, and she *told* me. For an hour. You know I couldn't care *that much.*" It was a silly point to be making at all, he realized, much less to Lafayette.

"No, no," Lafayette said, scarcely listening to him, smiling at lady-in-waiting number four, a beautiful woman named Mademoiselle Giradeau, who brushed against him as she walked by.

"After all, there are social rules in life," Richie continued, "and one of them permits us to ask polite questions without being burdened with replies."

Lafayette commented that Richie's situation here was much improved over the one in the tower. "This place more closely resembles the palace of the Tuileries," he said.

"Yes, it's similar to that," Richie said.

"Take care," Lafayette said, laughing, using the

laugh as an excuse for wandering off in the direction lady-in-waiting four had taken.

Richie went off to find Vorono. Mirabeau stopped him, asked after his health. Richie at once launched into a story. He was in a reminiscent mood, recalling important people he had known, a sign of nervousness, as he was aware. "I did an evening's benefit, a reading from Shaw, in 1944, and Sam Goldwyn phoned next day and asked how much fee to send. I started to say, 'Just pay the rental on my suit, Sam,' making a joke of it, but before I could even speak, he said, 'Will thirty thousand dollars do?' "

Mirabeau was studying Marat contemptuously. "Did you invite *him?*" he asked. "And who is that one?"

Richie tried to see over the heads of the other guests. "I think he plays a barber. Won't be in the film. I'm going to insist on that scene being killed."

"Not a discriminating list of guests, certainly," Mirabeau said, and wandered off to find someone to his liking.

Frances walked by, holding Marat's arm. "I'm only waiting for the chance to kill you," she said, giggling.

Vorono was just now arriving. Richie took his arm, ushered him into the kitchen. "Where is he?" he said.

"Out in the car. Praying," Vorono said.

"Did you tell him?"

"No, but maybe the Lord did."

"Take him up the back stairs, keep him up there until I need him."

"Whatever you say, but it's a long way from home, seems to me." Vorono started out through the entrance hallway.

"Vorono." When he had come back inside the kitchen, Richie said, "At the party talk up the Irish film."

Vorono shrugged, nodded.

"They seem to be ignoring me on that one," Richie said. "How much would I lose?"

"Oh, not much—and it's deductible."

"Talk it up. Mingle. Be discreet."

In the entrance hall he saw Annie, tried to move through the crowded room to her. The Prime Minister waylaid him, asked after his health.

Richie asked him if he had heard anything about the Irish film.

"I really can't say," the Prime Minister said.

"They tell me Kolisch might try to keep this cast together," Richie said.

"French in Ireland?" the Prime Minister said, watching him closely.

"The underground," Richie said.

Kolisch was talking as Richie went by: "Up to now I've always tried to infuse comedy into everything I've done, but this is not a day for comedy," he was telling Annie.

"We've gone from Garbo to Mia Farrow in one generation . . ." Annie said.

Richie interrupted. "Annie, I've got the lad."

"No, Richie," she said, stunned, pained at once. "No, don't."

"Well, it's going to be quite worthwhile," he said, ignoring Kolisch.

"Richie . . . dear . . ." She was frustrated and anxious, perhaps more for him than anyone else.

Simon, the guard, caught Richie's arm, swung him around. "How's the old boy getting on?" he said.

"I'm in need of nothing, really," Richie said gently, surprised by the fellow's friendliness.

Kate pushed her way through, said to Kolisch, "When do my retakes get shot? Vorono says we might all go to Ireland."

THE Spanish couple were wandering through the crowd, she on his arm, both of them obviously intoxicated with alcohol and pleasure. The Portuguese dresser arrived, couldn't find a hanger for his coat. "Put it on the stairs," Richie said. Somebody had spiked his drink. He had never felt such an effect from three high-balls in his life.

Kate handed him a fourth in passing. "Evanes-cence," she said.

"I've got the lad," he told her simply.

She stopped, came back to him, studied him care-fully. "What?"

"From Florida. You remember, in the report."

"Where?" she said.

"Never mind," he said, and pinched her cheek. It did do his soul good to see that she was impressed.

Wandering on. Lesher talking to Kolisch near the drapes. "If you're already half a million over budget," he was saying, "how can we afford all those additional exe-cutions, and a church scene to boot?"

To boot. To boot. Interesting verb form, or what-ever it was; playful, Richie thought. To boot. Might ask him about it. Richie cleared his throat near Kolisch's ear. "Of course, he didn't do his first film at all. The Florida one was done by a suicide named—uh—Roma, as I re-call."

The two producers turned to stare at him.

"What in the world are you talking about?" Kolisch asked.

"The lead actor. I have that boy here and will in-troduce him this afternoon."

"Whatever reason for?" Kolisch said.

It was annoying to be depreciated like that, to have reports of one's own best plans resound meaninglessly. "Vorono," Richie abruptly called across the crowded room, "bring Sigler's boyfriend down."

Kolisch, like most everybody else, grasped only part of the meaning, but from Richie's voice he could tell that some further revelation was intended. All in all, Kolisch would prefer not to have any surprises just now; it was difficult enough to stay abreast of what Lesher was up to. As for Lesher, he cleared his throat uneasily, excused himself from Richie's company. The crowded room became respectful, enlivened by the murmuring and whispering of those with speculations to pass along.

Vorono appeared at the top of the stairs, came quickly down. The lad stopped at the top, apparently startled to see that the people below were all watching him. He considered them one by one, as if questioning each one, wondering why he was of any consequence to them. When at last he saw Richie, he came tentatively down the stairs. He paused on the bottom step, stood there staring at Richie with his doelike eyes.

Annie went to him, took his hand, but the boy pulled it free, moved around her and stopped before Richie.

"Several of us have seen your Florida film," Richie said. The angelic expression of the young man was disconcerting.

The young man's dark, inquisitive gaze turned on Kolisch. "Who are you?" he asked.

Annie said, "Richie, don't go on."

"A marvelous film, isn't it, Kolisch?" Richie said. "Used it as Exhibit A whenever Sigler's abilities were proclaimed. But it is confirmed that he never did the film at all, and his treatment of this young man, even to the matter of contract and screen credit—"

Kolisch belched, covered his mouth as he turned away.

Annie took Richie's hand. "Please," she said.

"Lesher," Richie said doggedly continuing, "come meet the star of Sigler's first film."

Lesher held his place near the buffet, speculating about the young man and what Richie had in mind. As a producer he preferred to stay with his own problems.

The scene was not going as Richie had planned. It seemed to be bickering its way along. "My friends, this lad here will tell us during the course of the afternoon about the making of the Florida film. Welcome him as one of us."

"You son of a bitch," Kate whispered to Richie as the guests began uneasily wandering off, giving the young man room.

Richie irritably told her, "I thought Sigler might as well have all of his friends here."

LESHER was talking to Kolisch. "If Sigler didn't get a signed option, then who did? We were offered the property by him. I do happen to know that several other novels about the I.R.A. are to be published."

"Well, let's assume I can get the property," Kolisch said. "Can Sigler and I do the film for the studio?"

Lesher shrugged. "I'm cautious. Who wants to see a film about a subject that's always on television?"

"Sigler wants to," Kolisch said. "Sigler has a passion for this *Storm in the North* novel, by Dunstan or somebody, that's slipping away."

"Television is free," Lesher said. "As a TV documentary—"

"Sigler's film won't resemble television," Kolisch said bluntly. "I assure you."

Lesher shrugged uneasily. His gaze idly followed the young man from Florida as he moved across the terrace. "I—I would imagine not. Would half a million do for it?" he said finally.

Kolisch exhaled deeply, relieved to have a glimmer of hope. He began at once to tell about the opening scenes, but Lesher moved away toward the terrace.

Richie stepped in front of him. "I remember the old days more and more," Richie said, "when my friend Thalberg was alive—"

"Decided not to wear your costume?" Lesher asked.

"Not decided yet, have I?" Richie said.

The Florida lad appeared in the doorway, confronting Richie. "Where is he, where is Doug?" he said.

"Now," Richie said soothingly, "don't be overly anxious."

"Is he here?"

"No, not yet." Richie saw that more guests were arriving, but Sigler didn't appear to be among them. "Tell Mr. Lesher how he stole Roma's film."

Lesher turned away abruptly and began serving shrimp onto a little cocktail saucer. As Richie and the Florida lad watched, he put two small sausages beside the shrimp—"In honor of my German ancestors," he said to Richie. He dabbed mayonnaise on the plate, topped the dab with a radish. "Takes a strong stomach to make films," he said. With a nod to the boy, he moved onto the terrace.

SLOWLY, with immaculate care, Richie crossed the hallway, speaking briefly to two or three guests. He tried to open the front door of the house, could not, began to grunt and groan annoyances at it. One of the palace guards' officers hurried to his side and unlatched it for him. "Your Majesty," the guard said.

"Where's Sigler?" Richie asked him.

"Who is that?" the guard said.

"Must be here by now." Slowly Richie made his way as far as the stone wall, a short, blunt terrace wall. He noticed that the sundial was incorrect. "Be more careful," he told it. Along the bottom of the marble was *Tempus fugit.* "Run, you're late," he murmured. He couldn't open the garden gate. Somebody on the outside heard him, swung it toward him, and at once the sleepy sun-warmed fans were aroused like bees. "Sigler, you here?" he called out.

A Volkswagen horn replied.

"Come on, come on," Richie commanded.

The fans began shouting information to one another—There he is! Where's my book? Somebody stop him! Even as Sigler pushed his big body out of his little car and came heavily, solidly toward the gate. Other lesser bodies were in the way, but Sigler burst through and Richie slammed the gate shut in the fans' faces. "Get a drink inside," Richie said. "Someone I want you to meet."

Sigler hurried to the main door of the house without even a second glance at his drunken host.

Walks incredibly fast, doesn't he, Richie noticed. Devilishly difficult to walk on these infernal stones. Not the least bit even, not made of the same rock apparently. He sat down near the sundial to rest, moaning. "What's Sigler doing?" He pushed himself to his feet, made his way to the main door, stood there knocking with his right hand and holding to the ivy with his left. Didn't know the French had ivy. He knocked at his own front door until it opened. The Finance Minister pressed a lean forefinger against his lips.

Richie slipped into the entrance hallway, and from there he could see that the guests were—almost all of them—watching Sigler and the Florida boy. The boy was weeping in long, heartbroken, childlike wails, his arms around fat Sigler's neck. The boy was weeping into fat Sigler's shoulder, blubbering apologies, entreaties, criticisms, pleas, was bubbling with emotion and pain. The guests were entranced, embarrassed. Sigler was as embarrassed as anybody, but even so, he had a smile pasted on his face. Suddenly he gave the boy's shoulders a pat or two, winked at Kate. "Here, take him," he said, and unloaded him onto her shoulder, the boy still broken, sobbing. Sigler, with a hapless gesture, began to pretend that he was weeping, began to mimic the young man's

weeping, to grimace for the benefit of the guests. When
at last his confused audience laughed, Sigler also turned
from them with a shrug, and moved to the bar, where he
proceeded, in spite of the bartender's entreaties, to mix
a drink for himself.

Richie was stunned. Audaciously Sigler had carried
off the confrontation, had ridden out and stamped out
the humiliation. It was the Florida boy who had failed.
Now Sigler was measuring out five drops of vermouth,
his hand as steady as a rock. The man had not reacted
as expected, and the lad had crumpled, which for some
reason, far-fetched as it appeared to him now, he had not
expected.

Sigler was mimicking the boy once more, this time
for the amusement of two Swiss guards.

ANNIE helped Kate and the Florida boy out to the
terrace. "Sun will help anything," she told them. The
boy stopped moaning once he was perched on the edge
of a chaise longue; he whimpered less, anyway, seemed
to be regaining his composure. Kate was the delinquent
now; wan and pale, the lines on her face deeper than
usual, she had a haggard look. She sat beside him, her
mouth open, her breath coming in little puffs of air and
spittle.

Annie knelt before them on the tile floor. "Now, I'm
going to get each of you a drink."

The young man shook his head irritably.

Kate seemed not to hear. "They'll only keep hurting
one another."

"Didn't seem to hurt Sigler," Annie said.

"He enjoys the fight so much," Kate said.

"Sigler?"

Kate seemed to hear the single word. She emerged
from the protective coma; her eyes focused on Annie,

then on two court ladies watching her with silly grins on their faces. She got up at once. "I mean Richie," she said, and walked to the rock banister wall and vomited across it onto the flowers.

Sigler came out the door just in time to witness it. He watched her casually, his martini in hand, his expression as unconcerned as if he were waiting for a train to arrive in a station.

Annie left them to each other. They were tougher than she was, she realized. She also admitted that Sigler had won out in the confrontation with Richie. If anything, Richie's tactics had backfired, and now he was even more vulnerable than ever. It had also been his idea, from what rumors said, to bring Lesher to Paris, and even that plan had gone astray.

Just now Lesher came out of the house, approached Sigler. "If you can finish this church scene in two weeks on fifty thousand—I was wondering what schedule would be practical for starting the Irish film."

UPSTAIRS in the bedroom, Richie sought the costume Kolisch had sent earlier, and put it on. Of course, it was far too big, but in spite of that he did not intend to put on the hot padding. The costume drooped, folded, hung, much like a clown's costume in the old days, back at the start of his acting career. Well, he felt rather much like a clown. He had twice played Polonius on the road. He was aware that one current school of criticism contended Polonius was a wise old man, but such a view was merely a reflection of a modern tendency to make fools wise and wise men fools. He turned to his full-length mirror, faced himself, " 'My liege, and madame, to expostulate what majesty should be, what duty is, why day is day, night night, and time is time, were nothing but to waste night, day, and time, therefore, since brevity is the soul of wit and tediousness the limbs and outward flourishes, I will be brief.' "

He winked at himself in the mirror, pleased with his interpretation of the garrulous old man. " 'Mad let us grant him, then. And now remains that we find out the cause of this effect, or rather say the cause of this defect, for this effect defective comes by cause. Thus it remains and the remainder thus. Pretends.' "

He could hear in his mind's ear the laughter of audiences in Liverpool, Edinburgh, Leeds, Croydon . . .

He straightened. He turned his head to show off his nose in profile: Cyrano's. " 'You remember when Beauty said "I love you" to the Beast, that was a fairy prince, his ugliness changed and dissolved, like magic. But you see I am still the same.' "

In a falsetto voice, he replied, " 'And I—I have done this to you! All my fault—mine!' "

In his own voice: " 'You? Why no, on the contrary! I had never known womanhood and its sweetness but for you. My mother did not love to look at me—I never had a sister. Later on, I feared the mistress with the mockery behind her smile. But you—because of you I have had one friend not quite all a friend—across my life, one whispering silken gown.' "

"Well, if you're not a sight!" Annie said from the bedroom doorway.

"You startled me," Richie said indignantly.

"I missed you."

Richie resumed as Cyrano, playing to the reflection of himself and his droopy costume. " 'But a man does not fight merely to win! No—no—better to know one fights in vain!' "

"I'm afraid you do fight in vain, Richie. Lesher will pay for the church scene."

" 'Yes, all my laurels you have driven away.' "

"Are you drunk, darling? What if the Harrisons come? Or Burton?"

" 'And all my roses; yet in spite of you, there is one crown I bear away with me . . .' "

"Lesher says it's too good a chance to let slip by, pulling religion in. Look at *The Exorcist*, he says."

" 'And tonight when I enter before God, my salute shall sweep all the stars away from the blue threshold—' "

"Yes, I know, Richie, you'll have only one thing left—"

" 'Without stain, unspotted from the world—' "

"I only wish—"

" 'My white plume.' " He closed his eyes, stood blind before himself, admitting in the moment, or at least threatening to admit the absurdity of himself, the sweet sad sorrow of his predicament.

"Richie, let's get away from here while we can."

"Yes, of course, darling," he said, his eyes still closed.

"Before the torture starts, Richie."

"Yes, of course. But can we afford to run from them?"

"We can drive off now, Richie, and have a wonderful dinner on the road to Cherbourg."

"Do you think so?"

She took his hand, kissed it. "Please, let's try it."

He looked at her as if from a far distance, wondering about her.

"I have the children at the door. And I have no luggage this time, none."

"Escape from Paris, 'Toinette?" Richie said. "I wonder. A road leads on, through woods or something." Suddenly he embraced her, threw his oversized sleeves comfortingly around her. "But whatever you want, darling."

She kissed his chin, his cheek. "This way."

He freed his arms, adjusted his oversized costume

squarely on his frame. "We won't get through the crowd, I'm afraid," he said.

Proceeding down the stairs, her hand rested on his arm. One of the Swiss guards opened the door for them.

"Will you ask Count Fersen to drive, darling? I'm a bit too far gone," Richie said.

She went running off to find Fersen, and Richie carefully followed into the main room, made his royal way, his actor's mind reciting to itself in a lilting fashion: " 'Now my co-mates and brothers in exile, Hath not old custom made this life more sweet than that of painted pomp? Are not these woods more free from peril than the envious court?' "

"Richie, where have you been?" Lesher said, advancing on him, hand outstretched.

"I've been to London to look at the Queen," he said, and shook Lesher's hand formally.

"The church scene ought to be a real slash at the end."

"An extraordinary image," Richie said, moving on, bowing to lady-in-waiting number one, who was tittering at his "uniform," as she called his costume.

"What the hell did he mean by that?" Lesher said, looking after him.

Richie, passing close to lady-in-waiting three: "Go on—you never will be ugly—go!"

"You *are* funny, sir," she said.

Vorono talking to Kolisch: "So TV took over the audience for melodramas in America, and all that's left is a sophisticated audience that's on the make for more and more exceptional experiences."

Kolisch, nodding, was looking about to see who might relieve him.

"Vorono, you've been drinking," Richie said, moving past him.

"A beautiful woman is balm to a man's spirit," La-

332 : John Ehle

fayette was telling lady-in-waiting four.

"I wish I had you in the raspberry patch," Richie murmured to her. He heard her giggle as he wandered on. Be as delicious as the Princess de Lamballe, he thought. To Lafayette he said, "We are waiting, sir."

His Portuguese valet descended on him. "Pins, get me pins," he told the Spanish couple. "Sir, you look absurd."

"Let it alone," Richie told him, patting his face affectionately. "It doesn't matter." He found Antoinette and the two children. In his mind:

> Love seeketh not his own! Dear, you may take
> My happiness to make you happier,
> Even though you never know I gave it to you—

Somebody had begun projecting the work print of the film. What an absurd idea, he thought. *Onto* a pale yellow, paneled wall, too. Nobody paid much attention to it, fortunately, and the sound was turned down low.

Through the hallway Richie moved, his costume dragging the floor. He took down his tweed topcoat, which he folded over his arm. He selected a hat. Kate started toward him. "We're leaving now, Antoinette and I," he told her. "Where are your coats, dears?" he said to the children. Lafayette was trying to straighten Richie's costume. Richie saw that Annie and Count Fersen were watching the work print. "Darling, it's time for us to go," he said, and held out his hand to her.

He led the way out of the house and to the street, his costume askew. At the gate he came upon a sizable crowd of fans waiting, maybe seventy people. Annie was holding to his arm, Lafayette on the other side was holding him up. Simon suddenly appeared beside them.

Annie gasped. "Get away. You don't belong here."

"My dears, my dears," Richie was saying to the

crowd. "This is my wife, my two children. And you know General Lafayette, I'm sure. This shy fellow here is Count Fersen."

The fans moved closer, touched Richie's hand, his royal sleeves, his Louis XVI cuffs. He withheld his hand from touching, but seemed to be blessing them as he tottered toward his hooded convertible. "I do so want to fall in love again," he told Annie.

"Out of the damn way," Lafayette shouted, bullying the crowd. Fersen moved forward, pushed people aside. Richie paused at the side of the convertible, held to its top for support, too drunk even to look for the key. Count Fersen sought it in his topcoat pockets, found it in the left one, helped him into the driver's seat. "He's drunk," Lafayette said. "Move over there, Louis," he said.

Richie moved to the next seat.

"Into the back, Your Majesty," Lafayette said to Annie. He got the two children inside, pushed Count Fersen into the driver's seat. "Now clear the damn road," Lafayette shouted at the crowd. "Clear the road."

Fersen started the drophead, even as citizens began playfully rocking the car.

"See here," Richie said, rolling down his window.

Other citizens, laughing, joined in.

"You must do something, Louis," Annie said. "If we don't escape Paris now—I recall with considerable dread—"

Richie touched a button and the top rolled back, which startled and intimidated the citizens. He stood, he regally swayed before them. They were quiet for him now. Even Lafayette became respectful. In a firm voice Richie said, "It is the King's road, and you will clear a way." As they laughed, his famous, friendly smile appeared, the ingratiating smile known throughout the world. "Will you please," he said modestly. "I am—I really must leave Paris now. It pains me more than you can know."

"A song, Richie," a woman called.

"A song," others called. There was suddenly a loud chorus of demands for a song.

"Order them to leave, Louis," Annie said.

But he sang a few verses from *Morning Song*, and they, tears in their eyes, swayed arm in arm to the music, and asked for a song from yet another film, and after that was sung, the crowd was so dense around the car that no hope of driving away remained.

"It's no use," Lafayette told him.

"No, of course not," he said. He opened the door and stepped onto the road, held out his hand for his Queen. With the two children following, he pushed his way through the crowd to the garden gate, where he turned, almost falling because of the costume's hem, and bowed to them all. "I'll meet my judgment without regrets," he assured them.

As he reentered the big hall, he said to Annie, "I told you it wouldn't work."

Kate had been watching from the garden and came hurrying to him.

"I told her we couldn't get away," he said to her.

"Richie, I'm to be third lead in the Irish film, Sigler promised," she said.

"Ahhhh, how beautiful," he said. He was feeling rather gallant just now. "There's something about the Irish film that I really should tell you, dear one."

"And all the French actors are to be part of the Irish underground . . ."

LESHER had been going about meeting everyone, finding out who each person was, what part he had played, telling each one what he thought of his perfor-

mance and what he might want to play in the church
scene or the Irish film. The marvel of it was that he could
remember every detail of each conversation.

Richie found Marge sitting off to herself on the terrace and joined her. Maillard was sitting near them, Maillard being particularly dour. "Why should I play another
revolutionary?" he said to Richie.

"I hate parties like this one, don't you?" Marge said.
"Everyone drunk. Poor Eddie shouldn't drink so much."

"Quite a crowd outside the gate, wasn't there?" Lafayette said, pulling up a chair. "The Harrisons arrived
and couldn't get through."

Richie saw Lesher wandering about. "Oh, Lesher,"
he said, "I was suggesting to Marge here that she and I
do the Book of Job in modern dress."

Lesher stopped. "In blackface?"

Richie found that amusing. "I heard you had a sense
of humor. From Mankiewicz."

"Not in May and October," Lesher said, sitting
down. "My job is only a business. You have all the fun."

"Do you like France, monsieur?" Lafayette asked
him.

"France? Yes, why not?" The question had taken
him by surprise. "Is there some reason not to like
France?"

"Only Frenchman I ever felt sorry for," Richie said,
"was a French priest sent to Wyoming to serve a Catholic
church named Our Lady of the Grand Teton."

Marge roared with laughter. Lesher had to do a bit
of translating first, then he laughed modestly.

Lafayette remained reflective. "How well will this
motion picture succeed?" he asked Lesher.

"Oh—" Lesher frowned at the impertinent fellow.
"How does anybody know these days? Even with Richie,
I don't know. Even Elizabeth Taylor's not sure-fire these
days. If we make it shocking enough—after all, with his-

tory on our side we won't have problems with censorship. We can touch the big button this time. Even the
inference that Brando might put his pecker into an unknown girl's anus—well, that film will gross untold millions. And she's a total unknown. Not bad figures for the
May board meeting," Lesher said.

Richie unfolded his pocket handkerchief, dabbed at
his forehead. "My Lord," he said.

"Even Lady Macbeth is naked. Nobody seems to
know quite why. First time, and the play was written in
1599, wasn't it? But nudity is old hat now."

"Old hat?" Richie said, mildly amused by the use of
the figure of speech.

"Where will it end?" Lafayette asked.

Lesher frowned at him for a moment, then he
smiled, an answer occurring to him. "Probably what the
little unknown actress asked in the Brando film," he said.

Richie, embarrassed, cleared his throat. "You might
think I'm prudish—" he began, his voice rising.

"A penis in the anus and a crucifix in the vagina,"
Lesher said.

"But I maintain I don't mind people doing as they
please, so long as they admit it's either right or wrong.
We must have standards."

"Noticed yesterday some French bikinis are sheer,"
Lesher said. "How's that for a standard?"

"Really?" Marge said. "It's getting hard to shock me
any longer."

"Got to give the people what they want, or out we
go, don't you know?" Lesher said. "It's a competitive
business." He noticed Lafayette's perplexity. "My
friend, these are times of the anarchists. Just as yours
were."

Lafayette stared at him gloomily. "I know."

"I—I know," Richie began, once more trying to get
his thoughts in order. "I enjoy breaking the rules and I
enjoy keeping the rules, but that requires that there be

rules. The people without rules don't seem to enjoy anything."

"No, they're too busy blowing up everything,"
Lesher said. "Anarchists aren't interested in solving anything."

"Yes, but where are they taking us?" Lafayette said.

Lesher shrugged. "My casting people predict the
next superstar will look unattractive, will be uncouth,
will scratch his balls on screen, will be incoherent when
he talks, so much so you'll think he—he—" Lesher
stopped in the middle of the thought, sat there staring
at Sigler, who was hugging Kate at the terrace doorway.
"That fellow Sigler, I wonder did he ever do any acting."

COUPLES going off through the garden, ladies-in-
waiting and officers of the guards, Frances with the
Florida lad, having ditched her skinny boyfriend. The
Spanish couple were still walking about arm in arm. Lafayette haughty, Mirabeau rude, Maillard bilious, Kolisch
relieved, Sigler pawing Kate even as Richie watched. The
Prince and Princess sat beside him on the chaise, one on
each side. He had his arms around them and was trying
to tell them about life, but his mind was disorganized.
"We come finally to see that all a gentleman can do is
persevere," he told the children. "We can't easily fight
them, because they have all the slogans. Equality, liberty,
fraternity."

The Princess tittered, delighted with his hesitancies
and slurrings.

Annie, apparently upset about something, came
outside, found him, hurried to him. "Richie, help me."

"I was just telling our two dears about this—deplor-
able situation."

"Richie, they promised me I could decide which take
to use."

"I told them to be careful or the apes will get them," Richie said.

"Wednesday when you left to go get ready for your dinner with Kate—"

"What I really should say, dears—"

"Sigler talked me into doing one take where I— more or less offer myself to Simon. It's absurd, I realize now, but I was beaten down—"

"I could have stopped them, if I had only known," Richie said to the children.

The Princess giggled, amused at his drunkenness. The Prince frowned at her, at her insolence.

"All I have ever asked of Kolisch is that things go back to being what they were," Richie said.

Annie stared at him dismayed. Of course, she realized he was drunk. "I don't want to be in Sigler's Irish film, Richie," she said, sitting down in the chair opposite him.

"Oh?"

"I *am* Irish, you know. And Lesher says I must, I really must." She turned in her chair to stare at the doorway. "They're almost to my scene. If they use that awful take."

"Almost killed me by now, have they?" Richie said good-naturedly.

"Nobody's watching the film anyway. Thank God."

"Did I tell you, Antoinette, I have the most—the most marble stairway."

They heard Kolisch's voice: "Richie's best in comedy, in Shaw for instance, but it's simply not the world for comedy now."

"He's t-t-t-too 1950's," Sigler said.

"You go ahead and finish up this film, Sigler," Kolisch said. "Make it as new as the morning."

"See how they treat me," Richie said to Annie.

"You're too kind to them," Annie said.

"What can I do?"

"Order them," she said.

"They won't listen to me."

"If they show that last take, you won't look, will you, Richie? Or you children, either."

"Perhaps when it's over I will go to England," he said.

"England?" she said, astonished.

"I know it sounds peculiar."

"England?" she repeated.

"Yes, I'm really serious, Antoinette. We English ought to visit England."

"Maybe I should go home to Ireland," she said dubiously.

"It is a matter of pride with me that we English still have a royal family, for instance. The civilized society requires tradition, even among the common people. I recall my Uncle Charlie, who was a grocer, going out to shoot grouse on holiday, always wearing a white carnation in the buttonhole of his tweed hunting suit."

"We could have a marvelous vacation in England," she said dreamily. "But can we get away from Paris?"

"Did they leave my will in the work print, Antoinette?" he said.

"No, darling. I'm afraid not," she said.

"Are you sure? I expressly told them to."

"It was too talky, I suppose, darling," she said.

"My dear girl, talk is beautiful. I never look at you, but there's some new virtue born in me, some new courage. Do you begin to understand, a little?"

"Sir?" she said, astonished.

"Cyrano de Bergerac."

"Oh."

"London. 1938. Before the war, the awful bombing. Before we realized about the people being gassed. Before we all went out to kill each other. I played it at the Lyric."

"Did you say you loved me?" she asked.

Lafayette came forward to congratulate Richie on his death scene, which had just been projected. "A rich quality, beautiful," he said. "Lesher's gone up to a hundred and ten minutes for the film's length."

Annie rushed to the door to see if her scene had begun. Richie got to his feet unsteadily, smiled down at the children. The Princess giggled; she and the Prince got slowly to their feet. Richie led them into the crowded room where the drunken faces were rising, falling, laughing. Lafayette took his arm to steady him. Richie saw Annie's picture on the paneled wall, her breasts bare, and he stopped, stunned. On the screen Simon was undressing her. Before the screen Kate and Lesher and Annie were standing, watching; Kate's arm was around Annie, holding her.

Sigler appeared at the edge of the group of viewers, his gaze on Richie, not on the screen.

Simon touched Antoinette's breast. She closed her eyes, consenting. His hand, his soiled fingers moved over her white skin.

Sigler watching Richie.

Simon's lips moving toward her lips. He touches her cheek, her nose, he suddenly bends and sucks her breast.

Sigler watching.

Richie swung around, pushing the children before him. It was too much for him. He would have given a great deal to have brazened it out with Sigler, come what may, but he turned and made his way past Lesher and Kolisch, between the lady-in-waiting number four and Lafayette, and found the sunlit air.

DUSK. The camera truck was passing by again. From the raspberry rows, Richie could not see it, and of course it could not see him, which was more to the point, but he could hear its whining transmission. Must be French-made, he thought.

He rested on the grass path, his head on his bull-dog's ribs. "Somewhere I read that hunters in pioneer days slept with their head on one dog and their feet on another one," he said, speaking to his daughter. "In this manner, Charlotte, they were protected from bears, painters—the big cats, not the artists—and snakes."

Charlotte was sitting nearby, in the next row. Annie must have seen them, for she came along now, walking mournfully, and sat down near his feet. "I looked every-where for you," she said. "Wasn't it awful?"

"My dear, don't you worry about that scene. After all, it's only reflections on a screen."

"Don't make me cry," she said. "I can't forgive them for this."

"I'll order them to destroy it."

Their son, Charles, saw them, came running along. "Sigler wants you," he said to Richie.

Annie cringed. "Wants me?"

"Papa," Charles said.

Richie readjusted his head on his dog's ribs. "Yes," he said comfortably, "of course he does." He made no sign of rousing himself. "Lie quiet, Horace," he said to the dog. "Charles, sit down. Have a pruned raspberry."

"Kolisch is coming now," Annie said.

"Charles, go tell him to send Sigler or to send no one," Richie said.

"Sir?"

"Go, at once."

Charles took off running, and he must have been an adequate messenger, because Kolisch paused in the mid-dle of the big lawn for a baffled moment, then made his way to the house.

"Annie," Richie said, extending his hand, drawing her down at his feet. "My dear girl, you know what I've been thinking."

"No."

"How different the French are from us English."

342 : J O H N E H L E

"I'm Irish, Richie."

"A Frenchman prefers to be impersonal. While he spends hours making his best soufflé, he couldn't care less who turns up to eat it, would as soon serve it to a stranger as not. It is the dish itself, the act itself that interests him passionately."

"I think Sigler's coming now," she said.

"On the other hand, the English are only willing to do their best work for those whom they know very well, preferably members of the family, which helps to account for the abominable treatment given strangers in restaurants."

"I rather like the Connaught," she said.

"But the Connaught knows its guests. Call up and ask for a reservation if you want to find out."

"Sigler's got his shoulders hunched, his head lowered," she said. "He's angry, Richie."

"Won't even let you take a room, unless they know you."

"And Vorono is with him," she said.

"I don't doubt that he is." He lay there comfortably stretched out on the ground. Languidly he sought out a dried-up raspberry and plopped it into his mouth. As Sigler arrived, he said, "From here one can find a few berries, even yet, Sigler, so it's all a matter of point of view, isn't it?"

"You t-t-took my film," Sigler said angrily, and swept into a spate of angry sputtering and stuttering. "You know w-w-w-who has my movie rights," he said.

"Who?" Richie said.

"H-H-H-Horace H-H-H-Hall."

"Yes. So he does."

"Who i-i-is H-H-H—"

"My dog," Richie said simply.

Sigler straightened as if a blow had been received on his forehead. He stood quite erect and stiff, and stared down open-mouthed at the relaxed actor.

"I can think of nothing more appropriate," Richie said. "Horace owns my estate in the South of France, the house, the land. He owns—"

"He owns the furniture," Vorono said.

"He owns my Rolls drophead," Richie said. "He owns the—"

"He owns the film rights to many properties, including one by G.B.S.," Vorono said.

"George Bernard Shaw," Richie said. "Shaw rather enjoyed the idea. Of course, I was to play in the film. And he owns the film rights to several Irish properties."

"It's th-theft," Sigler said.

"Here," Richie said to Annie, offering her a raspberry. "Now, Sigler, let's arrange a time when you and Horace and I are sober, to discuss our Irish film."

A guttural growl came out of Sigler.

"And we can talk about the Paris film at the same time," Richie said. "I'm rather determined that it be an excellent one."

LATE dusk. The film truck was gone now. Richie came up from the raspberry canes, Annie helping him, his children and his dog following. He stopped to look at the near-full moon. He kissed Annie. "A good sign to kiss a pretty woman at a full moon," he said. He noticed that several guests were watching him from the terrace. "How fortunate I didn't succumb to Louis' illness, Annie," he said. He could make out Kolisch and Kate and Marge. "Wonder if Lesher has flown home, to preen his feathers there," he said.

Kate came to help him up the steps.

"Once more into the breach, dear friends," he said to her. "Ah," he said, seeing Lesher standing behind the geraniums. "One of your wife's old favorites has come home," he said.

In the kitchen he and Annie found a warm beer

apiece. Both Spaniards were asleep on the back stairs; Carlos' mouth was open, his head now and then bobbing. Richie made his way to the main room, where Sigler stood by the bar eating prawns with his fingers. Kate was talking to him in a soft voice, but she stopped when she saw Richie enter. She also released Sigler's hand.

Lady-in-waiting number two or three—Richie never could be quite sure of those two—said to him, "Do you think I might get a part in the Irish film, sire?"

Richie paused. Sigler had heard her ask—no doubt of that—and Richie watched him for a moment, before answering. "Why not?" he said, and made his way by Sigler's elbow, barely scraping it, as he and Annie went back onto the terrace to rejoin their guests.